Totally Bound Publishing books by M.J. Klipfel

Crossed Souls
Blood Promotion

I0526153

Crossed Souls

BLOOD PROMOTION

M.J. KLIPFEL

Blood Promotion
ISBN # 978-1-80250-965-6
©Copyright M.J. Klipfel 2022
Cover Art by Kelly Martin ©Copyright July 2022
Interior text design by Claire Siemaszkiewicz
Totally Bound Publishing

BLOOD PROMOTION

Dedication

To my soul and heart families, Anna, Merunicorns, and Podlings, thank you for all your support. You're legends. To Tia, this book would not be without your awesomeness. Here is to more chocolate cake and words ahead! To all writers — Dream big. To the readers — You're epic. Enjoy the ride.

Chapter One

Crusty armpit stains. That was the reason why I'd missed date nights with my sofa and coffee. After three months of running my editor's shirts to the dry cleaners with his nasal whine echoing in my skull, *"Make sure they use extra starch,"* I'd had enough. Tonight, my life would change.

A blast of late autumn wind rattled through the pine forest bordering Glenwood Park. My impromptu hiding spot, a bush, provided dismal shelter against the elements. Exhaling a puff of breath at the cloud-covered sky, I fished out my phone. No need for night vision — the dilapidated streetlamp gave off a sufficient amount of light. Giddiness bubbled through my freezing bones. To ease the stiffness creeping into my limbs, I wiggled my toes, triggering a horrid case of charley horses burning through my calves. Shivering rewarded me with a branch poking the back of my head. Afraid of being ratted out by the bush, I didn't dare tug my ponytail free.

To distract myself, I panned left and took a practice shot of the biohazard sign warning that Silver Lake was off limits, then I brought the empty bench overlooking the contaminated lake into focus. *Perfect.* My location gave me a balcony view for the shitshow about to commence. All I needed was for everyone to show up before I froze to death.

Right on time, two men hustled down to the lake. One I recognized as the mayor's bodyguard. Crouching, he checked underneath the bench with a flashlight.

"Check up top," he said.

Grumbling, the other man trudged up the hill. Each of his stumbles brought him closer and sent my heart slamming against my ribcage. When his gaze traveled to the bush, his brows pinched.

Adrenaline shot through my body, urging my tense limbs into a giddy-up and go. *Not tonight.* Gritting my teeth, I remained still.

With the approach of heavy footfalls against the jogging path, the man's attention snapped from the bush to his partner, who was signaling for him to return.

After the men dashed away, I let out my breath. I'd have been lying if I didn't admit to finding the danger invigorating. Writing obituaries lacked the whole pulse-pounding, undercover reporter, breaking news vibes.

A different group of shady meatheads walked over to the bench. After a few mumbles and a half-assed survey, the group parted, revealing the CEO of Safe Waters—the city's water treatment facility. Tim McKay loved flashing his green credentials. However, his hired goons had taken it to a new level.

I cringed in remembrance of our interview. How his halitosis had tickled my earlobe as he leaned over me, sneaking a peek down my shirt. *Ugh.* I shook the memory from my head, focusing on the creep.

Setting his briefcase on the bench, McKay pursed his lips. A phone chirped and he shifted his weight to dig it out of his coat. The screen's glow illuminated his plump face, reddened from the chill. Rolling his shoulders, he straightened up.

The two men from earlier escorted the mayor, muttering under his breath, over to McKay. As the bodyguards shifted to let him through, Mayor Brown transformed into a politician with a fake smile and puffed-out chest. With a confident swagger, he approached McKay.

"Sorry," Mayor Brown said. "I got tied up."

Flashing the mayor a tight-lipped smile, McKay gestured to the bench. The two men could've been twins, right down to the matching comb-overs and trench coats. I poised my numb finger, waiting. McKay handed over his briefcase while Mayor Brown pulled a manila envelope from his coat.

With the press of my finger, I landed the story no reporter had dared to investigate for fear of incurring the mayor's wrath. After all, his brother owned the city's newspaper. So much as an inkblot against the mayor's squeaky-clean image and a reporter could kiss their career goodbye.

"How much longer?" The mayor unclasped the briefcase.

My interest piqued, I snapped another photo.

"Not much," McKay answered, scanning the contents of the envelope.

Nodding, Mayor Brown closed the case. "Good."

The men stood. After a firm handshake, they sauntered off in opposite directions with their bodyguards in tow.

Rubbing my hands together to move heat and blood back into the prickling digits, I forced myself to stay put. As minutes passed, the chattering of my teeth drowned out the soft lapping of waves and the rustling of leaves.

So far, the bodyguards had stayed out of sight and hearing. When I dragged in a satisfying breath, a rich aroma flooded my nose. Cologne was my first thought. A deeper inhale nixed that idea. The mystery scent wasn't one of those drugstore deodorant sprays that men doused themselves with daily. No, it was something raw from nature and it smelled damn good.

Patting my windbreaker pocket, I hit on the cold metal of my pepper spray. An overreaction by far, yet a comforting one. Glenwood, New York, barely made city status with its population statistics. Most of our law-abiding citizens were snug in their beds watching sitcom reruns by nine, not waiting in the park shadows to grab me.

As I took another sniff, the musky lake odor jumped to my nostrils. The familiar stench marked the final all-clear to get moving. Groaning through my stiffness, I stood. No amount of frostbite would've kept me down. *I got the bastards.* Mayor Brown and McKay were covering up something at Safe Waters. Every fiber of my being believed it was the water contamination.

While blood flowed back through my legs, I sent the photos to my email. When the satisfying *ping* of a received message echoed through the deserted park, I stuffed my phone inside the windbreaker's pocket and attempted a half-assed stretch before taking off.

Frigid air scraped my cheeks and stung my lungs as I crested the park's tallest hill in record time. Overhead, the half-moon sent a silver glow across the frosted landscape. With the lengthening of my stride, I fought the impulse to stop and appreciate the scenery. The overpass tunnel came into view. Home stretch. Excitement propelled me into a full-out sprint. Nothing could have pulled the smile off my face except a patch of black ice.

In a series of violent somersaults, I plunged down the hill. My attempts to stop rewarded me with loose gravel embedded into my palms. To salvage the remaining layers of my flesh, I shifted onto my side. My hip smacked against the blacktop, grinding me to a halt inside the overpass tunnel.

As pain hammered my body, I shoved my bruised ego to the side and struggled to move. While my sharp inhales and ragged exhales bounced off the walls, an airy rhythmic sound filtered into the pitch-black tunnel.

Panting.

As I struggled to my hands and knees, an intense burn shot through my palms. With my groans and movements, the panting ceased.

Sweat trickled down my temples while I waited for the prankster to reveal himself. Since the high school stadium was a block away, I had seconds before a juvenile delinquent jumped out at me. "Go ahead. Pick on the klutz. Hope you recorded it," I muttered.

The panting continued. Louder. Faster.

"Quit it," I said.

A rapid clicking joined the panting.

I strained my eyes against the darkness. A huge mass charged me. Unable to move fast enough, I hunched over, bracing for impact. Avoiding a head-on collision, the ball of yellow fur adjusted its course, darting around me. Behind its tucked tail, a chain leash bounced and skipped along the blacktop.

"Bad dog," I whispered through my clenched jaw. When I slumped backward to sit, my palm landed on a sneaker. A wiggling of my toes confirmed both my sneakers were snug on my feet. "Hello?" I asked.

Silence answered me. I tugged experimentally at the shoe attached to a foot. No movement or protest. Stretching my fingers to grasp around a pant leg, I gave it a sharp tug, and with minimal resistance, I pulled a severed leg over my lap.

Shoving the limb off my thighs, I scrambled backward. Pain erupted from my right ankle, which gave out. Once more, I crashed onto my hip. Instead of a gravel landing, something solid and squishy broke my fall. I righted myself as a warm liquid soaked through my running tights. A brush of my fingertips across a sticky mess of jagged bone and denim sent a scream crawling up my throat.

Terror froze me to the spot as my eyes grew accustomed to the darkness. Lumpy shapes littered the tunnel. My attention locked onto the shredded remains of a varsity jacket.

It took three tries to shove my blood-soaked hand inside my windbreaker. Relief raced through me as I touched my pepper spray. Clenching the metal cylinder to my chest, I dug back in for my phone.

Gone.

"That was quite a fall," a masculine voice said.

I dragged my attention away from the body parts and up to a looming shadow which blocked the tunnel exit. The moon kindly made an appearance, outlining the stranger's tall frame.

Unable to move or think, I sat there blankly gaping at the man—who was wearing a freaking three-piece suit—until a breeze rushed past my face, carrying the rich scent that I'd wanted to snuggle with minutes ago.

"I hit my head." I nodded to myself. "This is a dream."

"I assure you"—his voice curled around me—"you are not dreaming."

"Really? What kind of guy wears a damn suit to go strolling in the park?"

He cocked his head. Confusion drew his brows tight. "I am not a guy."

"I'm dreaming," I whispered. Still, the blood soaking into my clothes and the pain throbbing through my bones yelled otherwise. Using the wall as support, I eased upward. When I added pressure to my right ankle, I gasped.

He took a step toward me.

I scrambled to aim my pepper spray at the stranger.

"Skittish?" His dark laughter sent goosebumps screaming across my body.

"Don't move," I warned.

He ceased his laughter, but a smile parted his lips. "You *want* me to move."

Blood rushed to my ears, and my head spun at his words. Some minuscule part of me was happy to agree with the stranger. I aimed the pepper spray at his face. "I've called the cops."

"I call your bluff. Remember, I saw you fall." The smile slipped from his face. "Put that contraption away."

Once more, his words assaulted me. The pepper spray took on the density of a twenty-pound dumbbell and I struggled to keep it leveled at the stranger's face.

"Impressive"—his eyebrow arched—"yet foolish."

"I'll scream," I gritted.

"No one will hear you." He gestured at the severed leg. "No one heard him."

I weighed my dismal escape options. The overkill suit showcased his physique—he clearly outmatched me in strength, and he stood at least half a foot taller. A fight for freedom? Nope. A turn-and-run was also out, thanks to my injuries. Which left me with smarts as my one-trick-pony for survival. Rubbing the pepper spray trigger with my thumb, I cleared my throat. "Are you going to attack me or—"

He cleared the ten feet in a blur. No time to process or move—he shoved my back against the wall, pinning me by my shoulders. Freeing my hand between our bodies, I fought to get the spray to his face. He easily snatched it from me and tossed it over his shoulder.

My gaze locked with his black, mirror-like eyes which held my terrified reflection captive. I became weightless. If it weren't for the man shoved against the entire length of my body, I'd have thought that I had jumped headfirst off a cliff. My heart hammered against my ribs as I forced myself to look beyond my reflection and into the dark abyss of his eyes, sucking me under, pulling me into—

The touch of his chilled finger trailing down my cheek snapped me from the trance. I tried to squirm away.

"How are you fighting me?" He grabbed my hair, pulling my head to the side.

Gasping for breath, I locked onto the lifeless gaze of the teenager whose body was nearby. His expression was frozen in surprised terror. The killer hadn't played with him.

I must be lucky.

My attacker's deep inhale over my throat cut through my thoughts.

"What are you?" His lips brushed against my neck.

"Stop—"

His needle-sharp teeth jabbed into my throat. Agony raked through every cell within my body as the frigid air surrounding me turned into an inferno. My ears popped with pressure. Energy swelled within me, prickling along my insides. In an explosion of light, it escaped my body and slammed into my attacker.

Unlatching from my neck, he shoved my back against the wall. "Who are you?" Blood speckled my face from his question. "Answer," he ordered, digging his fingernails into my shoulders.

Taking advantage of his momentary lack of control, I bottled up my terror, then rammed my knee into his groin. He let go.

My palms and knees smacked against the blacktop. As I scrambled to the tunnel's opening, he snagged my ankle and dragged me backward. When his other hand clamped onto my thigh, I twisted over, kicking with my free leg.

My foot slammed into his nose, sending his head upward with a crack. His grip tightened on my thigh, and I sent another kick to his throat. He released my leg to grab his windpipe.

I flopped to my stomach, crawling over the dead teen's leg, then out of the tunnel.

The ice-slick hill greeted me. *Shit.* I'd ended on the wrong side of the tunnel, heading back to the lake and away from the city. If my attacker recovered, he could watch me slip and slide. Abandoning the path, I dove into the knee-high weeds bordering the forest. Clawing the frozen earth between my fingers, I waited for the pounding of feet through the underbrush.

Silence.

Inch by painful inch, I crawled, panting into the dirt with the hopes that my breath wouldn't act like a smoke signal to the psycho. Still, it coiled upward against my best attempts while dead weeds groaned with each of my movements, tangling in my hair and snagging on my clothing. When I paused for a quick survey of my progress, I regretted it.

Blood trickled down my throbbing neck, slipping underneath my jacket then pooling between my breasts. When I glanced at the wetness darkening my windbreaker, the metallic scent of my blood filled my nose.

"Stop," my attacker said from behind me. "I will not hurt you."

"The hell you won't," I snapped.

My attacker jabbed his index finger at the forest. "They most certainly will."

At the edge of the tree line, moonlight reflected off clusters of glowing orbs. Eyes. At least four large animals dodged and wove through the weeds.

Either from a crazed biting man or a pack of rabid beasts, Death was coming for me. Dropping my cheek to the dirt, flattening myself as much as possible, I hoped the beasts would see the psycho above me as the easier target.

The man yanked on the back of my windbreaker, flipped me over and tossed himself on top of me. When his lips grazed my ear, I screamed.

He covered my mouth.

Running on instinct, I sank my teeth into the heel of his palm.

"You fool," he growled.

Snagging his free hand through my hair, he held me firm to the ground. I glared at his chest while flailing my arms. He easily dodged my blows, giving my hair a tug for my efforts. My teeth shredded into his flesh, but he still shoved his palm against my mouth.

"Drink." His revolting order brought on a panic-induced awareness to the shot glass worth of blood rolling around in my mouth. Smothering me with his hand, he forced me to swallow.

As his blood slid down my throat, an electric current surged through me. In the same instant, the psycho tensed, hissing through his teeth.

Shifting his pale face an inch from mine, he entrapped me with his soulless eyes. "Do not move. Be silent." He tore his hand from my mouth.

I tried to lift my arm, my leg… Nothing worked. My throat fought to produce a scream, but only air escaped. Breathing became labored. With each breath, an invisible chain tightened around my chest.

After a nod at my pathetic escape attempts, he moved off me.

Ear-splitting animalistic noises surrounded me, drowning out the thundering of my heart. Frozen in place, helpless, I stared at the cloud-covered sky. The ground vibrated against my spine from the impact of something large landing next to me. Trying to distract myself from the thing creeping its way over to me, I recited the different types of clouds.

Cumulus.

Hot breath fanned my fingertips.

Nimbus.

Grass exploded upward and the screaming beast was hurled across the sky. My fingers numbed from the absence of its breath.

Cirrus.

Tears blurred my unblinking eyes, while above me, a small shape pirouetted on the wind. It landed on my cheek, soft and wet.

Fur.

"I killed one." The psycho paced back and forth, no longer attempting to be quiet. "The rest scattered."

Another wet clump landed on my lip. More tears fell. Minutes ago, he was all about tearing out my jugular. Now, the asshole was making me wait so he could take a call.

"We have a problem. They made a kill," he grumbled while leaning over me. Tilting his head, he paused. "Understood." My attacker held no phone. He was freaking talking to himself. "I will return before dawn."

As blood trickled down my neck, a sick satisfaction came to mind—if he waited any longer, I'd bleed to death on my own.

"You're a mess," he said to me, not his imaginary friend. Crouching beside me, he plucked the fur off my cheeks and lips.

You're a psycho.

"What am I to do with you?"

Let me go. Call 911. Order me a pizza.

"You have placed me in quite a predicament." Carefully, he brushed away a freezing tear from the corner of my eye. "You may blink."

I did, and half wished I hadn't. Through the shredded remains of his suit, a deep gash ran the entire length of his sternum. Bile burned the back of my throat. Forcing my gaze away from the white of bone glistening in the moonlight, I focused on his face. His nose bent at an unnatural angle. Point for me. Apparently, he had a high threshold for pain, because he smiled.

To drive up the psycho factor, he parted his lips, revealing bloodstained fangs which he pricked his index fingertip against. Blood welled up and rolled down his finger.

"You will do all that I command." He brought his bloody digit to my temple and traced an arch across my forehead. His blood seeped into my pores and raced through my veins. "You may speak. What is your name?"

Unable to refuse his question, I whispered, "Tessa Sanders."

His finger slid to my neck and massaged over his bite while he spoke. "Tessa Sanders, you are under my protection."

"I'll pass on that." I glared at him.

"How naïve you are." He lowered his face to mine. "You fell while running tonight."

"No shit."

In a swift movement, he brushed his lips across mine. No lust. Just a slap in the mouth, because he was in control. As his thumbs touched my temples, a flash of light blanked my racing thoughts. Once it dimmed, a picture show flipped through my mind. As if I were a bystander, I watched myself fall on the ice. It became imperative for me to remember the event playing in my head. Struggling to remember anything different about the fall, all I recalled was the out-of-body experience.

Fear poured through my veins, freezing my blood. He controlled my body *and* my mind.

Finally, his lips left mine. Dipping his face against the crook of my neck, he inhaled. "Your fear is intoxicating," he said.

When he pulled away, our eyes locked. My terror mixed with his hesitance, catching us both off guard. I clenched my jaw. His eyes narrowed. In an instant, smoldering hate rolled between us.

"Forget me" — his words flowed like a stream through my mind — "and go home. Once you are there, you will sleep. When you awake, you are to leave town." The stream turned into a current that swallowed me whole. Darkness enveloped me as his last words echoed through my mind. "Never run at night again."

Chapter Two

My eyes flashed open to a deep red halo illuminating the gold-plated picture frame on my nightstand. Behind the fingerprint-covered glass, my family smiled back at me. Blinking away the familiar sting of approaching tears, I peered around their picture to my clock. My gaze locked onto the digital numbers — six-fifteen p.m.

Willing the p.m. to turn to a.m., my heart jogged to my throat. *How did I flipping sleep the day away? I missed work. I'm so screwed.* Deep in my still-asleep brain, a nagging thought tried to rise. I sat up. *Exhausted* was a pale word for how I felt. My hand trembled as I peeled my sweat-soaked hair away from my face. A loose strand fell in front of my eyes and with the back of my hand, I brushed it away.

Yuck.

My forehead had a grainy texture to it. I squinted at the granules of a rust-like substance covering the back of my hand. For further examination, I lifted my hand to the sunlight spilling in from the window. The specks began to lose their color and texture. They became a grayish powder. I brought my hand to my nose, taking a sniff.

Ash.

"What the f—" Wincing from how my voice scratched my dry throat, I swallowed some bloody saliva. I struggled to move. I glanced at the sheets tangled around me. The black material of my tights stood out against their whiteness. My blurry eyes narrowed. I never slept in my running gear.

If I thought sitting took effort, standing took courage. With the room spinning around me, my uneasy step triggered my right ankle screaming at me.

Limping into the bathroom, I flicked on the light. The fluorescent glare stung my eyes. Hanging my throbbing head, I reached for the tap and a washcloth.

The ice-cold water tore through the cloak of sleep. Gasping awake, I pulled the washcloth away from my face and stared at the mirrored vanity. Dark circles highlighted my bloodshot eyes and chalk-white skin, which paired awesomely with my lips, still covered in the ashy powder. I plucked a twig out of my tangled hair.

"What happened to me?" I asked my hot mess reflection.

My fall on the ice replayed through my mind. I concentrated. Something was off. The same image ran through my mind. I knew that was what had happened, but for the life of me, I couldn't remember before or after the fall.

Did I hit my head? I swept my hair away and stumbled backward. A half-ash-half-bloody arch dripped down my forehead. I ran the washcloth over my forehead and hissed, dropping the cloth with a fleshy plop into the sink. Blood oozed from my raw, gravel-peppered palms.

"Tess!" Ben, my best friend, banged on my front door.

Holding my breath, I willed him to leave.

"I can hear the water running." Underneath his frustration, worry laced his voice. "Tessa."

"Yep." Wide-eyed, face still covered in blood and ash, but nothing jacked up my panic more than Ben freaking out. No way was I going to face him before pulling out of the mental fog and giving myself a once-over. "Give me a few minutes."

"You have one," Ben warned.

Against my body's protests, I peeled off my sticky clothes.

Dry mouth quivering, pulse hammering at my temples, I traced my fingertips through the rivulets of dried blood decorating my chest.

Over and over the memory of my fall replayed.

"Open up." Ben pounded against the door. "Now!"

"I said, I'm coming." Eyeing the heap of bloodstained clothing at my feet, I crouched and tossed them inside the sink cabinet. From the sharp sting pulsing through my swollen ankle, I groaned as I straightened and snagged my robe off the bathroom door.

Grabbing the washcloth, I wiped my face and chest clean. Having had my share of falls, I confirmed that the road burn and twisted ankle matched up with the blacktop encounters from my past. But the blood....

Ben pummeled the front door.

Wincing, I turned off the tap. As soon as I calmed Ben, I'd send him on his way. While getting ready for job number two, I'd retrace my faulty steps which had led to the congealed blood nesting between my breasts.

Has to be from my hands. Yes. While I slept, blood dripped from my torn-up palms onto my chest. Huffing, I tossed the washcloth into the cabinet, then struggled into the full-length robe. A final glance at the mirror proved I had hidden the remaining bloodstains.

Shuffling out of the bathroom, I swept my hair away from my stiff neck. The brush of my wet fingers against my throat sent white-hot pain flaring through my body, falling against the wall, my vision tunneled and went black.

"Tessa!" Ben's voice jolted me back into consciousness.

Shaking, I stared at the wall. The sensation of fingertips running along my neck had me tripping to the door. Not trusting myself not to scream like a lunatic, I bit my trembling lips.

The doorknob rattled.

In the attempt to quell the terror flooding my nervous system, I gulped a deep breath, forcing my limbs to loosen enough for me to peer through the peephole. Ben paced the narrow hallway, raking his hands through his hair.

In his charcoal pea coat, khakis and rain-dappled penny loafers, he'd raced over right out of work, not even taking a second to discard his lanyard labeling him as a Glenwood Press reporter.

At the click of the deadbolt, he swiveled toward the door and flung it open. "Where the hell have you been? I was two seconds from calling the cops." He stormed past me. "Andrea's been texting me, says your phone's off. I tried and got the same message."

"Andrea—" My voice cracked. I'd lied—when it came to panic-induced heart palpitations, my pissed-off friend trumped a freaked-out Ben. "Call her. Right now."

Ben turned around, chewing the inside of his cheek while giving me a mental pat-down. "You look like crap."

"Nice to see you too," I grumbled. At least his glasses were off. "Please, call Andrea. She'll send the damn SWAT team over here."

"I'll text her." He pulled his phone from his coat. Ben's fingers swept across the screen in his mad texting skills. Then he looked back at me. "Didn't drink the tap water, did you?"

"No." *That* I knew, at least. Definitely didn't drink from the tap. I felt and looked like crap, but I was still able to stumble out of bed. "Although, if you want to watch another season of *Buffy*..."

"Never again." Ben pulled out the barstool. "Have a seat."

I sat as he retrieved the last bottle of water and coffee canister.

"You're going to send me to my grave." Annoyance replaced the fear in his voice. "Answer your damn phone. Okay?"

Where the heck did I leave my phone?

"Tess?"

"Will do," I said. "Sorry I scared you."

"You'd think after three years I'd be used to it." Ben rustled around with a coffee filter. "Rob's ticked."

"When is he not?" I mumbled about my editor.

With the snap of the button, the coffee maker sputtered to life. Instead of my usual countdown to wakefulness, my stomach clenched. I didn't want coffee. Something was seriously wrong with me.

"You were supposed to send him this week's obits by ten this morning."

"My procrastination never caused you to ruin a pair of shoes." I nodded at the road salt crystalizing on Ben's loafers.

He released a dry chuckle.

Unimpressed with his response, I said, "Spill it."

"Fine." He drummed his fingers against the counter. "Last night, after Andrea and I left, tell me you didn't go to the park."

"Shit." Tearing through my hazy memory, my fall replayed in my mind. Digging my nails against the raw flesh of my palms, I welcomed the flicks of pain shooting up my arms. I deserved them. Last night was my chance to catch scumbag McKay red-handed. "I blew it. I didn't get the photo."

Ben let out a frustrated sigh.

"Stop." I glared at him. "Think of the dead fish odor that wafts into your apartment through your windows and faucets."

Ben opened his mouth.

"How you had to sit through a *Buffy* marathon while I groaned in misery and tossed my cookies. Seriously, how many people went to the hospital? How many can't afford their medical bills?" I asked, glancing at my leaky kitchen faucet. "I know it's the water. If I got the photo—"

"After you took it upon yourself to interview McKay, Rob warned you to leave the story alone. You'll lose your job. Your apartment."

"Unlike you, Mr. Salaried Reporter, I'm a lowly freelancer." I smirked. "Fifty bucks for jazzing up the obituaries. I work at the bar to rent this crap hole."

"Okay, smartass." Ben set to pouring a cup of coffee. "Let's talk about safety. Why would the mayor meet with McKay, at night, in the park of all places?"

"No cameras. Less potential witnesses. To be super shady together."

"Absolutely." Ben sat the mug in front of me. "You could have gotten hurt."

A chill crept up my spine with his words. Splaying my shaking hands on the counter, I muttered, "It would've been just a photo."

"It's never just a 'just' with you." Ben's fingers brushed my knuckles and before I yanked my hand away, he flipped it over. "Shit."

"I'm fine."

"What happened to you?" He spun the stool, forcing me to look into his eyes. "Answer me."

"I fell running last night."

Ben sent his phone skidding onto the counter as he dug back into his jacket for his glasses. *Countdown to meltdown Ben in three, two —*

"Fall? You look like someone beat you against the blacktop." Ben softly touched my shoulder, his eyes crinkling in concentration. "Why do you have pieces of fur on you?" He pulled a patch of brown fluff off my shoulder, letting it float from his fingers onto the floor.

"Fur. What happened to me?"

"Hold up. You don't remember? You just said you fell."

"I did fall…" Fear clenched my throat.

"Tess, what aren't you telling me?" He reached for my arm.

I flinched.

"That's it. We're going to the hospital."

I rolled my aching shoulders, composing myself. "No."

"No? Really? Fine. Sit tight and I'll call an ambulance. They can haul your ass out of here."

"Ben, I'm okay, just banged up." I went to grab his phone to keep him from calling, and to start my damage control with Rob.

Ben intercepted the phone.

"I need to call Rob and beg for forgiveness."

"No need." Ben hung his head. "I already covered for you."

"You're my hero." I sighed. "What did you say?"

"The flu. By the looks of it, you can pull it off. Now, getting back to the hospital." Ben moved his finger over the screen, then glanced up, leaning against the counter. "Get dressed. I'll drive you."

"I'm not going."

He turned the phone to show me *911* ready and waiting. His phone flashed *Incoming Call*. Looking at the screen, his brows furrowed. "I've gotta take this." He pushed off the counter and headed down the hall. "Look." Pause. "No. You listen," Ben whispered angrily. "I've no clue who—" Pause. "You don't know her." Pause. "Bite me, asshole." Ben stomped back into the kitchen with his hands slicking his hair flat to his head.

"Who was that?" I asked.

"Some guy who didn't like my investigation on his roach motel of a diner." Ben's gaze darted around my kitchen, avoiding me.

"Well, I guess the *bite me* was called for then." My horrible joke fell flat. "Who's *her*?"

Ben's phone lit up, and he set it on silent. He usually hid nothing from me. Curiosity had me leaning over the counter before he had a chance to hide his cell. Its screen glowed with *private* on the caller I.D. He huffed, shoving it in his pocket.

"I'll be back." Again, he headed down the hall to the bathroom.

While I stared at the stained countertop peeling at the corners, my pity party commenced. "Screw it. The story. McKay. You too, kitty coffee mug." Glaring at the photo of a fluff ball on the mug sitting in front of me, I sank deeper into my thoughts. Running away had become a favorite pastime of mine. I shook my head. *Nope.* Not ready to travel down memory lane. I had enough disappointment right in front of me. All my hard work was for nothing. I'd missed the chance of a lifetime. Each of my failures pounded within my head. I closed my eyes.

"Leave town."

"What did you say?" I called out to Ben.

Silence.

I opened my eyes. "Great. Now I'm hearing things."

Ben stomped out of the bathroom all red-faced and ticked.

"Would you grab the ibuprofen for me?" I asked.

Sighing, I dropped my forehead to the cold counter. I had a hundred fifty-eight dollars to my name. Enough for a bus ticket to nowhere fast.

"The road kicked your butt, and you're wallowing over a photo?" Ben asked.

"Yes." Reluctantly, I lifted my head off the counter to meet his eyes.

"You can still send the story. You have enough with your investigation alone."

"All I have are citations that could be discredited with a simple *'they're phony.'* A list of sick people who refuse to be interviewed about their projectile vomiting. McKay's desktop calendar with a decrypted note on yesterday's date." I huffed. "Easy enough for McKay and the mayor to deny, or say it was a coincidence they had functions on the same day."

"Still, it's too coincidental. It would be enough for someone to investigate—"

"Yep. That someone was *me*." I groaned. "How did I screw up?"

"Tess—"

"Back to Rob's dry-cleaning duty."

"Take some time off. Get yourself checked out and pulled together. We'll hit the story hard on Monday. I have an interview with the mayor. You can come along and snoop." Ben bumped me with his knee.

"Tempting." I nodded. "As for now, I've got to get going."

He perked. "Good. I'll get my car."

I looked at my scraped-up palms. "No doctors. It's just road burn." I mumbled under my breath, "The martinis are gonna hurt like hell."

"You're not working at the bar tonight," Ben said in his firmest voice. "Shit, you can't even remember last night. You could have a concussion."

"Well, I haven't forgotten my rent is due in two weeks. It's the Halloween party tonight. If I'm lucky, I could make half my rent tonight alone."

"You never listen...."

To muffle Ben's protests, I grabbed the remote next to me, on my so-lovely counter, and turned on the TV. The local news station had finished recapping the breaking news of the evening. More claims of stomach bugs—big surprise there—and a missing seventeen-year-old and his dog.

Ben stepped in front of the TV.

I waved him from my view of the missing teen's photo. Haunting blue eyes smiled back at me. I shivered. "I've seen him...before."

Ben barged in front of me.

"Move."

He slapped his hands on his hips before taking a backstep away from the television. Unfortunately, the screen displayed the three-day forecast — rain, rain and more rain. I went to snag the ibuprofen, but Ben beat me to it, twisting off the cap and giving me back a taste of my attitude.

"You're supposed to take that stuff with food. What do you have to eat?" he asked.

As I shrugged my shoulders, pain throbbed through my arms. To mask my groan, I faked a yawn.

Ben pursed his lips. "Add a sore stomach to that attitude-memory-loss combo and you'll *really* bring in the tips tonight." He headed toward my bedroom. "Go shower. You're late as it is. I'll get an outfit together."

I slid off the stool, taking three pills dry. They raked the inside of my parched throat, causing me to gag as I limped to the bathroom. To catch my breath, I stopped and leaned against the wall. Through my coughing tears, the hallway's overhead light reflected a soft glow onto my coffee table littered with unopened bills and my scribbled notes on dirtbag McKay.

Copper glinted in the pale light. An image popped into my mind of Ben spinning a penny across the table and the coin landing on heads. I walked over to the lopsided table and glanced down. My heart skipped a beat. The penny was tails up. "Ben?"

"What?" He came out of my bedroom with his eyes glued to his phone.

"Last night, we coin-tossed and the penny landed on heads. Right?"

"Yep." He glanced up from his phone. "You won. Instead of heading to Andrea's for a chick-flick night, you were *supposed* to catch up on some sleep."

"See?" Guilt tickled my gut. I'd blown off my friends for the opportunity to spy on McKay. I'd counted on the coin to do a better job at buffering my guilt. After all, it was the stupid penny's fault for landing in my favor. "I'm getting the night back by the minute."

Ben turned toward my bedroom. "You've got about fifteen minutes to get it all back."

I scooped up the penny. The cold metal soothed my burning palm as I closed my eyes. "What happened to me?"

Darkness answered.

I concentrated, focusing on my fall. My head throbbed, every pulse intensifying. I refused to give in. Clasping the coin, I hissed into the pain. A flash of light engulfed my vision.

As it dimmed, my living room took on a hazy, dreamlike state. I squinted at my couch where a man in a torn-up suit sat.

With his bloodstained index finger, he reached for the penny on the table. "You would let a coin choose your fate?" he asked. "Careless." He tilted the coin to tails and stood. Then he walked over to the window and opened it. "May our paths never again cross, Tessa Sanders." When he glanced over his shoulder, his stare caught mine. "It will end poorly for you."

The penny clattering against the floor jarred me awake. Alone in my dark living room, I shivered as a breeze caressed the side of my neck. Turning toward the draft, I faced my half-opened window.

Chapter Three

As the shower's cold water pelted my face, fatigue whispered through my limbs, tempting me to turn the faucet to hot. Refusing, I placed my forehead against the wet tile. Mud, leaf litter and pink-tinged water slipped down the rusty drain while my thoughts consumed me.

Ben knocked on the door. "All you have that's edible is a bagel. No clue how old your leftovers in the fridge are or the thing that was once a fruit. An apple. Orange. Beats me." His phone chirped. He paused to text a response. "I'm sending Rob a message saying you'll call him in the a.m. Where's your phone anyway?"

"Good question," I said. "Check under the bed."

"Already did." He cleared his throat. "Not there or between the couch cushions, the coffee table, the kitchen—" His phone chirped. "The battery probably died. I'll check your desk for the charger." Mumbling under his breath, Ben headed toward my bedroom.

"Great, missing memories. Missing phone. I have the best luck ever." While I turned off the faucet, my hand shook with an unknown dread. I continued backtracking my night. I remembered the coin toss. The fall. Then blank. "Shit." I toed a leaf suctioned to the drain. The memory of a bush poking against the back of my head flashed before me. As I focused on the leaf at my foot, the memory of the bodyguard trudging up the hill hit me.

Holy crap.

Before the last of the water slipped down the drain, I snagged a towel. My teeth chattered while fear bubbled up from the pit of my stomach.

Please let Ben find my phone.

As I rushed to dry off, a sharp burn erupted from my torn-up palms. Gritting my teeth, I dropped the towel, now marked with fresh blood splotches. "Tessa. Get in here!"

I tossed on my robe then rushed out of the bathroom. The setting sun had sucked the last of the warmth from the day, which made my damp skin prickle while my heart drummed away with a false hope that Ben had found my phone.

The glow from my laptop highlighted Ben's bleak expression as he hunched over my desk. When the floorboards creaked under my feet, he looked over his shoulder. "You got it." Raking his hands through his hair, Ben sucked air between his teeth. "Holy shit, Tess." He stepped aside, allowing me a clear view of the screen. Front and center was a photo of Mayor Brown and Tim McKay exchanging money and a manila envelope.

I swallowed hard.

Ben started to pace, his deep-in-thought habit. The office carpets had a *Ben path* from his brainstorming. I knew better than to pull him out of his process. Still, I dug my toes into the carpet, holding myself firm from grabbing him and shaking him by the shoulders.

After the tenth silent pass, I moved to the laptop. Ben grabbed my wrist over the keyboard. "What are you doing?"

I looked from Ben's hand to his frown. "Sending the story and photo to Rob."

"No. Not safe. Anyone can hack into Rob's email."

I raised an eyebrow. "You mean you."

"And that says a lot. I barely scraped by in computer science." Ben's attention darted to his cell an inch from my fingertips.

"Did you find my phone?"

"No."

"That means I lost it when I fell." I studied the fear seeping from Ben's eyes. "That means someone could have found my phone." Fear turned to panic in his peepers. I knew then. "That means the person that has been hounding you on your phone has mine."

I went to grab his phone.

He beat me to it. Muttering under his breath, Ben turned away from me.

"Start talking." I folded my arms to keep from slapping him. "Why keep that from me?"

"You're hurt. Upset about the story." He plopped onto my bed. Hanging his head, Ben pinched the bridge of his nose. "I needed time to think this through. Make a plan. But he kept calling. I couldn't focus."

"Do you know who he is?" I walked over to the bed. As I sat on the opposite corner, the frame groaned with the extra weight it wasn't used to. Unable to look at Ben, I stared at the photo of my family.

"No. The arrogant S.O.B. didn't give me his name. He has a deep voice with a southern accent," Ben grumbled. "No one around here talks like that. I could pick the bastard's voice out in a crowd."

I looked away from Mom's smile to the scowl on Ben's lips. "What does he want?"

Ben stared straight ahead, no doubt trying to phrase his wording in the most delicate way to say, "*Tessa, you're fucked.*" "For you to stay here and be alone."

I smirked. "So he can off me?"

"Not funny." Ben glared at me. "He said he'd give your phone back. No questions asked."

"Yep. Right *on* my dead body left in the dumpster." I nodded to myself. "That's why you want me to go to the hospital. So a random security officer, a handful of cameras and overworked nurses can babysit me, while you try to bargain with this person?"

"Look at your hands. And don't think I didn't notice you limping. You need medical attention" — Ben smoothed the wrinkles out of his pant legs — "and a couple of dozen cops, too."

"Tell me everything," I demanded.

Lifting his gaze, Ben sighed. "He said he'd hand over your phone to the mayor if you did not follow his order."

"Order?" I raised an eyebrow. "Like, 'obey me'?"

"That's what he said."

"Who is this tool?" I chewed my lip in concentration while Ben sat rigid, waiting on my words. "He's not a cop. I'd have been hauled out of here for questioning already."

Ben grunted in agreement. "I think he's a bodyguard for the mayor. The jerk said he'd give your phone to the mayor."

I shook my head. "No. He'd already have given the phone to the mayor, and I would've been answering my door to some PR offering a latte and an explanation."

"The mayor would want to keep this a secret. That's why he's been on the down-low."

"He wouldn't have allowed me to go to work this morning without some kind of PR block."

"Okay. Not working for the mayor." Ben sighed.

"Wait. Accent. Not from town—" I jerked my head back to the laptop's screen. In the left-hand corner of the photo stood a large man. A snapshot of my vague memory hit on the three meatheads flanking McKay. I looked back at Ben. "Last night, McKay had some men with him—"

"Fucking Tim McKay." Ben shoved to his feet.

"It makes sense. The mayor has his money, and my clumsy ass just gave Tim a way to get it back." As my pulse hammered at my temples, I gave myself a mental beating. Even if I followed the tool's orders, there wasn't a chance in hell that McKay would let Ben off the hook.

"What are we going to do?" Ben asked.

"You're going to send the story and photo to your email. Once sent, you delete my file. I'm going to get dressed and ready for work." Limping over to the chair, I grabbed the outfit Ben had assembled.

"Tessa—"

"The bar will be packed. And you said it yourself—you could pick his voice out in a crowd."

"Shit. What if he—"

"He'd be stupid to try anything while I'm at work."

"We should leave for the hospital, now." Ben paced to my closet where a half-full bag of my clothes sat on the floor. He tossed in a pair of jeans.

"No." I put some force behind my words. "This tool needs to be caught. They all do."

Minutes later, dressed and almost ready to go, we sat on the couch while Ben bandaged my hands.

"There. That should hold." Ben yanked the last of the sports tape from its spool. Attempting a basket with the cardboard roll, he missed the trash completely, scattering papers from the coffee table across the floor. In a perfected stalling tactic, he gathered up the mess, then proceeded to stack my bills in alphabetical order.

"You missed one." I pointed at my rent bill halfway under my couch.

Narrowing his eyes at me, he retrieved the envelope covered with my scribbled notes. Once Ben stuffed it between my electric and student loan bills, he sighed. "Are you sure you want to do this?"

I nodded.

"Fine." He pulled his keys from his pocket. "I'm driving."

"I can—" Within Ben's eyes, an epic meltdown on the cusp of being unleashed had me retracting my retort. I lived a brisk five-minute walk from Oblivion, the bar Andrea and I worked at. I had been looking forward to the fresh air. Now, I'd be stuck in Ben's car with a lavender air freshener and country twang.

Yuck.

I grabbed my overnight bag. Until the story aired, I had agreed to stay at Ben's apartment. Since the bad guys—living and phantom—knew where I lived.

As we neared my door, I glanced around my patchwork apartment. The curtains lifting in the breeze caught my attention. "Wait a sec." Shuffling over, I hid the limp from my ankle while counterbalancing the bag on my shoulder.

Ben rounded the couch ahead of me. "Why's your window open? It's freezing outside. You could set the place on fire with that P.O.S. furnace running."

I shrugged my free shoulder, nearly tipping myself off balance. Masking my awkward spill, I huffed and picked the stupid penny off the floor. "I needed fresh air," I said, shoving the coin in my pocket along with my bottle opener.

Ben started his fight with the window.

"Put your back into it," I offered.

As he groaned, his face flushed. "How the heck did you open this with your hands?"

Oh, I didn't. The creep in my subconscious did. Instead, I said, "I opened it before I went to get the photo."

Ben jumped and forced the window closed. Step one. He sighed, then started on step two—struggling with the lock. The little knob gave a good fight, seeking its reward with a broken nail and a curse.

The lock snapped into place, and Ben cursed. "Let's go," he moaned as he shook his hand out.

Chapter Four

To free myself from the lavender and country, I about jumped from the moving car while Ben was pulling up to the rain-slick curb.

"Tess—" His hand landed on the empty seat instead of the arm he was going for.

Tuning Ben out, I glanced around the empty service road. During the brief ride over, my focus was on the rearview mirror, watching for tailgaters, while Ben kept his attention on the road. No stalkers. No goons. Nada.

Anticipation wound me up like a jack-in-the-box, with the blackmailing tool and phantom taking turns at my crank. I wanted the night to be over, bad guys in jail, Ben safe and my memory back.

Ben leaned across the passenger seat, staring at me over the rim of his glasses. "Did you hear me?"

"Not over the yodeling."

"I said, I'll be in after I park."

A muted song about a cowboy crying over his pickup truck filled the tense silence between us. Tired, annoyed and a tad scared, I blurted, "You should go home and publish the story."

"I programmed the story to publish at five a.m., regardless of whether we catch him."

"Good."

Ben blew out a puff of breath. The steam curled around his head while he shifted the car into drive. "Give me five, and I'll be in." Groaning, he drummed his fingers on the steering wheel. Ben's idea of a stellar Saturday was pizza and a dozen episodes of old sci-fi flicks. To confirm the misery he'd be enduring, bass music pulsed through the bar's brick walls and vibrated down to my ribcage.

"No fiddles in there," I warned.

Ben's jaw tightened. "I can live through a couple of hours of crappy music."

"A couple of hours?" I grinned. "I work until four."

"You owe me."

Once Ben's car was out of sight, I turned to the building. Phil, the owner of Oblivion, stood at the front entrance, barking orders at the bodyguards towering over him. Heck, even when I wore flats, I had a perfect view of his toupee. Phil had most of us on the girth aspect, though. Dressed as a Wild West sheriff, big white hat and all, Phil waved his pudgy hand in a shooing motion at his employees.

I crept to the side door, giving three solid knocks to signal a worker. When the door opened, I shuffled in before Phil's beady-black eyes landed on me.

"You're late." The head of Oblivion's security's baritone voice cut through the music. Shutting the door, Sam turned to face me. While he crossed his arms over his broad chest, he visually scanned me head to toe. "Andrea said you fell."

"I'm fine." Kudos to me for speaking in a full sentence. Usually, I avoided one-on-ones with Sam. His dimples buddied with intelligence made me…girly. Not cool. Dropping my gaze, I shimmied past his six-foot-two, solid-mass frame.

Ahead, Oblivion's eighties decor rose from a sea of dry ice. Across from the DJ booth, the bar's lit shelves illuminated the liquor bottles in a spectrum of color, while fog rolled around their silver spouts. The bar had the appearance of a mad scientist lab. By nine p.m., it would take on the persona as well.

"Nice ambiance." Sam winked.

"Big word." I smiled at him. "Cracked open the thesaurus while you polished your bald noggin?"

Grinning, he slapped the side of his neck. "Your snark monster's got some bite. That big word was a hint, you know?"

"I know." I did a turn, showing off my black tee and pants. "Dressed up as a bartender."

When the front doors opened, cold air spilled onto the dance floor, scattering the dry ice fumes, close behind, the rest of the staff poured inside. One person stood out, blazing at hyper-speed over to us. Andrea's spiked chestnut hair hid beneath a red pointed hat, her wrath zoned in to her target.

"Good luck." Patting my shoulder, Sam strolled past me.

"Thanks a lot," I mumbled behind a strained smile.

Andrea came to a halt, jabbing a black lacquered nail at me. "Did ya lose your costume, too?" Slapping her hands on her hips, the wicked witch snapped her cinnamon gum at me.

"You're about to lose your left boob." I pointed at her ample bosom, ready to jump out of the pleather corset.

Andrea's scowl never wavered. "Phil's gonna be pissed. He said not an option."

I muttered my gratitude to the partnership between the ibuprofen and my knee-high boots, because my sore ankle gave little protest as I distanced myself from Andrea and her skintight micro-miniskirt.

In a hip slide, I pushed myself over the bar. Too bad I'd forgotten about my road burn. To hide my cringe, I ducked to store my jacket behind the kegs. "Did you take stock yet?" I asked.

The swing door slammed against the wall. I looked over my shoulder, and my gaze landed on Andrea's thigh-high, laced boots. "Bathroom. You. Me. Now."

Before I could object, her petite hand grasped my forearm, dragging me upward then toward the bathroom.

Once inside, she sashayed me over to the sinks. "You stay." Andrea spun her back to me, banging her fists against the three bathroom stall doors. "Get done and out." Her witch hat jerked with a sharp nod, hearing no activity from behind the doors. She pivoted and cocked her chin up at me, all of five-foot-three with nostrils flaring. Not even Sam stood a chance against her in this state.

I backed up, bumping my butt into a damp sink, my hands braced against the porcelain. With the contact, a dull throb ran up my arms. I thought I knew then why we were having bathroom-chat time. "Ben told you I fell. Right?"

"Yeah. Not buying it. The punk harassing Ben do that?"

"What're you talking about?"

Andrea grabbed me by the shoulders and spun me to the mirror. "You want to tell me now?" She yanked up the capped sleeves of my shirt, displaying five scabbed-over crescent marks on each arm.

I leaned in, blinking a few times. Along with the slices in my skin, black and blue bruises encircled them.

"What the hell." Andrea let me go. "You're hurt, lost your memory, some creep is after you and you want to play fucking detective?"

"I need to." I looked into the mirror, locking stares with Andrea. "I have to."

"Why?"

"No one else has. Or they were threatened and gave up."

"Smart people—"

"*Scared* people." I turned to face her. Fear was a luxury I couldn't afford at the moment. I killed all emotion from my voice. "This story being released—"

"Won't bring your family back from the dead." Her eyes widened. "Tess, I'm sorry, I just…"

"Don't." I bit my lip. Ben and Andrea were the only souls who knew about my past, even if it was the watered-down version. Taking a deep breath, I refocused. "All this tool is doing is talking smack."

Andrea pointed at my arm. "And *those* marks are from helping hands?"

"I fell."

"Newsflash, Ms. Reporter, you scare the shit out of me. I've had it with your I-got-this-I'm-fine crap." She slapped her hands on her hips. "This is how *we're* going to handle this asshole. You don't agree, then you can take your sweet ass out of here and straight to the cops. Got it?"

"All that texting back and forth while I was getting ready—I should have known you and Ben were plotting."

"What did you think I was doing all this damn time? Baking cookies?" She folded her arms. "I've been here, watching for some thug looking to mess with my friends."

"I'm sorry." My temples pulsed to the beat of my racing heart. My plan had only made it to Ben signaling the tool. Leave it to my pals to make the plan free of chaos. As I stared into Andrea's eyes, fear nibbled at my gut. She had signed herself up as a target for the tool. To keep my friends safe, I'd go along with their plan, until I came up with...something that didn't involve them. I sighed. "Fill me in."

"Ben will lift his beer when he identifies the asshole." She slipped her fingers between the gap of her boot and thigh, fished around for a second then retrieved her cherry-red phone. "I call the cops."

"What if the tool catches on?"

"Sam is on stand-by."

I groaned. "You told Sam?"

"Not the *whole* story." She hesitated then covered with, "He likes you. A lot. Something you *should* investigate after this shit gets settled."

Mentally adding Sam to the target list, I glanced at the floor. "Look, I appreciate the help, but this is my mess."

"You're not alone." Her voice softened. "Me, Sam and Ben. We care about you."

"That's why you *all* need to let me handle this." I straightened to my full height of five-foot-seven—thanks to my boots.

Eyes smoldering, Andrea snapped her gum at me—her go-to stress vice since she'd quit smoking two months ago. Cinnamon permeated the air between us. It was a lingering scent inside my apartment, a constant reminder of our long nights of banter where Andrea had pleaded with me to leave the Tim McKay story alone.

I sucked at the friend thing.

"No more vigilante," she ordered. "You see shit going down, you call over the headset 'Fool's brew kicked.' Got it?"

No able body drank the dark brew. The only time it kicked was when it needed to be tossed. There'd be no confusion if I gave that warning. Tipping my chin at the water-stained ceiling, I sighed. "Let's go."

Andrea's arms and legs spread, blocking the door. "I'm not done," she snapped. "After this asshole is taken away and the story is published, you are going to the hospital."

"I'm fine." I shoved my hands under my armpits. "Why don't you believe me?"

And just like Ben earlier, her dainty and hell-bent finger moved across the screen of her phone. *911* waited for her command. Andrea's perfectly hot-waxed eyebrow arched. "So. Are you going to follow the plan or not?" The door bumped against her backside. "Watch it," she yipped.

"Sorry," Sam not-too-apologetically said. "Open in ten. Phil wants a rundown on the bar."

"We're coming," I answered.

"Not yet." Andrea tucked her phone into her boot. "Dress up's not an option *and* both our rents are due."

Minutes later we left the restroom. Andrea grinned ear to ear while I emerged with some of my dignity still intact. Explaining that my pants hid my injuries had saved me from stuffing my ass into a miniskirt, while an offer to break down the bar after hours had saved me from changing my form-fitting-tee into a boob-strangling corset. Annoyed, I brushed a strand of hair out of my face. For the sake of the costume, Andrea, the stylist from Hell, had demanded my crazy locks free.

"There's Ben." I nodded at him huddled over his cellphone, swiveling on the barstool closest to the entrance. "He sticks out like a sore thumb—" I flinched when the fog machine sputtered next to us.

"Jumpy?" Andrea asked. Her focus was on solo Ben as well. "Once the bar fills, he'll blend." She batted fog away from her face while she bounced on the balls of her feet.

"Glad you're certain." I flexed my bare fingers around the pair of black gloves covering my bandaged palms. The satin material sucked at my flesh from hands to elbows. Andrea had done well with camouflaging my injuries. She'd hidden the bruises on my upper arms under a red satin caplet. I ran a finger underneath the silk ribbon keeping the cape in place. Sweat already dampened my skin.

"You take stock for the shot girls," Andrea said. "I'll prep the minibar. Phil's been filled in by yours truly. Off you go." With a slap to my ass, she sent me on my way.

When I made it behind the bar, I patted the pocket of my pants, feeling the penny. "Let's see if you're any luckier tonight."

Chapter Five

Ten minutes after opening, Oblivion became a sea of gyrating bodies. I worked the opposite end of the bar from Ben, who sat wedged between a devil and a bearded tooth fairy. Andrea topped off a round of shots in the middle while Sam's bald head bobbed at the front doors. Confident the tool wouldn't slip past us, I allowed my racing mind to focus on work.

"Out of the house gin," Andrea's voice crackled into my headset.

"I'll get Sam," I answered. Sweat plastered hair to my cheek and annoyingly slipped between my ear and the headset. A low buzz answered me back. *Great. Must've shorted the headset.* I lined up a row of longnecks while taking a sweep of the bar—now four deep.

"Didja get that?" Andrea's muted voice crackled. "I...." The connection succumbed to the buzzing.

I tapped the battery pack attached to my hip. The buzzing increased. Giving the knob a few turns caused the buzzing to stop. "What?" I asked, taking my opener to the first bottle.

Andrea's finger poking between my ribs, made me almost dump the beer into a guest's lap. "It's yours. Not mine." Her hand slipped to my battery pack, giving it the same workout I had. "Battery's dead. I'll get another."

The patron couldn't wait a flipping second for his beer. When I pushed the bottle to the edge of the bar, he grabbed my wrist. "Hey." With me jerking my hand free, the bottle tipped over and rolled down the bar, spilling its brew.

"Alcohol abuse!" the crowd cheered.

"I got this." Andrea huffed and turned to grab the cowbell. When she lifted it above her head, the crowd pounded at the bar in a drunken drumroll.

And to think, it was only ten.

I glanced at Ben, whose lips pressed into a grim line while sweat darkened his shirt around his pits and collar. The poster child of misery cringed as the bearded tooth fairy slapped him on the back. Ben's glasses bounced off his nose. As he recovered them, he shook his head at me. The tool so far was M.I.A.

I turned to the waiting crowd with their eyes glued to the liquor bottles held by shot girls prancing across the bar.

"Free shots," Andrea belted while ringing the bell. Simultaneously, the shot girls poured liquor into eager mouths.

I took the opportunity to take off my useless headset and swing over the bar. The bottle of gin wouldn't restock itself, and Sam had his hands full with a couple of fake IDs at the front door.

Stumbling, I blamed my utter loss of equilibrium on the twenty-degree temperature change generated by the heat radiating from the sweaty bodies jostling me about. Latching my focus onto the glowing exit sign by the DJ booth, I made slow progress toward the cellar until a pair of excited dancers sent me slamming against a man's hard chest.

To recover my balance, I snagged ahold of his dress shirt. His hands covered mine, pressing my palms flat across his pecs. The world spun while the music faded into a muffled echo. When the man intertwined our fingers, everything came to a halt.

Lifting my focus from our hands, I shamelessly roamed my gaze along his exposed throat, then settled on a great set of lips. Before I did something stupid with mine, I swept my attention to his eyes.

Colossal mistake. My pulse revved from the intensity blazing within his stare. Never had I experienced a look filled with such concrete desire. Terrifying. Exhilarating. Making it so much better and worse, he leaned into me. As his exhale rushed coolly across my lips, scattered images of this stranger kissing me swirled through my mind.

Again, the dancers crashed against us. The impact was enough to knock my senses back into me. Taking another look into his eyes, I was certain we had never kissed. Thankfully. Lips like those could make a girl forget her name...let alone a breaking news story. Regaining my focus, I plastered McKay's nasty face to my mind.

"Sorry." I tried to pull away, but the stranger held firm. Mentally, I kicked myself. There was no way he had heard me over the music, and he must've mistaken my wandering hands and googly eyes as an invitation because he dragged me into the heart of the dance floor.

As I tugged in the opposite direction, my heels skated along the beer-slick floor. To keep me from falling he clamped his hand onto my wrist, pulling me tightly against his back. With my nose shoved against his spine, his rich cologne drifted into my nostrils. Catching myself in a deep sniff, I shook my head from the effects of this man. In an attempt to hinder his movement, I hooked my leg around his.

Flawlessly, he countered, spinning me to face him. The stranger locked his glare with mine. "You will walk with me" — beneath his commanding tone, a musical lilt accompanied his deep voice — "now."

"Are you…Scottish?"

He didn't answer but his hand tightened around mine. Knowing the only exposure, outside of New York, Ben had ever had was with the Discovery Network, any sing-song accent could've been southern to him.

"It's you — "

Too fast for me to follow, the stranger's lips brushed against my ear. Over the deafening bass, I heard his whispers clearly. "The wolves have come for you. Can you not see them? Smell them? Because they see you. Smell you." He abruptly turned me around, slipping a hand to my hip as his other draped across my shoulders. With my back molded to his chest, he swayed us to the music, mimicking the other dancers. Everywhere our bodies touched hummed with a sensitivity only awarded to lovers. Desire, searing me from the inside, demanded I press every inch of my stupid body to his, while fear tore through me, keeping me rigid and in check. The stranger's arm loosened around my shoulder, allowing his fingers freedom to run along my collarbone. Once more, his voice caressed my ear. "Look."

Through the slivers of space between dancing bodies, my attention locked on the far back wall where three huge men stood with their stares fixed on me. When they took a step toward us, I rotated in the stranger's grasp.

"Go," he said, forcing me toward the emergency exit.

"I'm not leaving with you." Twisting my wrist, I dislodged his grip. At the loss of his resistance, I stumbled backward and smacked into another hard chest.

"You okay, Tess?" Sam pulled me behind him while the stranger retreated to the exit. "Is that…?"

"I think so—"

Sam barked into his headset, "Forty-seven. Back door."

A group of bouncers moved at a quick clip toward the door. Sam maneuvered his torso, giving me a clear view of the stranger's confrontation with the bouncers. Without issues, he walked out the door with the group.

Grabbing onto Sam's arm, I glanced over my shoulder to the empty brick wall, wildly scanning the rest of the dance floor. The three men had just disappeared. Goosebumps chased the cold sweat running down my spine.

"Cops are coming." Sam moved in front of me. With eyebrows drawn together, he scanned my face. He tracked my gaze, snapping his attention over his shoulder at the wall. Slowly, he turned back to me. "You okay?"

"I'll be fine." Terror rolled around in the back of my mind. Even if my imagination was making up phantoms, it did have a point. *Too easy*. The stranger had gone with the security guards without a fight.

"Where's your headset?" Sam asked.

"Oh." Absently, I tucked a strand of hair behind my ear. "I took it off."

"Keep it on. Got it?"

"They don't work."

Concern flashed through Sam's eyes. "Stay behind the bar until we close. You need out sooner, call me."

I nodded.

Dodging past Sam, Ben wrapped his tense arms around me. "You scared the shit out of us."

I looked past Ben's shoulder to Andrea's scowl as she jammed a spout into a new bottle of gin. Glancing back at Ben, I said, "We got him."

His face lit. "Where is he?"

"They took him out back," Sam answered. "Cops should be here soon."

"I'm gonna watch what goes down," Ben said to Sam.

Sam leaned over me. "I don't want a scene."

Ben nodded.

"Head out the front," Sam continued. "I'll have one of my team escort you around back."

"I'll return as soon as he's in the cop car." Ben's arms slipped from around me.

"No." I grabbed onto Ben's forearms, forcing him to focus on me. "Something's…off."

Ben's eyes widened, and, denying him the opportunity to blast me with a dozen questions, I pulled him to me, whispering against his ear, "I don't think he's working alone. Follow the cop car that they stuff him in."

"Gotta move." Sam tapped my shoulder. "We need you safe behind the bar."

I let go of Ben.

"All good, Sam?" Rick, one of the bouncers, came up behind Ben.

Sam raised an eyebrow at Ben.

"I'm okay," I mouthed. "Go."

With Ben's shallow nod, relief spiked my adrenaline.

"Sam, you'll drive Andrea and Tessa to my place," Ben stated. The look on Rick's face proved no one gave orders to Sam.

"Will do." Sam took a hold of my hand. "Rick, you stick with Ben until I head over there."

While Rick ushered Ben toward the front door, Sam cleared the way through the dance floor to the bar.

When I slid over the counter, Andrea received me with crossed arms and a death glare. "Ummm, where we at?" I asked, slipping on the headset.

She stood there, smoldering until the bargoers took up drumming on the bar. "There's a—"

A high-pitched screech blasted through the earpiece. Wincing, Andrea pulled off her headset and tossed it into the tip jar. I mirrored her. Our means of communication would be hand gestures. She jabbed a finger at the end of the bar. I gave a nod and turned.

"Huge fucker," I huffed to myself.

With his hands splayed on the counter, the man took up enough space to squeeze in three more guests, yet all stayed a body length from him.

I ignored the waving bills in my autopilot to the end of the bar, still shaking off the heebie-jeebies from the stranger's rants about wolves and his phantom posse. Taking a calming breath, I inhaled sandalwood. The behemoth was oozing the dominant scent. I kept my head down. A good-smelling man had gotten me into trouble a time or…like ten minutes ago.

"What can I get you?" I asked his onyx ring.

"Something red," he replied.

I glanced up from his ring to a handsome face with blond hair tied back, allowing for a very nice view. Until I looked into his amber eyes. That was where the good looks ended, and wickedness began. My gut instinct kicked into overdrive, screaming, *Run.*

"Is there something wrong, Red?" He cocked an eyebrow.

"Yes. Guys thinking they're slick, nicknaming redheads Red." I narrowed my eyes.

"Such an attitude." He tilted his chin upward and his nostrils flared with a deep inhale.

"Did you…just *sniff* me?"

"I did." His grin parted his full lips. "No perfume. Good."

"What? You can—" I shook my head and the glint of his ring captured my attention. I could play nice long enough to grab a tip from the guy. "Just tell me what you want to drink."

"I like the taste of vanilla." His tongue slid across the tips of his teeth. "Warm. Clean. Weak. Perfect."

I opened and shut my mouth. The urge to tell the jerk to *taste* my boot heel had me counting to three. "Whatever, dude." I turned and reached on tiptoes for a top-shelf whiskey. My shirt lifted with my efforts, exposing my midriff. Cold air prickled my belly as heat scorched my back. When I glanced over my shoulder,

Mr. Sex's amber eyes were locked onto my ass. Slowly his gaze swept up my torso and settled onto my lips.

Looking down, I stole a peek at his chest through the gaps between the black buttons and red silk of his shirt. Tightening my fingers around the bottle with the thought—I could've easily traced the plates of his muscles.

"Enjoying the view, Red?"

"You lost a button," I said, shrugging my shoulders. While he was preoccupied with checking out the non-missing button, I poured a shot.

His manicured fingers slipped to his chest, pinching the button between his pecs. "I have them all. Yet"—his voice dropped—"I don't have a drink."

"Here, on me—*no*. I mean—"

The *ting* of the button hitting the shot glass in my hand and whiskey splashing onto my wrist had me sinking my teeth into the flesh of my lip. Mr. Sex, less one button, leaned over the bar.

"Serve me my drink." The rush of his exhale slapped his minty breath against my cheek while he snagged the wrist of my hand that was holding the shot. Jerking my arm to his lips, he dug his finger into the pressure point at my wrist, causing my hand to release the glass, spilling the shot down my arm.

Soaking through the glove and bandage, the whiskey found my torn-up palm. I groaned at the pulsing pain. Any attempt to struggle free ended when his mouth sealed over the heel of my glove. Rolling his gaze to mine, he lapped the whiskey up.

"Let go—"

With the graze of his teeth against the soaking fabric, flicks of heat shot to my belly. Shocked, I froze. Not taking a hint or care for my discomfort, he dragged the flat of his tongue down the underside of my arm.

"Now," I gritted, half-wanting and half-not wanting him to listen to me. Some stupid part of me wanted to pick a fight with the asshole, forcing my glare from Mr. Sex—enjoying his shot—to my bottle opener resting on the bar. Not that I wanted to stab him. However, a jab with its hilt to his solar plexus was an option. My fingers curled around the sticky metal.

Mr. Sex nipped the underside of my elbow.

I swung the opener.

He defused the blow, grabbing my wrist. "What kind of service is that?"

"You licked me."

"You moaned." His hold tightened, shoving his fingers between the bones of my wrist. The burst of pain caught me off guard, and the bottle opener clattered against the counter. "You reek of want, Red."

"Oh, hell no—"

"Yes." Mr. Sex's face morphed before my eyes, flushed with pronounced angles and bulging veins, stealing the last of my sanity. "And you're too scared to do anything about it."

I clamped my jaw shut.

"You're a coward." His words shattered the wall of badass I'd spent years constructing. "Only the weak attack the unarmed."

"Let me go—"

Jerking me closer, he slid his tongue up the side of my face, then with a laugh, he released me.

I staggered backward, wiping his saliva off my cheek. *Stupid Tessa, letting a man get to you. Let him laugh. Screw him. No. Do not screw him.* I turned away.

"Red," he called out, "I would've preferred tequila. It mixes better with fear."

I planted my hands on the sides of the cash register, staring at the number *three* while his minty spit dried in a smeared line down my face. When a pair of petite hands grabbed onto my hips, I cranked my neck around.

Andrea's sly smile disappeared. "What's wrong?"

I jerked my chin at Mr. Sex. "That asshole licked my face."

"I saw."

I glared at her.

"Hey." She held up her hands. "You flag Sam when you don't want the attention. Which is always. I'm just calling it as I see it...and you're blushing."

"Don't even."

"Well, it's been like what? Six months? No —"

I dragged a finger across my throat, which Andrea giggled at before turning heel. For a little comparison, if my reporting career was a nuclear bomb, then my love life was the apocalypse.

I glanced back at Mr. Sex. Two women wearing nylon catsuits clung to him. While his smug stare partnering with his shit-eating grin mocked me, he dipped his head, whispering something that made the women giggle.

Underneath my breath, I muttered, "Tool."

He laughed.

No way he heard that. Shaking off my nerves, I slipped past Andrea to the opposite side of the bar, giving her a nod that we were switching bar-ends.

Chapter Six

Four a.m. couldn't have come sooner. Neon lights flooded the hazy bar. I tossed my towel in the linen basket and dropped into a booth. Andrea sat across from me with the tip bucket. Sam joined us. Wedging me between the wall and his body, he handed over a chilled bottle of water.

"Thanks." I took a few swigs and closed my eyes.

"You two hungry?" he asked.

"Starving," Andrea answered between counting.

"Tessa?"

"I'm good." Putting the near-empty bottle on the back of my neck, I sighed into the coolness. With Sam's leg nudging me, I cracked open my eyes.

"To hear that sound again, I'll bring you all the water, Tess." Sam's killer grin took up my entire field of vision. He slid me another bottle.

My dry mouth popped open. Blood rushed to my cheeks, and I prayed the dim lights covered my blush. *Nope.* The dimple on his cheek deepened.

"So, not to be a third wheel or anything." Andrea winked at me. "Here's the shot girls' cut, Sammy Boy." Andrea pushed over a stack of bills.

"Whoa. Nice night." Sam scooted out of the booth. His eyes lingered on my too-warm face. "I'll be back after I lock up."

"See ya," I mumbled, slumping further into the booth.

"Girl." Andrea wiggled her eyebrows at me. "You're hooking up. Tonight."

"So not." Exhaustion made the plastic-covered two-by-fours comfy. Fatigue carried me into a flashback of the dark-haired stranger. His hands. Lips. That voice —

"Tess. Yo." Andrea tapped my shin underneath the table with her boot. "Wakey, wakey."

"Yes?"

"You look like shit."

"Thank you." I slanted open my eyes to her and giggled. "Take a peek in your magic mirror, witchy."

"I broke it." She smirked at me with mascara trailing down her cheeks and flattened hair. Andrea had lost her hat halfway through the night, about the time Mr. Sex had left with the slutty kitties.

I held out my hand. "Well, how'd we do?"

"Rent paid." She plopped the thicker pile in my palm.

"You had to give me all the ones?"

"I took the change." She shook her purse.

Glancing over at the bar, I willed my jacket to me. No luck.

When the front doors opened, a breeze whipped through the bar, scattering the stagnant air.

"We got company," Andrea mumbled around a sip of water.

Sam's back shielded us from the two men.

Andrea dipped below the table. "Cops."

I sat upright. Tiredness was an afterthought as relief and nervousness fought it out for residency in my brain. "Ben must've brought them back."

"No." Andrea returned to her seated position. "He sent me a text."

"What?" I glared at her. "You didn't tell me?"

"Sorry, it was balls-to-walls in here." She slumped against the booth. "I forgot."

"What did he say?"

"Car has a flat."

"Andrea! When did he send it?" I leaned over the table.

She tapped her phone to life. "Eleven p.m. Then he sent at eleven-fifteen — tow here. See you at the apartment at five." She spun her phone to me.

I scrolled through Ben's messages. "No way he'd let that man out of his sight." I looked at Andrea. "Either Ben's playing some kind of code charades or he's in trouble."

Andrea reached over and grabbed her phone. "Relax, Rick's with him. No one messes with that dude."

I struggled to untie the cape from around my neck. "Text Rick. See where they are."

Her fingers tapped against the screen. "Done." Drumming her nails on the table, Andrea's eyes narrowed to her phone. "Come on —"

The screen lit.

Her eyes widened.

My fingers stilled at the knot. "Is it Rick?"

She nodded then turned the phone to me.

In bed. Want 2 join me?

As I launched to my feet, Andrea slapped her hand onto mine. Her attention shifted over my shoulder.

"Ladies, this is Detective Miller and Officer James." Sam pointed at the men.

Officer James' baby face betrayed his neutral expression. Miller, on the other hand, had stone-cold down. Years of questions and answers hid behind his tired eyes. I knew most of the law enforcement in town from both jobs. Yet I'd never seen these two.

Hiding my face from the cops, I looked at Andrea.

She gave them a blank stare and asked, "What's this about, gentlemen?"

"We have some questions we need to ask Miss Sanders in private. Shouldn't take more than a few minutes," a calm, professional voice answered. I rode on a hunch the voice belonged to Miller.

"Is it about the jerk you hauled out of here?" Andrea asked.

"It's a confidential matter, Miss," Miller answered. "Sir? Sam, is it? If you would, please?"

"We lock up in ten." Sam gave a reassuring nod to me. He had my back if need be. He patted Andrea's shoulder. "Sweep the restrooms for me."

"Sweep 'em yourself—"

Sam glared at her.

"Fine." She scooted out of the booth. "Yeses and nos only."

I nodded as Andrea brushed past Sam, who cracked and popped his neck while staring down at the men. Tapping my foot under the table, I wanted the cops to take their report—fast. I needed to get the hell over to

Ben's. *He's safe. He never lasts past midnight. I'm so going to wake his ass up and give him a ration of shit —*

Miller dragged a chair in front of me. As he settled in, my nose tickled with his overpowering cologne — juniper. Talk about a bad Christmas present. "Miss Sanders, you know why we are here?" he asked.

"Yes." *I could do the yes and no.*

"And?"

"And what?" *Fail. Why prolong the inevitable?* "You and your officer are here to question me about the man who grabbed me this evening."

Miller nodded. "Tell us what happened."

"He grabbed me on the dance floor. I said let go. He did. And Sam had him escorted out."

"I see." Miller rubbed his chin. "Now, Miss Sanders, how long have you worked here?"

I paused my foot's tapping with his question. "A year or so."

"Have you had men advance on you before?"

"Yes."

"Hmm." Miller took a long pause. "What happens?"

"We have Sam kick them out."

"And then?"

We take them out back and play patty cake. I took a deep breath. "That's it."

The corner of his thin lip twitched. "I see."

"See what?" I wanted to rip Miller's hand from his chin.

"Well. I find it interesting that, in this instance, the man was taken into custody." Miller leaned in. "Don't you?"

"No."

"Why not?"

I shrugged my shoulders and looked at Sam.

"Gentlemen," Sam said, "we gotta lock up."

"Wait." Miller nodded over to James. The officer, happy to be of service, pulled a photo out of his pocket and a clear bag marked, *evidence*, inside was the casing to my phone.

Fuck.

James placed them in front of me as Miller shifted in his seat and retrieved a pen from his breast pocket. He clicked its push cap, once, twice. A long pause, then he asked, "Miss Sanders, do you recognize this?" Miller pointed at my cracked cover with his pen.

"It's part of a phone," I whispered.

"You're right. Miss. Sanders, do you recognize this person here?" He lifted his pen to the photo.

I glanced at the missing teenager from the evening news report. Instantly, needling pain crept through the base of my skull, and I clenched my eyes shut. A flash of light engulfed the darkness behind my eyelids, and my lost night played in rapid forward, still blurry and skipping parts. I took a shaky breath and the vision slowed and cleared. The teen's lifeless eyes gazed at me while someone sank their teeth…fangs into my throat.

My eyes shot open. "No," I uttered while gripping my knees under the table, fighting the urge to rub my neck, which was tingling from the memory.

"Interesting." Miller stood. "You don't seem so well. Perhaps some fresh air would do you some good?"

I didn't take his bait. I kept my eyes glued to the smiling — now torn into bits and pieces — teenager.

Sam's hand engulfed my trembling shoulder. "You got your answers, gentlemen. Time to go."

"I have one more to ask," Miller said, looking at Sam with a slack expression. Then Miller sharpened his gaze on me. "Where were you last night, Miss Sanders?"

Sweat rolled down the small of my back as I answered, "Home."

He leaned toward me with his potent juniper cologne and judging eyes. "Let me tell you what makes a good detective." Miller's lips curled into a grin. "They can see a lie a mile away."

"Tessa," Sam said, "get up."

Miller nodded to Officer James, who moved closer to the table. Miller returned his focus to me. "You know what makes a great one?" He tapped the tip of his nose. "One who can smell a lie."

"Move it, Tess." Andrea snagged my coat from behind the bar and stormed back to the booth. "We're out—" She tripped over Sam's foot, falling against the table. The half-filled water bottle sloshed over the dead teen's photo and into my lap.

"Dammit, Andrea." Sam hoisted me up, knocking into the table, which sent Andrea's bottle emptying onto the front of Miller's pants. "Watch where you're going."

"Watch your big-ass feet," Andrea countered.

While Officer James fretted over Miller, Sam turned toward Andrea. With his back blocking my view of the cops, Andrea peeked around his arm, catching my attention. She glanced at the bathroom.

Grabbing my coat, I gave a subtle nod, then slipped away from the table.

Once inside the restroom, I locked the door. "Now what—" Sam's keys sat on the counter. Scooping them up, I shoved them into my pocket. A cold breeze hit the nape of my neck when I raked my hands through my hair. I spun in that direction. The window over the third stall was open. I tossed on my coat, then climbed onto the lid of the toilet.

Groaning, I attempted the first pull-up of my adult life. The window's metal frame cut into my injured hands. My grip slid from the mixture of sweat and blood while my boots slipped against the brick wall.

Miller's muffled voice behind the bathroom door gave me the strength to flop my ribs over the frame. I struggled to escape through the small window, scraping my stomach and hips along the way. Outside, a seven-foot drop to the pavement greeted me.

Clenching my jaw, I groaned into the added pressure to my hands as I maneuvered myself to hang, then fell feet first. I was unable to favor my bum ankle as I landed, so pain stabbed at the joint. The pounding of Miller's fist against the bathroom door had me sucking up my tears and limping through the alley.

Real smooth. Nothing says innocent *like running away.* I shook my head. *They can arrest me at Ben's for…whatever. My messed-up memory, the photos, the stranger yacking about wolves as he attempted to abduct me.* I tried to move my feet into a trot, but my ankle gave out, knocking me against the wall. *Nope. Can't even run. Stroll. Mosey on down this alley. When the cops meet you at the end with the cruiser, you can thank them for warming it up. Yep. Just hop right in and spill your guts.*

Inching my way along the damp wall, I held my breath. Even the frigid air couldn't mask the stench rising from the dumpster guarding the dead end. Wrinkling my nose at the musky scent of the forest mixing with the garbage bouquet, I swept my gaze up the wall to the fire-escape ladder a good eight feet up. Digging Sam's keys out of my pocket, I neared the only exit for a limping fugitive.

The parking lot.

I peered around the brick wall. In the middle of the lot, Miller's unmarked car sat underneath the streetlight. Sam's red pickup truck was no more than a few steps from me. Ben's rust bucket sat abandoned between the two.

I limped to the truck. Once I was flush against the driver's side door, I forced my hand to unclench Sam's keys. Their cold metal stuck to the pads of my fingertips. I paused at the lock, knowing that the dome light would shout my presence. Through the driver's side window, I studied Ben's car. No new dents, no broken windows and the doorknobs were still in the locked position. I crouched. All the tires looked fine to me. No flats.

As Oblivion's back door swung open, a flashlight beam swept across the wet pavement. Behind the front tire, I squeezed myself into a ball, facing the alley.

"She's gone," James said.

"Take them," Miller snapped. "I'll track her on foot."

"You can't be serious," Andrea said. "We have rights."

"Yes, you do. James," Miller ordered, "read them their Miranda Rights."

The car purred to life, muting Andrea's protests.

"Wait." The beam of light cut the alley in two. "What's down there?" Miller asked.

"The dumpster," Sam answered.

Dress shoes scuffed at the pavement, and the beam grew brighter, showcasing the dumpster.

"Sir," James said, "a call came in. There's been a break-in at an apartment complex."

"And?" Miller stopped, training the light right over the hood of Sam's car.

"On Delwood. The renter is Tessa Sanders."

"You two, get in, now," Miller ordered. The beam bounced along the pavement with Miller's jog to the car. Sirens echoed within the parking lot while the taillights bathed everything in a crimson hue.

My mind raced to make sense of what had just happened. Someone had broken into my place, proving that the stranger was not acting on his own. Thankfully, I'd had Ben delete everything I had on the story. They'd find nothing before it published in less than an hour. My relief was short-lived. Andrea and Sam sat in the backseat of a cop cruiser while Ben was missing.

Still crouching, I turned toward Ben's car. A shadow passed left to right beneath the vehicle. I slammed my back against the tire while digging into my pants for my bottle opener. Once I retrieved it, I flipped it open.

Click. Click. Click...

I tried to sort out the noise. Not dress shoes...almost like claws. I grasped Sam's keys and bottle opener in my fists at the memory of the dismembered body. No human was capable of that. It had to have been a large animal. Maybe a bear.

A low growl to my right broke my concentration. Something jumped onto the roof of Sam's truck and the undercarriage scraped against the pavement. My eyes locked onto the alley's brick wall, which displayed the shadow of Sam's truck and a massive creature.

Definitely *not* a bear.

With every sniff and snort, my chance of survival diminished. I gave Sam's keys a final squeeze before hurling them down the alley.

The impact with the dumpster sent the creature bounding off the truck. I scrambled to the left as a black mass of fur jumped from the hood of Ben's car and almost collided with me.

As I threw myself forward into a run, my legs straight up refused to move faster than a shuffle.

"Never run at night again," said the stranger in my mind.

My vision tunneled onto Ben's rust bucket—so close, yet so far away.

Growls bounced off the walls around me.

I concentrated on the distance to the car.

Five feet.

An ear-piercing howl silenced the growls.

Four feet.

Once the howling ceased, a gust of wind blew an empty chip bag across the blacktop. Each scrape and crunch the foil made repelled off the walls and muted the beasts' heavy breaths.

I stole a glance to the right, meeting sets of glowing eyes that watched me quickly divert my tear-filled eyes back to the pavement.

Three feet.

A low growl broke my forward movement. I held the bottle opener to my side in a death grip. As the wind grabbed my hair, tossing it away from my face, I lifted my gaze.

A massive white wolf stood on the car roof. The beast's amber eyes focused on me.

A wolf as large as the monster in front of me rounded the car. I didn't dare take my eyes away from the white wolf. Another paced behind me. A sniff from the right was close enough to warm my hand. A pack of tiger-sized wolves circled me—holding a bottle opener as my only weapon.

Lowering its body, the white wolf flattened its ears to its massive head and catapulted off the car. The impact cracked the back of my head against the pavement. Stars flashed across my vision while I struggled to breathe. I was pinned beneath the wolf. The intense pressure to my left forearm grew into searing agony.

Above me, blood arced across the predawn sky. Tracking the spray, I rolled my head to the side. The wolf ripped into my flesh, snapping the bones between its bloodstained jaws. With adrenaline buzzing through me, I impaled its neck with the bottle opener.

The beast unlatched from my arm and thrashed around wildly. With a twist, the wolf freed itself from my bottle opener.

I scrambled backward, slamming my vertebrae against a wheel. While the wolf lapped my blood from its jowls, I looked the beast in its glowing amber eyes. "I hope you choke on me," I gritted.

The wolf tore after me.

I braced against the tire and readied for the killing blow.

The wolf went air-born, but instead of slamming into me, it sailed in the opposite direction. Fighting against the blood loss and the intense agony tearing through my body, I lifted my heavy eyes to the stranger.

He wasn't alone. A group of men flanked him.

Hell broke loose around me. Fur, blood, skin and God knew what else decorated the parking lot. With his eyes trained on the pool of my blood, the stranger kneeled. Giving no warning, he gathered me tight to his chest and stood.

"Stay alive," he whispered.

Chapter Seven

Stay alive…easier said than done.

Agony ravaged every nerve ending as molten fire coursed through my veins. To escape, I sank into a restless sleep and each time its darkness surrounded me, the stranger consumed my nightmares.

A white light penetrated my eyelids. As the brightness intensified, a low-pitched hum filtered into my throbbing skull. After a few blinks to clear my hazy vision, I glanced past the white sheet covering the length of my body to a pair of floor-to-ceiling windows. Outside, the twilight sky held an almost-full moon.

As the rest of my senses came online, I kept still, not trusting myself to make any sudden moves. I might've screamed in pain, and I needed to prepare for whoever could bust through the doors on the other side of the bedroom — which was the size of my entire apartment.

I glanced around the sparse room. Besides the four-poster bed large enough to sleep three linebackers comfortably and a nightstand holding a brass lamp, in the center of the room, three wingback chairs in a semi-circle sat on a fancy rug facing a mammoth-sized fireplace.

That's new. In the dark, halfway across the room, I saw the weave pattern of the chairs' fabric. *My vision's HD.*

I peeked between the chairs to the hearth, where the charcoal remains of massive logs glowed amber. They would've taken at least a day to burn through.

Keeping my growing unease in check, I studied the rest of my surroundings.

Behind the bed, the stench of chemically processed citrus drifted from underneath the bathroom door. I chewed my lip, realizing I was smelling soap behind a closed door, a good fifty feet away.

After another sweep of the room and no new pains from flexing my toes or rolling my shoulders, I struggled to sit. My breath hitched from the cold air slipping between the sheet and my naked body.

Where the hell are my clothes?

Curling into a ball, I snagged the sheet tightly against myself. Nausea rolled through my stomach from the jarring movement. To distract myself, I shifted my focus to the play of light and movement inches from my face.

Moonlight reflected prisms off specks of dust swirling within a draft. I lifted my trembling hand to the crystal-like particles. When my fingertips brushed through the light, they heated and tingled. As I stretched my fingers further into the light, the sensation traveled along my exposed arm, causing the fine hairs to stand on end.

Drugs. I've been drugged. With my heightened senses, it was the only acceptable answer. *With what? Why?*

I shivered. A sweat-soaked strand of hair fell in front of my face. As I batted it away with my free hand, rough cotton scraped my eyebrow. I lowered my left arm. It had been bandaged from wrist to elbow. Four crimson splotches stood out against the white material — two on the top of my forearm and two matching spots on the underside.

In vivid detail, the memory of the wolf attack plowed through my mind. Shaking my head, I tried to sort fact from fiction. After all, I should have been dead, and men didn't pop out of thin air to save a chick from a pack of wolves. *And what's with the moon being so freaking bright?*

I glared at it.

When a cloud slipped in front of the moon, the humming ceased. *The moon was making that noise?* Without the hum acting as a buffer, my heartbeat, breathing, and every sound a person not on drugs would pay no attention to ricocheted through my skull. I hung my head, focusing my attention away from the deafening white noise and onto the bandage.

It was coming off.

Wedging the tip of my index finger between the tape and my sweaty palm, I bent the nail sharply backward. "Shit."

"Tess?"

If not for my enhanced hearing, I'd have mistaken my name for the draft. Snapping up my head, I locked my gaze onto a vertical pole a few feet away from the foot of the bed. From my prior position, the bedposts had blocked the horrid centerpiece. Chain links hung from a metal loop at eye level. Dark speckles marred the pole's metallic surface.

"Hello...?" I whispered.

"You okay?"

I know that voice... "Sam?"

"Present." He inhaled sharply. "You're going to want to move slowly. The fever takes a toll on your body."

I didn't listen.

The exertion of struggling to my knees had my throat burning from sucking in oxygen. Cold air rolled over my tongue, tasting of rich chocolate and sweet wine. It was unnerving—I tasted a scent. Sniffing, I tracked the aroma. When I leaned over, Sam's bald head came into view.

He lifted his honey-colored eyes to me. Deep gashes and bruises covered his swollen face. "Tess, stay calm, and listen to me."

"What happened—" I glanced down the length of his defined torso. Five deep gashes crisscrossed his bare chest. With every breath he took, the wounds opened and oozed blood.

The sheet vibrated with my shivering, and I gripped it tighter against myself. If Sam didn't receive medical attention soon, he'd die. Worse, that delicious scent came from him. My stomach clenched into a tight knot. *What's wrong with me?*

Sam cleared his throat. "We don't have much time."

I snapped my attention to his face. Blood trickled from his split lip and for some sick reason, I wanted to lick it off. "Stay away," I warned.

When he leaned forward, metal scraped against the pole at his back. "Not going anywhere. You need to get out of that bed and hide behind me."

"No." I imagined nuzzling the juncture of his neck and broad shoulders until the throbbing of my gums pulled me out of the warped fantasy. "I've been drugged. Something's—"

"You won't be able to protect yourself."

"What the hell, Sam. You're the one who needs help."

He looked at me for a moment. "Trust me." He ticked his chin at the doors. "Men are on their way. They're killers, Tess. Don't let their bullshit charm fool you. They want nothing more than to tear out our throats. Hear me?"

I wanted to argue the point that we were still alive, but the blood rolling down his abdomen and pooling in his navel stole my thoughts. Each of his breaths made the bloody puddle overflow and trickle down to the seam of his grungy jeans. As my thick tongue unlatched from the roof of my mouth, my stomach rumbled.

Clarity hit. Sam was half right. He was meant to have his throat torn out. His mistake was that some psycho outside the room wouldn't be doing the dirty work.

"Tess?"

"I want to…" I looked down at my fingers digging into the sheet over my breasts. "I'm really messed up."

"It's a lot to take in—"

"Stop." Every time Sam breathed, spoke or moved, more of his sweet scent carried on the air to me. "I need to think." *And to stop imagining I'm eating you.* I inched toward the brass lamp.

"I was stupid. I should've known. It makes so much damn sense now. Your scent…"

I shot over my shoulder, "What the hell are you going on about?"

Sam answered in a soft voice, "We are the same."

"I think your blood loss is getting to you." *And to me.*

He watched me with a blank expression. "Don't let the hunger run you."

"Run me? Look, you're hurt. I'm drugged. Ben's missing. Andrea's—"

"She's alive." Sam took a shallow breath. "They can't hurt her. She's human."

"Listen to you. Human? Of course she's human. Where's Andrea?"

"She's here." He locked his stare with mine, dropping his voice. "Somewhere."

"Not good." I gulped. "No way Andrea would let someone hold her hostage. She has to be hurt or drugged or..." I left my next thought silent and instead asked for an answer. "What happened when the cops took you away?"

"When the *fake* cops were on the way to your apartment, we were attacked by vampires."

That was enough for me. Sam was drugged out of his bald head, or it was the combination of his beat down and blood loss—both were terrifying conclusions. For the past year, I had worked with Sam almost nightly. No one who valued their face picked a fight with Sam. The numbskulls that did took a trip to the ER with a baggy holding their teeth.

Vampires... Shaking my head, I grabbed the brass lamp. The makeshift weapon in hand spiked a surge of confidence. I yanked the cord from the wall. "Try to rest, I'll be back."

"You can't leave the room," Sam said.

"You need help."

"You can help me." He looked down at his chest to an injury in the shape of two crescent marks on his left pec.

As my enhanced vision traced over each tooth imprint, I squeezed the lamp post in my trembling hands. "Who bit you, Sam?"

"Help me."

"How?" I whispered.

"Your—" He jerked his head toward the doors.

"Sam?"

"Get off the bed." He snapped his attention back at me. "Now."

I swung my legs over the side of the bed, but they buckled underneath my weight. In a heap of tangled sheets, I fell on the hardwood floor. Without letting go of my weapon, I gathered the sheets around me and scrambled into a crouching position between the wall and bed.

"Get over here. Hurry," Sam whispered.

I shook my head. When I was at his level, his scent overpowered me. A vision of me lapping the blood away from his chest burned into my mind. "No."

Footfalls scraped against a carpet outside of the room.

Sam closed his eyes and rested his chin on his chest.

"Hey," I whispered.

He didn't make a peep. He just stayed slumped over. Couldn't have said I blamed him playing possum. I glanced under the bed toward the doors. On the other side, a pair of black dress shoes stood facing the room.

Just walk by. Go. Leave.

No luck.

I shot Sam a glance. His shoulders bunched with tension. When he pumped his fists, the metal cuffs around his wrists stretched like taffy. Biting my lip, I hoped the sting would wake me from the drug's effects. Nope. I eyed the windows blocked by Sam's body.

A drawn-out sniff from the other side of the doors kicked my heart into my throat. I gripped the lamp tighter.

"She-beast," a man on the opposite side of the doors said. "I can hear your heartbeat."

Something sharp scratched down one of the doors.

I hunched over to protect my ears without letting go of the post.

The object stopped its travels against the door.

"Your fragile heart pleads for silence." The man paused to inhale. "I can smell you, too."

The screeching continued to travel across the door, toward the glass doorknobs.

Frantically, I backed up, knocking my spine against the wall.

The doorknobs turned.

A whimper raced from my sealed lips, causing the knobs to snap back into place.

"What's the matter?" he mocked. "Do you not like me?"

"Nope."

"Let me in."

"Not gonna happen."

"You're teasing me." He laughed softly. "Is that a proper repayment for someone who has spared your pathetic life?" His laughter swirled around my head, making me dizzy. "I shall tell you what you smell like." He paused for another inhale. "You are sweet." He dragged out each word. "I'm...going to...devour... you."

"No—"

The doors opened.

I dropped to my belly. From under the bed, I had a clear view of the man standing at the threshold. He was no taller than me, and his slender build tipped the scales in my favor. *What besides his blond hair, outdated suit and pale skin could he attack me with?*

As the man's gaze landed on the bed, the tips of his pearl-white fangs protruded from his curling lips. "Death would be a great favor to you." He cocked his head down at me, locking his black mirror-like eyes with mine. "You are alone. Weak. Broken."

His words dug into my brain, pulling memories from me like a film in reverse. The image of my family's upside-down car, engulfed in flames, slammed into me. Screams surrounded me.

"So much sorrow and death follow you. Such heavy burdens for an insignificant girl to carry."

Tears stung my eyes.

"Guilt. Shame. Cowardice," he said. "You cannot run from memories. Come to me, and I'll give you the peace you so crave."

Like a siren's call, his words summoned me. When I stood, the sheet cascaded around my feet. The cold air dried the sweat from my body while the brass lamp hung from my trembling fingertips.

A sneer wrinkled his face. "Such a disappointment you are."

How right he was. The truth I'd fought to change, hide and forget rolled effortlessly from his tongue. He promised me peace...an end.

With my forward step, the lamp slipped from my fingertips, crashing to the floor. The lightbulb's shattering rang through my head, snapping me out of the self-pitying B.S.

"No more pain." His voice raised, "No more sorrow —"

"Stop." I slammed my knees against the glass-littered floor. "Get out of my head."

"No more emptiness," he hissed.

From my nails digging into my palms, blood welled up between my fingers. A single drop escaped my fist.

The man's verbal assault ceased.

In dead silence, the crimson droplet splattered against the floor. Heat washed over me while a current of energy raced through my veins, meeting over my chest, intensifying with each heartbeat. I concentrated on the sensation building within me.

"Stop!" He crossed into the room. "I will not be merciful—"

With a force violent enough to shake the walls, something crashed into the hallway. The man's eyes widened a split second before a streak of black appeared behind him. Pale hands with claws grabbed him by the shoulders, ripping him out of the room.

Inhuman shrills cut short by the explosion of glass sent me into action. Stumbling to my feet, I spun around and found myself nose to bloody chest with Sam.

He grabbed me.

"Get to the windows. We can't be more than a story up." I tried to squirm out of his hold. "Sam? Let go."

"We can't leave." He moved us toward the bathroom.

"What are you doing? No. Stop!"

I clawed and kicked wildly at him. His counter-movements opened his injuries, spilling his hot blood against my skin. Escape no longer mattered. I couldn't care less about the monsters in the hall. All that mattered was the raw craving for Sam's blood. I lunged for his chest.

He shifted his hold, one hand to the small of my back, the other tangled in my hair, pulling my head away from his injury. "Try to relax." Even though his body shook, he spoke calmly. "It's easier for you to gain control."

I let him think I bought that. I went lax, and his hold loosened from my hair. As I launched forward, our stares locked.

His voice echoed inside my head. *We are the same.*

Hunger darkened Sam's eyes.

"No—" I fought harder against him.

His hands were always a step ahead of my next kick or jab. I twisted in his grasp to elbow his jaw. With blinding speed, he dodged the blow then grabbed my upper thighs. The shock from the intimate touch caused me to tense, giving Sam the advantage. He scooped me into a cradle-like hold.

"Please," Sam whispered against my hair, "trust me."

I had spent my *short* reporting career as a fact seeker. Stats, studies, photo evidence—I got behind those. I for damn sure never followed a gut feeling or listened to my heart, both of which screamed – trust Sam.

As he jogged us across the room, my lips brushed his shoulder. He swayed in his step. "Almost there."

Closing my eyes, I listened to the drum of his heartbeat. The need to be closer to his heart had me trailing my lips over the bite. I couldn't help myself—I licked. Blood mixed with sweat rolled across my tongue, and my throat convulsed around the droplets.

"I'm thirsty...so thirsty." Sweat broke out across my shivering body. "I'm going...mad," I panted.

Sam kicked open a door. "I need you to take deep breaths for me."

He sat me on a cold marble counter, and its chill bit into my ass, snapping me out of the urge to sink my teeth into his flesh.

Gently, Sam tugged me away from his chest. "I need you to—"

I jumped.

He stopped me.

"Listen to me," Sam said, moving his body between my legs while cupping my face with his hands. Sweeping my sweat-soaked hair away from my face, he wiped a stray tear from my cheek with his thumb. "You need help controlling the hunger. I'm going to help."

When he placed one hand on the base of my neck and the other planted next to my thigh, our gazes locked.

"What are you doing?" I asked.

"Trust me." Sam's face flushed beet-red and his eyes began to glow.

I struggled, pinned between his body and the mirror. Clamping both my hands onto his wrist, I tried to hold him away. "Sam!" My grip slipped from his wrist. "No—"

The door slammed against the wall.

Sam stilled yet kept a tight grip on my neck.

I stole a glance over Sam's shoulder to the man who had grabbed me on Oblivion's dance floor and saved me from the wolf. Unlike the blond guy, he didn't look like he'd be petting bunnies on a warm summer day. Crushing skulls under his heel seemed more like his go-to hobby. His blackhole eyes glared at Sam's back. "Get away from her," he said.

Sam turned slightly over his shoulder and spoke to the stranger, "Leave."

"I will not. If she dies—"

82

"She won't." Sam turned to me. "I'm going to…."

I couldn't breathe or much less make sense of Sam's words. Black spots punched holes in my vision as my body vibrated with intense hunger.

Sam cupped my chin. "Trust me."

Before I could protest, he slanted his lips across mine. Wrapping his arms around me, Sam pressed his body against mine. When his tongue coaxed my lips to part, a growl escaped his mouth.

Every inch of my skin prickled and flushed with heat. I tried to pull away, but Sam kissed me deeper, reopening his split lip in the process. Blood coated my tongue. I snapped, sinking my teeth into his swollen lip. With my loss of control, a surge of energy shot up through my belly and out of my mouth, crashing into Sam.

As he stumbled backward, a flash of light consumed Sam, and I closed my eyes.

After a few heartbeats, I took a deep breath. The air no longer held wild energy. I inhaled the scent of crisp pine while I rested my head against the mirror, hungrily taking in air. *What just happened?* I licked my quivering lip. *That was one hell of a lip-lock.* I wiggled my toes. At least my body was mine to control again. Also, the raw hunger had disappeared. I cracked open my eyes.

Sam was gone.

The stranger, however, was not. He stood at the bathroom's threshold, his expression hidden by shadows.

Something stirred below my dangling feet. Pulling away from the mirror, I glanced over my knees to a massive brown wolf lying on the shredded remains of a pair of blue jeans.

Chapter Eight

The wolf opened its eyes.

I scooted backward, pressing my spine against the cold mirror, then tucked myself into a ball to hide my limbs and nudity.

In a sequence of graceful movements, the wolf stretched, flexing its sharp, thick claws while giving a yawn that displayed canines as long as my index finger. After rising to his full height, he stepped around the scraps of jeans to stand in front of me.

No way this is Sam. The simple thought of his name made my face flush. I chalked up the girly reaction to the drugs I'd been given.

"Sam?" I whispered.

With his glowing eyes latched onto mine, the wolf lowered his head the slightest amount.

"No way," I said, even though I knew the unrealistic truth — the wolf was Sam.

"Wolf, stay." The stranger I'd mentally put on the backburner stepped into the bathroom. At least his mirrored monster eyes were gone. He scowled at me. "Tessa Sanders, you will walk to the bedroom and sit on the bed," he ordered.

I curled further into a ball. "If you think I am going to—"

"Now."

"No way." I shook my head, glaring right back at him.

The stranger lifted a pale hand to me. "I call your blood to my command, Tessa Sanders."

Pain crawled up the base of my skull. My limbs shook with the need to move. I forced my attention away from the man and back to the growling wolf. No. It was Sam, who had turned into a wolf after I had kissed him.

Still had a hard time wrapping my mind around that event.

"What kind of drugs did you give me?" I asked the stranger. "Why am I here? Where's Andrea? And where the hell are my clothes?" I almost thought he was going to answer. His lips moved, and he shifted in his stance. Then he got a grip on his macho self and went all stone cold.

"The pain only gets worse," he said, curling his fingers in a beckoning motion. "The wolf can't harm you. Come now."

Pressure pulsed at my temples, my teeth throbbed to the beat of my heart, tears burned my eyes and I couldn't hold out a second longer. Folding my arms around my hunched form, I scooted off the counter. When the balls of my feet made contact with the tiled floor, the pain ebbed. I chanced a glance at Sam, who ruffled my hair with his snorts. One inch more and his wet snout would've touched my forehead.

"Stand with your hands to your sides," the stranger ordered.

I glared at his blank, handsome face. *Handsome?* For letting that description wiggle into my brain, I wanted to slap myself stupid.

"I said—"

"I heard you the first time, asshole." I unfolded my arms from around my breasts and dropped them to my sides. Cold air raised goosebumps across my flesh as Sam's hot breath pelted my ribs.

Heat raced to my face while tears prickled my eyes. Standing stark naked in front of Sam and the stranger, I wanted to crawl away and die. Unable to do either at the moment, I shifted my glare from the stranger's eyes to his chest.

He looked like he'd brawled with a lion. The remains of his white dress shirt sported a bloodstained dye job. It clung to the deep gashes across his chest. The injuries matched those of the human Sam.

I shivered. The blond creep accessorized with claws and fangs could've been waiting outside the bathroom. I was human. I would not survive almost losing my torso. My gaze met the stranger's emotionless eyes. "Don't make me go out there."

He stepped out of my way. "Go."

If I could've used my middle finger, I'd have given him the bird.

Sam stayed facing the counter, giving a soft whine as I passed.

When I crossed the threshold, I got a whiff of the stranger's dark, rich scent blending with the metallic stink of blood staining his clothes.

Eww.

He followed behind me.

Swaying on weak knees, I gathered the courage to glance toward the doors. My throat clenched in my silent cry of relief. No blond guy and the doors were shut.

Men spoke in hushed voices outside of the room. I tried to tune into their conversation, but the stranger caught on. "Pay no mind to the hallway. Keep walking to the bed." After he spoke, the chatting abruptly ceased within the hallway.

Since the stranger somehow controlled my body, I had to climb onto the bed without using my hands. Epic fail. My knees knocked into the wood frame. Groaning, I tried again and failed.

"Can I have my hands back?" I asked, shooting a glare over my shoulder at the stranger.

He gave a shallow nod. "You may use your hands."

"Pity. It would have been amusing to see how she got on the bed without them." The blond monster sat in the center wingback chair, facing the fire. A tuft of pink-tinged hair masked his profile.

In one fluid movement, the stranger in control of my body pulled a sheet off the bed and wrapped it around me. When his fingers brushed my bare arm, goosebumps raced along my skin, kicking my heart into my throat. Sheer terror filled me. Not because the monster had his hands on me. No. Because it felt...good. *Yep.* My life had taken a nosedive. I dragged my wide eyes to his face, meeting the same reaction. His throat bobbed. And I'd be damned if he didn't squeeze my arm, testing my reaction. I denied him. Squinting my eyes, all I could do was glare at him as he picked me up. He shifted me in his arms to create as much distance as possible between us, then sat me on the bed.

"If you make any attempts to escape, or to harm yourself or others, I will make you lie on your back until morning." He turned toward the blond. "Nathaniel, I made it clear. You were not to come into this room."

"Perhaps my head being bashed against the pavement gave me a lapse in memory." Nathaniel peered around the chair. He wasn't kidding. The left side of his head had a distinct dent. Blood and dirt covered his road-burned forehead.

"How is he alive?" I asked.

"It speaks." Nathaniel jerked his chin toward me. Blue irises highlighted by blood-red pupils glared at me. His grin grew, stretching across his fangs. "Boo."

I bolted backward, unfortunately slamming the back of my head against the headboard. *Great.* For the third time that night, I had a headache.

Nathaniel laughed.

"Enough." The command the stranger used in that single word sucked the air from my lungs.

The fanged grin fell from Nathaniel's face. "Her fear smells wonderful." In a blink, he turned the chair around to face the bed. Nathaniel caught me gawking at the fractured ribs jabbing out of his blood-soiled suit. He made a point not to cover the mess as he relaxed into the chair, shifting his attention back to the stranger. "Tell me, Derek, what are our plans this glorious evening?"

"Derek?" I quirked an eyebrow. "I was kidnapped by a Scotsman named Derek?"

Derek flicked his glare at me before settling it back on Nathaniel.

"I take your silence as you wish for me to choose our agenda." Nathaniel cocked his head at me. "Let's feed."

Derek stepped in front of me. "Wolf, guard her."

"She didn't eat him?" Nathaniel asked.

Sam charged out of the bathroom. Stopping a foot from the bed, he turned to face off against Nathaniel.

"He's healed?" Nathaniel narrowed his eyes at Derek.

"Leave," Derek said.

Ignoring Derek, Nathaniel waved his hand at snarling Sam. "This is not good. Kill it."

"Go, Nathaniel," Derek ordered.

"After you kill the wolf" — Nathaniel leveled his gaze on mine — "kill her."

"Nathaniel — "

"You have brought the final death to us all." Nathaniel stood. "You sit her upon a downy mattress. She so much as spills a drop of blood tomorrow — "

"She will not," Derek said.

"You know our queen. You *both* are fools." Nathaniel pointed a long, sharp, black claw at me. "Thinking you can bind her."

Derek broke his casual stance. "I have. She is under my control."

Nathaniel sighed. "Said the last idiot who tried to cage a Wolf Born."

"What's a Wolf Born?" I asked, and if looks could kill, I'd have been dead from the scowls on both their mugs.

"Tessa, you will not speak another word this evening," Derek said. Before I attempted, he turned back to Nathaniel. Derek's shoulders rose with a deep breath which he held, then expelled with his words. "She is under my protection."

Nathaniel's eyes widened. "You *are* mad. When?"

"It does not matter."

"Yes, *it* does." Nathaniel shifted his attention to me. "Was it before or after the wolf attack?"

"After," Derek answered.

"Lucky you." Nathaniel slumped back into the chair. "I'm not up to beheading you tonight." He drummed his claws on the armrest. "I can only aid you for so long, Derek. The queen will find out sooner or later. And if I was a betting soul, I'd say tomorrow night." His lips tugged into a grin. "When the queen slits open her throat."

Derek took a step toward Nathaniel.

"Kill the hound," Nathaniel said. "If one of her minions sees that he still breathes, let alone made a full recovery—"

"She needs it still." Derek's voice sharpened.

"As you have incessantly reminded me for the past three hundred years, you are a hunter. So hunt for another wolf. I'll keep her entertained." Nathaniel rose from the chair.

Derek stopped a foot from Nathaniel. "You did not return to this room after our disagreement. You did not see the wolf healed."

"*You* have a death wish." Nathaniel tilted his chin up at Derek.

"You will tell our queen, as she instructed, that you tested the Wolf Born. Her powers were minimal at best." With inhuman speed Derek grabbed Nathaniel by the throat, lifting him to his tiptoes. "You will never enter this room, again."

Nathaniel stammered out a chuckle from around Derek's nails embedded in his windpipe.

Derek tossed him toward the doors.

Effortlessly, Nathaniel recovered his balance. "Until sunset." He tilted his head, then turned to face the doors, which were opening on their own. "Kill them, Derek. Or the queen plays tomorrow."

With three steps more to clear the threshold, Nathaniel disappeared into thin air. Then the doors closed and locked by themselves.

Derek stood facing the doors. Sam did as well.

I tried to sit still and take it all in, but being a reporter, I asked, "What does Wolf Born mean?"

Derek didn't answer. However, his shoulders tensed with my question.

The way Nathaniel and Derek reacted to the term affirmed my guess that Wolf Born wasn't a pleasant thing to be called. I would've received a better response if I'd said root canal.

Except for Sam's fur standing on end, he made no noticeable movement or sound.

Time to leave this joint.

Unfolding my legs, I inched my way to the edge of the bed. "Keeping us here is a bad idea all-around," I told Derek. "How about you let the wolf and me go?"

"Wolf, stay." As black claws formed from Derek's fingernails, he paced toward Sam.

"No!" I stumbled off the bed.

Derek pivoted.

Air whistled past my ears, and my feet left the ground. The back of my head hit a pillow.

"This is your doing." Straddling me, Derek pinned me to the mattress. Once again, his touch stirred my stupid heart. Damn me if he didn't flinch, too. His voice tightened. "Your burden."

"Get off," I gritted.

He grabbed ahold of my hair, yanking my head to the side. His chilled breath crept along my neck while I stared at Sam thrashing around on an imaginary chain, trying to get to me.

Derek's lips touched my neck.

"Don't kill him," I whispered.

"You ask for the wolf's life?" Derek pulled away to stare into my eyes. "While your own death looks down on you?"

Staring at my weak, pale reflection in his black, mirror-like eyes, pissed me off. "You don't want me dead," I whispered.

His lips drew away from his fangs. "You're gravely mistaken."

"You had your chance at the bar." It took all the courage I had left to see past my reflection and into his soulless eyes. Pain stabbed at my temples as the memory of the phantom sitting on my sofa popped into my brain. "Missed your opportunity at my apartment as well."

As fast as Derek had been on top of me, he now stood in front of the doors. "Wolf, watch over her." He stormed out of the room, and the doors slammed behind him.

Sam leapt onto the bed. While he stood over me, the mattress vibrated with his growls.

"You know, 'watch over her' doesn't have to mean literally." I shifted my legs, and he snapped his head down at me.

He grumbled.

I had no clue what to do. I wasn't a wolf whisperer. "Easy, Sam..." I reached up with a shaky hand and touched his neck. His body relaxed against my palm. It scared the hell out of me, because the touch calmed me, too.

He allowed me to sit.

"Thanks." I let my hand drop.

He huffed and leaned over me.

"Hey!" I shoved at his chest, and his dense fur swallowed my hands to my wrists. Warmth crept up my arms and for a second, I wanted nothing more than to bury my face in his coat. "You're crushing me."

His snort ruffled the stray hairs against my forehead.

"Move it."

Sam shot his attention toward the doors.

"What is it?"

Lifting his head, he gave a few sniffs.

Mimicking Sam, I inhaled. *Pancakes?* If I weren't so dehydrated or eluding death, I'd have drooled all over myself.

Metal wheels clicked down the hall.

Jumping off the bed, Sam stalked over to the doors.

I flopped off the bed, almost tripping over the discarded lamp. Snatching up the post, I was ready to pound anything that came close.

The doors opened.

Chapter Nine

An old geezer pushed a serving cart into the room. I assumed the man wearing an ill-fitting three-piece suit was a butler. Not that I was one to talk about fashion. I must've looked ridiculous, draped in a bedsheet while holding the lamp like a baseball bat over my shoulder. He never batted an eye as he flicked the light switch next to the doors, illuminating a huge chandelier.

Tears stung my eyes in the harsh light. I didn't dare blink. So far, I had concluded anything could stroll through those doors — like a murdering grandpa.

Thinking it better to treat the senior citizen as a killer, I pointed my weapon toward him.

His sharp, intelligent eyes regarded me for a moment. Then they dulled with cataracts as the whites of his pupils yellowed. Before my eyes, the man's face aged another decade.

What is he?

Already relying on my drug-enhanced senses, I inhaled through my nose. Along with the aroma of pancakes, the man smelled of freshly turned earth. While he continued his way to the center of the room, Sam moved to my side, growling — which caused the thin thread of my sanity to fray.

Sam's a freaking werewolf.

When the butler stopped in front of the wingback chairs, I glanced over his head to the empty hallway.

"Your dinner is served." At the sound of his pleasant voice, I snapped my attention back to the butler. With a slight nod of his chin, he turned toward the hallway.

Once his bony spine was to me, I raised the post.

Sam gave a soft grumble. Even as a wolf, he was the play-it-safe one.

Ignoring Sam, I curled my sweaty fingers tight around the post. A distance of a couple of feet and the butler's cranium was mine.

I'll just give him a light tap.

When the butler paused, I jerked to a halt. Glancing over his hunched shoulders, I lowered the post.

Derek stood outside the room. His stare locked with mine. And there was that look again, the inner debate. One half would've been glad to hold the doors open while we moseyed on out. The other half wanted to eat me. Choices. Choices.

"I made it clear what your punishment would be if you harmed anyone." Derek moved past the butler.

"Actually, I was looking out for his wellbeing." Letting the lamp rest against my thigh, I shrugged my shoulder. "Didn't want him to trip on it and break a hip."

"He never came close to the lamp."

"Close enough," I mumbled, shifting the sheet from around my legs.

With the butler exiting and shutting the doors, the opportunity for escape slammed in my face. There was no running past Derek. He'd just scoop me up and bite me. The thought of his lips next to my jugular sent a chill crawling down my neck to my numb toes.

Derek glanced from me to the dying fire. "You're cold?"

"I'm standing in a room with no heat, naked and shivering. So, yep. Great guess."

Sam snorted as he padded over to the serving cart, giving it a few sniffs.

Derek crossed the room. While he passed me, I wondered where he had gone when he had left in his hissy fit. He'd made a slight alteration to his wardrobe by losing the suit jacket. However, his white dress shirt was just as bloody from the back as the front. My gaze slipped to his butt. *Nice. No, bad.* I looked away and down to my bandaged arm.

Sadly, I was stuck with the gauze and tape until someone could help me take it off. Sam had paws, and no way would I have asked Derek for a hand. With those instant claws he had displayed for Sam earlier, he could've sliced my arm off.

Derek opened a door across from the windows, one I hadn't seen while I was on the bed. The damn bedposts blocked everything. Metal clicked together. *Clothes hangers.* I stretched up on my tiptoes, trying to see inside the closet, although the pole Sam had been chained to blocked my view. Through the dangerous amounts of blood splatter, its steel finish gleamed within the room's neon light.

Again, I raised my weapon.

Derek emerged from the closet, holding a woman's slip.

"Are you kidding me?" I eyed the black silk lingerie. "How is *that* going to make me all toasty warm?"

He narrowed his eyes at me, obviously not understanding my sarcasm. As he walked over, he held out the flimsy piece of fabric. "Here."

Gripping the sheet tight to me in one hand, I pointed the lamp at Derek with the other. "That's close enough...bloodsucker."

"You will show respect when—"

"I bash your skull in."

Sam lifted his head from the cart, watching us.

Derek and I stared at each other, neither of us bending to the other's nasty looks.

"If you prefer to be nude"—Derek tilted his head—"give me the sheet."

"Wait," I said more to myself. Better to escape in a slip than being naked. "Can you and Sam leave, so I can get dressed?"

"No," Derek answered.

I wanted to scream.

Sam was decent enough to turn away, although he did swivel his ears toward me.

"Give me the lamp, Tessa." Derek held out his free hand.

"No." I gripped the post tight to my chest.

"Tessa, I command you to give me the lamp." With his words, the annoying headache pounded at my temples.

I slapped the post into his palm.

"Get dressed," he said, letting the nightgown slip from his fingertips as he brushed past me.

When the silk nightmare landed on my curled toes, I had the urge to throw something hard and sharp at Derek. My lamp sat on the floor next to his leg. So I settled for mentally hitting him over the head with it, repeatedly.

Derek clasped his hands behind his back, resting them on his derriere as he peered out the windows. He looked pretty stupid in his disheveled clothing, trying to hold the posture of an aristocrat. "Your food grows cold," he said over his shoulder.

"Whatever, *Sir*. I'm not eating anything from here." I bent down and scooped up the vile thing.

"You will." He rolled his shoulders.

"Nope." I threw the slip over my head. It left nothing to the imagination, clinging to my hips and breasts. I glanced down. I looked like a pink zebra. Sam's blood striped my exposed skin, which contrasted against the shiny black material. I pulled the lace hem tautly down, barely covering the top of my thighs. With my movements, the little spaghetti straps slipped off my shoulders. I shoved them up, then folded my arms across my breasts while I continued venting inside my head at Derek. His choice of clothing was as piss-poor as his attitude.

As I stepped free of the discarded sheet, my stomach grumbled.

"You will eat." Derek walked past me, toward the serving cart.

I'd had enough of being bossed around by him. "I. Said. No."

That stopped him in his tracks. "You will obey me."

"Why? So I'm tastier for your queen?"

Over his shoulder, he gave me a bewildered look. "What?"

"You know, like Hansel and Gretel. Feed me, then eat me."

His eyes widened before he turned away, and maybe it was the play of light on his back, but I could've sworn his shoulders shook with a stifled chuckle. "Do as you're told and she won't."

Sam snarled.

"Mutt," Derek spoke at Sam, "retrieve her."

Stopping mid-growl, Sam trotted over to me, lowering his head to my hand.

"Do you not understand the definition of n—"

Sam took my entire wrist in his jaws. He didn't bite, just mouthed, but there was pressure to it.

"Hey." I glared at him, and he let go.

Dropping his head, Sam turned to expose his neck to me.

"He is sorry he frightened you." Derek circled the cart. "He gives you his neck as a sign of trust and acknowledgment that you are dominant over him."

"Well, aren't you all Discovery Channel," I grumbled, rubbing my slimy wrist.

Derek looked over the cart at me. "We would not want you to do anything careless."

"Like what?"

"Kill your watchdog."

"Dog?" I glanced at Sam. "He's like three hundred pounds with fangs." If my mind wasn't completely on the verge of hysterics, it appeared that Sam's eyes held hurt from my comment. With my shaky hand, I gave a pat to his neck.

Apparently, that was what Sam was looking for. He nipped and tugged on the hem of the slip, pulling me toward the cart. The material groaned under his teeth. I'd have been naked, again, if he hadn't let go.

"All right, Sam. Easy," I said.

Derek moved away from the chair and stood on the opposite side of the serving cart. As I sat, my stomach barked at me. It felt like I hadn't eaten in days. Sam sat next to me with his head level with my chest.

"Eat," Derek said.

I glanced away from the werewolf and across the makeshift table to the pissed-off vampire. If I had to partake in the dinner party from Hell, then I was going to get something out of it. "I'll eat *after* you answer my questions." I didn't wait for Derek's response. "Where's Andrea?"

Derek tapped his foot as he watched me drop a cloth napkin into my lap. "Here."

I arched an eyebrow. "Kinda vague there, Derek."

He lifted a pitcher filled with orange juice, then poured a glass. "I gave you an answer." He nodded to the crystal flute he had filled to the brim. "Drink."

"How is 'here' a good answer? More detail. Like she is in the next room or down the hall—"

"If you find my answer is not to your satisfaction, then be more specific with your questions."

I sighed, holding up the flute. "Cheers." I had it down in five gulps. Fresh squeezed and chilled—I shuddered from the relief it gave my sore throat.

"She is staying in another building on this estate," Derek said.

"Staying. Funny way to put being held hostage. Is she okay?" Instantly, I facepalmed. "Wait. No, let me re-ask."

"She is okay," Derek answered.

"I asked for a redo." I slumped against the seat as Derek removed the silver platters' tops. The first two plates held breakfast—eggs, toast and pancakes. The other two—meat, meat and more raw meat. The poor animals had been breathing two minutes ago before they found their way onto the plates. I settled for the carbs. Since there was no silverware, I rolled up a pancake. "Not really finger foods."

"We do not need you to harm yourself." Derek intently stared at me as he spoke.

I caught the *we*. Too hungry to protest or ask about the identities of *we*, I took a bite. As much as I wanted to plow through the pancakes I restrained. "Andrea's not physically harmed." I forced my concentration away from the food to Derek.

"Andrea has not been harmed." He tapped his fingers on the cart. "Eat the meat."

"Nope."

He tilted his head. "I answered your question."

"I made a statement."

He grinned. "Clever." The glimmer of emotion fell as fast as it came to his face. "You will not best me again."

I chewed the inside of my cheek, thinking about my next question. Andrea, for the time being, was alive and a hostage. Derek had never said differently. As he put it, Sam was my watchdog, so Sam was safe as long as I kept breathing. I was here because some queen wanted to tear my throat out while Derek had me under his protection—"What does *under my protection* mean to a…vampire?"

Derek stared at me. "Eat."

"You didn't—"

The black of his pupils swallowed his irises. "I said eat." At his command, my hand moved to a glob of scrambled eggs. He leaned over the table, and Sam rose. Derek snapped his black mirror-like eyes at Sam. "Wolf, go sit in the closet."

Sam curled his lips from his fangs before he obeyed, stalking over to the closet. Once Sam was inside, Derek grabbed my chin, turning my head back to him.

"Protection is no more than a sentence of servitude," Derek said, glaring into my eyes. "Do as I say. Act the way I tell you to, and in return, I will keep you alive."

Without warning, he let me go, and I fell back into the chair. Derek paced in front of the fireplace, muttering under his breath. An odd feeling that I had seen him arguing with himself before tugged at my subconscious. To focus on his words, I stared at the flames while tuning out the white noise of the room.

"What photo?" Out of the corner of my eye, Derek stopped and glanced at me. "Nothing can be linked to her. I made sure of it."

A faint whisper carried to my ears. Closing my eyes, I focused on the voice.

"The whole bloody debacle is on the front page of the city's newspaper," Nathaniel's echo-like voice responded. *"A Benjamin Wright was the reporter. And here's the jolly part. The fellow is missing. Perhaps you could stop playing with the dogs and put your skills to use, hunter."*

My mind spun. *Where is Ben? Is he hurt? Alive?*

Cold hands covered mine, gripping the armrests. Flashing my eyes open, I pressed my back against the chair.

"What are you thinking about?" Derek asked, lowering his face to an inch from mine.

"Lots." I gulped.

Slowly, his monster eyes returned to a human-like dark brown. "Remember my rules. Do not try to escape or harm yourself or others. I will return for you tomorrow evening." After giving me his *do not do*-list, he lifted his hands from mine and stormed out of the room.

Once the doors shut, I glanced over to Sam, whose eyes glowed within the depths of the closet.

While I dodged confrontation, both Andrea and Sam had found themselves in trouble a few thousand times. Yet they thrived under the pressure. Always finding their way out. However, against bloodsuckers…well, we all still breathed. *Go us*. But Ben…he had run from a Girl Scout—twice. Both times, he was caught, heckled then bought six boxes to buy her silence.

Please, stay safe, Ben. I'll get us all out of this. Somehow.

Chapter Ten

There were some things I had never wanted to see my friends engaging in, such as hooking up or falling apart. Top of my list — seeing them change from a wolf into a man.

On the rug in front of the fireplace, I hugged my knees to my chest. My palms still stung from pounding on the doors while my throat burned from screaming for help — which never came.

Another groan erupted from the closet, and I slapped my shaking hands over my ears.

After Derek had left, Sam had grunted and growled. Worried that he was hurt, I had gone to check on him. As I neared the door, static-like energy, similar, yet more intense than when I had kissed Sam, prickled along my skin. I should've taken that as a warning to back away, but curiosity had me peeking inside.

A mangled mass of flesh and bone had writhed on the floor. When I had gasped, it had jerked upward.

Razor-sharp teeth had snapped at me from a wolf's head covered in human flesh.

Another growl—more human-sounding than animal—pulled me out of the flashback of Sam's metamorphosis. I chanced a look at the closet as the growl turned into a scream. It then changed into a moan and ended in a harsh exhale.

Silence filled the room.

I let out a sigh, wiping the half-dried tears from my cheeks. Stopping mid-swipe after noticing a sweet smell covering my hands, I assumed it was syrup from the pancake I'd eaten. I gave my fingers and wrists a few sniffs. The scent oozed from my pores.

"Tess?" Sam's voice cracked.

Dropping my hands from my nose, I glanced over my shoulder. Sam stood there in a robe loosely tied around his waist. All thoughts wiped from my mind. What muscles managed to peek out from the white terry robe glistened with sweat, and not a single bruise or scratch marked his flushed face. I should've asked if he was all right, if he needed to rest or have a drink or two. But all that came out was, "You have hair."

At my observation, he raked his hands through the newly acquired, light-brown hair that brushed the tops of his wide shoulders. "Yeah, it's a pain in the ass. Have to shave this shit every time I...I'm sorry you saw that." Dropping his gaze to the floor, Sam sighed. "Sorry you got dragged into this mess."

An ugly cry-chuckle climbed out of my throat. "I'm the sorry one. It's my fault we're here. You heard—"

He lifted a finger to his lips and glanced at the doors. I shut my mouth, mentally kicking myself in the head for not thinking about potential snitches listening to us.

Sure enough, once I focused on the doors, I could hear someone pacing up and down the hallway.

Sam padded over to me. Each of his steps made his joints crackle and pop. At my cringing, he abruptly stopped. "I haven't changed—I mean I'm still the same badass you've been hanging with."

"Except you're a living Chia Pet." I looked away and started picking at the fray of my bandage. "Why didn't you tell me?"

"And you would've believed me?"

"You'd be surprised." I shrugged my shoulders. Spade-for-spade, I didn't have a right to be mad at Sam for his furry secret. It wasn't like I had opened my closet for him to dance with my skeletons. I looked away from my arm and toward the fire. Phantom screams echoed within my skull as the flames turned and rolled across a log the same way they'd torn through my family's car three years ago.

I snapped my eyes shut.

"Hey." At Sam's tap on my shoulder, the memory disappeared. "Can I join you?" he asked.

I patted the rug before he finished his question. Groaning, he eased down to the floor. Heat radiated off his body, and when his arm brushed mine, I caught myself leaning into him. After all, I wore a slip, and he had a comfy-plush robe that smelt of pine. At least that was what I convinced myself. Not the fact that touching Sam instantly calmed me.

"Tess?"

"Yep." I brought my attention back to the bandage, zoning in on the four crimson splotches. *Please don't talk about the friend-zone breach. Or that you saw me naked and crying...*

He gave my shoulder a nudge with his. "You're handling this solid."

"That's me, go with the flow." I lifted my bandaged arm. "Get mauled by a wolf and then wake up in hell's penthouse—no problem. Find out my pal is a werewolf, and another is a hostage to vampires, all the while my best friend is missing—just peachy." I smirked. "Oh, and I'm Derek's puppet. I really should thank him for getting me out of taking my soon-to-be-ex editor Rob's pit-stained undershirts to the dry cleaners." I glanced at Sam. "Extra starched."

"*Just* like I said, solid. No cracking. You'll keep it together." He paused. "It blows. Not gonna lie, I'd love nothing more than to pull you into my lap and tell you it'll all be good. But that's bullshit, Tess. People will die if you sink into a piss-n-moan routine while sitting on your ass—which is a fine ass, I must say."

Before I could counter, Sam stood, offering me his hand. "We got lots to talk about," he said. "But first, you need a shower. You stink."

I raised an eyebrow. "At least I don't smell like a pine forest-scented candle."

"True. You reek of that vampire and a dose of fear." He glanced at my arms, which were still striped with his blood. Swallowing hard, Sam looked away. "Besides, the water will make the bandage come off easier. Afterward, we're going to have a heart-to-heart."

"Then what was that motivational speech about?" I huffed.

"Orientation," Sam said, raising his eyes to mine.

"To?"

"Your new reality."

* * * *

Freshly showered and in my own fluffy robe, I sat in a chair with Sam sitting across from me, his knees touching mine. There was no escape as he tried to be gentle while removing my bandage. He managed to get the first few layers off with minor grunts and ouches from me.

The four crimson spots grew in circumference with each layer removed. Finally, only a rusty-colored pad hid the injury below.

Besides my arm hair and a layer or two of skin being peeled off, I felt no pain from the hidden wound. I flexed my fingers and wrist, wiggled my arm—nothing.

Sam pinched delicately at the pad, and sighed when it stuck firm to my flesh. "Sorry, but I have to rip it off."

"Wait." I tugged my arm out of his hand. "What if there's stitches, or glue, or...."

He leaned back in the chair, glancing at me through his bloodshot eyes. "There are no sutures. Just the pad."

"How do you know? You saw me being patched up?"

"I didn't have the best seat in the house, being chained to that pole behind you." Sam looked at the pad. "But I heard what he was doing and what he was saying as they worked on you."

With me imagining what kind of wacko patched me up, fear crept into my voice. "Who?"

"Mostly Derek. Nathaniel had to keep me...distracted." Sam held out his hand. "Delaying isn't gonna make it feel better."

I obliged, giving him back my arm.

"Brace yourself." He ripped the pad away.

I clenched my teeth against the stream of cuss words bubbling up from my throat while tears blurred my vision.

Sam gave my shoulder a soft squeeze, then turned to the serving cart. He dampened a washcloth. "You ready to learn about your new title?" He glanced over his shoulder at me. Smart man, he'd used my weakness — curiosity. Before I could look at my arm, he started again. "It has been three hundred years since the last Wolf Born lived." Holding his stare with mine, he moved the chair facing me to the side, then settled onto his knees in front of me. "Give me your arm."

He carefully wiped away the blood staining my skin. I studied the four shiny, pink puncture-shaped scars in disbelief. "After that bite...I shouldn't have an arm...but..."

"Tess."

"That kid was torn apart. He's not walking around..."

"Listen to me."

"It's the drugs. I'm dreaming. This is —"

"Tessa!" Sam shook my shoulders, jolting me from a near meltdown. "Look at me. Deep breaths for me." As I did so, he slid his right hand down my arm. His thumb traced my scars absently. Immediately, I stopped trembling. Once again, he'd chilled me out with just a touch.

With my newfound calmness, I asked Sam, "What's happening to me?"

"You were bitten by a werewolf, in wolf form." He talked slow, holding eye contact, "Your Change has begun."

"My what?"

"You are the Wolf Born."

"What does Wolf Born mean?"

Sam just stared at me.

"Answer me!"

"We are the same," he whispered.

I shook with anger, fear and denial. The last thread of sanity left me as I answered my question. "Werewolf," I whispered. "Let me go."

Sam's grip didn't waver.

I glared at him. "Now."

"Listen to me, please." He brushed his thumb over my scars.

I wouldn't fall for his calming trick again. "Let me the fuck go."

The second he released me, I bolted from the chair and stumbled to the windows.

Through hot tears, I peered out of my prison. An escape by a three-story swan dive would land me dead on the stone pavers below. I strained my neck to the left, then to the right to see the corners of the building. The place was massive.

"The vampires use compulsion, mind control, to hide their dwellings," Sam offered. "We're still somewhere near the city. I heard a guard talking about the interstate."

Forest and cow fields surrounded Glenwood. The bloodsuckers had their pick of prime real estate for their magical hidey hole. *Vampires. Werewolves.* My chest tightened. Before hysterics took me for a trip, I focused on a spotlight illuminating the ground below.

A pair of men, dressed head-to-boots in black, walked along the white crushed-stone path leading into a garden. The hedges were fourteen feet tall, at least, and formed an interknit maze—one a person could become lost in for hours. In its center sat a marble fountain illuminated by lights. I rose to my tiptoes. Only the top of a stone head was visible. Beyond the maze, a long stretch of manicured grounds bordered a vast forest. No city lights. No layer of smog. Nothing but trees and the night sky stretched as far as I could see.

Sam stepped up behind me. His body heat reached me, but thankfully he kept his hands to himself or else I'd have crumbled into a sobbing fit. Composing myself, I wiped away tears with the back of my hand. Crying wasn't getting me anywhere. I had to put on my newly acquired big-girl monster pants, and figure a way out of this colossal mess.

"Help me wrap my mind around all of this." My temper warmed my blood. So much for cool and collected. "I was bitten. Now I'm a werewolf?"

"Not *now*. You've always been."

"Explain."

"The blood of the wolf runs through your veins. You're a miracle, a gift to our race. You are the Wolf Born."

"There's that damn title again." I looked over my shoulder at Sam. "I was born human. Not fuzzy."

"Until now, the magic has lain dormant in your blood."

I shook my head because he was being dead serious. "Magic?"

He nodded. "It was passed down from your mother."

"Let's leave my mom out of this."

"I can't," Sam said. "You need to know."

I narrowed my eyes at him. "For as long as I can remember and up until she died, Mom spent her days working as a bank manager and taking care of our family. At night she played cello for the community orchestra. *Never* did I see Mom running on all fours and barking at the moon."

"She wasn't bitten. If she were, the race would have known when she made the Change..." Pausing, Sam shifted his weight. "The first time when a werewolf turns into their wolf."

"*I* would have known." I spun back to the window as fresh tears leaked from my eyes. "There were no secrets between us."

"Listen to me, Tess." Sam softened his voice. "Maybe, like you, she didn't know about her bloodline. Or, she could've kept hidden from the wolves if she was half as clever as you."

"I'm clever? Shit, Sam, if I was so smart, you'd think we'd be here right now?"

"Tess—"

"Stop." I smoothed the stray hairs away from my face and took a deep breath. *Treat this like an interview.* I looked at the moon falling below the treetops. "You said Mom wasn't bitten. So, the bite is a catalyst to something inside of my blood that makes me a Wolf Born?"

"The something is magic, and yes, being bitten starts the Change," he answered.

I turned to face him. "Can it be stopped?"

"No. The only option is to accept it. I'll help you." He reached out to me, and I jerked away, bumping into the cold glass. Hurt spread across his face.

My stomach twisted with the urge to offer him comfort, but instead, I clasped my hands in front of me. "How many Wolf Borns are there?"

"One. You. Your bloodline is the only one that can produce females able to survive the wolf bite. All other werewolves are male."

"So, my chromosomes, bloodline and a bite gave me the title," I muttered. "I can only imagine what the job perks are."

"The magic in your blood links you to all werewolves." Sam's voice deepened. "That title, Wolf Born, makes you the leader of our race."

"*If* Mom knew, that would explain the wanting to stay hidden and unbitten part." I came from a noble line of introverts. The room started to tilt around me. "How many werewolves are there?"

"Our numbers have dwindled since the vampires came over from Europe a couple of hundred years ago. If you hadn't gathered from your first meet-and-greet with the dirt sleepers, we don't get along. In the States, we're lucky to hit a thousand in numbers."

Before I could process the information, Sam added, "But you'll rule over the entire werewolf race. Worldwide, our numbers near twenty thousand or so."

"I'm not a leader." I chewed my quivering lip. "I'm a runner, as in — run the other way."

"You will learn. Remember? You don't have a choice. The alpha took that away from you."

"Alpha as in top dog? The one who mauled me?"

Sam nodded. "Alphas are the leaders of a pack. Only their bite can turn a human into a werewolf." A strand of hair fell in front of Sam's face, triggering my memory of Mr. Sex. His long blond hair had highlighted his monster face when he hoisted me over the bar.

I looked into Sam's eyes. "I know who bit me."

"Who?"

"The huge blond guy from the bar that licked my face." I nodded to myself. "I'd never seen him before that night."

"I told you to call me if you needed help," Sam grumbled.

"How? The headsets went down. You never would have heard me over the music."

"I would have."

"See?" I huffed. "Should've told me you're a werewolf, then."

"Did you notice if the jacked-up blond wore a ring?"

"Yes, a huge oval-shaped onyx one."

Sam made a sour face as he spat out the name. "Jason."

"You know him?"

"Yes." An inner fight played behind Sam's eyes. "Are you positive?"

Thinking back to the way the wolf had licked my blood from its fangs, I superimposed the memory of Jason licking his teeth when he had told me I smelled weak. "Positive."

Air hissed between Sam's teeth as he muttered profanity that would make a sailor blush. He turned away from me with his hands fisted at his sides. After a few seconds, he glanced over his shoulder at me. "Never leave that vampire Derek's side. Do everything he says."

"Why?"

"Because his queen, the one who slaughters werewolves for shits and giggles—Jason makes her look like a toddler playing tiddlywinks."

I swallowed hard. "How is Derek going to keep us alive?"

"Being under his protection, your life is his." From the evident confusion on my face, Sam explained, "He gives his energy to you. Strength. Speed. You'll be harder to kill. When you draw on his protection, it weakens him. He needs to feed often to support you both."

"Yeah. No worries there. I won't *draw* anything from him."

"You've been drawing from the bloodsucker since Jason attacked you. You can't control it."

"There has to be a way to shut it off."

"Yeah. One. You die, and he turns to a pile of ash." Sam pinched the bridge of his nose. "He better value his undead life."

"So if he dies, then do I as well?"

Sam's eyes darkened. "You and the entire werewolf population."

"Why would every werewolf die?"

"From what Andrea told me about your family, you're the only living member. That means all the magic has funneled into you." Sam stilled. "Since the magic within your blood links you to each werewolf. Cut the power source and…."

"Lights out." My knees buckled, and I slumped against the wall. "It's not Derek I need to win over." I stared at Sam. "It's the queen. If she wanted the race killed off, she would have slit my throat as soon as she could, but for some reason, she's holding out." I nodded, certain that there was more to my life's extension. "Whatever it is, I've got to make it worth her while to keep us alive."

Sam shook his head. "Tessa—"

"You mean *Asset*." I held his stare. "Any ideas on how I will do so?"

Sam's jaw tightened. "There is one way."

Chapter Eleven

"You're joking." I folded my arms under my breasts while staring at Sam. "I'm going to take a nap, hope that Jason shows up in my dream and then agree to his demands. That's how I'm going to win over the Vampire Queen?"

Sam nodded. "I'll wake you up if anything happens."

"Like what? I drool?"

"If you become restless, I'll wake you."

"You don't understand..." A chill danced up my spine. "I don't dream about rainbows and unicorns."

"I know."

"Know?"

He rubbed the back of his neck. "Andrea told me you have some pretty detailed nightmares."

"What the hell, Sam? Stalker much?"

His brows narrowed. "Stalker?"

"You asked Andrea about my family. You know I have nightmares. Anything else you would like to know about me without scampering off to ask Andrea?"

He rolled his neck. "I wouldn't have to ask if you weren't so damn secretive."

"Oh. I see. I should broadcast my dirt to the world like every other twenty-something female." I flipped my hair over my shoulder. "I'm an Aries. I hate math. I love eighties music." I tapped my foot while making air quotes. "Can I get a — like — ?"

Sam's eyes crinkled. His chest vibrated. He laughed. And God, did it sound great. I bit my cheek to keep from grinning like a smitten teenager.

"Not so hard, right?" he asked.

"Could've been worse." I dropped my gaze when his darkened.

An awkward silence filled the room. Thankfully, Sam broke it. "I ask about you because I…"

"What?" I glanced up in time to see him blushing. Which dumped more awkwardness into the situation. We were fighting for our lives, not fumbling through a first date. In an attempt to dodge the pink elephant in the room, I looked at the windows. "Umm…there's just about an hour before sunrise."

"It's just a dream." He must have taken the tremor in my voice as fear about what I needed to do. "Jason can't hurt you while you sleep."

When I turned back around, Sam's face was a normal hue again. "That makes it so much better. You think he's going to give me a high-five when I barge into his mind?"

"Well, maybe, if you hadn't tried to stab him in the back with your bottle opener," Sam grumbled.

I'd had to fill Sam in on my bar encounter with Jason at least three times before Sam had reluctantly agreed to tell me about the — cold chance in Hell — way to stay off the queen's Tuesday list of people to kill. He also informed me that I had been in and out of consciousness for the past two days, hence Tuesday's kill list comment.

"I said I was going to *hit* him. I'd never stab a person." I grinned and added, "I stabbed him in the neck when he was a wolf."

Sam's eyes widened. "Why did you leave that out?"

"If I didn't, you'd never have told me about using this magical-link thing to tap into nighty-night alpha's mind." In a bold move, I took a step toward Sam and touched his fisted hands. Shock replaced the tension in his face while below my hands, his fists loosened. "You said this is the only chance we have."

He lowered his stare to meet mine, and in a bold move, he used his inhuman speed to capture my hands with his. Sweeping his thumbs across my knuckles, he lowered his voice. "I can't let you do this."

"It's not your decision to make." I held his gaze, and he made no signs of bending to my will. After realizing he was as stubborn as me, I gritted my teeth and whispered, "Help me, please."

"Is it that hard for you to ask for help?" He squeezed my hands. "News flash, Ms. Reporter, you can't win a war by yourself."

I opened my mouth, and he cut me off.

"And this is a war." He dropped my hands, then walked past me to the closet, mumbling over his shoulder, "You're gonna want to put on some clothes."

* * * *

"Just an observation, Tess. Maybe if you stop wiggling your feet, you'll fall asleep."

"If they weren't freezing due to lack of socks, I'd stop." I flexed my numb toes. The vampires had made sure Sam and I wouldn't get any ideas about running away. Since it was around thirty-two degrees outside, and we had no clue where we were, frostbite became another invisible ball and chain.

I drummed my fingers on the sheets below me. Being under them, I felt constricted and too warm. From what Sam told me, whatever I fell asleep in was what I'd be wearing when I met up with Jason in my dream. So the more clothing between me and Mr. Sex, the better.

Sam trumped Derek on clothing options. Still, the black lace undergarments got a raised eyebrow from me and a grin from Sam. The jeans fit me perfectly, whereas the V-necked hunter-green sweater hugged my breasts a little too snugly for my taste. It was, however, ten zillion times better than the nightie. These clothes had been hanging next to that thing Derek had selected. He'd done it to mock me—I was sure of it.

"Vampires suck," I grumbled.

Sam groaned. "Kill the awful puns."

When the mattress sank from his weight, my eyes popped open. "What are you doing?"

"Chill." He kept on climbing across the bed toward me. "I'm going to help you sleep."

"No thanks. I'm capable of—"

Without warning, Sam rolled me onto my side, facing the wall. His arm draped over my torso as he spooned me. Blood rushed to my ears as my lungs screamed for breath.

"Relax, Tess. I'm not going to cop a feel. Here." His hand slipped to mine, and I grabbed hold. "You know what you have to do?"

Nodding, I repeated in my mind the name *Jason,* over and over.

Sam lowered his voice. "Good. Now, listen to my heartbeat, my breath. Loosen your limbs. Close your eyes."

I took a deep breath and inhaled Sam's pine scent. His warmth seeped into my skin, and I eased my spine the slightest bit against his chest.

"There you go." He yawned and his breathing deepened. "I got you, Tess."

I glanced over my shoulder. His eyes were closed, face relaxed, but I knew he was putting on a show for me. Turning back around, I closed my eyes then tuned out the white noise buzzing around my skull. Sam's heartbeat carried me to sleep.

* * * *

Warmth crept across my face while light shone against my eyelids. I opened my eyes to the soft glow of sunrise. Dew dampened my cheeks and hands as mud squeezed between my toes.

Turning in a tight circle, I scanned my dreamscape. Woods. Woods. Gravel road. Abandoned-looking two-story cabin. To add to the creep factor, an unnatural blend of stillness and silence clung to me. Movement from the building's moss-covered roof grabbed my attention. Smoke drifted upward from a stone chimney.

"Let's get this over with," I said, fisting my hands around the sleeves of my sweater.

When I stepped onto the porch's first weathered step, it groaned. I winced and forced my feet onward. Once my heel touched the third step, my foot crashed through the rotten wood. I braced myself against the railing.

If that doesn't send an ax murderer running…

Wiping the sweat from my brow, I pulled my foot free of the hole. Red speckles offset the gray floorboards. I licked my dry, trembling lips. "Paint, Tessa. It's just red paint."

I stole a look behind me. Muddy tire tracks covered the gravel driveway. Not wanting to wait around for anyone to return, I tiptoed the remaining steps to the screen door. As my fingertips brushed the rusty handle, my hair rose along the back of my neck.

Jason was inside. His sandalwood scent stuck to the inside of my nose while a tugging sensation sank into the pit of my stomach, beckoning me to open the door. To make sure I wasn't imagining it, I braced my hands against the sides of the door's frame and the tugging increased. Holding my breath, I ventured inside the cabin.

Flies buzzed around stacks of food-caked plates scattered across the fifties-era kitchen countertop. Dead ahead, yellow-tinted water dripped into the rusty sink basin, splatting onto a mold-covered milk container. Hooking the crook of my arm up to my mouth and nose, I gagged at the stench of rotting meat and curdled milk.

I strained my ears against the silence. Jason's whereabouts remained unknown. Still, the tugging pulled me onward. I shuffled around the kitchen table and into a dank living room. Windows covered in tarps gave me false hope that if someone or something attacked, I'd have multiple escape routes. Along the back wall, a fireplace brought the only light into the room. Flames casting shadows created the illusion of long, mangled fingers reaching for me.

Backing away, I knocked into a moth-eaten recliner. The chair swiveled and bumped into an end table. When I glanced at its dust-covered top, my heart jumped.

A pair of wire-rimmed glasses with a bent frame from pinching a nose in continuous worry rested on the table. My fingers unclasped around my sweat-dampened sleeves. Just as I reached for Ben's glasses, a door slammed.

Snapping my head up, I squinted in the direction the sound had come from. As I did, the relentless tugging grew stronger, pulling me toward the long stretch of a dark hallway.

Doors lined both sides of the narrow passageway. Pausing at each, I listened for Ben. No pacing, talking...breathing. I raced to the next. My common sense took a hike. Halfway down the hall, I started opening doors.

My heart seized before I turned the handles. Dizziness spun through my head when I looked inside each identical, vacant room—bed, nightstand and a case of bottled water.

Where are you, Ben? When I twisted the next doorknob, the damn thing fell off into my hand, and I chucked it over my shoulder. Cringing, I waited for its contact with the end table or chair. Instead, water hitting a steel basin filtered down the hallway.

Glancing over my shoulder, I eyed the last room to the left. Steam tumbled from underneath the door. I tiptoed over, placing my ear to the cold wood, hearing no movement. However, the tugging became a pulsating ache. The longer I fought the internal battle over whether to open the door or not, the sensation increased.

Unable to stand the ache a second longer, I pushed open the door. Steam billowed into the hall, blinding me. My limbs locked while the pounding of water deafened me.

As the steam escaped, the contours of the bathroom came into view. The room was a tight squeeze for even one person — sink, toilet and a rust-stained plastic shower curtain hiding a garden tub.

With my shuddering breath, a sweet scent, almost like fresh-baked chocolate chip cookies, greeted me. Tracking the smell, I stepped into the room, then pushed the shower curtain aside.

Staring ahead at the damp, brick wall, I deeply inhaled the aroma which had caused my mouth to water. A glance down shattered the utopia.

Blood coated the tub basin. My heartbeat revved but instead of turning heel and bolting, against all logical reasoning, I sank to my knees and traced my index finger through the blood.

Fresh and warm. It glided like silk against my fingertip. Before I could stop myself, I brought my finger to my parted lips.

Sweet like honey. The blood sent a shiver of hunger through me. Plucking my finger from my mouth, I stared at the digit that I'd sucked clean.

No! I stumbled away from the gore, crashing my back into the sink. Spinning around, I grabbed the counter for balance and glanced at the mirror.

Something caught my attention.

When I wiped the condensation from the mirror, my breath hitched. Ruby-red blood dripped from my bottom lip. *No. No. No.* With the back of my hand, I scrubbed away the mess, stopping mid-motion.

My eyes. I blinked a few times, hoping it was a trick of light, dust, anything. Still, they glowed a deep emerald.

If I hadn't been so enamored, I might've escaped the pair of large hands grabbing me from behind. I glared at the reflection of a tall, wet and *very* naked Jason. From the scent of sandalwood pouring out of his skin, I crinkled my nose. "Let me go."

"Not this time. You're in my territory, now." He pressed his naked flesh against my back. As I struggled against his rib-crushing embrace, he laughed. "Still weak for a wolf." Jason grabbed my arm, shoving my sleeve up to reveal my scars. His calloused thumb scraped over the marks. "You should be thanking me, Red," he said, nuzzling my neck. "I made you."

"A monster," I whispered.

"Not yet." His lips stretched into a smile against my throat. "Not even close. I'm enjoying playing with you," he said, moving a hand to grab my hip, while his other wrapped around my shoulders, pinning me to him. "I've missed it."

I spoke through clenched teeth. "Can't say the same."

"Such a tease." His tongue lapped across my pulse. "You're the one who came to me."

My stomach tightened. "I need your...assistance with escape."

Groaning, Jason pressed himself tighter against my spine. Loosening his hold on my hip, his hand wandered up my side, then slipped underneath my sweater. At his commanding touch, goosebumps raced across my skin. Forcing myself to act unaffected, I went still.

He smirked at my response. "All work and no play" The jagged skin of his thumb snagged on the lace bra as he traced the underside of my breast. He worked his finger into the hole he'd created while he asked, "Where are they keeping you?"

"In some estate, at least three stories high, bordered by woods." Because of his teasing, the information just flowed out of me. To gain control, I looked at my white-knuckled fists gripping the porcelain sink. Still, his rough caresses caused my mouth to dry. I stammered out reasons for him to let me go. "I need fresh air. I'm claustrophobic."

He cupped my breast. "Are you alone?"

"No," I groaned.

"Who is with you?" He squeezed.

"Stop—"

"Answer me," he growled against my ear.

I struggled to think. "Sam."

Jason's teasing ceased. "Samuel Lyncourt?" The slight widening of my eyes was all Jason needed for his answer. "You think you can outsmart me?"

"Yes." I glared at Jason's reflection.

His face reddened and elongated, stopping my flight with a voice two octaves lower, "If you struggle, I will tear out your throat." With his warning, he nipped my earlobe.

"You'll die, too."

He grinned. "Sam's been teaching you," Jason said, placing a firm kiss on my throat. "Did he tell you about me, Red?"

"That you are dangerous, smart, an alpha..." After each attribute, his grin deepened. Seeing his weakness for gloating, I added, "The Vampire Queen is no match for you."

"I like Sam," Jason whispered. "I'll take my time killing him in front of you."

The porcelain underneath my fingers cracked. When I released my hands from the sink, the broken pieces crashed to the floor.

Jason laughed. "Yes. That's what I want. Your hate." He nipped at my jaw while giving my breast another squeeze. "Your madness. And once I am done with Sam, I'll start on that rat of a human, Ben."

I dropped my gaze, and Jason let go of my breast to grab my chin, jerking my head back, so I was forced to keep looking into his eyes.

"Don't you dare pity that scum." He dragged his thumb across my bottom lip. "I'm going to stuff this pretty mouth with the bitterness of betrayal. Do you think it was by chance that I found you?" Jason asked, releasing my chin. Then he snagged a fistful of my hair as his voice took on a southern drawl. "No, I reckon a smart reporter like yourself wouldn't believe something so peculiar. Ben led me to the bar. Left you alone. Watched on as I tore into your flesh."

Blood roared through my racing mind while I sharpened my focus onto Jason's jugular. Each word he spat made the fresh star-shaped scar dance. The scar I'd made on his perfect body.

From the abrupt yank to my hair, I gathered he wasn't pleased I had tuned him out. My scalp stung and my eyes filled with tears, yet I remained still and silent.

"Do I bore you, bitch?" Slowly he rubbed against my backside. My breath hitched, and he growled into my ear. "Tell Sam we will be at the Gathering. I'll handle the queen."

"I don't understand—"

"Mine." He shoved against me, making my hips smack into the sink. "Do you understand that?"

I remained still and silent.

"Answer!"

"Yes."

He yanked my hair again. "Yes, what?"

"I understand."

"Obedient *and* weak. Good." He pulled me sharply to him. I went to tiptoes as he tilted my chin back to him. He spoke over my lips. "Tell Sam, if he tries to fuck you, I'll rip his heart out and eat it."

He sucked my bottom lip into his mouth, biting it.

Blood trickled down my throat, and I moaned in disgust because I enjoyed—no—relished the copper tang of my blood. A primal need for more had me scraping my tongue across his sharp teeth.

Jason growled into the kiss. "See, Red? You're no better than me. You crave the kill. The pain. You know what? I'll let you have at Ben for your first Change."

"No—"

"Yes." Drawing away, he licked his bloodstained lips. "After you kill him, with your throat raw and your limbs burning, I'll have you crawl to me." Jason paused, waiting until my glare connected with his reflection. Through his sneer, he whispered, "I'll laugh over your cries."

Rolling his head back, Jason stretched open his mouth. Then he struck, burying his fangs deep into my shoulder.

White-hot pain tore through my body as my screams shattered the world around me.

Chapter Twelve

If waking up choking on a mouthful of blood while Sam used his massive body to pin me to the bed wasn't a precursor to a bad day, then the searing shoulder pain from Jason's bite, and the terror of not trusting myself around anything with a pulse because the thought of tearing out their throat made my stomach growl surely was. Lucky me, both scenarios played out simultaneously.

"You're safe, Tess." With the morning sun at Sam's back, shadows masked his face and caused his eyes to glow as bright as a set of headlights. When he lowered his face closer to mine, his hair brushed against my tear-streaked cheeks.

I still wasn't used to his hair or how I could hear his heart beating at the pace of a jackrabbit's, pumping blood through his jugular that throbbed a mere inch from my lips.

"Get away from me." I squeezed my eyes shut, turning my face against a pillow.

"I'm going to sit you up." He spoke in a calm tone, even though I knew he was anything but. "See? You're okay."

No good. He sat me in his lap. His robe hung open to his navel from struggling with me. I averted my eyes.

"Let me go," I begged.

"Trust me."

"I don't trust *me*." My voice shook. "I want to tear out your throat."

"But you won't." Without warning, Sam's arms tightened, holding me flush to his chest. He arched his neck toward my mouth, so close that his pulse caused his flesh to brush against my lips.

I groaned.

"I know you won't hurt me," he whispered. "You will fight the hunger, Tess."

I didn't dare utter a word, fearing if I opened my mouth, I'd latch onto his neck. In a last-ditch attempt to harness my urge, I closed my eyes and thought about my brother.

Drew had always bailed me out of trouble. Afterward, he'd warn me that it was the last time he'd come to my rescue. And of course, immediately following his speech, he'd use the incident as blackmail for getting out of his chores. The punk had never scrubbed a toilet in his short twenty-four years.

"That's it," Sam whispered.

Still not ready to return to the present, I clung to the image of my brother. Each time I allowed myself to think about him, the angles of his face were a little softer, and the emerald green of his eyes not as defined. Grief killed the hunger while Sam's hushes and scent offered comfort.

Sighing, I rested my forehead on Sam's shoulder. "Why did you shove your neck at me?"

"Two reasons. First, *you* needed to know that you wouldn't hurt me."

"That's a stupid reason."

He ignored me. "Second, I've witnessed your saint-like control when you're at work. Contrary to popular belief, you've got a temper that puts Andrea's to shame." He chuckled. "The way you chew your lip and stare daggers at the back of Phil's head after he makes a jab about how your reporting career is working out. Then, in the split second that he turns around, your face lights up with a smile."

"To keep my job, I smile instead of telling Phil to shove his wig up his ass. To get a lead on the story, I smile instead of shoving a mint in Tim McKay's mouth." I pulled back to look Sam in the eyes, forcing a smile. "Sorry to burst your bubble, but you're staring at a grinning coward."

"B.S., Tess." He lowered his voice, squeezing my arms. "B.S."

Turning his head toward the bathroom, my gaze landed on the smudged bloody imprint of my lips on his neck. It was a reminder of how wrong Sam's demonstration could've gone.

"Don't *ever* think differently about me," I said.

His arms slipped from around me, and he straightened.

"And she says she doesn't like chick flicks."

I jerked my head in the direction of the fatigue-laced, recognizable voice.

Andrea, still wearing her witch costume, with her arms folded under her breasts, leaned against the bathroom door frame. "Seriously, Tess. Lifetime called, and they want their drama back."

"Andrea—" I tried to scramble out of Sam's lap, but he pulled me back.

"When a vampire bites you, they can control you," Sam whispered. "Look at her throat. She's been bitten."

Bruising and raw puncture marks covered Andrea's neck.

"I want my boots back, secret agent wannabes," she yelled, jabbing a finger at the doors. "Those guys are freaks. Who wears three-piece suits these days?"

Sam squeezed my arm, snapping my attention back to him. "She doesn't know it."

"Know what, Sammy Boy?" Andrea walked over to the serving cart. "That you're packing?"

With her comment, I pushed out of his lap.

In a sing-song voice, she said, "Awkward."

How does she not know she was chewed on? Self-consciously, I touched my neck. As the pads of my fingertips grazed my skin, the blurry memory of the tunnel where a bloodsucker stuck his fangs into my throat flashed before my mind.

Liquid trickling into a crystal flute shot me back to the present.

Andrea stared at me while pouring the pitcher of water. "You okay, Tess?"

"I slept wrong." Pretending to rub a kink out of my neck, I glanced at Sam, who no doubt was jotting a mental note down to ask about my neck later.

I gave him a slight nod, understanding his remark on how the vampire who had bitten Andrea now controlled her. She was too calm, too fine with everything.

Sam glanced back at Andrea, signaling I should do the same. With some distance between us, his scent wasn't all-consuming. Testing out my enhanced nose, I sniffed, picking up a familiar dark-rich aroma drifting from Andrea.

Derek.

I studied her, unable to accept that the bloodsucker had bitten and brainwashed the strongest, most badass woman I'd ever known. In the sunlight, her pale complexion took on a greyish undertone, while the dark circles under her eyes showcased her vacant, bloodshot gaze.

Cold hate for Derek filled me. To keep it from seeping into my voice, I whispered, "Are you okay?"

Andrea dropped into the chair. "I've been better. The room I'm in is half this size with the only window walled off."

"Walled off?" I asked.

With her faint smile, I saw a glimmer of my friend. "My first night, I used the lamp to smash through the window." Her grin grew. "They thought plywood would keep me inside." She lifted her right foot where her cut-up heel peeked through a hole in her fishnet stocking. "I made it to the driveway before they hauled me back inside. After that, they came with brick and mortar."

"They?" I asked, walking to the edge of the rug.

Close behind, Sam chimed in, "Ladies, I suggest lowering your voices."

"I don't remember," Andrea whispered as she focused on the floor. "My nights are blurry. I think they're slipping me drugs. During the day, I'm bored as hell. No phone. No TV. To keep from going nuts, I'm reading musty books covered in animal flesh. Finally got through *Macbeth*. Talk about depressing. At least the food's good." She took a sip of water, then raised her glass to the steel beam. "And I don't have a stripper pole in my room." She squinted at the pole. "Is that..." Her voice trailed off as she worked around a lump in her throat. "Blood?"

"Paint," Sam answered as he moved over to the pole. "Never used a primer before painting it. Look, it comes right off when you touch it." He wiped his hands along its surface, bringing away flakes of what he identified as paint.

"Well, I know Tessa wasn't licking paint during her nightmare." She poured another glass of water. "I wasn't even here for ten minutes, and Sam *orders* me into the bathroom for my safety. You're not joking about those nightmares, Tess. You tossed his ass off the bed a few times. And that scream...." She shivered. "Here." Her hand shook as she held out the glass to me. "It'll help wash that nasty metallic taste from your mouth. I'm surprised you didn't bite a hole through your lip."

I twisted my sleeves around my fingers, instead of shoving my hands up to my face to palpate my lip. But curiosity won out, and I slid my tongue along its swollen flesh, stopping mid-lick once I noticed Sam staring.

He shifted his attention to Andrea. "Do you remember what line of B.S. they gave you for holding you here?" he asked.

"Witness protection," she answered, handing me the glass. Both of us were careful not to touch the other, and to avoid getting to the reason why, Andrea kept on telling her story to Sam. "Said those cops from the bar were fakes. Then I said, 'No shit.' The tall, dark and uptight guy blinked like he had no clue what I was saying."

"Derek." The pressure of my grip snapped the glass stem in two and before the pieces hit the floor, Sam caught them. We spared each other a scolding side-glance as he set the pieces on the bed. Less than a minute and I had about outed my promotion to *monster*.

Wide-eyed, Andrea continued, "Sure, Derek—the uptight. Anyhow, last night he stormed into my room and demanded to know about Ben." She huffed. "By the way, shitty friend move there on Ben's part. Taking all the credit for your story. Derek showed me the article."

"It's not like that," I mumbled.

"Really? That's what it looks like. You put all the work in, and Ben slaps his name on the end product. Then he ditches you at the bar where you were attacked by a creeper—" Her mouth fell open. "It was him, Derek, the creeper."

I nodded.

"Whoa." She cocked her head. "Makes sense then why he told me to find out how familiar you are with the story."

"Tess," Sam interjected. "Don't say a word about the story, Ben or about anything since you last saw Andrea at the bar."

We both looked at Sam.

"Derek's using Andrea, and he'll force her to tell him everything."

"Sam, what kind of shit are you on?" Andrea rubbed her flattened, spiked hair. "Besides the Rogaine. Do you think I'd flap my mouth off to the first person who threatened me? Which reminds me." She glanced at me.

"Tess, you gotta stop pissing people off. That chick has a hate-on for you."

"Chick?" I asked.

Sam muttered a curse under his breath.

"The short brunette who runs this show. She goes ballistic when Derek even mentions your name. And don't even get me started on the blond. The little prick thinks he's so witty. But he's on borrowed time. That woman doesn't like him." Andrea slumped deeper into the chair.

"Did she talk to you?" I asked.

Sam stepped in front of me. "Don't answer her, Andrea."

"What the actual hell, Hercules?" she demanded. "Yes. And that's one convo I'd gladly forget."

I dodged around Sam. "What did she say?"

"The less you know, the better," Sam about shouted. "Damn it, Tessa. Listen to me."

When he touched my shoulder to spin me toward him, I snapped, "Back off."

"Heightened emotions" — he lowered his voice — "cause your eyes to glow."

With a glance at the steel pole, I caught the contorted reflection of my glowing eyes. Before I turned back to Andrea, I shut my monster eyes and hung my head.

"Tess?" All confidence left Andrea's voice. "What happened to you?"

"Tessa's sick," Sam answered.

I cracked open my eyes. Keeping my head down, I watched Sam's feet as he moved toward Andrea. The chair scraped against the rug as she scrambled away.

"Bullshit," she spat, shoving the serving cart between them, sending plates crashing against the floor. "No puffy eyes or dull skin. Come to think of it,

I've never seen her look so good. I'd say the dry spell is over."

Snapping my head up, I glared at her.

Andrea went rigid, and the last bit of color faded from her face. "What's wrong with her?" she whispered at Sam.

He stood with his back to me, silent.

I took a few slow steps, stopping when I was next to him. "What did the brunette say?" I asked.

"As soon as she gets an answer from you, I'm free to leave this place," Andrea answered. "Shit. Your eyes are glowing."

"What about Sam?" I asked.

"She didn't say." Andrea looked at Sam. "Just that I need the answer."

"What *answer* does that bitch want?" he growled.

"She wants to know who Tessa thinks is behind the Safe Waters contamination."

"Contamination. I knew it. Someone is deliberately poisoning the water." Pushing the story mentally to the side, I glanced at Sam. "How positive are you they can't hurt Andrea?"

His jaw tightened. "The longer she is here, the harder it'll be for them to erase her memories. She already knows too much…"

Andrea's alert, wide eyes stared at Sam. "I don't know what you think I know, but she promised me."

A sweet aroma drifted off Andrea, triggering my saliva glands to fire. To focus on Sam and not Andrea's revved heartbeat, I latched my gaze to the floor. "And how are vamp—they with keeping promises?"

"If the queen gave an oath, then she must keep it," Sam said. "But they are deceptive and twist words—"

Andrea cut in. "Yep, she said that oath thing. In front of the blond guy." She raised her voice, mimicking the Vampire Queen, "'I give my oath to you, Andrea Garwin, that you will be set free with the name given by Tessa Sanders'."

Two names tossed around my mind. Closing my eyes, I focused on the photo I'd taken at the park. My skull throbbed as I forced myself to remember before my fall. To keep from whimpering, I sank my teeth into my lip. When the blood trickled down my throat, light burst before my eyes, and the memory played inside my head in slow motion.

Tim McKay and Mayor Brown sat on the park bench overlooking Silver Lake.
"How much longer?" the mayor asked.
"Not much," Tim said.

The memory disappeared, and my eyes snapped open. "I know who it is."

"Are you sure?" Andrea asked, backstepping toward the doors.

"Yes." I forced a faint smile at her. "The queen will get her answer tonight. *After* you're out of this place." I looked at Sam. "And you, too."

He locked his stare with mine. "I'm not leaving you."

Footfalls stormed down the hall toward the room.

"Time to say your goodbyes," Sam said, dropping the broken glass into the chair.

Andrea took that handful of seconds to make it to the doors. While her knees knocked together, she balled her fists. As if she felt my attention on her, she glanced over her shoulder at me.

"Screw goodbyes. Raise hell, Tess. Fight." She offered a faint smile. "You're not getting out of next Saturday's chick flick marathon."

Before I could cross the distance between us, Sam grabbed me, spinning me around so I faced the morning sun instead of the opening doors.

"What are you doing?" I squirmed.

"It's for your safety," he gritted.

Catching Sam off-guard, I relaxed. With the created space between his arms and body, I slipped out of his hold, dropping to my knees. I'd enough time to spin around and look past his legs, toward the closing doors.

Andrea was gone.

Chapter Thirteen

In a frantic crawl, I lunged for the doors. I'd be damned if they thought they could take Andrea away. A shadow crossed over my head, and Sam landed inches in front of me, blocking the doors.

"Move," I screamed.

He snapped his red face down at me. "They'll kill her. And you!"

I glared into his glowing eyes.

He growled.

I sank into a crouch. Rage drove me, and my destination was the hallway which was momentarily blocked by the doors and a pissed-off werewolf.

He knocked me off balance.

Surging to my feet, I raised my face to his. "Get out of my way."

"Make me." He took a firm step toward me, shoving his head down so his nose bumped mine.

Even with his hot breath hitting my face and his labored exhales causing his chest to press against my breasts, I didn't budge. For the first time in my life, I refused to let fear manipulate me. "I'm *really* getting sick of you invading my personal space." My voice deepened into a full-fledged growl.

Growling?

It must have surprised Sam as well. In a swift, fluid movement, he went to his knees, placing his palms on the floor, then continued to lower his head, touching his forehead to the floor. "Forgive me. I forgot my rank, Wolf Born."

With his use of the title, my stomach turned sour. Hoping it was a slip and not a calculated move on his part, I asked, "What do you mean by rank?"

"I am your servant. I will protect you by any means. Your life above all others." Sam paused. "The only way you're going to get through these doors is for you to kill me."

While he waited for my response, his breath fogged the polished floor.

"You and your *rank* can kiss my ass." I pivoted on my heels and stomped away as he continued doing the bowing thing.

My trip was a short one, ending with me inside the dark bathroom. I slammed the door behind me then took a few strides to the furthest point of the room, to some sort of dressing space. Growling again, I plopped down on the chair in front of a towering antique vanity.

What light had managed to slip underneath the door dimmed from Sam standing silently on the other side. *Good for him, not trying to come in after me or say anything.* Although, he still held a high ranking on my top-twenty shit list.

A soft green glow illuminated the room. *Where's that light coming from? It's a flipping furnace in here.* I swung my hair over my shoulder and fanned myself haphazardly. My movements in the mirror caught my attention.

Looking at the reflection of my glowing irises, I screamed until my throat went raw. Pressing the heels of my hands against my monster eyes, I sucked in a ragged breath. The scent of vanilla crept into my nostrils. Such a perfect, weak stench and all too recognizably my own.

Lowering my shaking hands, I glanced at the tiled floor to where I'd disposed of the nightie. Derek's spicy scent lingered on the fabric.

Snatching up the stupid garment, I tore it to pieces. The shoulder that Jason had sunk his jaws into throbbed from my assault on the nightie. Just having the sweater against my tender flesh was excruciating, so I ripped it off, tearing it to shreds, too. Material particles floated around the room while I continued my path of destruction. Grabbing the chair, I hurled it against the vanity.

In slow motion, the vanity toppled over, crashing with force to shake the walls and floor. The mirror exploded, shattering glass everywhere while the vanity drawers splintered, leaking their contents across the tiles. Perfume flooded the air. I prayed it was expensive shit.

My haggard breaths slapped against the walls. In. Out. In. Out. Each repetition tugged me into a restless trance while the green glow from my eyes dimmed. As darkness engulfed the bathroom, I sank to the floor, sobbing.

When the door cracked open, sunlight pooled inside, casting ugly shadows across my destruction. It was so worth the seven years of bad luck. They would fit nicely in front of the years I'd already had.

Sam's pine scent curled around me.

"Why? Why...me?" I asked, glancing up at him.

"Because of who you are. Who you will be." He lowered to his knees, opening his arms to me. With my slight movement, Sam closed the distance, gathering me to his chest.

"My head's spinning. I can't control myself. I can't do this," I whispered. "I don't even know what *this* is."

Gazing into my eyes, Sam brushed my sweat-soaked hair away from my face. "We'll take it one step at a time. Okay?"

I laughed bitterly. "Well, we can't *step* that far, can we? We're stuck in this room."

Before I could blink, he picked me off the floor. Effortlessly, Sam navigated around the shattered bottles and wood. Outside the bathroom, it was at least twenty degrees cooler. Then again, it didn't help that I'd trashed my sweater. Not much warmth to be had from a lace bra. Shivering, I pressed tighter against Sam until the bare skin of my breast touched his pec. I glanced down at the bra. My flesh peeked out from the hole Jason's calloused finger had made.

"Stay put, you're covered in glass," Sam said, sitting me on the chair in front of the fireplace.

After I drew my legs up and rested my chin on my knees, I caught him staring at my shoulder. I glanced at the fading imprints of four puncture marks. "Those are from Jason." I gingerly touched my shoulder. "Looks like I take *living the dream* to a whole new level."

"Piece of shit alpha. He shouldn't have been able to hurt you." Growling, Sam turned to the serving cart. He grabbed a napkin and dipped it into the water pitcher. His strained knuckles matched the crisp white of the cloth that he wrung into a tightrope. "I was fucking careless. Forgetting what — who you are. That the alpha's link could affect you differently. I shouldn't have let you — "

Voices filtered down the hallway.

Sam snapped his head toward the doors. "Armed guards are coming. I need you to trust me. Do what I say." He glanced in my direction, careful not to look me in the eyes. Still, I caught the anxiety he shoved behind his badass persona. "Don't worry about me," he said.

While I scrambled from the chair, my legs turned to jelly. I wanted to grab ahold of Sam, cling to him for protection. Instead, I moved behind the chair, gripping its back to the point the frame snapped. Below my feet, the floor vibrated from the pounding of boots down the hall.

The click of the locks had Sam pivoting around, blocking my view of the doors.

I shuffled with weak knees to a few feet behind his shoulder. I thought it better to leave some space. We might've had an opportunity to escape. Taking a sweep around the room for promising weapons, my gaze landed on Sam's hands. His nails elongated into four-inch, blade-sharp claws. I was mid-step, backing away when two men barged through the doors.

Huge and dressed in black from their berets right down to their shit-kicking boots, they reminded me of some type of soldier. A blood-red band with an embroidered black symbol in its center encircled their right forearms.

While red lasers skated around the room from their guns, nine more men stormed into the room. If I closed my eyes, I'd have mistaken my surroundings for a battlefield. They smelled like dirt and their gruff, staccato voices carried over their heavy footfalls. My gut instinct screamed that something was off about these men. Their eyes held madness and a dark hollowness of loss. One by one, their gun beams landed over our hearts.

Tilting his profile slightly toward me, Sam kept his eyes trained on the men. "Don't move. Do not speak to them."

I'd never had a gun pointed at me. The saying was true — my dismal life flashed before my puffy eyes. I struggled to breathe, let alone attempt to talk.

While the group fanned out, circling us, the two guards in front parted for a man to walk through.

Shorter, leaner and with a silver buzz cut that stood out like a sore thumb amongst his drones, the military general from the bowels of hell pinned me with his ice-cold, grey eyes.

"Get on your knees," he ordered, pointing his gun at my heart. "Raise your hands to the ceiling."

Sam faced the man. "Leave her al —"

Behind Sam, a guard cracked the butt of his pistol against the back of Sam's head. Falling forward, he crashed onto his face, out cold. Blood ran down Sam's neck and soaked into the collar of his robe.

Sinking to my knees, I leveled my stare at the silver-haired man. "You're no general. You're like my boss, hiding behind false power."

The corner of the Boss-man's lip pulled upward. Then he nodded to the person behind me, who snagged my arms, twisting them against my spine.

I clenched my jaw, refusing Boss the satisfaction of my pain.

"Check the bathroom," he told his lackeys.

Two of the guards broke away and headed for the bathroom. Only the sound of glass crushing under their boots and my hitching breaths filled the crowded room.

Sneering, Boss looked me up and down. His finger curled around the trigger like I was going to jump any second, and he'd have the pleasure of shooting me.

The men exited the bathroom and walked over to Boss, forming a V with their bodies. All three trained their guns on me.

"Sir, he did a number in there," the man to the right said. He looked like GI Joe on steroids.

"Sir, may I have permission to make him talk?" the man to the left asked. He was just as huge as GI Joe. His dark eyes dropped from my face to my holey bra. Clearing his throat, Boob Man pulled his gaze away from my breasts and set it on Sam.

"Perimeter," Boss ordered. "Check for potential weapons."

Both men nodded and lowered their guns. They worked the room in opposite directions. One opened the door to the closet while the other looked under the bed.

"Glass on the mattress," Boob Man said, grabbing the broken flute. "Clear now."

"All clear, sir," the other said.

Boss nodded to Sam's limp body. "Chain him."

There was no way I'd let Sam take the heat for my recklessness. But my mouth protested, refusing to form words, only allowing a whimper to escape through my lips.

Boss's full attention snapped back to me.

"I did it," I whispered.

The man at my back twisted my arms further, scraping my knuckles against my spine. Tears threatened to fall, clouding my vision as a full-blown scream waited to be unleashed.

"I didn't ask you to speak, princess." A mocking tone accompanied the pet name the Boss had slapped me with. "You follow my rules during daylight. Do you understand?"

I glared at him.

"No more than a whisper is to come from this room. Any more of your tantrums" — he ticked his chin at the blood-splattered pole — "and I will personally chain you to that post."

I shivered.

"Do you understand, princess?" he asked.

I nodded.

A guard standing at the doors moved to let the decrepit butler pushing an industrial-sized hamper through. No emotion crossed his leathery face as he headed into the bathroom with the guard following close behind.

While a broom scraped against the tile, pushing around the wood and glass, the hot breath of the asshole at my back made my stomach turn. Boss passed the minutes by clicking his gun's safety. Off. On. Off. On.

When the butler reappeared with the hamper full to the brim, the guard followed. Sweat crawled down his forehead while he paused to adjust his grip on the vanity. Grinding his teeth with the veins on his neck bulging, the guard dragged the vanity out to the hall.

Tipped pretty easily for me. At first, I credited my adrenaline during my meltdown. Then a minuscule particle of hope wiggled into my thoughts. *Am I stronger than these psychopaths?* I wasn't about to test the idea with Sam unconscious and the room full of guns cocked and ready to blow holes through our hearts.

Another guard entered the bathroom. When he emerged, he nodded at Boss. "All clear, sir," he said.

Boss gave a sharp nod to the man behind me, who gave one final squeeze to my arms, before letting go.

"Fall out," Boss ordered.

As the guards backed out of the room, half of them leveled their guns at me while the others pointed theirs at Sam. The last to leave was Boss. His glare locked on me while he shut the doors.

The three locks fell into place. Then a chair bumped against the doors and its frame groaned under the weight of a man sitting.

I crawled over to Sam and brushed my fingertips across his neck to find a strong pulse. Relief flooded me. I grabbed the wet napkin from the floor that Sam had meant to use on my shoulder.

"Please, wake up," I whispered, patting at the gash on the back of his scalp. Blood slid between my fingers, turning the white fabric crimson. "Come on, Sam. Stop bleeding."

I wildly glanced around the room. When my gaze landed on a terrycloth robe inside the closet, I let Sam's head rest on the floor. Stumbling to the closet, I snatched the robe and raced back to Sam. Slamming down onto my knees, I tugged the robe's tie free. As tightly as I dared, I wrapped the robe around Sam's head, securing it with the tie.

Still, his blood soaked through, warming my hands below his scalp. The coppery aroma aroused the sick hunger within me. I focused my attention solely on Sam's steady breaths. "Please, wake up," I whispered, cradling his head in my lap while his blood seeped into my jeans. I gathered him closer, my teeth chattering violently. "Please, please, wake up."

Chapter Fourteen

"One hundred ninety-nine." I paused in counting Sam's breaths. The red beam of sunset now spotlighted the steel pole. Running my fingers across Sam's forehead, I willed him to wake before the beam slipped to the floor.

My stomach growled. *Not. Good.* Focusing on his breathing passed the time for the first hour. But my attention…hunger always drifted back to Sam's injury. Thankfully, Sam had stopped bleeding some time ago, and although unconscious, he'd groaned when I tried to move.

Closing my eyes, I tuned in to the activity happening within the hallway. For the most part, the men were silent, only using code words to communicate through their walkie-talkies. I assumed *pit* was code for break. No more than a minute would pass and the guard would be replaced by another. *Check* was self-explanatory, with the entrance of three guards jabbing firearms at me as they surveyed the room. Checks happened every thirty minutes or so. I gauged their timing by the digital beep on the guards' watches before they entered.

With each inspection, I acted surprised, hoping that they'd not catch on to the fact I was studying their patterns while testing out my new abilities. My fear, however, was genuine. Boss, cold and alert, always made an appearance. He was silent in his approach and his timing was random, never predictable.

I glanced toward the doors and sniffed. If I shut my eyes when the guards came through, I could pick out how many just by scenting them. True, they all smelled like dirt, but below the stench lingered the subtle trace of the soap they used. What they had eaten for lunch clung to their breaths.

One guard had a love for blue cheese. When I shoved my nose against my shoulder to escape the reek, I made another scent connection. Werewolves had a base scent from nature. Sam was pine. Jason was sandalwood. As for me, a weak vanilla.

Vampires, on the other hand, I hadn't thought to, nor did I want to, get within sniffing range to find out. Well, there had been Derek and his dark-rich scent.

Shaking my head, I ticked off a gaggle of reasons to loathe the dirt sleeper. Still, he smelled…

I sighed, rolling my stiff neck and shifting my legs underneath Sam's head. I rocked my hips side-to-side. My butt was completely numb. It would take me some time to regain feeling, and I had about fifteen minutes before the next check happened. I chanced a look at Sam. His feet were still in the same relaxed position, pointing toward the pole. My check-over came to a screeching halt at his robe that parted enough to give a great view of a muscled thigh. As I glanced at the sliver of exposed skin from his hip to his pec, heat prickled my cheeks.

Which brought front-and-center the stuff that sucked about being a werewolf—hormones, rage and a killer appetite. In a nutshell—PMS to the tenth power.

Tracing my fingertips across his forehead, I glanced longingly at the food cart that was delivered during the last check. If I couldn't eat, then I'd settle for some aromatherapy from the pancakes. Big mistake. My nose hit on the scent of blood, causing my tastebuds to hum with the memory of its sweetness.

Holding my breath and squeezing my eyes shut, I focused on Sam's heartbeat. Huge mistake. Instead of distracting myself from hunger, I became hyper-sensitive. The pads of my fingertips brushing across his skin caught against each dried speck of blood.

"Any harder and you'll rub my skin off." At the sound of Sam's pain-laced voice, I stopped my aggressive petting. He gazed up at me with one dilated pupil and the other one no more than a pinprick. Yet he was the one asking, "Are you okay?"

"I am."

"Good." He struggled to lift his head.

"Take it easy. You got hit hard."

"I've been hit harder."

He tried to sit up, but I pushed at his chest to keep him still. Leaning down, I whispered against his ear, "There's a guard outside the room. They'll be in here within the next ten minutes."

Nodding, he rolled to his side, leaving a bloody imprint of his head on my jeans. He paused to look at the mark. "Scalp wounds bleed a lot." His observation sounded more like self-reassurance than fact.

As he sat upright, the robe slid off his head. His light brown hair looked more auburn than mine. Through the blood-caked mats, the white of bone stuck out.

"Sam...umm, the back of your head..."

He slapped his hand over his skull, groaning as he touched the injury. "Just a flesh wound. No fracture." He sighed, dropping his hand. "It'd heal faster if I made the Change, but I'd have to stay a wolf for the night."

"Do it. Please!"

He grabbed my hand as I went to stand. "No."

"No?"

He ticked his chin at the door. "I don't trust them around you. Besides, the bloodsuckers will rise soon. You don't understand...I won't be able to protect you."

"I've handled the guards the entire day by myself." I tugged my hand out of his and stood, pointing at him. "As for the vampires, I'm not the one resembling a bloody pig-in-a-blanket."

Sam glanced at his blood-soaked robe. "I can fix that." To prove his point, his hands dropped to the tie at his waist.

"Don't you dare—"

Outside, a group of guards walked the grounds. Both of us turned to the window, listening. Unfortunately, a truck's engine revved to life, muting most of their conversation.

"I can't hear a damn thing," Sam mumbled.

I cut him off with a finger to my lips as I crept to the window.

"Patrol. Risen. Feed," I said.

I wasn't a fan of those words, nor was Sam by the way his shoulders tensed. He went to move, and I held up my hand.

"There's one more." I dampened my trembling lips before speaking the word Jason had spat at me. "Gathering."

Gathering received a full-throated growl from Sam.

"I can't believe it." He bolted to his feet, but his right leg buckled.

I was a clear six feet away from Sam. I raced to his aid, but my stomach somersaulted as the room blurred around me. Sam's back brought my momentum to an ungraceful stop. When I rocked into him, he launched forward, and before he kissed the floor, I caught him under the arms. Lifting him to his feet, I went to my tiptoes, ducking under his arm that I draped over my shoulder while supporting his weight with my body. In a clumsy shuffle, we moved to the center wingback chair.

Excitement whirled through my mind, which I kept from showing outwardly. I needed to prove to Sam I could handle myself around our enemies. If it appeared I'd known about my speed, perhaps he'd feel more confident in my ability to protect myself and go furry.

His chin brushed my temple as he whispered, "Do they know about your speed?"

"No."

"Keep it that way. What about your strength?"

I hesitated. "Maybe."

He planted his feet while raising his one working eyebrow. "Tess?"

"They wanted to hurt you."

"You told them you were the one who went all *Hulk Smash* on the vanity." He grumbled, "They know. Soon the vampires will."

"I wasn't about to let them beat you." I tugged him the last few steps to the chair.

"I told you not to worry about me."

"Must have slipped my mind." I poked his chest. "Sit." As soon as his ass hit the cushion, I stated, "You have minutes, at most, to tell me what you know about this Gathering. Afterward, you're turning wolf."

Folding my arms under my breasts, I glared at him, hoping my demeanor came across as leader-ish and not freaking out—which I was. Rivulets of fresh blood trailed down Sam's neck, and his eyelids kept drooping while his head tipped to the side.

He sighed. "Every fifty years, the vampire council, which consists of all the big bad bloodsuckers from around the world, get together for one night—the Gathering." He coughed and gripped his head. "Think of it as a legislative assembly—fights over land, laws, forging alliances. However, the combatants really do lose their heads."

"So the vampire council is meeting to bitch and then kill each other. Seems like a good thing."

"Wish that was the case. These monsters are powerful. Some can kill with just a glance. Inflict pain with their voice. Control a small army of men with just a thought," he said, lifting his gaze to mine. "Power that will strengthen when the vampire drains its opponent of their blood."

"How many council members are there?"

He shrugged. "Not sure of the exact number. A couple dozen, maybe. Our race makes sure to steer clear of these gatherings. Having a bunch of bloodsuckers drunk on power, and then toss in werewolf blood…" His voice trailed off. Attempting a recovery, he pitched in some good news. "Thankfully, their self-preservation trumps their greed in most cases.

The last time a council member lost their head was over a hundred years ago."

"What happened?"

"The Great Chicago Fire."

I tilted my head. "The fire caused by a cow?"

"The fire that covered up over three hundred human bodies drained of their blood by some ape-shit-crazy vampires on a power-high. Once they were bloated on blood, they used compulsion—mind control—on all the survivors, hence the O'Leary cow story."

"I always thought the cow explanation was unbelievable."

He chuckled. "And a group of vampires draining a city dry is more believable?" His laughter turned into a dry cough that wouldn't cease, causing blood to trickle out of his nostrils.

I grabbed the pitcher of water and handed it to him. "Glenwood's a speck compared to Chicago. If the bloodsuckers go berserk, there will be no survivors."

I glanced at my bloodstained jeans. My memory of the torn-apart teenager morphed into hundreds of corpses.

Sam paused mid-gulp, then slowly lowered the pitcher, setting it on the cart. "Tess?"

My attention fastened on the droplets of blood mixing with the water sloshing inside the pitcher. "What does werewolf blood do to a vampire?"

He looked away, lowering his voice. "It's bloodsucker ambrosia. A deadly combination of hallucinogen and adrenaline."

"That's it...our blood." I gulped. "What if the queen is keeping us alive for the Gathering? She could drain us, and then take on the council."

"I don't think so." He gave a forced smile. "It would take the blood of several werewolves to affect a single council member."

"But my blood links me to all the werewolves."

"Still... don't take this the wrong way, but you're not enough to go around. With their numbers, the council still would overpower her."

I fluttered my fingers down to my twisting stomach. "I never got a chance to tell you what Jason told me." My dry mouth caused my voice to crack. "They will be here for the Gathering."

All color drained from Sam's face. "Jason's mad. He's sending his pack to the slaughter."

"How many are in his pack?"

"At least forty." Sam rose from his chair. "You are escaping right now. When the guard comes through, I'll—"

"Get shot. If not by him, then by the other two behind him, and if you can manage to hold them off, Boss will sneak in and kill you." I glared at Sam. "Besides, if I get away, you and Andrea are dead. The Gathering will still happen. Jason will still crash it. And Glenwood will become the vampires' blood bank," I said. "Now, go wolf."

Sam answered me with a scowl.

I took my clenched lungs and thundering heartbeat for a walk to the windows. As I glanced outside to the twilight sky, a draft snaked across my midriff. Shivering, I drew my arms tight around me. At the sound of Sam's footsteps heading into the closet, I glanced over my shoulder.

Instead of his moans of pain, hangers clicked together.

"It's not that easy." He reemerged holding a black turtleneck and a pair of charcoal slacks. "And as you saw, changing forms doesn't tickle."

"How much does it hurt?" My voice wavered.

With a harsh sigh, he hung his head. "I'm an idiot."

"No sugar coating."

He held out the turtleneck, which I wiggled into.

"Each time you pray it will be your last." He raised his eyes to mine. "But you are different. When we kissed, your wolf called to mine."

"That volt thingy that shot out my mouth and into you, that's my wolf?"

"Yes and no. That was your wolf's energy. *Your* power." He nodded to himself. "One second I was human. The next, wolf. No pain."

His eyes lit.

I wanted in on his inner conversation, but a humming sound filtered into the room.

"Do you hear that?" I asked.

"Yes." A soft smile crossed his lips. "That's the moon song."

When I turned to the window, the nearly full moon bathed me in a soft glow, warming my face and setting every nerve ending to buzz. "It's making me all tingly, too."

"It will. Every night it sings to us. The closer to the full moon, the louder its call. The song is at its strongest during the full moon, when it claims us and our wolves take over."

Between Sam's calming voice and the moon's song, I barely heard the guard's watch beep.

I spun around. "Change, now —"

"Tessa." Sam's firm use of my name, and his slow advancement, shut me up.

With my counter-back steps, I bumped into the window.

Sam came to stop an inch from me.

I held my head high and added heat to my words, "I gave you an order. Change."

"And I'm following it." He dipped his head to mine. "Kiss me."

"Are you nuts?"

"Please." His deep voice grew to a coaxing rumble against my lips. "Help me Change."

And I'd be damned if my hormones didn't wake right up...until the scent of fresh blood hit my nose. Hunger consumed me. As fear screamed through my mind, I pushed at Sam's chest. "I might kill—"

The doors opened, and for the first time, I was relieved to see a vampire.

Chapter Fifteen

The hallway's harsh light silhouetted Derek's rigid frame. "Release her," he ordered, stepping across the threshold.

Before Derek's stare locked with mine, Sam spun me around. With my back flush to his chest, he then turned us to face the windows.

"Don't look at him," Sam said.

Sam's warning came too late. The hall's electric light against the backdrop of the clear night sky turned the window into a mirror. I wanted to look away from Derek's reflection, but my brain failed to fire off that synapse.

Still, it didn't matter how sleek and sexy Derek looked in his suit or the sultry way his accented words rolled off his tongue—he had messed with Andrea, and now he'd deal with the consequences.

I relaxed in Sam's hold, giving me enough space—
Busted.

Being a quick learner, Sam caught me mid-drop in my escape. With a squeeze to my arms, he dragged a smidge of my attention back to him. "Look at the moon. Not at him. Focus on its song. Not his voice."

"Step away from her," Derek said, glancing down at his finely pressed jacket.

Sam didn't budge.

Derek lifted his head and with a flick of his wrist, the doors closed. "Turn around, Tessa."

My skin crawled with the need to obey. I shimmied in Sam's hold, managing to move nose to chest. His arms tightened around me. Pressing a hand to the back of my head, Sam kept my face to his chest while he turned toward Derek.

"Let her go," Derek ordered.

"You," Sam growled, "let her go."

Derek's dress shoes clicked against the floorboards. Each step he took shot cold adrenaline through my veins. My spine prickled with his nearness. I struggled to turn, but Sam held me firm. I knew this was his way of protecting me, by keeping me from looking at the vampire or allowing me to do something stupid — like jumping out the window.

The metallic clicking from the serving carts' wheels shot my heart into my throat. Derek stood mere feet away from us. "Didn't care for your dinner?"

"As much as I care for you," I mumbled into Sam's robe.

"The feeling's mutual," Derek continued in a low voice. "If you think more fondly of the wolf smothering you, tell him to step away."

Sam pressed me harder against his pecs. "Not happening."

Derek rapped his knuckles on the chair. "Wolf, you're of no value to us anymore. You do me a favor by disobeying."

"Still gotta go through me to get to her." Sam's voice deepened. "A warning, bloodsucker — you won't be the first or the last vampire I dust."

"You wolves are such a passionate race." Derek smirked. "But fools all the same. Think on this — if I kill you, who will protect her during the day?" His voice lifted. "Then again, by your appearances, she seems to have dealt with the guards better than you."

I jabbed my finger at Sam's rock-hard abs. "Ohhh, let me go *deal* with him."

Both men ignored me, Sam by silence, Derek by running his mouth.

"Yet, if you end up dead, I fear her temper would compromise her safety," Derek said. "There are only so many pieces of furniture for her to assault before Anthony corrects her behavior."

Filling me in with what I already gathered, Sam mumbled, "Anthony is the captain of the queen's day guards."

A.k.a. Boss.

Loosening his arms from around me, Sam then dipped his head to mine, capturing my eyes with his. "If I let you go, can you keep calm?"

I glared at him. "I'm not the one crushing your spleen while holding a pissing match with a vampire."

"If you go crazy on him, you'll lose, and we die."

That one sentence held a trifecta of my greatest fears — loss of control, failure and death. Perfectly executed manipulation on Sam's part to keep me safe. I let out a ragged breath. "I'm fine."

"You suck at lying." Sam's gaze shifted from my eyes to my lips and before I could put together a plan on how I was going to flog the vampire, Sam kissed me.

With his fingers tangling in my hair, and his lips moving against mine, I gave in, sinking into the rhythm of his kiss. Shuddering against the warmth of his exhale, I fluttered my eyes open to his intense stare. He cupped my face in his trembling hands, which kept me from escaping the raw emotion filling his eyes.

"Still angry?" he asked.

"N—nope." Desire raced through my veins, setting every inch of my skin to heat. My mind swirled. Never had a kiss stirred such a feverish want within me. Pulling my gaze away from Sam's, I knew I was in deep trouble.

Sam's killer grin highlighted his dimples. "Good."

"Why didn't you?" In the presence of Derek, I let the rest of the question fall silent. Sam could've used the kiss to heal himself by turning wolf.

"I'm not going to wait until sunrise for another kiss." Sam's tone grew serious. "Remember, don't look into his eyes. If his voice puts you in a trance, focus on *my* heartbeat. If he ticks you off, I want you to remember that kiss."

Sam released me and took a step back.

With fisted hands, racing heart and tingling lips, I turned to face Derek.

He stood feet from me, with his eyes drawn into slits aimed at Sam. "Come to me, Tessa."

Every bone in my body hummed with his order. I looked at my toes curling against the floorboards. *Stay. Don't go.* Useless. They walked me right to the vampire. Keeping my stare trained on the floor, I stopped once my gaze landed on his polished shoes, which reflected my wide eyes and trembling jaw.

"Look at me," he said in a flat voice.

I searched for a loophole and came up with *looking at* his shin.

"My eyes, Tessa Sanders." As my last name left his lips, my eyes were on his. Not a hint of emotion crossed his unwavering stare. "I will not burden you with pain if you answer my questions."

My mouth gaped. "What a way to start a conversation."

"Perhaps, if your wolf had listened the first time, you would not be in this situation."

With Derek's icy breath hitting my chin, still warmed by Sam's facial stubble, my memory snapped back to our kiss...no, not the kiss a moment ago with Sam. But the lip lock with Derek. The hazy park memory focused. I relived every movement of Derek's lips against mine in full-out detail. I slapped my hands over my mouth. "Oh no. In the park. You—"

"You will tell me all you know about Safe Waters." Derek's words swam through my mind. Fighting against the intoxicating effect of his voice, I shook my head. Dizziness attacked me. "Do not fight me, Tessa Sanders."

"Fight him." The roughness of Sam's voice broke through Derek's trance. "He's using compulsion on you."

Still glaring into my eyes, Derek spoke at Sam. "Keep your mouth shut." After a silent pause, Derek's voice constricted around my mind. "Tessa, answer."

Even though the less painful thing to do would've been for me to spell it all out, the story was Andrea's ticket to freedom, and I wasn't about to let some discomfort ruin her chance. The queen would get her information from me, not her vampire bitch-boy.

Channeling Andrea, I cocked my chin up at Derek. "No."

As he narrowed his gaze, pain hammered at my temples. Distracting myself, I focused on the flecks of gold in his dark hazel eyes. Until blackness spread outwards from his pupils, consuming his irises.

"You cannot fight me," he said.

"Watch…me," I whispered.

With a tilt of his head, my stomach dropped like I was on a rollercoaster to hell.

As I took a seat on the floor, a movement behind Derek's leg caught my attention. A shadow pulled away from the wall, then took a step toward us. Not trusting my eyes, I blinked, and upon opening them, Nathaniel stood beside Derek.

Short, blond and deadly peered down at me. "I see you taught your pet how to sit."

Derek curled his lips around his elongating fangs. "Nathaniel, I ordered you to never enter this room."

"A fine night to you too, Derek." Nathaniel's baby blues never left me as he spoke. "Queen's orders trump the hunter's. I'm to dog-sit while you take your pet to her." A grin tugged at the corner of his lips. "Might I suggest the next trick you teach is how to extend her neck for proper feeding."

When Derek spun toward Nathaniel, a hand covered in brown fur clamped onto my shoulder. Moonlight glinted on the razor-sharp claws dragging me backward.

Not wanting to have my arm ripped off, I moved with Sam as he yanked me to my feet. A sharp sting flared at my shoulder, and what I forced myself to believe was thick, copper-scented sweat rolled down my arm.

"Let her go," Derek ordered. "You will kill her."

Sam's claws bit deeper into my shoulder.

"You spill her blood," Nathaniel said as his gaze tracked the droplets falling from my fingertips to the floor.

Sam sniffed.

Instantly, his grip disappeared from my shoulder, then a shove to my back had me stumbling over to the vampires. I braced my heels against the floor, stopping myself halfway between Sam and the bloodsuckers.

Tension crackled in the air from Sam's approaching Change. I chanced a glance at him. Agony contorted his beet-red face as he hunched over. With a series of wet pops, his neck lengthened.

"Tessa," Derek called out.

I jerked my head back to him, and his black mirrored eyes caught mine.

"Tell your wolf to stay in his human form. Or I *will* kill him."

Not trusting Derek, I kept my attention on him while I whispered at Sam, "Listen to Derek."

Sam growled.

Derek twitched his fingers at his sides. His nails grew long, black and sharp.

"No." I looked away from Derek to Sam, who opened his mouth to make room for his canines. "Please."

"Fool," Derek spat.

"Stop." I tossed my hands out, holding back the monsters. "None of you want me dead." Behind Derek's right shoulder, Nathaniel lifted his index finger in protest, so I added, "At the moment."

"That is why you will come to me." Derek held out his claw-accessorized hand.

"No." I narrowed my eyes to his chin. "Both of you bloodsuckers will move back toward the doors."

"Why would we do such a thing?" Nathaniel asked.

Keeping my attention on Derek, I answered, "Because you have no option."

Sam snarled, and the hair on the back of my neck stood on end.

Derek spoke just above a whisper. "That animal at your back smells your fear. Your weakness. He'll soon be blind to his human half, and the need for flesh will overrule the desire to protect you."

How I wanted Derek's words to be a bluff, but below Sam's growls, his stomach rumbled. When I took a shuddering breath, vanilla punched me in the nose. I smelled like a freaking cookie factory.

Nathaniel inhaled. "Her scent...."

He took a step toward me, but Derek muttered something under his breath, halting Nathaniel's advancement.

Derek spoke at me. "Move slowly to the bathroom. Shut the door and cover your ears. I'll make it quick."

"I won't let you kill him," I said.

Sam moaned. "Comm...and...me." His words sounded more like an animalistic howl.

"What?" I asked.

"He'll eat you alive," Derek answered.

"I got that the first time you said it. I'm not talking to you."

"Wolf Born." Sam gasped for breath. "Command me."

With his use of my title, energy coursed through my veins as heat rolled around me, through me. While I looked into Sam's glowing eyes, I mustered all my strength into my words. "Sam, I *command* you to remain human."

He stilled in his Change. Then in a seamless reverse, Sam returned to his fully human self.

The command left me jittery and cold. I rubbed away the chill creeping up my arms. When my fingers brushed across Sam's claw marks, pain shot down my arm.

"Good dogs," Nathaniel mocked.

Balling my hands into fists, I spun to face the bloodsucker.

"Oh, she's going to attack." Nathaniel exaggerated a shiver. "I quiver with anticipation."

"Nathaniel," Derek warned. "Sit by the fire while I speak with her."

All giddiness dropped from Nathaniel, who walked over to the chair then turned it around to face us. Slowly, he lowered himself, glaring at me. "I told you to take care of *her* last night."

Derek's full attention was on me again. "Who taught you to command?"

"My inner awesomeness," I grumbled.

"Who taught you?" His words flowed through me, searching for the answer. "Tell me."

He'd be sorely disappointed. Commanding was more instinct than something I needed to be taught. After a lap around my mind, Derek's compulsion drifted away.

"What an interesting wolf you are," he said.

"I'm not a wolf." I glared at his chiseled jawline. "Stay out of my head."

"I will for now," he said.

"Golly gee, Mr. Bloodsucker, how kind of you."

"You haven't an idea." A ghost of a smile tugged at the corners of his pressed lips. "I give my oath to you, Tessa Sanders. I'll not use compulsion on you for the rest of the night."

"Well, that could've ruined the evening." Nathaniel scowled at Derek. "Lucky there is still one vampire who wishes to keep his head." His voice crept into my skull. *"You will answer — "*

"Did the queen's orders instruct you to use compulsion on the Wolf Born?" Derek asked.

"No." With Nathaniel's answer, his compulsion loosened its grip on my mind. Still, present enough for me to know he was ready and waiting to make me go puppet.

"Then you will not use compulsion on her or her wolf while Tessa is in this room and under my protection."

Nathaniel gave me a final brain squeeze before releasing me entirely. "Behave, she-beast."

"My name is Tessa."

"Okay, she-beast," Nathaniel muttered.

Derek looked past me toward Sam. "Go stand watch at the doors."

In three strides, Sam stood a foot away from Derek. To anyone placing a bet on a throwdown, Sam appeared the obvious winner, towering over Derek and outweighing him. However, Derek was a vampire, and the back of his skull wasn't jabbing out of his scalp.

"The second you hear movement, alert me," Derek said to Sam.

With a sharp nod, Sam moved to the doors not even glancing at me as he passed.

Nathaniel tapped his claws on the armrests. "You're running out of time, Derek. Our eager queen will be here within the hour."

Derek walked toward me. "Tell me all you know about Safe Waters."

Rolling my uninjured shoulder, I faced off the vampire. "I will tell the queen."

His jaw tightened. "Why do you defy me?"

"Andrea."

He sighed. "The queen gave an oath. With the name, the human will be set free."

"No," I corrected. "Her oath stated she wanted *me* to tell her. Not you."

"I was witness, Derek." Nathaniel steepled his hands under his chin. "She-beast is correct."

Derek muttered a curse. "If you go before the queen, I cannot guarantee your safety."

"Wolf Born—"

"Don't call me that," I snapped at Sam.

"Listen to him." Sam's gaze intensified. "Think of the greater sum."

"The greater sum, Sam? What the actual fuck? Andrea is your friend."

"She is." His eyes narrowed. "But you have a responsibility."

"You're right. To Andrea."

"To our race."

Clapping his fingers against his open palm, Nathaniel silenced us. "The queen only stated she wanted to know who your pet thought was behind the water contamination, Derek." Nathaniel glanced at me. "You may speak of everything else, and that hellspawn's freedom will still be granted."

I shook my head. "Like I'd trust you."

Derek shot a look at Sam. "Did you not teach her about vampires today?"

"Are you bloody kidding me?" Nathaniel straightened. "You would allow him to snitch on our race? To her?"

"Only about certain things." Derek glanced at Nathaniel. "I'd not put us at risk."

"Knowledge is deadlier than a stake to the heart." Nathaniel covered his mouth. "Oops." When he lowered his hand, he smiled at me. "Not like you could get close enough."

Before I had a chance to test that theory, Derek cut in. "Vampires cannot bear false witness."

"Sure." I folded my arms. "I'm totally convinced."

"Nathaniel, speak falsely." Derek glanced at him. "As the queen's hunter, you will obey my order."

Nathaniel's grin fell from his face. Utter hate pooled from the look he tossed my way. "I hope that you live through this night, she-beast."

He launched from his seat, eyes widening while muffled snaps and crackles came from his sealed lips. In vampire speed, he made it to the serving cart. Smoke drifted from his nostrils as he grabbed the carafe of orange juice. He took a swig, then spun to the fireplace, spraying the flames with juice. Smoke rose over his head. When he turned around, his mouth was smoldering.

"Open your mouth," Derek said.

Smoke rolled out of Nathaniel's mouth. After the haze cleared, his fangs and jawbone glistened in the firelight. He coughed, and his chalk-white tongue disintegrated into a puff of ash.

"Do you take my word for truth now?" Derek asked.

Still eyes wide on Nathaniel, I nodded.

Derek stepped in front of me, and I dropped my gaze to his shoes, covered in the remnants of Nathaniel's tongue.

"Then tell me all you know."

Chapter Sixteen

I'd hoped to never hear Nathaniel's sing-song shrill again once he was without a tongue. Like a mosquito trapped between my hair and ear, his tenor voice buzzed inside my skull. *"My, my, my, what a little muckraker. Good luck protecting her."*

For some reason, I heard only his side of the vampires' mind-to-mind conversation. Each stared at the other across the room, neither breathing nor blinking. The only gauge I had to Derek's take on my story was the slight tightening of his fists.

I gave a glance at Sam. His shoulders had risen to his ears with tension. He'd smartly kept his mouth shut and eyes to the doors.

While I stared at him, guilt jogged laps around my mind. Without hesitation, Sam chose the lives of thousands over Andrea. Like a true leader. Unlike me. Everyone would die waiting for me to *not* choose.

Nathaniel snapped his fingers at me. *"I swear, these animals have no attention span. She has shared nothing we did not already know."* As he tilted his head, his gaze almost caught mine. *"Pity, my tongue is on your shoes and you gave your oath to not use compulsion. The stupid she-beast will die tonight if you do not find something of interest for Adele."*

With Nathaniel's lack of respect by dropping the queen's name, I added him—momentarily—to our side. Yes, he wanted me dead, but from what Andrea overheard, the queen wouldn't cry over the loss of Nathaniel. He needed to keep me breathing just as much as Derek and the entire werewolf population.

"We need collateral for your safety." Derek turned toward me.

"Well…why is Safe Waters important to Queen Bloodsucker?" I asked.

"Best tell her to watch her mouth. A wolf's tongue does not grow back."

"You will address her as Queen," Derek said. "She has a vested interest in who is behind the contamination."

"I get that. But I asked *why*."

"Do not tell her. You do, and Adele will have your head." Nathaniel waited for Derek to look at him before he spoke again. *"This Benjamin, the missing human, she has avoided any mention of him. If he is not dead by human hand or filling the belly of a wolf, perhaps she may have some knowledge of where he's hiding."*

Derek glanced my way. "Andrea's mind did not offer much information on Benjamin."

"Offer?" My nails bit into the flesh of my sweaty palms. "You wormed your way into her mind. You brainwashed her. You terrified her."

"And fed from her." Derek paused, letting that image fester in my mind. "Tell me about Benjamin."

Cold hatred caused my vision to tunnel onto his neck. With the urge to tear my teeth into his porcelain flesh, I struggled to remain on my side of the room. "Ben—"

Sam cleared his throat.

When I looked at him, Sam held my stare. Derek had changed tactics by trying to use my emotions to flush out information—which he almost had. Smartly, Sam caught on, and with his distraction, I regained control.

Derek sidestepped, causing me to look away from Sam to keep both vampires in my line of vision. "Do you know where Benjamin is hiding?" he asked.

"No." Wonderful thing werewolves could bluff. Truth, I'd no clue where Ben was. Fib, I knew where his glasses were and that he'd partnered with Jason.

I gritted my teeth.

"Before Benjamin betrayed you—"

"He did not."

"Before entering the bar, he conversed with the alpha. Benjamin betrayed you." Derek's abrasiveness cut deep. "Now, was there anything pertaining to Safe Waters that you did not discuss with him?"

"No. He knows everything." I tried for a flat, uncaring tone and failed as my voice wavered. Each time someone mentioned how Ben had stabbed me in the back—hurt. And each occurrence had me doing a mental what-if-they're-right. Not giving two shits about the no-staring-into-a-vampire's-eyes rule, I looked right into Derek's as I said, "Ben didn't betray me."

Derek held my stare. "You trust too much. Care too much—" His eyes widened the slightest. "Why did you begin your investigation of Safe Waters?"

"Armpit stains."

"Explain." Derek lifted his hand to silence Nathaniel, who slouched against the chair.

"I saw the story as my way out of being my boss's errand runner."

Sam shifted his position, keeping his ear to the doors, and eyes to me.

"Perhaps, that's the reason you wanted Benjamin, Andrea...yourself to believe." Derek stepped closer, lowering his voice. "What was the real reason, Tessa?"

"I wanted the truth."

"About?"

"What was causing certain people who drank the tap water or swam in the lake, to become sick."

"Enough, Derek. Steer her away from the illness."

"Did you become sick, Tessa?" Derek asked, ignoring Nathaniel.

I nodded and looked at Sam, who had also prayed to the Porcelain God after drinking from the water fountain at Oblivion. The pieces slammed together. "The sick. They're not...human."

Derek nodded. "Anyone not entirely human who ingested the contaminated water became sick."

"What do you mean by not entirely human?" I asked.

"There are other races."

"Others like?"

"Others will serve for now," Derek said. "Regardless, their blood has been weakened throughout the centuries from breeding with humans. Their offspring are deemed half-bloods. They possess no powers. No heightened abilities."

Narrowing my eyes at him, I rocked on my heels. How many people were like me, having no clue that, they, the tee-ball players, lawyers, stay-at-home dads and business moms were supernatural?

"Is someone or thing targeting them?" I asked.

Derek just stared at me.

"A little help from the audience?" I glanced at Sam, who went back to staring a hole through the doors. Concentrating, I zoned onto the bloody spider web covering his robe. "Blood. Catalyst. Others like me—"

Nathaniel stood. *"Derek, silence her racing mind."*

"The list." All three focused on me. "Ben has everything except for the list."

"What list?" Derek asked.

"Any time I got word someone became sick, I jotted their names down."

"Of course she did." Nathaniel hung his head.

"Has anyone else had access to this list?" Derek asked.

"The city's health inspector. Anyone who went to the hospital after encountering the water supply had their charts reviewed by the inspector. It took him a week to dismiss the sickness as a stomach virus." To keep from losing track of my ideas, I paced across the rug. "His reasons were—Safe Waters had a perfect track record of inspections, the illness affected such a small population of the city and every case cleared up within a matter of days."

Nathaniel stuck his leg out, almost tripping me. Instead of his usual look of twisted amusement, an expression of intense concentration crossed his face.

"But there's more, isn't there?" I asked Derek.

"The queen—"

Nathaniel snapped his face at Derek. *"I've sworn to kill any who speak of her interest."*

Derek gave a curt nod at Nathaniel before rerouting the conversation. "Nathaniel erased the files from the hospital's database as well as any human minds that were part of the research or investigation. Then he took care to strip the minds of the rest of Glenwood's citizens."

With the nonchalant attitude Derek had about Nathaniel's ability to brainwash an entire city, I carefully sidestepped away from Blond. "Compulsion. Makes sense," I mumbled. "Everyone bought right into the stomach virus and algae bloom stories."

"You did not." Derek stepped closer to me, and before I could gauge if he was leading me into a clue, he continued, "Before we were able to confront the health inspector, he…left the city."

Nathaniel smirked. *"That's an interesting way of saying murdered."*

Rigid, I pretended not to hear Nathaniel. "Just a guess, the inspector *left* with his research — the medical files."

Nathaniel made a sound that resembled a groan, confirming my fear.

I snapped my attention between the three silent men. "The half-bloods, they're in danger."

"Nothing has happened to them," Derek said.

"Yet." I raked my fingers through my hair. "We need to warn them."

"Yes, you do that, she-beast."

Without losing eye contact with me, Derek grumbled at Nathaniel, "Enough." When he returned his entire focus to me, Derek's voice softened but still held authority. "How many names are on your list?"

"There were at least twenty from the hospital and another dozen more, like me, who toughed it out at home."

The vampires faced each other while I looked at Sam, who shook his head. How I wanted to tell him to trust me. No way were the bloodsuckers getting my list.

"Where is this list?" Derek asked.

I searched my memories, hitting on Ben filing my bills that he'd knocked off my coffee table. When he lifted my rent bill, on its backside were my chicken scratches of names.

"I'm not sure...maybe on my desk," I said.

Nathaniel sighed. *"Her dwelling was ransacked. The list is lost."*

"Take us to her apartment." Derek caught my wrist, pulling me toward Nathaniel.

"The one broken into by werewolves? Watched by all sorts of spies?" Nathaniel grinned. *"Finally, some entertainment."*

"You will return to watch the wolf. This search won't take more than a few minutes. I'll signal when to gather us," Derek said to Nathaniel.

"Two round trips. I'll need to feed." Nathaniel eyed Sam.

I dug my heels against the rug. "I can tell you where it was last. My apartment's small. You'll find it. I'll stay with Sam."

Derek glanced down at me. "Why so frightened?"

Because Blond wants to chomp-chomp on Sam. Instead, I said, "The way Nathaniel's looking at Sam."

Derek turned his attention to Nathaniel. "Unless he attacks, you'll not kill the wolf in our absence. Now, be quick." He snaked his arm around my waist, dragging me toward the closet.

Even with my inhuman strength, Derek's iron grip outmatched my struggles.

"Leave her." Sam fought against the invisible leash of Derek's compulsion that kept him guarding the doors. "Take me. I know her apartment. From the busted living room window to her lopsided nightstand."

One look at Sam's guilt-ridden face and I knew he wasn't rehashing details from Andrea. No. He'd seen my shithole firsthand, and I had never invited Sam to my apartment—ever. Anger won over self-control as I snapped at him, "I'm supposed to *trust* you?"

"Andrea worried you were in deep with this story. I told her I'd check up on you, so I went to your place to see how much trouble you were getting into. I wanted to help. I swear on my life, it was only to keep you safe."

"You could have asked!"

"And you would have let me? No." He snapped his head to the doors. "We'd have still ended up here."

"Correct," Derek said.

Nathaniel peeked out from the closet. *"Can we go?"*

Derek increased his stride, bringing us to the closet threshold.

"In there with you? I think not." Kicking my legs out, I shoved my back against his chest and planted my feet on each side of the door frame.

"Nathaniel will use the shadows to take us to your apartment." Derek gave me a shove that failed to dislodge me. "The darker the space, the easier for him to do so. He can move two with great effort, but I'm unsure how he will manage with three."

"She's a wisp of a thing."

"Car. Bus. Taxi. All are wonderful means of transportation." Flexing my legs, I locked my knees.

"We do not have the time," Derek said.

"Or permission."

"Tessa." Derek's lips brushed my ear. "Your list will keep you unharmed."

It wasn't about saving my neck. The news story I'd risked my career and life for threatened innocent people. I needed to find that list and destroy it. Staring into the dark closet, with Derek's chilled breath crawling along my skin, I let my feet slip from the frame.

Chapter Seventeen

Inside the closet, Derek spun me around, pinning me flush to his chest. "The discomfort will be brief," he said against the top of my head.

Nathaniel jabbed a finger against my back, sending a jolt of energy through my body.

The sensation of being weightless, bodiless, then what I imagined were my atoms mixing with Nathaniel's took over.

"You have minutes at most."

Instantly, I was a solid, freezing and gasping for breath crazy woman who'd crawled up Derek's torso. Nathaniel wasted no time disappearing from my living room, while I detached myself from Derek.

"Wait here," Derek whispered.

Then he took off down the hallway.

Left alone, my heightened senses crippled me. White noise pounded against my head while the reek of spoiled milk assaulted my nose. The worst was seeing my dark, trashed apartment in HD.

Not a thing had escaped intact from the break-in. Overhead, part of a barstool hung from the living room fan suspended by a frayed electrical cord. Where the stool should have been, the kitchen countertop curled like an orange peel, obscuring my view of the leaky faucet — still dripping away.

Glancing down, I toed a piece of porcelain, flipping it over to reveal the smiling kitty from my coffee mug. While I looked at its beady eyes, numbness crept into my heart. For the past three years, I'd rebuilt my life while collecting my second-hand items. Piece by piece, they had made this crummy space in the universe mine. Then in an instant, both my life and my space had been stolen from me. Again.

"Focus on finding the list," Derek said from behind me. "It will help dull your senses."

Almost starting where it would have been, under my broken-in-two-upside-down coffee table, I turned, coming face to face with Derek. Something about the way he looked at me with a smidge of sympathy heated my blood. "You know, you could act human. Make noise. Blink. Breathe now and then."

He took a deep breath.

It was my turn to stare. With a flick of his personality switch, Derek transformed from an uptight, heartless bloodsucker into a wiseass.

As his chest deflated with his exaggerated exhale, I brushed past him. "Bedroom is this way."

He grabbed my arm. "Follow me, and keep your voice at a whisper. If a human was to wander up here to investigate, I would kill them."

"Why not brainwash them?" I asked.

"Too much energy."

"And killing a person requires less?"

"Yes." He paused. "The entire city believes you ran away. That this…place belongs to an elderly man. If you are seen…"

"I cause even more of a pain in Queen Bloodsucker's ass."

He dropped my arm with a nod.

"Got it," I sighed. "Ninja mode."

Confusion crossed his face. "There are no ninjas." He took the lead down the hallway. "Watch your footing, there is glass everywhere."

"Total bummer, I don't have shoes." Puffs of breath rose above my head. Hugging myself, I added, "A coat, hat, gloves…coffee."

No response came from the vampire inspecting a dust bunny.

When I dodged around him, he snagged my pant leg, knocking me off balance. To keep from landing on him, I fell back against the wall.

"Reckless." Derek cringed as his fingertips brushed the dirty sole of my foot.

"A splinter isn't going to kill me." I tried to tug free.

"Your blood will attract a wolf from a mile away."

I looked at my shoulder that Sam had sunk his claws into minutes ago.

"Fresh blood," Derek added. He let me go, then stood. "Be observant of your surroundings."

Never had I hated the hamster tube of a hallway as much as at that moment. An inch separated us. To keep from locking stares with Derek, I studied his nose. As far as sniffers went, his was a fine specimen. The slight bump at its bridge hinted he'd broken it a while back. He made no move to let me pass, instead, he just stood there. With each tight inhale I took, I struggled not to deepen my breaths, because his dark, delicious scent coiled around me, making my knees go weak.

He tilted his head, mocking. "You know, you could breathe once in a while, Tessa."

"I would if you and your stink moved it."

With a shrug, he turned toward my bedroom. "Wolves and their sensitive snouts."

"So, werewolves have a better sense of smell than bloodsuckers?"

"Barely. *Vampires* are faster, stronger, possess higher intelligence, immortal—"

"And plagued with pale skin, a limited diet, awful fashion sense and a blinding ego."

"Have you looked at your reflection as of late?" He set the bedroom door against the wall, then faced me. "I confuse your pallor for that of the moon. As for my suit, it's a dress code. I believe you are versed in dress codes because when I saved you from the alpha, I recall you wearing a polyester cape. Although it was an improvement over the windbreaker from the prior evening."

He cursed with his slip—which had me grinning.

"Blinding ego. Gets them every time." Before he had a chance to backpaddle, I asked, "What happened to me at the park?"

He just stared at me.

I tapped a finger to my temple. "I know you were there and that you messed with my mind."

His jaw tightened.

My attention slipped to Derek's lips. Heat crawled through my belly, spilling into my veins, sparking a blush to creep up my throat. Swallowing, I whispered, "Why did you kiss me?"

He squared his shoulders, boxing me in between his chest and the wall, his gaze lowered to my neck. "Find the list, Tessa." Slowly, he backed away.

Adrenaline buzzed through my body, leaving my limbs trembling. Sucking in a breath, I continued to the bedroom. It was evident when he'd disappeared earlier, Derek had taken a tour of my ransacked bedroom. His scent lingered in the stagnant air. "Thought you could find the list without me?"

"Good to observe you're using your new skill sets. I was checking for threats." He walked past me, stepping over part of the mattress, and continued to the window.

Through my disheveled blinds, the streetlight's yellow glow streaked across Derek's face. A nanosecond earlier, I had thought his nostrils were the cat's pajamas. Now, he looked like two-day-old roadkill.

"Even a vampire looks like death under fluorescent lighting."

His sunken eyes scowled at me. "Put your nose back to work, before I send word to Nathaniel that Sam is on the menu."

While I hobbled to the wood kindling that once was my desk, I took a deep inhale, hitting on a cluster of scents. Some vampire. Some werewolf. And one— recently here—lover of lavender-air-fresheners human.

Ben.

Happy he wasn't with the werewolves but scared he was still hanging around town, I shoved my emotions to the back of my mind to track my best friend. From Ben's scent, I knew he had been on an in-and-out mission. He came through the window, went over to the crunched bed frame leaning against the wall, then right back out the window.

What is he looking for?

Scanning over the wreckage for clues, I filled Derek in with some of my observations. "My laptop's gone, taken before they trashed the place, or else there would be bits of Dell everywhere. Too bad for the burglars, Ben removed my work files. All the vampires gained on me was my unhealthy love of eighties music."

Derek watched me settle to my knees in front of the desk's remains. "Why vampires?"

"The queen's guards smell like dirt. Nathaniel smells like earthworms. There is a faint mixture of the two here."

"Earthworms." He chuckled. "Best not say this to him." Derek's face relaxed. "Keep searching, while you inform me about the other scents you pick up on." His voice deepened. "One lie or delay could cost someone their life."

I set my glare to the junk on my lap. "Next was a werewolf. Then you. Not sure about time passage, but I know the order from how strong the scents are." My fingertips brushed over a pencil. Shoving my arms up to my shoulders in the pile, I wiggled the pencil into the sleeve of my shirt.

"Correct in your observations." Derek sounded amused. "Tell me about the wolf."

Just because I'd no warm-n-fuzzy feelings toward Detective Miller didn't mean I'd put him on the bloodsuckers' radar. I wrinkled my nose at his juniper scent. "He searched this pile."

"Why do you think that?"

"Because his scent is on these clean socks." With my free hand, I lifted the balled-up socks from the debris.

Derek nodded approvingly. "Detective Miller is his alias. He's the werewolf you climbed out a window to escape from."

Dropping the sock, I sighed. Of course, he had pulled the incident from Andrea's brain and more than likely Sam's too. I drifted off into my thoughts. Sam had to have known Miller was a werewolf, certainly. The vampires who kidnapped Andrea and Sam from Miller's car would have as well.

"Why did the bloodsuckers let him go?" I looked at Derek.

"Miller belongs to the alpha who bit you." Derek took a step away from the window. "He has been quite useful."

"Compulsion." I swallowed on my suddenly dry throat. "You're using him as a spy."

Two nasty thoughts came to mind. If Jason smelled the vampires on Miller, he'd not hesitate to kill Miller. And if the stench went unnoticed, then the bloodsuckers might've known about Jason's plan to crash the Gathering.

Derek dropped his gaze to my buried arm. "You tremble."

"I'm freezing." Curling my fingers into my sleeve, keeping the pencil concealed, I pulled my arm free from the pile.

"A truth amongst a lie." He leveled his stare to mine. "Who smells like an old woman's perfume?"

"I don't…"

His eyes flared, and his mouth tensed into a flat line.

"You already know," I whispered.

"What was he looking for?" His voice sharpened, "You lie once more, I will hunt Benjamin down and kill him myself."

"I don't know!"

Derek lunged at me, his hand tangled in my hair, dragging me up to my feet. "Benjamin went from the window to the bedframe." Using his grip at the back of my head, he pointed me at the wall. "Just above the frame, there is a message."

Squinting, I read the one-inch space covered with Ben's perfect penmanship. "I sat through *Buffy*."

"What does it mean?"

Blinking back hot tears, I answered with utmost certainty, "Besties for life."

Derek growled. "What does *that* mean?"

"Friend. Get with the times, bloodsucker."

A shimmer of gold from underneath the bedframe caught my eye. Staring at the empty picture frame, I knew then what Ben had come for. My prized possession, the only remaining photo of my family.

"Your friend is an idiot who risked his neck to scribble a note which may have never been seen by you. It's only a matter of time until we hunt him down. Think of him as your dead bestie."

Along with Derek's deteriorating looks, his strength was dissolving. His hand shook on my scalp. As he turned me around, I could've broken away, but I wanted him weaker.

His fangs jabbed out from his thinning lips, momentarily catching me off guard. Freeing his hand from my hair, Derek slid his fingertips along my temple, while he brought his other hand to circle my waist. "Show me the list."

A flash of light followed by my memory of the coin toss flickered across my mind. Derek pressed deeper into my subconscious, streamlining what I desperately tried to hide, lurching to halt on the list in Ben's hand as he set it on the coffee table.

The brush of Derek's nose next to the crook of my neck snapped me out of the memory.

"Why do you lie?" His breath dragged across my throat.

My turn not to speak. Not that I could. Fear of having my throat torn out stole my voice, while the ridiculous craving to have Derek's lips brush my skin vibrated a breathy sigh from me.

Groaning, he grabbed my hip with pressure enough to bruise, yet not to bring me closer to him. "I'm trying to protect you."

Slowly, I uncurled my fingers from my sleeve, letting the pencil slip into my palm. A quick alteration in my grip and the #2 was ready. "Funny way of showing it. Kidnapping me. My friends. Having your fangs—"

His eyes went to mine. Within his intense stare, I met the desire he had gifted me with on the dance floor. His body shook, lips parted. "I cannot lie. I *am* protecting you from the queen."

"What about from you?"

"No." Searing heat filled his voice. "No one can or will protect you from me."

Folding my bottom lip into my mouth, I rationalized my next move. For the opportunity to save the half-bloods…Ben, and maybe a thread of deadly curiosity, I pressed my lips to Derek's.

His control shattered. Caging my face between his hands, Derek stole my soul with his kiss. Lips, teeth and tongues danced in a punishing rhythm. One I never wanted to end, even with my lungs screaming for air. The damn reflexes severed our kiss. Gasping for breath,

I snapped back my head. Stupid. Derek's mouth fastened to my neck. Fangs skirted along my jugular. The need to sate the passion burning through me ravaged my sanity when he pierced my flesh. Digging my nails into the pencil, I rooted myself in my mission, plunging the makeshift stake into Derek.

He jerked. Bringing his blood-slick lips to my ear, he whispered, "You...missed."

"No, I didn't." I gave him a shove. He stumbled away from me with the pencil lodged in his stomach just above his navel.

Yanking out the makeshift stake, he dropped to his knees. Blood sluggishly darkened his dress shirt, rolling down his thigh to pool onto the floor. His arms hung loosely at his sides while his head bobbed side to side as he fought to keep it aimed at me.

"Stay," I said.

Being in such a weakened state, all I had to worry about was the leer he gave me as I stumbled to the hallway. My legs felt like lead. Any time I tried to pick up the pace, Derek's prior set compulsion taunted inside my head. *"Never run at night again."*

Tossing the coffee table to the side, I glanced at the papers speckled with fresh blood. When I swept my hand across my neck, I flinched. *Oh no.* Dropping to my knees, I tore through the pile, smearing blood on everything I touched. "Come on," I muttered. "Yes!" Relief buzzed through me as I grasped ahold of my rent bill. I turned it over. A list of names ran from top to bottom.

A floor below, one of Mrs. Peterson's cats hissed, then another growled while the other screamed. Countless times I had received the same greeting when I passed her apartment. Closing my eyes to focus my hearing, the faint sound of swift steps touching concrete echoed within the apartment's stairwell.

Mystery solved — cats hated werewolves.

Forcing my wobbling legs into action, I shuffled down the hall. Just as Derek limped into the hallway, I swung into the bathroom.

Aside from the medicine cabinet busted on the floor, the room still was intact. Lowering into a squat, praying that I found a loophole in Derek's — no running at night — compulsion, I launched myself at the toilet.

Pieces of glass embedded into my right heel from my hard landing. Wincing, I looked into the water-filled bowl. Careful not to read any of the names, in case a vampire used compulsion to force the information from me, I shredded the list, letting the pieces flutter into the toilet.

I was in mid-flush when two things happened simultaneously — the front door crashed to the floor, and Derek grabbed me around the waist.

Claws clicking against the kitchen floor joined pursuit with the pairs of boots storming toward the bathroom.

Derek spun me toward the sink, curling over me.

The shower wall exploded.

Nathaniel rolled through the crater-sized hole. Springing to his feet, he shot his hands out, grabbing ahold of Derek's limp body and snagging my wrist.

Pain flared throughout my body. Nathaniel was not as flawless with the transition as the last time — I screamed. Every inch of my skin felt like a hot poker had pressed against it, followed by a razor blade dragging across my seared flesh. As the encroaching darkness rose around me, Jason tore into the bathroom. His glowing eyes met mine. With claws and fangs, he came at me. When he sliced through my ghostlike body, he threw his head back, howling.

"I should leave you to the wolves," Nathaniel hissed at my ear. "But that would be an act of mercy."

Chapter Eighteen

Back in the prison room, Nathaniel dropped me against a wall. It took all my concentration to focus on the plaster-covered vampires in front of me. Nathaniel dragged Derek by his ankle across the room to the pole supporting Sam.

Bruised arms chained behind his back and slumped over with his robe bunched around his hips, Sam looked like he was the one who rolled through a brick wall. At his neck, deep punctures drooled blood.

All my locked limbs refused my attempts to move out of the crouched position I had landed in. Forcing air into my freezing lungs, I coughed up a dust cloud of plaster.

"Sam," I wheezed.

Nathaniel whirled around. "Do not speak another word in my presence. Move only to take breath." He stormed toward Sam. Releasing Derek's ankle, Nathaniel muttered a string of curses in French. My reason for studying the language in high school came to fruition. At that moment, I understood the vampire had called me a scum dog, a bitch from hell.

He sliced one of his claws across the inside of Sam's elbow. Cradling Derek's head, Nathaniel angled Derek's mouth to the wound.

Sam groaned, then cracked open his eyes. His groan turned into a throaty growl as he fought to free his arm from the bloodsucker.

Going against Nathaniel's order, I shook my head. Struggling with a vampire latched onto an artery—not smart. My movement attracted Sam's attention.

Locking his glowing eyes to mine, Sam stilled.

Keeping his mouth sealed to Sam's arm, Derek pulled himself to his knees.

"The hound still has use. Take only what you need." Nathaniel stood. "Guards are on their way to provide you with proper nourishment. The queen's arrival is delayed due to a pack of werewolves scampering around the city. I assured her—"

"Tessa?" Derek uttered between gulps.

Nathaniel tensed. Still watching Derek, he spoke at me, "Unless she wants to explain to the queen why she is covered in plaster, she will make her way into the restroom where she will shower and then dress in the garments provided."

Careful not to put weight on my injured foot, I used the wall for support as I stood. A group of guards trudged down the hall toward the room. As much as I didn't want to leave Sam, Nathaniel had a valid point. I'd flushed my golden ticket out of the torture session with the Vampire Queen. Knowledge of my field trip would only make it worse.

When I closed the bathroom door, a group of guards entered the room. Not one peep came from the men.

"The wolf attacked. The fight landed them through a wall." A master of blurring the truth, Nathaniel kept his new tongue from turning to ash as he spoke to the guards. "Send a cleaning crew to the library. This is to be handled before our queen arrives. You. You. And that tall one by the door, come here. Pull up your sleeves. I need the rest at their backs."

After the guards' footfalls moved into the ordered positions, silence followed.

Peeling off my clothes, I caught my reflection in the mirror. I looked like a deflated powdered doughnut. My stomach grumbled, not because I was thinking about doughnuts but from the aroma of fresh blood slipping underneath the door.

Hair wrapped in a towel, foot pulsing with pain, I fumbled with the thin straps to the cream-colored antique from the roaring twenties. "Am I gonna Charleston my way out of the queen's visit?" Glancing at the three-piece suit hanging on the clothing rack, I pulled my hair free of the towel. *Blond didn't specify which garments....*

The door opened.

"Hands to your sides, she-beast," Nathaniel ordered as he ushered Derek, who refused to look at me, inside.

If he had been, then he could have avoided brushing his knuckles against my arm. A static charge snapped against my flesh. Gripping at the fringe covering my thighs, I fought not to rub my tingling arm.

Nathaniel shifted his glare from my face to Derek rubbing his hand on his pant leg. "Queen is at the gate. You have minutes, Derek." Nathaniel grabbed my arm, yanking me out of the bathroom.

Tugging free of Nathaniel, I froze. Sam's chained wrists kept him from falling all the way forward while his shoulders rose with shallow breaths. I was so hell-bent on saving Andrea instead of the lives of thousands of werewolves. Yet I had potentially sacrificed Sam over the safety of a couple of dozen half-blood humans. Staring at his bloodstained hair and slack face, I shivered.

"He'll live." Nathaniel shoved me onward, then into the chair facing the fireplace. He dropped a rubber band on my lap. "Secure your hair away from your neck."

Once my drenched mass was in a ponytail, rivulets of water slid down my neck to the small of my back. The bone marrow chill I'd been fighting all night took a backseat to the terror kicking my heart into flight mode with the conclusion that I'd prepared my own neck for the queen to tear into.

Nathaniel smirked. "No witty comments?"

Fidgeting with the fringe at my knees, I mumbled, "Saving them for Queen Bloodsucker."

"If you wish to live, keep your trap shut." Placing his hands on the armrests, he leaned in, blocking my view of the fireplace. "You're not human, Wolf Born. The queen has endless ways to bring you to the brink of death. Ways that would kill a human three times over."

"Good to know." My breath hitched, and the room tilted around me.

His eyes lit. "You...still think you are human."

"I am," I whispered, hoping he'd not hear the lie that I desperately still believed.

He laughed. "Because you have yet to make the Change? Because you have not given in to your beastly ways?" He grinned, showing his fangs. "All in time, and I'll have a front seat when you do." Tilting his head, he quipped, "That's if you survive tonight."

Derek emerged from the bathroom, shirtless. His taut-muscled abdomen was ruined by the bloody lesion from my pencil.

"A wolf. Three guards. Why have you not healed?" Nathaniel asked.

Derek ignored the question, lifting his chin at Sam. "When the queen calls, stay with the wolf."

The armrests groaned under Nathaniel's grip. "When did Derek bite you?"

"Back away from her," Derek said.

Nathaniel turned his full attention to my throat. "Tonight. I smelt your blood. Saw it on your hands. Felt its wetness on your wrist." Heatedly he ordered, "Show me."

I ran my fingers along my neck where Derek had bitten me. Sighing inwardly as I probed my unmarked skin.

"It was an accident," Derek said.

Slapping the armrests, Nathaniel pushed away. "She just stumbled onto your fangs? And you, not on purpose, tasted her blood?"

"No." Derek leveled his stare at Nathaniel. "There was a purpose."

"You bound her blood to you." Nathaniel jabbed a claw at Derek. "I felt it in the bathroom when you touched her."

"If she escaped, I had to be able to track her."

"Wicked, vile little accident, indeed." Grabbing my wrist, Nathaniel turned it over and sliced his claw across my palm. "Oh no. Tsk-tsk. Seems I had an accident myself." He dragged me out of the chair and over to Derek. "Give him another *taste*, she-beast."

"No." Although Derek took a step away, he held his gaze steady to the blood pooling in my cupped hand. "I'll feed on another guard."

"Go in front of the queen, bleeding, she will know about this..." Nathaniel waved his free hand at me. "Abomination. Take enough to heal you."

Derek's stare met mine. "I'll hurt her."

"Call it a tit for tat. It'll only be the second time you feed on her."

Guilt flashed across Derek's face. Too fast for Nathaniel to wrangle me away, Derek sealed his mouth to my palm. With each hungry pull, a current of energy swelled between us. I wanted it to hurt. Gross me out. Make me hate bloodsuckers more. Anything but the euphoria coursing through my body as my mind whimsically drifted into a drunken state.

"Tessa?" Derek swept his tongue across the cut. His lips lingered until I rolled my heavy eyes up to him. Gently, he propped me against the wall while reaching a hand back, grabbing his shirt and suit jacket from Nathaniel. In less than a heartbeat, he was dressed to the nines.

"When?" Nathaniel asked.

"Does it matter?" Derek asked. "She destroyed the list. There is nothing to save her from the queen's attention."

"You will feel her pain tonight." Nathaniel's uncharacteristically serious tone held both Derek's and my attention. "Let this lesson be learned. Hard. So that you never bind blood again."

Both vampires went rigid.

Dread sliced through my dizziness which took me aback because the emotion was not mine. Looking at

Derek's blank face, I'd never have known he was scared. "What did you do to me? I can feel —"

He snapped his hand out, gripping my chin, holding my face toward his. "Do not question or speak about our — the bond. Since you did not behave, tonight I take back my oath." His compulsion wrapped around my mind. "You will not try to escape. You will not speak unless I give permission. Follow me," Derek ordered.

My mind, held with Derek's compulsion, dragged my feet forward. Cringing, I waited to feel the stabbing pang in my foot. After three steps with no discomfort, I stole a glance at my healed foot. My awe was short-lived as I crossed the door's threshold. Searing pain, like I had walked into a swarm of hornets, stung me. When I was fully in the hallway, the pain faded.

Ahead, Derek flinched as if he'd felt the stinging as well. Straightening he said, "The threshold is lined with silver."

Nathaniel leaned out the doorway. *"How does silver feel to a werewolf, Derek?"*

"Unpleasant," Derek mumbled under his breath as he started down the long stretch of an empty hallway.

Brass sconces on beige walls lit the way, while under my feet a scratchy maroon floor runner ran the length of the hall. As we passed by closed doors lining each side of the hall, I strained to hear any noise from within the rooms. I heard nothing. Relying then on my sense of smell, I sniffed. My nose twitched and my eyes watered from the overwhelming scent of dust. Nothing learned. Nothing gained. I continued behind Derek.

Our prison sat at one end of the hallway, and a huge walkout balcony, minus its glass doors, stood at the other. *So that's where Derek tossed Nathaniel.* Blocking the potential escape route stood two guards and a machine gun aimed at the prison room. A camera mounted over the balcony's entryway pivoted toward me. Sam wasn't kidding. We had eyes, ears and an Uzi constantly on us.

If I weren't on Derek's mind control leash, I'd have stayed, sucking in the fresh air while buying time. My thoughts raced back to Andrea's pending freedom and Sam injured while under Nathaniel's watch. With a deep breath, I picked up my pace.

In the center of the hall, Derek made his way down a staircase.

A cold draft crept up my body, and I fought the urge to hug myself, clasping my hands into fists instead as I followed obediently behind the bloodsucker.

The dirt-stench of guards saturated the second floor. "Hunter and prisoner, second floor," one of the guards standing at the stair landing said into his radio. The device crackled with static, and a voice responded.

If I'd stopped, I knew I could've picked up the full conversation. I glanced over my shoulder. Their faces were blank, but their white knuckles grasped the hilts of their guns. Their full attention was on...me.

Derek continued his brisk pace onward. Not once did he turn to look or speak to me.

My hope for escape diminished with every step. The estate was more like a fortress, all doors closed within the halls. A pair of guards stood at each stairway or window while overhead cameras panned, following our every move.

As Derek descended the final staircase, cold sweat beaded along my forehead.

We stopped at the mid-landing which overlooked the foyer. A three-tier chandelier as large as a dump truck illuminated the white marble floor. My gaze traveled upward to a pair of marble statues. The lifelike male lions stood ten feet tall with their stone facings polished to a sheen. They held guard at a set of double doors.

I choked back a fear-induced giggle. I was about to enter the lions' den.

When Derek's foot cleared the last step, the doors opened from the inside. A musky stench hit me full force in the face, and I death-gripped the banister while planting myself firmly in place.

Derek turned to me. "Come."

My body betrayed me by descending the remaining steps. As the icy marble floor stung my bare feet, I bit my lip to keep from hissing. Still, I'd rather freeze than enter the room.

When a breeze ran across the back of my knees, I turned my head toward a dark hallway. Knowing that was the way out of this hellhole, I jerked my feet in its direction.

Derek grabbed my shoulder, facing me back around and steering me through the doorway.

Candles lit a room about half the size of my prison. The musky stench poured out of the two vampires who stood in the shadows of the doors. Only their eyes sparkling in their pale, stone-like faces proved they weren't statues.

With a slight squeeze to my shoulder, Derek got me moving through another set of doors and into a viewing room. As my vision tunneled onto the woman seated in the center of the room, I wished my name were Buffy.

Chapter Nineteen

Hyperventilating, I looked past the petite monster sitting on a mahogany throne — large enough to seat a geared-up hockey player — to the wall of glass overlooking the courtyard. Outside, three guards passed by the windows. Their shadows crawled across the room, which was rapidly filling with vampires.

Dressed in identical three-piece suits, and similar to Derek in height and muscle mass, the vampires assumed their positions. Six flanked the queen's throne. And just in case I thought I could get around Derek and the two door openers, a barricade of vampires blocked the exit. Silent. Emotionless. They stood with hands behind backs, feet slightly parted and their black, mirrored eyes watching me.

Only one heartbeat in the room of near twenty.

Between forgetting how to breathe and daydreaming about acrobatic fight combinations which resulted in the annihilation of all the bloodsuckers within the room, I'd stopped moving. Derek squeezed my shoulder, snapping me into cold reality and motion.

With a *clunk*, the doors sealed me in with the monsters. My heart slammed against my ribcage as every bone in my body screamed at me to get the hell out of there. I dropped my gaze to the floor. I was going to lose it if I looked up again. When my toes touched the white Persian rug, Derek's hand tightened on my shoulder to hold me in place.

"My Queen," he said as he pushed me down to kneel. He kept the pressure on my shoulder, his silent warning for me to remain kneeling. "Speak only when addressed, Wolf Born." Slowly he removed his hand and compulsion.

It felt like he'd wiped himself free and clear of me. Why this bothered me was beyond my grasp. I mentally stomped on my hurt and readied myself. I was about to fight for my life for the umpteenth time.

"Derek." The queen acknowledged him with a low, silky voice. "Look to me, female," she spoke with a firm order.

Reluctantly, I raised my eyes, letting my gaze first land on the bottom step of her throne. The tips of her blood-red satin slippers peeked out from the hem of a forest-green dress. The gown, embroidered in gold and rubies, fit her like a glove.

Between the GQ-upped vampire guards and her ensemble, I might as well have been wearing a burlap sack instead of the fringe and sequins. The weight of my tied-back, damp hair reminded me of the true nature of this meeting.

I *was* fine dining.

Fisting my hands, clamping my jaw shut, clenching my thighs, I failed at controlling my shivering body while the queen lounged on her throne.

Candlelight reflected off her pointed nails which tapped on the armrests. A huge ruby sitting on her ring finger bounced in time with the drumming. Underneath her alabaster skin, a delicate webbing of blue veins ran up to her un-beating heart. The plunging cut of her dress showcased her breasts cradling a gold pendant of a roaring lion head. Its ruby eyes sparkled at me.

Her lips parted in an amused grin, revealing the tips of her fangs. Not ready to meet her eyes, I skipped over her face to her braided crown of ebony hair. She was beautiful in a psycho-killer-monster kinda way.

"Look into my eyes," the queen said.

Unable to procrastinate any longer, I leveled my gaze to her eyes. In her stare, I met pure evil with a capital E — a monster the bogeyman had nightmares about. She brought a fingernail to her lips while her cold gaze assaulted me. I was an insect for her to dissect then squash under her satin slipper.

"I believe the saying is all wrong." Her throaty laughter bounced off the walls. "I have a sheep dressed as a wolf." The queen's laughter ceased as quickly as it started, and the room fell silent, except for the ticking of the grandfather clock standing in the corner of the room.

Tick, tick, tick... Each tick, louder than the last, hammered against my ears. My jaw ached from clenching my teeth together. *Tick, tick, tick...* Clenching my hands into fists made my fingers numb. *Tick, tick, tick...* I wanted to scream at the top of my lungs. *Tick, tick, tick...*

At a discreet sniff from her upturned nose, the queen's fangs elongated. "Derek." Her voice filled with venom as she darted her glare at him. "She has bled recently."

Serves you right, jerk, I huffed to myself while looking back at the rug.

"From an incident earlier, she was able to confiscate a wooden splinter," Derek answered in a neutral tone.

He'd carefully chosen his words, steering her toward my fight with the vanity and away from the trip to my apartment. I concentrated on the ticking clock. I didn't want the queen's attention on me if she became wise. That wasn't the whole story.

The jewels of the queen's dress clinked against the throne with her movement. "Incident? She destroyed a piece that was very dear to me."

I felt her hard stare on the top of my head.

"I have my hunter as her guardian. Over five dozen human guards during the day and over six dozen vampires at night to keep watch over that room. Yet the sheep still manages to fool you all." She paused. "How will the penniless sheep repay me?"

"She will exchange the information you have sought this evening for the destruction of your property —"

"No." Realizing what Derek offered, I spoke up. "I will only share the name for Andrea's freedom."

Derek snapped at me, "You have nothing else for her —"

"I accept the original terms of our exchange." The queen tilted her chin at a door to her right. "Bring the human out to the courtyard."

Outside a spotlight illuminated a group of guards escorting Andrea shivering and limping to the wall of glass.

Derek slapped his hand on my shoulder, holding me down. Having removed his compulsion, I was ready to go ballistic with a verbal assault, but I smartly bit my tongue. I wouldn't have Andrea suffer anymore.

Andrea squinted into the room. When her eyes widened, and her mouth started running, I knew she'd seen me.

"She's going to kill you. Tess, run!" Andrea pleaded, "Go…"

Speaking over Andrea's screams, the queen ordered, "Give me the name I seek, sheep."

I kept my eyes to Andrea's as I traded another's life for hers. "I have no firm evidence he is behind the water contamination. You only sought who I think it may —"

"I know what I asked. Tell me now, or I'll have her shot." The queen lifted her hand above her head, making a fist.

The guard behind Andrea kicked the back of her legs, knocking her to her knees. Then he shoved a pistol against her temple. When he clicked off the safety, Andrea cried.

"The CEO of Safe Waters, Tim McKay," I blurted. "Please let Andrea go. Please!"

With her fist still held high, the queen sat through a series of my frantic heartbeats, staring at me. "With this name, I uphold my oath. Let the human Andrea be set free." The queen opened her fist, splaying her fingers.

I shot my attention to the guard engaging the safety. As he re-holstered the pistol, I looked at Andrea. Tears streamed from her wide eyes. Abruptly she was yanked to her feet. As the guards dragged her away, struggling, she screamed, "Fight, Tess! Fight!"

In the direction she was hauled away, an engine revved to life. When the vehicle drove away, the queen lowered her hand. "I require payment for my vanity, sheep."

"For payment," Derek said, "I pledge another century to you, my queen."

"Guards, leave." She kept her eyes on Derek while they filed out of the room through the doors on each side of her throne and through the main entrance.

Once more the doors shut with a *clunk*.

Tick, tick, tick…the clock said.

"A prized offering, Derek. It pains me that your original servitude is complete come the full moon. However, you did not destroy my property."

"Physically, I did not. But I failed to take the proper precautions throughout the day to keep your property safe."

"True. For your careless behavior, Derek, I accept a new servitude in the amount of two centuries."

Derek's fingers tightened on my shoulder.

"What's two hundred years to an immortal?" She leaned forward. "Am I not a just queen? Do I not care for you, servant?"

Still keeping his hand on me, Derek lowered to his knee, placing his free hand over his heart. "I pledge two hundred years of servitude to you, my queen."

"Accepted." She sat back, lifting her head high. "Bring her to me."

Derek rose to his feet. "My qu —"

"You try my patience, hunter." Her eyes narrowed to slits. "Give her to me."

"I won't have *anyone* serve me to you." Scrabbling to my feet, I batted away Derek's hand.

A smile curved her cruel lips. "The sheep has more fight than the hunter. Come to me, female."

There was no way around Queen Bloodsucker. Her vampire crew was behind the doors, and outside, guards passed by the window. My anger propelled my feet to the steps of her throne. Stopping just out of her reach, I waited for her move.

"Let me see your wound."

Slowly, I opened my fist. No dried blood. No cut.

"Your foot, sheep." She glared at Derek. "Tell me, hunter, is she as clumsy as the rest of her race that she would injure herself, twice, on the same splinter?" She didn't wait for Derek to answer. "Show me, sheep."

I lifted my healed foot.

"Come closer." Her voice quivered at the sight of my dried blood.

I thought it better to stay where I was, thank you very much.

She pounced, snagging my arm, forcing me to kneel before her. I darted my gaze to her blood-red eyes glaring down at me. She brought my palm that Derek had licked clean to her mouth. I struggled to get out of her grasp as her tongue parted her lips. Cold, sandpaper-like, it slithered along the flesh of my hand.

The queen drew away, examining the full length of my arm. "She heals faster than the males." She swept her fingers across the silvery-pink puncture scars from Jason's bite. Releasing me, she sat back.

I sighed.

Her irises flashed red, fangs unsheathed. She released a roar which I answered with a blood-curdling scream that she cut short, attacking me.

The jewels on her dress dug against my torso when she yanked me up the length of her body. As she grabbed my ponytail, the rubber band snapped. Fisting my hair at the base of my skull, she forced my chin upward.

"I want to see your beautiful terror, sheep," she whispered, brushing a strand of my hair away from my eyes.

As I stared into her eyes, fear blazed through my body, rendering me motionless. Sinking into her hypnotic trance, I felt a tugging at the back of my subconscious. A flash of light spiraled me away to a vision of a red wolf charging toward me. Its emerald eyes lifted to mine as it slammed into me. Adrenaline shot through my body, snapping me out of the queen's trance. The reflection of my emerald eyes flickered aglow within the abyss of hers. Grasping her pendant, I shoved it against her throat.

"You dare attack me?" She growled as her nails dug against my back. "I'll have you plead for me to end your life."

Not thinking, I arched my spine away from the pain, giving her full access to my throat.

Twisting her grip on my hair, she jerked my neck to her cold lips, pressing a kiss to my jugular. "You owe me a vanity, sheep."

Abruptly she dropped me.

I tumbled off the throne steps, then landed on my ass. Clambering backward, I slammed against Derek's legs. Snatching me up, he pinned my back to his chest and my arms to my sides. There was a split second where Derek's relief flooded my mind.

"Guards." The queen assumed the same unmoving pose that she'd held when we had entered the room.

As the vampires filtered in with their musky stench, I caught another mixture of scents trailing into the room — mint and juniper.

My attention latched on to the owners of the scents, Detective Miller and Officer James. They wore ill-fitting suits with the price tags still attached to the sleeves. As they staggered past us, Miller kept his stare to the floor. Officer James darted his glossed-over gaze in every direction. He was pale and suffering from shock. Each step he took, a bloody footprint blemished the marble floor. From mid-thigh down, blood saturated his right pant leg.

Taking a sniff, I caught his base scent of mint. Hoping I was wrong, I looked into his eyes. They glowed a pale yellow. Dread rocketed to the pit of my stomach. James had been bitten by a werewolf. His human card was forfeit.

The vampires surrounded Miller and James, driving the werewolves toward the throne. At the edge of the rug, James's leg buckled. Miller caught him under the arm, propping James against his side.

"Kneel," the queen ordered.

Miller raised his eyes to her. "We don't take orders from a corpse."

Power filled her voice. "Kneel."

Instantly, Miller and James fell to their knees, clawing at their throats.

My skin prickled with her repulsive energy, and I struggled not to breathe any more than needed, revolted by the thought that each breath I took, a part of her slipped inside of me.

Out of the corner of her eye, the queen watched me. Then she lifted her attention to her right where the decrepit butler shuffled through the door, carrying a silver tray with a letter on top.

"Is this letter from your alpha?" she asked Miller.

He struggled to speak through his blue-tinted lips.

The queen closed her eyes, and when she opened them, a translucent oily-black mass lifted away from Miller and James. It floated over to the queen, and she stiffened at its touch. Slowly, the oily mass seeped into her.

Discreetly, I lifted my gaze to her guards. None took notice of the mass, or else this was a regular occurrence with the queen.

Miller and James toppled over themselves, hungrily sucking air.

"Jason…" Miller panted. "Isn't — "

"Silence." She nodded at the butler. "Open the letter."

He placed the tray between his arm and side as he pulled a silver letter opener out from the pocket of his suit jacket. With a clean swipe, he severed the waxed seal.

The queen's stare roamed over the letter. She looked up with a blank face, nodding for the butler to remove the letter.

"Did you read this?" She spoke to the men, but her focus was on me.

"No. No. No," James gasped. "I woke up here. A monster bit me." He looked at Miller. "Tell her. Tell her what happened. I…."

Miller answered the queen over James' rambling, "No."

The corners of her mouth pinched into a grin. "Give the letter to the sheep," the queen ordered the butler.

He bowed, then shuffled down the steps.

Derek slid his hold to my shoulders, allowing me to lift my hands.

A deep inhale broke the silence, and I looked in its direction, meeting James and Miller's glowing eyes staring at me.

"Killing a human is one thing, Sanders. But cozying up to a bloodsucker." Miller spat on the rug. "Rot in hell."

"I didn't kill that teenager—"

"Take the letter," Derek growled. "Utter not one word more to the wolves."

The butler stretched out his arthritic hand holding the letter to me.

Taking it, I refused to look at the paper rattling in my hands. I'd seen the queen's attitude change after reading the letter. The scent of sandalwood rose from the parchment dampened by my sweaty palms. Jason's scent was concentrated on the blood-red seal. He had mixed his blood with the wax.

The queen stared intently at me. "Read it out loud."

My throat went dry, and my voice came out as a whisper while I read.

Queen Adele,

I, Jason, Alpha to the Still Water pack, claim the Wolf Born, Tessa Sanders. I send my gratitude to you for keeping her comfortable and safe until your Gathering, at which time I shall take custody of Tessa Sanders. Thereafter, the wolves of North America will swear loyalty to you. In bonding my word, I have sent you blood payments. One is given so that no physical harm will come to Tessa Sanders. The other, for the promise of loyalty.

My hands shook as I looked at the queen. "What does he mean by blood payment?"

She turned her head toward the butler, who had returned to her side. "Seek out Nathaniel. Tell him to respond to the alpha, 'Offer accepted'."

The butler bowed then exited through the side door.

I tilted my head to look at Derek, whose undivided attention was to his queen. "What's blood payment?" I asked.

"You are soon to find out, sheep," she purred while nodding to the vampires standing behind Miller and James.

I spun around in Derek's arms. Grasping the lapels of his suit, I searched his eyes for an ounce of compassion. He kept his emotionless stare upon his queen.

"Derek, turn her so that she may view the blood payments. Properly," the queen ordered.

He twisted me around, wrapping one arm around me while his other hand clenched my hair at the base of my skull, forcing my head toward the queen.

The damn clock chimed. Its slow, steady bong was in complete contrast to my erratic heartbeats. While the vampires dragged Miller and James over to the throne, I kept my sobs silent. I wouldn't give her the pleasure of watching me break down, nor show weakness to Miller and James.

The queen pointed at James. "Bring him."

Ceasing my struggles against Derek, my eyes burned with loathing for the queen and her vampires. She took note, and her vile smile widened.

With a high-pitched shriek, James bucked against the guards. He was no match for the vampires who easily handed him into the queen's lap.

Glancing over his neck at me, the queen tore her fangs into his throat. His wet screams silenced as the sweet, coppery scent of his blood flowed into the room. When his body went lax, she dropped him to the floor like a piece of trash.

Blood fell from her lips and ran in streams down to her chest, covering her lion pendant. With a nod, she motioned for Miller to come forward.

The numbness of shock took over my limbs.

"It's almost over," Derek whispered.

She grabbed Miller by his forearm, ripping it away from the socket with a wet pop. Still holding his dangling limb, she gave it a sharp twist, snapping the bone like a twig. Miller's arm rolled down the steps, landing on James's body with a thud.

Miller shook, and his face blanched. To keep from screaming, he sank his fangs into his lip. He kept his glare fixed on mine until the queen caught him by the throat.

Anticipation, thick with hunger, consumed the room from the cluster of vampires stalking toward the throne.

When the queen lifted Miller to his tiptoes, he twisted around, spitting a chunk of his lip at her face. She responded by sinking her fangs into his missing arm's socket. Miller's screams echoed through the room while the queen, bathed in his blood, rose from her throne.

Effortlessly and with no remorse, the queen tossed Miller to the waiting vampires. They descended, silencing his wet screams with their ravenous feeding. Ecstasy washed over the queen's blood-covered face while she floated down to her throne, giving a slight nod to Derek.

His jawline brushed against my ear as he whispered, "Do not speak or move. They will kill you." Derek lifted me into a deadman's carry over his shoulder. "Now, close your eyes and keep them closed."

Chapter Twenty

The burn of silver against my flesh announced when Derek had hauled me across the prison room threshold. Flashing open my eyes, I caught a glimpse of Sam, still unconscious and chained to the pole.

Nathaniel was missing.

Derek charged to the closet. Half dropping me inside, he glanced down. Rage twisted his face, showcasing his fangs. Yet it was the sheer terror in his eyes that made me flinch. He slammed the door.

While Derek tossed furniture against the closet, I scooted backward until the wall dug against my spine. Drawing my knees tight to my chest, I buried my face into my hands, shaking with silent sobs while overhead, garments brushed against the top of my tucked head.

Every corner of the estate erupted with violence. Inhuman shrills drowned out the screams of men. Guns fired. Orders shouted. Glass exploded. All the while, Derek kept a vigil outside of the closet. The blood-bond coursed between us. Rage. Worry. Hunger. I was unable to decipher which emotions belonged to who, until, when a surge of energy snapped into the room, both of our emotions unified into one. Terror.

"Bloodlust," Derek shouted.

"I warned you," Nathaniel growled.

"Nathaniel, do not—" Shoes screeched against the floor as what sounded like a fist connected with a gut. "Fool," Derek wheezed.

Sam groaned, then the aroma of his blood flooded my nostrils.

"If the queen's guards make it outside, they will attack the city in minutes," Nathaniel said. "Let them fight us first."

Thundering footfalls barreled down the hallway. What I assumed were the queen's guards crashed into the room. From the amount of screaming bloodsuckers attacking, I'd lost track of Derek and Nathaniel.

Abruptly the struggling ceased. Then silence filled the pitch-black closet. With the musky stench of vampire blood spilling under the door, I pulled my toes closer to me and clenched my eyes shut, focusing on the faint thud of Sam's heartbeat. He was alive, bleeding and chained up as bloodsucker bait, while I cowered in the safety of terrycloth robes.

Footsteps neared the closet.

Slowly, I stood. Flashing my concentration to the door, I grabbed a wire hanger, painfully aware of the slight clicking it made against the metal pole. I bent the hanger into a sword-like shape. Twisting its hook straight, I sliced my hand in the process. Blood oozed between my sweaty palms, dripping onto my numb feet.

"How bad are you hurt?" Derek asked.

"Say again, Derek?" Nathaniel shut the prison room doors, then strolled over. "Oh. For a second I thought you cared about my welfare." He exaggerated an inhale. "I'd say by the ratio of tears to blood, she'll live…for now."

"Silence," Derek ordered. "The day guards are making rounds."

The force of the nearing guards' steps vibrated the floorboards beneath me. Their revved heartbeats hammered at my eardrums. Off-putting yet refreshing that the assholes still feared something.

"Hallway, third floor, clear," Boss said. A door opened. "Storage, clear." A door shut as another opened. "Injury, human, second room from stairs, on right." The door shut. Boss was all business when he knocked on the doors of the room. "Hunter, do you need assistance?"

"Main room, clear. Two prisoners accounted for and detained," Derek answered.

Boss's intercom crackled to life. "Main room, clear." A twinge of anger layered his voice. For the time being, he'd have to wait to torture me. "Follow me, men."

The group stormed back down the hall.

"The queen will be quite perturbed," Nathaniel said. "Having to replace six personal guards before the Gathering, while werewolves run wild across her territory, and council members are already arriving, being the pests that they are…" Nathaniel paused. "This message she errands me with, what offer did our queen *accept*?"

"The alpha gave two wolves as blood payment. One was for Tessa's safety. The other serves as an agreement."

"Stupid dog." Annoyance rolled off Nathaniel's tongue. "What is this agreement?"

"At the Gathering, Tessa is turned over to the alpha and he swears the loyalties of the North America wolves to the queen."

Nathaniel snickered. "So the alpha is supplying the buffet for the council members. Our scouts have tracked only a dozen of his pack within the city. Hardly a threat. However, seeing what the blood of two wolves did to her guards...I fear another one of my *cow* stories will not serve in this day and age for a city ravaged by vampires and then buried with fire."

"There will be no need for stories," Derek said. "Tomorrow night, you will detain the alpha and then dispose of the pack."

Nathaniel threw his voice toward the closet. "When the alpha fails to attend the Gathering, the queen will kill your pet. Courtesy of the blood-bond, you perish as well."

"Only if Tessa has not made the Change," Derek countered. "When the queen threatened Tessa, she summoned her wolf. Her ability to hold off the Change for another night is nil."

"That she-beast *is* your final death, Derek," Nathanial snapped. "Provoke her Change."

With the brush of power along my skin, I knew Nathaniel had left. Except for Sam's breathing and faint heartbeat, a tense silence sank into the room.

The cursed blood-bond worked like an invisible ball and chain. I felt Derek's presence just outside the closet. Thankfully, he kept his emotions to himself. Wondering if he felt mine, I let my wrath flow freely.

"Morning comes," Derek said. "You are safe."

"Only from vampires." Preparing for him to bust through the door, I held the hanger straight out in front of me.

"The day guards will protect you from any — "

"That is who I'm worried about. They almost killed Sam."

"Follow their rules and — "

"Please. You said you would protect me. Even after I stabbed you. In a weird, twisted way, you've kept me safe. Let us go. There's still time." Through the blood-bond, a glimmer of Derek's emotions slipped. *Regret. For what? No clue.* In an attempt to use the all-too-human emotion against him, I blurted, "You're not like that queen — "

"I'm worse." And with that warning, Derek's footsteps carried him away from the closet and out of the prison room.

After a few unsuccessful attempts to dislodge the barricade in front of the closet, I gathered the hanger-sword tight to my chest. Numbness crawled through my limbs while I slid to the floor, letting my head rest against the wall. No one and nothing were coming to rescue me...us.

Metal clinked against the pole and relief sprang fresh tears to my eyes. Sam's breathing and heartbeat grew stronger. We would escape...somehow. That thread of hope kept me company until exhaustion pulled me into unconsciousness.

* * * *

The pungent smell of garlic kick-started my nightmare. A to-go container balanced on my jean-covered thighs tilted. When I righted it, steam from my dinner's leftovers warmed my trembling hands. A sharp bite to my lip failed to dislodge me from the memory I'd put on permanent lockdown. Once more, I sat in the backseat of Dad's car, speeding toward death.

Ahead, the headlights reflected off Oregon's notorious road sign, *US-101*. Only the full moon and a sparse amount of traffic lights guided the way through the cliff's twist and turns, while a ribbon of guardrail ran along the rain-slick road, providing false security from a plummet to the ocean below.

Tears burned my eyes as I relived the last moments with my family. I turned to Drew, texting away while laughing at Dad who was attempting his best impersonation of a synthesized voice. Sitting behind Dad, I could only see his profile. His dark hazel eyes crinkled as he smiled at Mom.

"Tessa." She glanced at me through the rearview mirror. "Happy Birth—"

A boulder smashed into the passenger side of the car. Time crawled by in slow motion while every inch of grinding metal pushed toward me. The vehicle slammed into something, causing the car to spin. During the violent rotations, my door peeled backward. Claw-like hands grabbed me, pulling me free and throwing me to the pavement. I rolled to my side, watching in horror as Dad's car plunged off the cliff.

A massive explosion lit the night sky. Stumbling to the cliff edge, I glanced over my sneakers. Pieces of metal strung across the beach in every direction away from the mangled car engulfed in flames. Pain flared in my arm. Through my shredded jacket, five slashes splattered blood against the road. Cradling my arm, I scanned the vacant highway wildly for my rescuer...monster. Forcing my tear-filled stare at the moon, gasping for breath, I choked on the stench of gasoline and burnt flesh.

* * * *

I snapped awake. Disoriented, I launched backward, hitting the back of my head against a wall. When my fingers skimmed over a metal object, my current predicament slammed into me.

Closet. Hanger. Vampires.

Furniture groaned against the floor, and I snagged the hanger, pointing it at the closet door. Taking a deep breath, I inhaled the scent of pine. *Sam.* Relieved, I dropped the hanger to clatter against the floor.

"Tess." Sam's voice strained with pain. "I'm going to open the door."

Sunlight washed into the closet, stinging my eyes. I blinked at his form as he slipped inside, closing the door behind himself. Biting my lip, keeping my pathetic whimpers quiet, I wanted to run to Sam and have him wrap his arms around me, but my limbs refused.

The light streaming underneath the door allowed me a perfect view of Sam. Still wearing his disheveled, bloodstained robe, he stood rigid. While he refused to close the distance between us, his scent traveled. Pine blended with blood and sweat to tickle my nose. I drew in another breath and caught a familiar, sweet smell rolling off him.

Fear.

"The vampires are gone," I whispered, "and the guards' muted voices hint they're down the hall. It's just the two of us. Yet...I smell fear."

Sam swallowed.

"You're afraid"—my gaze shot to his face—"of *me*."

"Never." Taking a step toward me, Sam cut his attention to the dried blood caking my palms. He stopped his advancement and the scent of fear intensified like cheap perfume covering shit. "It's not what you think. Blood this close to the full moon...."

A switch fired in my brain. Rejection turned off, and hunger snapped on. My gaze drifted to the deep gashes across his chest, and I noted he was favoring his left foot. *Easy prey.* Horrified by the thought, I shoved my face into my hands, heaving air through my clenched throat.

"Easy, Tess." He cleared the distance. "Deep, slow breaths."

"Scared." I panted.

Sam misunderstood and pulled me into his lap. "Don't be."

"*You're* the one who stinks of fear."

"Look at me." He tugged my hands from my face. "Please."

With my stare held fast to his clawed-up chest, I shook with hiccupping breaths. I couldn't bring myself to look into his eyes. He would see the wrongness in me. The monster. Once more, the switch in my brain snapped over. Tears streamed down my face, and my chest tightened.

Softly, Sam lifted my chin with his fingertips, capturing my gaze with his. "When I smelled your blood, I was afraid of what the queen did to you."

"She didn't hurt me...physically." I sniffled. "I live another day."

Sam dropped his gaze and his body tensed around mine.

"What?"

"I doubted you. I didn't think you could handle yourself around the bloodsuckers. That you'd end up getting yourself killed." He raised his eyes back to mine. "You proved me an idiot. You're a fighter."

"Fighter?" I looked away with fresh tears burning my eyes. "Instead of coping with my family's death, I fled to the opposite side of the country. Last night, I watched two men die, and I did nothing. Then I hid in a closet, crying, while Nathaniel used you as bait." Coldly, I stated, "I'm a coward."

"No. You *are* a fighter." He leaned in, forcing me to stare into his eyes. "You believe anything less, and that's when the dying starts."

"Sam, people die because of me. For that reason, you should fear me. You—"

Slanting his mouth across mine, he silenced my protest.

"*Never* would I fear you," he whispered.

"You should." I pulled away. "I saw you as food."

"It's your wolf." Sam rubbed his thumbs in slow, soft circles against my wet cheeks. "Let me help you control her."

My damn hormones stirred to life at his touch. One way or another, the monster inside of me would have her appetite satiated. To keep my fingers from exploring his pecs, I twisted the dress's hem into a tourniquet. Ignoring the evident lust in Sam's eyes, I shifted my focus to the prior night.

"There are cameras at every corner," I said. "Armed guards patrol each floor and block every window. Minus the six vampire guards that Derek and Nathaniel killed, there are at least six dozen more and the queen." At the memory of her leering at me as she tore into James's throat, I gasped. "She killed Miller and James. Blood payments. James was bitten by the alpha. Wait." I paused, trying to make sense of time and distance. "The bite was fresh but Jason was just at my apartment—"

"Men don't heal as fast as you." Sam leaned in, sniffing. "I smell that bloodsucker on you."

The convo flip spun my mind. Inhaling, I hit on Derek's scent, and instantly, my blood heated, taking me aback because it wasn't seething hatred but... Yeah. Not ready to deal with the development of those feelings, I shook my head. "He brought me here. Kept the other vampires from getting to us. I think he—"

"Will kill you." Sam caged my face between his hands. "You and me. We will get out of here. Understood?"

Before I could answer, Sam crashed his mouth against mine. Desire consumed my senses. Relishing Sam's attention, still, my thoughts spun to Derek. To our kiss. Fear prickled my skin. He'd made himself a spot in my brain and refused to leave. I forced my concentration to Sam. If anyone could take my mind away from the vampire, it was the man holding me. Struggling to free my fingers from the dress, I ripped the fringe. The sound distracted Sam long enough to glance at the ruined garment.

A killer grin spread across his lips as he slid his hands up my body. "May I?"

Eagerly, I nodded.

Fisting the front of the dress, he tore it in half, tossing the remains to the floor. Once more his lips sought mine. Sweeping his hands down my exposed back, he grabbed onto the swell of my hips. The heat of his caresses burned the numbness from my body. Craving skin-to-skin contact, I tugged the robe off his shoulders. With the brush of his chest against mine, a soft cry escaped from my throat.

Sam rolled us to the floor, pinning me underneath his taut body. His growl vibrated against my breasts and I arched into him. The adjustment bared my shoulder to Sam's mouth. Teeth pressed against my flesh, triggering the flashback of Jason pinning me to the sink, biting my shoulder.

"Stop." I scrambled from underneath Sam, coming to a halt on my knees facing the wall. "Jason said he'd kill you."

"No threat. No one. Will keep me from you." The rawness in Sam's voice rose goosebumps along my feverish skin. "I mean it."

Closing my eyes, Derek's image greeted me. His words echoed through my mind. *"No one can or will protect you from me."*

Sam coaxed me to turn and face him. Our stares locked. Lust tangled with trepidation and my shaking breath outed my fading self-control. Sam dipped his forehead to mine. His words raced across my lips. "Fuck. I want you. All of *you*."

Swallowing hard, I answered Sam with a kiss. Setting to the task of wiping everything Derek from my mind and body, I flattened my back against the wall and fought with the knot securing Sam's robe.

Sam pulled my hands away from the task, drawing them tightly over my head, holding them in one strong hand. Ravenous, Sam's mouth captured mine. Still, all that consumed my thoughts was Derek. How his body molded to mine. His breath along my skin. His voice. Lost in my mind, I mistook the strike of a fist against the room doors for the pounding of my heart.

Launching to his feet, Sam pulled me along. He released me and said, "Get dressed." Shoving the bloodstained robe back over his shoulders, Sam paused at the closet door. Then in two powerful strides, he covered me with his body and kissed me dizzy.

When a second series of fists pummeled at the doors, he abruptly stopped. "This is not over with," Sam warned before leaving me in the closet.

Lust ran hot through my blood while I struggled with the closest garment, a silk nightgown.

Chapter Twenty-One

It took a few blinks for my eyes to adjust to the sunlight flooding the room. With the bed and chairs shoved against the wall, nothing separated us from whoever might come through the doors.

Sam stood feet away with his robe gaping enough for a clear view of his torso. No wonder he had stopped me from tearing off his robe. His chest injuries were papercuts compared to the wounds just above his navel — five puncture marks — no doubt the handiwork of Nathaniel's claws.

Sam healed fast, but he could die. I had never met anyone who could heal from 'dead.' Vampires didn't count. No heartbeat equaled dead to me.

Taking a step, I skidded on a pile of ash. Glancing around the room, I counted six piles. Slowly, I sidestepped the final resting place of one of the queen's guards.

"Same as yesterday." Sam cut his attention to me. "No talking or sudden moves."

I nodded.

As Sam lowered to his knees, I mirrored him. When our hands touched the floor, three guards busted in the room with their guns drawn, close behind, with his gun out and lowered to his side, Boss entered. Two more guards filtered in behind him. They fanned out, walking the perimeter of the room. One went to check out the bathroom while the other walked behind us. He peeked inside the closet, then stood to my right side, giving a nod to Boss.

With his silver hair shimmering in the sunlight, Boss passed by the three guards aiming their guns at us, then stopped at the edge of the rug.

"Did you not hear my knocks, princess?" he asked. "Too busy with your beauty sleep?" He squinted. "No…not sleeping."

I glanced down to see what had tipped off Boss. The silk slip, smooth as butter, clung to my body without wrinkles.

From his crimson face and blanched lips, it was obvious Boss had figured out what had been happening between Sam and me. Quickly, he composed himself in front of his men, snapping his chin toward the guard who had gawked at my chest yesterday. "Bring the silver chains."

Recoiling I halted when a gun barrel pressed against the back of my head.

Boss's cold stare locked with mine. "Playtime is over."

"We did nothing—"

The guard disengaged the safety, shoving the gun firmly against my head.

"Remember my rules?" Boss's shoulders lifted with each punctuated word. "Let me remind you. One. No tantrums. Two. Speak only in a whisper. And since you act more animal than human, I'll add on three. No screwing around."

The boob-ogling guard pushed a metal cart through the doors — the type used in a hospital to hold medical instruments. Or, thanks to my imagination, the cart of doom used to display torture devices. Looking at Boss's twisted grin, I went with the latter.

My gaze froze on the cart's contents — four coils of thick, silver chain. The cold brightness of the metal reflected into my eyes, causing my temples to throb.

"Stand, princess," Boss ordered.

The guard held the gun steady to my head as I rose with shaking legs.

"Time for a demonstration in werewolf anatomy." Boss walked over to the cart. "Silver. Just a touch and it burns their flesh. Stare at it too long, and they'll burn their retinas." He paused, tracing his index finger over a chain. "Silver keeps these freaks from changing into the beast. Forward," he ordered the guard.

A mechanical, well-oiled click came from the steel wheels as the guard rolled the cart toward me. The sweetness of fear wafted off him, intensifying with each of his controlled steps.

"That's close enough. Fall back," Boss ordered.

The guard stepped away while pointing his gun, naturally, at my chest.

"Princess." Boss's voice lifted. "Take those last three steps to the cart."

Raising his hands to the ceiling, Sam stood.

Boss leveled his gun at my head. "Take one step, she's dead."

"Look at her," Sam said in a forced-calm tone. "Scare her. Push her, and she will start the Change."

Boss's thin lips tugged into a cocky half-grin. "As I was saying, princess, move."

The guard shoved the gun snugly against my skull.

Keeping my gaze trained on Boss, I obeyed. When my hips bumped the cart, I stopped. Sweat beaded along my forehead as my skin heated and itched. I didn't dare look at the chains.

"As you can see by the first-degree burns forming"—Boss ticked his gun at me—"in your case, feel. Silver instantly—"

"Leave her alone," Sam growled.

"Plan on it." Curling his finger around the trigger, Boss shifted his aim over my shoulder and fired.

The flash momentarily blinded me while intense pain rang through my ears. Falling to my knees, I pivoted toward Sam. Blood gushed between his fingers, which pressed against his shoulder.

When the guard snagged my arm, instinct took over. Using his momentum, I lunged upward, slipping out of his grasp. Before he could counter, I snatched ahold of his forearm, hurling him across the room.

Three guards charged me. Dodging them, I tore after my silver-haired target until a body slammed against my back, knocking me to the floor. My arms were yanked behind me where a knee pinned them to my tailbone. By the inhuman resistance I met, and from the blood dripping onto my shoulder blades, I knew it was Sam restraining me.

He mumbled into my semi-working ear, "He'll kill you. Stop. Please."

A pair of boots halted inches from my face. My tight exhale fogged their polished surface. Inhaling Boss's dirt stench sent me into a coughing fit. Between each gasp, a sweet scent filled my nose. I strained to lift my glare to meet Boss's face.

A conquering smile stretched across his lips. "It's only a matter of time until I put a bullet between those green eyes—"

"I smell…"—my voice cracked, but it was loud enough for everyone in the room to hear—"your fear."

The corners of Boss's mouth trembled. "No. Not fear. It is my utter *hate* for you," he spat in a deadly whisper. "This room is on lockdown. No food. No medical attention."

"Sir," a guard responded. "We were ordered to keep her from changing—"

Boss cut him off. "During the day, you follow my orders. Fall out."

In an organized stumble, the guards exited.

With his scowl and gun pointed at my face, Boss retreated from the room.

When the doors shut and the locks fastened into place, Sam rolled off me. His face scrunched with pain. "You okay?"

"Me?" Ignoring the aches and pains of being plowed into by a werewolf, I rose to my knees. "You're the one who's shot."

"I'll be all right." He groaned.

"The hell you will."

"Went clean through."

"You're pouring blood."

"Silver is a bitch. When I turn wolf, it'll stop." He blinked his glowing eyes at me. "Promise."

My attention shifted away from Sam's words and onto the way his blood slid between my fingers, how the cooling droplets rolled down my shoulder blades.

He grabbed my wrist. "Tess?"

Shuddering, I looked at the chandelier and breathed through my mouth. Still, the coppery tang of his blood caused my gums to throb. "Let me go."

"No." He tightened his grip. "Focus."

A splitting headache crippled me. Sweat erupted from every pore. I groaned.

"Hold it together. Think," Sam snapped. "Why did he shoot me?"

Shaking my head, trying to think past the pain radiating throughout my body, I blurted, "To kill you. Weaken you. Me. Us." As my skin flushed with a feverish heat, I glanced at Sam. "Control," I answered, "Boss wants control. He *wants* me to...make the Change."

Sam nodded. "If you change without Jason here to help you control your wolf, she will take over."

"That *is* what Jason wants," I whispered. "He wants me to be like him. A killer."

"All right." Sam gritted his teeth. "Let's worry about the assholes within these walls first. You make the Change, and the guards would have no choice if you attacked. They would kill you. Anthony wins."

Remembering last night, I added, "It's not just Boss. Nathaniel told Derek to provoke my Change."

Sam's eyes narrowed. "Why?"

"There was a brief struggle at my apartment where I stabbed Derek, and he nicked me with his fang." I glanced away from Sam. "Derek bound my blood to him."

Releasing my wrist, Sam cursed.

"There's more." Lowering my voice, I laid out the rest. "Then to stop Derek from bleeding, Nathaniel sliced my hand and shoved it to Derek's mouth."

Sam struggled to sit. "You let that *thing* drink your blood? Twice?"

"Did you *not* listen to me?" I glared at him. "I didn't have a choice..."

Panic crossed Sam's face. "He's only taken your blood twice. Right?"

"Maybe...I don't know—" A wave of agony tore away my voice.

The roar of blood pulsed at my temples as I fought to recall the flashback of Miller's investigation at Oblivion. I focused on the photo he had shoved at me. Staring into the dead teen's eyes had triggered the memory of the tunnel. Derek's face came into focus. In blurring speed, he stabbed his fangs into my throat.

"Yes." I gasped. "In the tunnel—"

"Three times. Derek's sealed the blood-bond." Sam raised his eyes to mine. "You never drank his blood?"

"No."

"Not even a drop?"

Glancing away from Sam, I stared at the remains of a queen's guard. "Ash," I whispered. Bringing my fingertips to my lips, I drifted back into my subconscious. Pain sliced through my head. Still, I kept focusing on a blurry memory of Derek, in the park, struggling with me. His hand covered my mouth, and I tore my teeth into his palm, tasting blood.

Searing pain screamed through my limbs. Crawling away from Sam, the room spun across my fading vision. He lunged to his knees, caging my shoulders in his grasp. Concern engulfed his eyes as his hands loosened. "You're burning up."

"I'm fine." I batted his blood-covered hand away from my face. "Watch where you wave your blood around—" Dizziness attacked me. Hanging my head increased the spin of the room and the throbbing at my temples.

"Tessa, try to—"

"I bit Derek."

Slamming his fists against the floor, Sam glared at the splintered board. "His blood contaminates yours. If Derek bites you and drains your blood before your first Change, you'll become—"

"A bloodsucker." I struggled to my feet. "That's not gonna happen."

Sam raked his hands through his hair. "You make the Change. Now."

"That's not gonna happen, either."

"It's the only way to break that bloodsucker's hold on you." With a deep sigh, he glanced away, attempting to hide a look that flipped between dread and guilt.

"What else?"

Slowly, Sam forced his eyes back to mine. "It's no longer important."

"Let me decide—" Agony flared through my body, and my knees gave out. I curled into the fetal position. Every joint stung while all my muscles tensed and tore. To keep from screaming, I sank my teeth into the meaty flesh of my lip. Blood slid down my hoarse throat, and I groaned as my gut spasmed and clenched.

Staring at me with a cold calmness masking the fear oozing from his pores, Sam whispered, "Tess, you're about to Change."

"No…no…no."

"I'm going to help. I'll make the Change first." Shrugging out of his robe, his glowing eyes locked with mine. "I'll keep your wolf from hurting anyone."

"Who will keep me from hurting you?" I gasped.

"Let's hope your wolf likes me."

Energy swelled off Sam, snapping against my flesh. Looking away from his back dislocating, I latched my attention onto the cart. Boss's voice rang inside my head, *"Silver keeps these freaks from changing into their beast."*

Taking a sharp breath, I worked to get my legs under me. When Sam lowered his head, I lunged for the cart. Claws grazed my ankle yet flicks of white-hot pain to my fingertips rewarded me for my achievement. Fisting the chain, I closed my eyes.

No time like desperation to beg for help from an enemy. "Jason... Ja...son..." I repeated his name while willing his face to my subconscious. As my flesh blackened and sizzled, a clash of howls and screams dragged me into unconsciousness.

Chapter Twenty-Two

Out of options, I took the risk of another Jason encounter to escape the Change. It was unlikely the jerk would still be asleep. I worried I'd not be able to connect with him, and that I'd end up in some hellish limbo between human and monster.

My worries were short-lived.

Overhead, sunlight penetrated through a row of dust-covered windows, spotlighting me — wearing the thigh-length slip — in a testosterone-filled gymnasium.

Plastering my back against a concrete wall, across the gym, I took in the bleachers packed with five hundred or so arguing men. From the energy snapping against my skin and the fact that all their eyes were glowing, it was a no-brainer they were werewolves.

Engrossed in their fights, they didn't notice me inching my way to a set of doors off to my right. The blistered skin covering the back of my hand caught my attention when I swept my hand toward the nearest door.

Holding my breath, I turned over my hand. Underneath charred flesh, blackened tendons surrounded the white bones of my palm. Letting my breath out, I wiggled my fingers, feeling no pain.

The doors swung open.

With his canary-yellow eyes focused straight ahead, Jason strolled past me. Dressed in hip-hugging jeans and a crisp cotton shirt, he'd have fit sipping a mocha in a coffee shop instead of a foray in a rundown gymnasium. Behind Jason followed two meatheads. Thankfully, their glowing eyeballs stared ahead at the bleachers lined with the werewolves and not at me.

Still unnoticed, I scrambled to slip through the closing doors. Missing the opportunity by a sliver, I sighed.

Jason froze. As he tilted his head, his nostrils flared with an extended inhale. His eyes narrowed. When his glare traveled the wall I was molded to, he skimmed right over me.

Can he not see me?

When one of the men following him started to turn, Jason made a slight movement with his right hand which had the man tracking his attention back at the bleachers.

Again, Jason's narrowed gaze swept across my body.

Cringing, I braced for him to stomp over and grab me. Instead, he shifted around and made his way to the podium in the center of the room. The meatheads followed. Stopping a few paces from the podium, they stood guard at his sides.

The entire gym watched Jason.

Can no one see me?

After a graceful bow of Jason's head, the werewolves in the back row sat. Like the wave at a sporting event, the next aisles followed.

"My Alpha brothers," Jason said.

Oh. Hell. No. These are all alphas?

Jason lifted his voice. "In two nights —"

"We demand to see her," a man in the back shouted.

"That is not possible," Jason answered.

I'm invisible. Still not trusting the first speck of good fortune tossed my way, I remained flush against the wall while searching for any geographic hints to my whereabouts. Cobwebs. Leaky ceiling. Moth-eaten basketball banner — *'Jamestown Regional Champs 1986.'*

The werewolves' meet-n-greet was a two-hour drive from Glenwood at the abandoned college. The campus, surrounded by farmlands and a ten-mile-wide swamp, had closed down in the early nineties. A food court, buildings and acres of land — they'd picked a prime spot... *but for what?*

"Explain," a man in the front ordered.

"She is being... held by the Vampire Queen," Jason answered.

The room threatened to explode into mayhem.

Above the men's heads, the window to the far right caught my eye. A face dusted with freckles watched on. I'd know that mug from a mile away. Ben.

Jason slammed his fist on the podium. "Enough."

The gym fell silent.

Jason's voice deepened. "The queen has guaranteed, through blood payment, that the Wolf Born will be safely returned to me at the Gathering."

The front row of men turned to each other, mumbling under their breaths.

In a cold voice, Jason interrupted the group. "I request you listen before making any rash decisions."

Their mumbles silenced.

"The attack plan has altered."

My mind reeled. If all these men were alphas, then they each had a pack. It wasn't just Jason's group of twenty heading to the slaughter. Glenwood would perish under the rampage of vampires drunk on a river of werewolf blood.

"The Wolf Born will be our distraction." Jason's attention locked on the men, who I assumed were the scale tippers to his master plan. "As we all agreed upon, my brothers, we attack the vampire council. In their ball gowns and top hats, they will be no match for our numbers, strength and power..." Eager voices rose to consume Jason's calculated drawl.

"You will be fighting with us. Risking your life. Your pack," a man sitting in the center of the front row said. "How do you plan on controlling her?"

"Her safety is above all else," Jason answered.

Says the asshole who mauled my arm, I mused.

The man rose, his dark eyes narrowed at Jason. "Answer the question."

"She is not alone. There is a wolf with her."

"If he is wise, he will kill her." The man turned over his shoulder, addressing the crowd. "We have not felt the call of her power. She has not made the Change yet. There is still time to save our race."

Running on a hunch, that trinket of knowledge was Sam's *"It's no longer important, go and make the Change."* I gritted my teeth. The link wasn't formed. If I died, it'd be just me. The possible reasons why Sam had lied about the link already being fused with the entire race buzzed through my brain and almost drowned out the heated conversation happening in front of me.

"I will control her," Jason growled. "We need her."

"You are foolish, Alpha of the Still Waters pack." An old man sitting at the end of the front row rose slowly from his seat. As he maneuvered his cane with his gnarled hand, he peered at Jason. "What happened three hundred years ago to the Old World packs after a Changed Wolf Born was killed?"

Tension built between Jason's shoulders. "They went insane."

The old man nodded. "What will happen to our *entire* race if she, the last, dies after her Change?"

"That will not happen—"

"Never say will not. Life is a game of possibilities." With the aid of the man to his left, the old man sat. "She must die before her first Change. Her death *is* the guarantee of our survival."

"I speak for all," the dark-eyed man said. "The Wolf Born must die."

A tense-filled silence consumed the gymnasium.

"For centuries we've been hunted, humiliated and killed by the vampires," Jason said bitterly. "When we have the power to eliminate them, you cower, so you can live in hiding for another day? What existence is that?"

Jason tapped a single finger against the podium. After each tap, he increased the pace. I fluttered my fingers up to my heart, beating at the same tempo.

"We are the predators. Conquers," Jason's voice bellowed as his energy plowed into me, fastening itself to mine. "Rulers."

To the beats of my heart, my energy was stolen and consumed by Jason. Gripping my knees, I struggled to remain propped against the wall while a glowing orb of light pulsed around Jason. When he rolled back his head, the aura exploded, slamming into the crowd.

Over their groans and attempts to regain composure, Jason spoke. "That is her energy coursing through you. Imagine if she makes the Change.

Nothing will stop us. We will take back our land. Our pride. Our lives. The vampires will fall."

Too clearly, I saw Jason's motive. He'd send them all to their deaths with his false promises. Never would Jason share power.

"He's lying," I gasped. "He gave his pack members over to the queen. He swore allegiance to her!" I could have tap-danced, on fire, across the room. Suddenly, being invisible sucked. Or not…

Once the alphas recovered, there was a wildness to them. Even the old geezer who had handed down my death sentence gave a toothy grin while opening and closing his un-gnarled hand.

"My brothers." Jason raised his voice. "Are we as one?"

In unison, each of the men in the front row stood.

"Rest your packs and wait for my call." Jason bowed his head to the alphas.

While cheers erupted, I glanced back at the window. Wide-eyed, Ben retreated. Once he was out of sight, relief flew through me. Ben had gotten out of Dodge before the werewolves dispersed.

When Jason turned toward the doors, one of his meathead guards took the lead while the other took up the rear. As the guard pushed open the doors, Jason paused. His nostrils flared. Once. Twice. With his focus trained beyond the doors, he said in a satisfied whisper, "Hello, Red."

Chapter Twenty-Three

Surging awake on top of a thin mattress surrounded by darkness was an improvement over the gymnasium filled with energy-sucking alphas. A brick wall dug at my spine while my face pressed against someone's cold, stiff back. Unable to move or see, I sniffed my bed-buddy. Derek.

Giving him a nudge with my knee sent him rolling off the bed. At the thud of his body smacking against cement, I winced.

No cursing. No graceful rise. Nada.

"That wasn't very nice," Nathaniel said, striking a match on the wall across from the bed.

With his chin pointed at his chest, he sat cross-legged on the floor. A coarse black cloak covered him from head to toe. Nathaniel lit a lantern next to his knee. The weak glow illuminated a room no larger than my apartment's bathroom.

In case he glanced up to entrap me with compulsion, I moved my gaze to his shoulder. "Is Derek all right?" I asked.

"He's...oblivious."

As I pushed up to sit, pain tore through my burnt hand. What resembled an oven mitt covered my fingers to my forearm. Just looking at the bandage, constructed from duct tape and a towel, made the throbbing worse.

"I had to improvise with the dressing," Nathaniel said. "Happy coincidence for you that Derek is overly cautious. Three levels underground and he still uses tape to seal the gap underneath the door."

"My hand...how bad?" I groaned.

"You'll live," Nathaniel muttered. "By sunset, you should make a near-full recovery. Unfortunately."

Picking at the outer layer of tape, I asked, "Where are we?"

"Derek's quarters."

"Quarters? More like a jail cell."

"*You have no idea,*" Nathaniel responded inside his head.

After hearing the bitterness in his words, less than a second passed while I debated letting the bloodsucker in on my mind-reading secret. "Why don't you leave then?"

His shoulders loosened as he gave a dry chuckle. "I know you've been eavesdropping on my *silent* conversations with Derek. It would be smart for you to keep this annoyance between you and me."

"Why?"

"Secrets keep heads attached to necks."

"Good reason. Which adds to my question, why do you stay? Why not ghost yourself as far away from that..." My anger robbed me of an adequate name for the queen. "Thing."

"I am her loyal servant." He sighed. "Alas, I never fancied freedom. Too many rules to follow. Do this. Not that. Here it's simple. Do or die." His voice softened.

"Freedom…that's Derek's dream. His *only* dream. The one *you* smashed amongst the perfume bottles." Nathaniel pushed off the wall.

I growled.

"Easy, she-beast. I'm lifting Derek onto the bed." When Nathaniel moved again, the backs of his charred hands poked out from his cloak.

"You're burnt."

"You don't say?" He laid Derek on the bed. "Touch him."

Ignoring Nathaniel's order, I asked, "What happened to you?"

Using the cloak to hide his face with shadows, he returned to the wall. "Forgot to apply sunscreen before rescuing an idiot from silver."

No signs of Nathaniel's tongue combusting. I knew he wasn't lying. "Thank you."

"Ha. I'd bring chestnuts to your roasting." Carefully, he folded his arms across his chest. "Derek's screams alerted me that my plan was botched. When I saw your hand melted to the silver chain, I learned how badly."

"I knew it was you," I said, gritting my teeth.

"Until you touch him, the pain will worsen."

Sparing a glance at Derek, I brushed my uninjured hand against his cold shoulder. "He looks…dead."

"Wonderful observation," Nathaniel grumbled. "And he will be until sunset. As will the other fifty-eight vampires within this building."

Forcing myself to keep my fingers touching Derek, I rested my back against the wall. I'd not openly admit it, but my burnt hand did feel better, which allowed my inner reporter to chime in. "Why are you still alive?"

"Awake," Nathaniel corrected.

"Okay, awake then."

"I'm special." He lifted his head. Burnt down to the last layer of bloody skin and bone, what was left of his face scowled at me.

Air hissed between my teeth with my stifled curse. In case Nathaniel tried to use compulsion, I dropped my stare to his nasal cavity. When his blackened lip ticked into a grin, I saw through his act—freak her out to shut her up.

"You wanted me to make the Change to destroy the blood-bond. I get that. What I don't understand is why you let Boss use silver if you knew it would affect Derek through the bond?"

"Anthony." Nathaniel spit his name. "If the threat of silver did not scare you into your Change, the fool was to shoot the mutt, and then leave the room *with* the silver chains." He sighed. "Never in his thirty years of servitude has Anthony made an error. Yet you have this effect that drives all...stupid."

"Greed for power makes people stupid," I answered.

"You're not as dumb as I thought, she-beast." Nathaniel lifted his charred index finger. "I still utterly and completely loathe you."

"Good."

He tilted his head. "I want you dead, Wolf Born. Where do you find *good* in knowing that?"

"I trust you." I let my words sink into his skull before I continued. "I know you hate me. You will always hate me. Your hate is the only certainty I can count on."

Nathaniel tipped his head to the other side. His mouth opened then shut. For once, the vampire was speechless.

Below my fingertips, Derek stirred.

"Sunset." Nathaniel groaned as he got to his feet. "Time to return to your mutt."

"No thanks."

The flesh above his missing eyelid crinkled. "A little soon for a lover's quarrel."

"Nope," I stammered as heat prickled my cheeks. "Sam's not my lover."

"That's not the story being whispered between the day guards."

"Get your tea elsewhere."

"If you do not get moving, it won't be tea spilling but your blood." With vampire speed, Nathaniel grabbed my wrist, dragging me over Derek, then off the bed. His blistered lips brushed my ear as he whispered, "Though the sight of Derek, driven by hunger, tearing into your throat, does warm my un-beating heart."

"But you won't let him because of the blood-bond. If Derek kills me, he dies and you—"

Nathaniel pulled me into a rib-crushing hold more to cut off my words than to keep me restrained. An action that cemented my belief that Nathaniel's weakness was Derek. Nathaniel had risked his life and his loyalty to his queen by keeping me alive for Derek. As long as I refused the Change, Nathaniel was my protector.

Derek sluggishly rose from his bed. When his black-hole eyes focused on me, he launched off the mattress. Before Nathaniel could react, Derek grabbed the bloodsucker by the throat.

"Let her go," Derek ordered.

Nathaniel's arms tightened around me. He spoke at Derek, but the warning was meant for my ears too. "If I do, you will kill her."

"I will control myself," Derek said. I wasn't reassured by his choice of words. Slowly, Derek removed his hand from Nathaniel's throat. "Leave us."

"Alone? I think not." Nathaniel backstepped us toward the door. "If someone was to learn she was here, we *all* would meet our eternal night. They will hear you. Smell her. Time is up."

"That is why you will make the feeding rounds." Derek stepped toward us. "Place compulsion for the vampires to turn away from here."

"Should you lose your control?" Nathaniel asked.

"I will send for you."

The two vampires stared at each other.

"Listen to him." I gulped around Nathaniel's vicelike grip.

"You are a fool." Nathaniel's voice echoed through my mind. In a quick alteration, he spun, dropped me on the bed then pulled his disappearing act.

Energy prickled along my skin. Absently, I rubbed at the sensation traveling through my arms. Derek's gaze tracked my movements. His brows drew tight as he stared at the makeshift bandage. "That is Nathaniel's compulsion you are feeling."

"It…" I hesitated as my voice bounced around the cell. Lowering my volume to a whisper, I continued, "Feels different than yours. His is like pins-and-needles."

"And mine?"

"Err…" I swallowed, thinking back to the sensation of his fingertips running along my throat. "Weird."

Derek's gaze flicked to my bandaged hand resting on my bare thighs. "I'll aid you in removing the dressing, after I feed."

I shoved my back against the wall. "You will never *feed* from me, again."

"I have no desire..." Derek froze. His lips pressed tight, keeping the lie from bursting his tongue on fire.

"That's what I thought."

While we stared at each other, tension buzzed between us. Finally, Derek broke the silence. "This wasn't supposed to happen."

"This?" I waved my bandaged hand. "You mean this?"

"No."

"Or did you mean this?" I jabbed a finger at my throat where he had bitten me.

"No."

"Hmm, you must mean this, then." I flashed my forearm where Jason's bite shone against the lantern light.

"No."

Unable to keep my voice and anger restrained, I growled, "Then what, Derek? What is not supposed to happen?"

"Nathaniel is right." Derek's energy brushed against my skin.

"No." I jumped off the bed. "Don't let him take me back."

Derek's gaze connected with mine. From both our erratic movements, we stood mere inches apart. His nostrils flared. Eyes darkened. "You bleed."

I clenched my injured hand while blood warmed my palm and dampened the bandage. "Yep, and you're going to control yourself long enough to answer my question." Taking a shuttering breath, I rooted myself to stand firm. "You sent Nathaniel away and kept me in here for a reason. Why?"

"To apologize. For last night. For today. For..." His fangs unsheathed. "You need to back up."

"No."

"Tessa." He groaned. "I will hurt you."

"No more than you already have."

He froze. Frustration struggled with the hunger burning in his eyes. "Last night, I gave my freedom to right my wrongs against you."

Tears burned my eyes. "Now we're both prisoners."

"That has been my existence for the last three hundred years." He closed the distance between us. "Come the full moon, your sentence ends."

I swallowed the sob forming in my throat. "In death."

"No." His hands cupped my face while his chilled fingers trailed down the sides of my throat. He stepped forward, ushering me to step back, pinning me between his body and the stone wall. "This is what was not supposed to happen." His words and mouth crashed against my lips.

Before I could react, Derek released the blood-bond. My emotions tangled with his, blending and weaving into want and desperation. I grabbed hold of his dress shirt, twisting it through my fingers, to keep his mouth against mine.

He severed the kiss, angling his chin, giving me access to his throat. I ran my tongue across his flesh. My gums throbbed to the wild beating of my heart. Forcing my mouth back to his, I clenched my eyes shut against the gnawing hunger.

"You can control it." He freed a hand to caress down my side. "Focus on me." At the touch of his chilled fingers running along my bare thigh, pleasure rolled through me, drowning out the needling hunger. "There," he whispered against my mouth.

Fluttering my eyes open to his intense stare, hastily, I asked, "Is this how you control your hunger too?"

"No. Touching you unravels me." His fingers slid along my inner thigh, setting every nerve humming with awareness. "I want to ravish you in every way."

Panic dumped into my system. If Derek lost control, I would die. Then there would be no need to keep Sam alive. Jason would still bust into the Gathering. The vampire council would go crazy on werewolf blood and attack the city. Ben remained on both vampire and werewolf hit lists. Too many lives would suffer if I gave in to what I wanted with Derek. "You can't."

Derek stilled. His energy raced across my skin. "Take her back," Derek whispered.

Instantly, Nathaniel appeared. Derek moved away from me, and Nathaniel wasted no time snatching me into his arms and disappearing.

* * * *

When we rematerialized inside the prison room closet, Nathaniel dropped me. The impact of my butt smacking against the floor triggered a growl from the other side of the door.

"I'd not be relieved to reunite with that wolf," Nathaniel quipped. "He has not eaten. Suffered an injury. His lover plucked from his protection—"

"Sam is *not* my lover."

"I said, *his* lover. Also, there is no *Sam* in that beast." Nathaniel glanced over his shoulder at the door. "Lucky you, mutts can't open door—" Splinters of wood grazed my forehead from the force of Sam's claws punching a hole through the center of the door. "Terrible for you, mutts can break through doors. Wish I could stay, but I have a pack of wolves to kill." Nathaniel ruffled my hair. "Now be a good she-beast and Change."

"Wait—"

Nathaniel disappeared.

Fumbling to my feet, I snagged a pair of jeans off a hanger. No way would I face death wearing a nightie. Again.

The doorframe groaned from another assault.

"Sam, it's me. I'm okay," I mumbled, tugging on the jeans. "Calm down."

Rapid digging at the door answered me.

As I struggled with the zipper, a wolf's eye peered at me through a jagged hole in the center of the door. Sam wasn't home. The animal staring at me saw me as dinner.

Abruptly, the wolf was gone.

Claws hammered against the floor, gaining speed as they neared the closet. With Sam's body slam, the door dislodged from its hinges. When he made another charge, I rammed the door at the same instant, keeping it righted while his claws sliced at my bandaged arm.

Energy swelled around me in response to his claws scoring my flesh. Losing control of my shaking limbs, I fought to keep myself upright. Giving the door another shove, I struggled to hold off the Change, knowing full well the wolf attacking me would not sit and wait for me to go furry.

Another wave of energy tore through me, triggering an idea. If Jason had used the link on me, then why couldn't I use it on him? Closing my eyes, I dove into my subconscious, allowing the energy to drag me toward Jason.

An image of Jason plowed into my mind. Sitting on the edge of a cheap hotel bed, he glanced up at me, slack-jawed, as I fastened onto his energy.

"Let's see how you like it," I muttered. Focusing on his heartbeat, I pulled his energy into me. Not as impressive as mine, but I worked with what the sleazeball had.

Snapping my eyes open, I jumped sideways. As the closet door crashed to the floor, I shoved Jason's energy at the charging wolf. The impact sent the wolf airborne, tossing him across the room, then rocketing him against the bathroom door—which exploded into a cloud of splinters.

Gasping for breath, I took a hard seat on the floor. My face and fingertips tingled with the traces of Jason's energy, while what felt like the ultimate caffeine-buzz hummed through my body.

The prison room doors slammed open against the walls. The force sent parts of the chandelier crashing to the floor. Derek bolted inside. When his glare landed on me, his confusion and panic raced across the blood-bond before he cut it off.

"Where's the wolf?" he asked.

"Bathroom."

As the prison room doors closed by themselves, Derek raced to where Sam had landed. A glass bead from the chandelier knocked against my toe, triggering my awareness. I gasped. Derek's exchange with me had taken less than a few seconds. I had that much time, if that, to warn Jason about Nathaniel's attack.

Still absorbing Jason's energy, I dove back into my mind. Instantly, I was again in the hotel room, standing at the edge of the bed where Jason was sprawled on his back. His foggy eyes widened as I leaned over him.

"A vampire is heading to Glenwood to kill your pack," I warned.

"I'm not there." Jason grimaced. "Only decoys."

"Get them to safety," I snapped. "Any more bloodshed on your orders and I'll take every last drop of your disgusting energy." Making my point, I tore his energy from him.

"I'll punish you for this, bitch," he wheezed.

"I don't think you'll have the energy—"

Jarring me out of my vision, Derek shook my shoulders. "Are you all right?"

Still alive. Still human. I nodded.

His sigh carried the coppery scent of blood, and his fingers held the stench of turned earth. Thankfully, Derek had indulged on a guard instead of me. I relaxed.

For the moment, I felt safe. No. Better than safe. In control. I had used the link against a raging werewolf while holding off my Change. Then, by turning the link on Jason, I had saved a pack of werewolves from Nathaniel's attack. Furthering my confidence came with the confirmation that Nathaniel and Derek were on my side until I went wolf.

I can do this. I sighed. *I'm not a coward.*

Derek's eyes narrowed. "How did you learn to use the alpha's link?"

I let a grin spread across my lips. "Because I'm special."

Chapter Twenty-Four

Outside, lightning cut across the sky as sleet pelted against the windows and roof. Inside, Derek was just as ruthless as the elements with his interrogation. Minutes ago, we had shared a mind-shattering kiss. Now, Derek stole my breath with his fury.

"The link." He leaned closer, forcing me to look him dead in the eyes. His fingers, gripping my shoulders, tightened. "Who taught you how to use it?"

"No one."

"Who taught you?" His dress shirt stretched tight across his expanding chest. A restrained scream threatened to escape his clenched throat if I dared to dodge the question again.

"Myself," I whispered.

His grip loosened, but he kept encroaching on my personal space. "If you had drained the alpha of all his energy, you would have killed him. Do you know what would have happened to you?"

Staring at the tips of Derek's fangs, I answered, "I'd have one less monster after me."

"You need the alpha to guide you through your first Change." Air hissed through his fangs as he released me. "If he dies, you will be torn apart."

Crossing my arms to control my shivering, I asked, "By who?"

"Your wolf." Derek shot a look over at the bathroom where Sam was in the process of changing into his human form. "Did that dog teach you anything?"

Derek was too kind to classify Sam as lupine. Sam was a rat. A conniving, sneaky…protective, tender… To gain control over my flip-flopping feelings for Sam, I focused on his most recent breach of trust. "Lies."

Derek snapped his head back at me. "What lies?"

"That every werewolf will die when—"

"*If.*" The tone Derek used to utter that simple word of opportunity, and the intensity of his stare proved he cared that I lived. Yes, his existence temporarily relied on my heart beating, but that *if* had a deeper meaning. He knew it. I knew it, and he seemed pretty hell-bent on covering it up. With his expressionless face and flat tone back in place, Derek said, "The wolf spoke the truth. You die. They all die."

"No. I am still human—"

"You are *not* human."

"As human as I'll ever be." A lump formed in my throat and my eyes burned. "I have not made the Change, therefore I'm not linked to the whole race."

Derek's eyes darkened.

"Of course." I sighed. "You were in on the lie."

"Vampires cannot lie."

"You can twist words. Be vague. Use compulsion on Sam to lie to me."

"There was no need to place compulsion. It was the wolf's idea." Derek paused until I looked back at him.

"If you believed your life meant others lived, you would fight to stay alive. Be cautious. Become more…controllable."

Movement in the bathroom caught my attention. Sam, fully human, with a towel wrapped around his hips, stood in the threshold. My stare connected with his glowing eyes.

"You get all that from snooping through my sock drawer?"

Derek stood.

Ignoring Derek, Sam kept his stare on mine. "I said it to keep you safe." He added softly, "You have to believe me."

"I don't." I looked away from his guilt-ridden face. "You can stop with the whole I-care-about-you routine—you care *only* about the greater sum."

"Tessa…."

I forced my stare back at Sam. "You mean *Asset*."

"Don't let my screw-ups have you siding with that bloodsucker. Please, Tess."

"And she should trust you?" Derek asked. "You almost killed her. You deceived her."

"Don't listen to him." Sam stormed into the room, then stopped. With his frustrated sigh, his shoulders shook while he struggled to maintain a controlled stance. "He's trying to split us up."

Calm and poised, Derek faced off Sam. "You are doing the job well enough, wolf."

"He's a killer," Sam snarled.

"As are we all," Derek countered.

"I'm not a killer." I stood.

Derek tilted his head at me. "Your actions put lives at risk. You could have killed the alpha."

"I didn't."

"That list you destroyed — those lives are at risk. There still is another copy which more than likely is in the wrong hands. Hands that will kill."

"And your queen would have protected the half-bloods?"

"Better a quick death than what could happen to them."

"A quick death? She tore Miller's arm off, and then tossed him to her vampires." I glared at Derek's expressionless face. "She smiled at me while she ripped into James' throat."

"I said quick, not painless."

Shaking my head, I looked around Derek's shoulder at Sam, hoping for some reassurance that I did right by destroying the list. Sam's jaw ticked as he lowered his gaze from mine. "Sam?"

"Sam *is* a killer," Derek answered.

"I get it," I snapped. "His actions could cause —"

"I have," Sam said.

"Excuse me?" my voice hitched, "Look at me, Sam."

He straightened to his full height, raising his stare to mine. "Last night, Jason gave two wolves as blood payment."

"Miller and James," I answered.

With his eyes darkening, Sam shook his head. "Miller and I." He held out a hand to keep me from talking. "Since the night we all were abducted, James was kept as bloodsucker food. Tortured nightly by them." With his voice deepening, Sam shot a glare at Derek, "That's what bloodsuckers do to their victims. Until they kill them."

"I've seen firsthand how ruthless they are, Sam." When he looked back at me, I kept my stare to his. "Stop diverting."

"If I stay alive, I can save our race by protecting you." Sam paused, taking a deep breath like he was preparing to hurl himself over the precipice of Mount Everest. "When you were at your apartment searching for the list, Nathaniel offered me a way out of becoming a blood payment. I could save myself by turning James."

"You said that a person must be bitten by a werewolf in wolf form. Yet you were human. You refused the Change, because you need time in between. Right? Or was that a lie?"

"No," Sam said. "You saw how weak that back-to-back Change made me."

My temples throbbed to the rapid beat of my heart as I tried to grasp and discredit what Sam confessed. "Only an alpha can turn a human," I whispered.

No answer came from his clenched jaw.

Sleet hammered at the roof, drowning out the tense silence inside the room.

"He is what your race calls 'a lone wolf'." Derek moved in front of my stare down with Sam. "An alpha cast out of his pack for committing a crime against the whole."

Locking my attention on Sam, I asked, "What was your crime?"

"Murder," he answered.

"How many?" Tears coated my cheeks as I shook violently. "How many people have you killed, Sam?"

"Two. Five. Twenty-six..." Sam's voice lowered. "What difference does the number make? You'll still hate me."

When Derek took a step toward me, I matched him with a stumble backward.

"Don't touch me," I warned. "Just get me out of here."

"That I cannot do," Derek said. "However, I can remove him."

"Do it," I whispered.

Derek nodded, then turned to face Sam.

"You gotta stop letting your emotions get to you." Sam sunk into a crouch while angling his right shoulder at Derek. "You need me. You don't know all their weaknesses. You need my protection."

"There is no need." Derek took a step toward Sam. "She is under *my* protection."

"What happens to your *protection* at the Gathering?" Sam asked, keeping his focus on Derek's torso. "Will you obey your queen and give Tessa to Jason? So she can be locked in a vault? Like the werewolves from the Old World did to the last Wolf Born? Never to breathe fresh air. Never to see or speak to anyone. She will go mad. Or, will you show Tessa pity and kill her yourself?" Snarling, Sam locked glares with Derek. "No. Not you. You'll damn her to hell."

Derek moved faster than I could follow, but Sam was a pace ahead. Rolling away in a somersault, Sam then lunged to his feet. Eyes narrowed, fangs out, they circled each other.

Remembering the old energy-sucking werewolf's warning to Jason about the risk of allowing a Wolf Born to live, and how Jason was confident he could control me, I knew Sam had, for once, told the truth. How long was my predecessor trapped in a vault, waiting for the chance to escape? Weeks? Months? Years? Decades? I'd been locked up for a little over a week and lost my sanity countless times.

"How did she die?" I asked.

Still keeping his focus on Derek's midsection, Sam answered, "She waited until her blood had rusted her chains enough to break loose. Then she drove her claws into her heart."

"Sam will stay in this room as my guard." The coldness in my voice had both men pause in their pacing.

When Sam looked into my eyes, he quickly dropped his stare. In a fluid movement, he went to his knees, lowering his head and touching his fists to the floor. "My life for yours." The matter-of-fact tone of his voice made my jaw quiver.

Sam had been my friend and as much as I denied it, I still had feelings for the murdering, lying alpha. Staring at Sam's shoulder blades, I choked back a scream. Stifling my rage sent energy skirting through my body. Pain sliced through my fingertips. Hissing, I lifted my trembling hands. Black claws jetted out of the oven-mitt bandage. From my bare hand, blood dripped off the three-inch claws protruding from my fingertips.

Derek stepped in front of me, then swept his hands over mine. With the touch of his cold palms, he opened the blood-bond. Calmness flooded my limbs and slowed my racing heart. I bit my tongue as my claws retracted back into my swollen fingertips.

Below our hands, a splattered line of blood glistened on the floor. A glaring reminder that no matter how much I thought I had allies, protectors, friends...after tomorrow night, I was on my own.

"Let me go," I pleaded, raising my stare to Derek. Sorrow filled his eyes while silence screamed from his sealed lips. I continued my plight. "I'll disappear. I'm an expert at running away. No one or thing will find me."

A tugging sensation from the bandage had me returning my gaze to our hands. His claws slid across the bandage, splitting it in two. Then he tore it off like a band-aid. While Derek turned over my wrist, I averted my eyes to his chest. I wasn't ready to see the damage which burned with the touch of cold air.

Immediately, Derek released my hand. A gust of stale air whisked across my face as he moved away in his blurring speed toward the doors. Once the doors shut, I glanced at the figure-eight brand across my palm.

Chapter Twenty-Five

The need to find something to preoccupy myself with, other than staring at Sam's muscled back, had me ducking into the closet. Tiptoeing around pieces of door and fragments of the dress Sam had torn off me, I spotted a shirt hanging in the back corner.

Leave it to me to be kidnapped by hoarding vampires. Skintight and yellowed with age, the blouse belonged in the eighteen-hundreds, and it should have stayed there. As I struggled to fasten the pearl button across my breasts, behind me, shoes crunched on the scattered debris. Muttering a plea to the strained button for it to do its job one last time, I turned to face Derek.

"Put this on." He held out a guard's jacket.

Wrinkling my nose at the dirt stench emanating from the coat, I folded my arms across my chest. "Why?"

His eyes narrowed. "I will use compulsion."

"Fine."

He lifted it so I could shrug into the nasty thing. Meant to fit someone of Sam's size, the coat hung to my knees. Shoving up the sleeves, I exposed the tips of my fingers.

"We have a short amount of time," Derek said, turning me around. "Do not argue. Do only as I say."

Zipping up the jacket, Derek then grabbed for my elbow, but the coat's padding kept him from getting a good hold. Trying for my forearm, he missed again. When he slid his hand down to mine, I pulled my fingers inside the coat.

"No need to hold my hand. I'll follow you," I said.

As we emerged from the closet, Sam lifted his stare. Avoiding his attention, I trained my focus on Derek's back. The vampire headed toward the doors. Puzzled, I paused. "I thought I couldn't leave the room."

"Things have changed," Derek said.

"Where are we going?"

"I said" —he shot a glare over his shoulder— "no arguing."

"I'm not." I dropped my hands to my hips. "What's your deal? Why can't you *ever* just answer a question?"

"Must you *always* be so difficult?" Turning to face me, Derek looked over my shoulder, then back at my face.

Confused by his vampire charades, I glanced behind myself and met my reflection in the rain-covered windows. Spinning around, I fought the urge to backflip. I was going outside. Fresh air. Freedom…well as much freedom as guards with itchy trigger fingers and bloodthirsty vampires would allow.

"Her feet will freeze," Sam said.

Derek glanced at my purplish toes. "It will be only for a few minutes."

"Enough time for her to catch frostbite."

"I've been stuck in this room, without heat, and most of the time I've just been in my underwear."

Both men shot their attention at me.

Patting my thighs and tugging on the jacket, I said, "Jeans. Long-sleeved shirt. Stinky winter coat. All major improvements. Besides, what's a little rain to a New Yorker?"

"Freezing rain," Sam added.

"While I'm gone, you can stop bowing and put on a robe." I stormed past him and stopped at the doors.

Derek moved to my side. "Same as last night. Follow me, and do not speak a word." He paused as the doors opened. "A suggestion — keep your eyes on my back at all times."

When he stepped over the silver-lined threshold, Derek shut down the blood-bond. Knowing he did it so he wouldn't feel my pain, I glared at him as I crossed over the threshold. Not even the puffy coat could buffer the sting. Derek waited for me to recover my breath before he started down the hallway.

Sometime during the day, the hallway had been restored to its former stuffiness. A fresh coat of lemon-scented furniture polish lathered the air, masking the coppery tang of guard blood soaked into the floor runner. At the end of the hallway, rain hammered at the balcony's new set of glass doors. In place of the guards and the Uzi, two of the queen's tuxedo-dressed vampires stood watch.

Ignoring his fellow bloodsuckers, Derek continued down the stairwell. My brief stall ended when their black-mirrored gazes shifted to me. Gluing my focus to Derek's shoulder blades, I followed close behind.

At the mid-landing, I froze. The second floor swarmed with human and vampire guards.

Derek turned to me. "They are preparing for tomorrow."

That newsflash didn't get my feet moving. Instead, my back knocked against the wall as my legs turned to jelly.

Sighing, Derek climbed back up the steps. "They are here to protect you."

"Sure they are," I snapped.

Derek closed the distance between us, which only made my heart thud louder and the sweet aroma of my terror rise from my pores. Tilting his lips to my ear, he whispered, "Calm your heart and pay mind to your fear."

"Kinda hard," I gritted, "when there's a vampire at my throat."

Pulling away, Derek looked into my eyes. His stare shifted to a lock of my hair that fell in front of my face. Tucking the wayward strand behind my ear, he brushed his fingers along my jawline, opening the blood-bond.

Instantly, I relaxed as my mind took on a drunken state. Before I got too comfortable propped between the wall and Derek, I pressed my palms against his chest, giving him a nudge to step back.

As he dropped his hand, he sealed off the bond. Keeping his gaze to mine, Derek spoke at the fanged audience gathering at the landing. "All leave this hallway until we have passed."

He gave me a nod, then headed down the stairs. Each of his footsteps echoed through the now-vacant hallway. The packed hall had cleared before the last syllable had left Derek's mouth, further unnerving me.

Easing my back away from the wall, I curled my fingers around the railing. Lightheaded, my concentration moved from the missing bloodsuckers to keeping myself from tumbling down the remaining steps.

Unlike last night, we passed the main staircase that led to the foyer and continued down the hallway. When Derek stopped, I peeked around his shoulder. Two human guards, dressed in their outside gear, stood in front of a set of glass doors that led to a walkout balcony.

"The garden is cleared," the guard to the right said.

When Derek nodded, the guard to the left unlocked the doors. As he pushed them open, a blast of frigid wind raced inside, stinging my face and the tips of my exposed toes. Desperate to breathe fresh air, I sucked in a lungful which simultaneously burned my throat and launched me into full alertness. When Derek's hand encircled my waist, I snapped my attention to him.

"There is silver in the doorframe," he said, scooping me into his arms. "I will be quick."

As he sprinted us across the threshold, the zap of pain left me writhing in his arms until the sensation of weightlessness took over. The wind howled past my ears as we plummeted two stories. The transition from air to earth was flawless. Continuing at the same speed as our free fall, Derek took off across the grounds.

Ice-like needles of rain stung my cheeks and lips. To escape the elements, I buried my face against the crook of Derek's neck. With the tip of my nose pressed against his jugular, I guiltily inhaled his scent.

He slowed his pace to a walk. "Did you just sniff me?"

"No...maybe."

As I pushed away from his chest, my heightened senses unleashed themselves. Raindrops hitting the stone pavers sounded like hammers striking against iron. Drawing in a breath sent me into a coughing fit. A potent mixture of pine, earth and the acridness of smog amplified by the rain rolled across my tongue. Nausea turned my stomach from my gaze tracking the slightest of movements. In sensory overload, I jerked my head to the sky. Just as I had trained myself while inside my prison room, I focused solely on one sense. My sight.

And in that fraction of time, suspended by Derek's arms, watching each crystal-like raindrop fall slowly toward the earth, I enjoyed being what I was becoming. While I acclimated to my other senses, I closed my eyes, listening for the moon song. Though muted by the thick band of cloud cover, its hum ran through my mind. As the fine hairs on the back of my neck stood on end, I shoved at Derek. "Put me down."

"Not yet. They can still see us."

When I flashed my attention toward the estate, at almost every window, eyes peered back at us, most through the scope of a rifle. "Move faster," I muttered.

"No matter my speed, there are always others who are faster. Stronger." Derek's voice lifted. "Now intelligence, that is on our side."

"There's that vampire vanity again," I grumbled.

He grinned down at me. "Be glad my vanity is aligned with you."

"Until I go wolf."

Instantly, his face fell back into emptiness. Kicking myself in the head for my snark monster surfacing, I fumbled for a recovery. "Anyways...don't they hear you dissing them?"

"Dissing?"

"Mocking."

The change in topic worked. His shoulders loosened, and he picked up the pace. "Those inside are deafened by the sounds around them. With the rain and their distance, the vampires outside cannot hear us. We may speak freely."

"What's to keep them from sneaking up on us?"

"I am the queen's hunter. Her assassin," Derek said. "All obey my orders when she is away."

"Where is she?"

He hesitated. "Greeting the council members who have already arrived."

"No chance of one of them dusting her before tomorrow?"

"No."

"Dang." The glare from the floodlights boarding the maze caused me to squint. "What were your orders?"

"While we are outside, no one is allowed within the maze or on the grounds. They are to stay along the edges of the property or remain inside the estate. If…"

When the harsh light dimmed, I opened my eyes and instantly tuned Derek out. Daedalus would have swooned inside this maze. Manicured to perfection, the fourteen-foot-tall hedges gave the illusion of solid walls. Stained-glass lanterns illuminated the walkways in a soft glow. Below, Derek's shoes crunched along a quartz path where prisms glinted off the pebbles' glass-like surface—

Derek pinched the back of my thigh.

"Ouch. What the hell was that for?"

"Nathaniel is right. You have no attention span."

"I have been trapped in that room for a week. Forgive me for taking a moment to not fear for my life."

"A moment?" Shifting his arms, Derek let me get my feet underneath me. "You have been looking at the ground for nearly five minutes."

Cold shot up the balls of my feet. I gritted my teeth. Thankfully, a marble bench sat three hops away from me. When I plopped down, rain soaked through my jeans, freezing my poor butt.

Unfazed by the rain drizzling down his face, Derek stood motionless in front of me. A curtain of mist drifted between us from my body heat freezing as it hit the air. He moved to the side so he could continue scowling at me. When he let out an annoyed sigh, his breath didn't fog.

Shivering, I mumbled, "Freaking vampires."

"What are you lamenting about?" he asked.

"How my life has faceplanted. Days ago, I took a photo that outed the mayor and McKay for the crooks they are. I should be in my apartment, celebrating with Ben and Andrea, dancing around my trashcan while holding the burnt remains of one of my boss's crusty, pit-stained shirts because some mid-sized paper called me with a job offer." I glared at a puddle. "Instead, I'm here, freezing my Wolf Born butt off while sitting next to a vampire—who bound my blood to him," I said, giving Derek a sideways glance. "Why am I here?"

"The queen plans to use you tomorrow evening to eradicate the vampire council and then the entire werewolf population."

"I meant the garden, Mr. Doom."

Derek straightened. "The wolf was right. You need to be prepared for tomorrow."

"Oh." I blew out a puff of breath. "You're going to teach me how to fight a group of powerful bloodsuckers?"

"Hundreds of vampires," he corrected. "No. I do not have the time or patience to teach you combat. I'm going to watch you find your way out of this maze."

Hope washed over me, bringing tears to my eyes. Then dread crashed the party. I glanced in the direction of the estate. "As much as I want to escape...I'm not leaving without Sam."

"That animal betrayed you," Derek snapped. "He'll do so at every opportunity. You know what happened to the last Wolf Born. Make no mistake, your *Sam* will chain and lock you away for the greater good of the wolves."

"I know." I glanced at Derek's scowl. "Doesn't mean I have to drop to his level of assholeness. I plan on ditching Sam as soon as we're free."

Derek leaned over, putting our faces inches apart. Refusing to budge, I let my hot breath slip from my lips to slap him in his sneer.

"You're a fool, Tessa Sanders." He straightened. "Besides, I said nothing of escape. I want to prove to you how completely helpless you are."

"You're such a tool." I shoved to my feet. "Peace out, Derek."

A spotlight from the center of the maze shone on the hedge tops. I'd use its brightness to gauge my progress. Glancing left, I chose to tackle the maze counter-clockwise. Curiosity to find the statue that I'd seen from the prison room gave me a distraction from the rain slipping underneath the coat collar and Derek's shoes crunching loudly on the path behind me.

Every twist and turn mirrored the last, except for the brightness of the spotlight. As long as its intensity grew, I knew I was headed toward the center. When I came to a turn I was sure I'd passed before, I'd sniff. At any time I scented Derek, I readjusted my course. Keeping his scent behind me meant I wasn't doubling back on myself.

Soon the spotlight's intensity caused me to squint. Sure that the next turn would be the center, I picked up my pace. When I rounded the corner, I jerked to a stop.

Dead end.

"Damnit." I spun around.

Derek blocked the narrow path. A flicker of copper sailed into the air then fell into his waiting palm. He lifted his gaze to mine. "Heads or tails?"

"Is this your attempt at a joke?" Curling my numb fingers around the coat's damp sleeves, frozen pine needles scraped my knuckles. I'd backed myself against the dead end. "Not funny."

"I assure you, this is no farce." His eyes darkened. "If not for your coin toss the night we met—"

"You attacked me," I corrected, pressing my back further against the hedge, I tested for weaknesses but instead met an impenetrable wall of ice and pine. "You bit me."

His lips twitched. "You were not to remember that."

"Well, I wish I didn't."

He took a step closer. "You broke my nose."

A fuzzy memory of me in the overpass tunnel, flat on my back, sending my foot into Derek's face as he lunged for me, crossed my mind. "You *so* deserved it." I glared at the bump on the bridge of his nose then at his fangs peeking out from his grin. "You forced me to drink your blood."

"After you bit my hand." He took a step, putting me within arm's reach. "You left me no choice."

"You could have *left* me."

"To the wolves?" He smirked. "No. Of course, *that* is the memory you don't remember."

Another hazy image of me in the park, on my back, watching a tuft of fur floating above me plowed into my mind then flashed to the one of Ben in my kitchen, picking the clump of fur off my shoulder. "In the park, why did you try to erase my memories?"

"To keep you...safe." Derek's eyes narrowed. "If you had left the next day, as I instructed, then you would not be in this predicament."

I shook my head. "Miller found my phone in the tunnel...my blood, too."

Derek opened his mouth.

"When Miller interviewed me at Oblivion, he knew what I was." I searched Derek's eyes for understanding but saw only his stubborn denial. "Don't you get it? Instead of being hostage to the vampires, I'd have already started my prison time with the wolves. There was no saving me." I bit my lip, struggling to hold it together. "There *is* no saving me."

"You are wrong." Derek shoved his loose-held fist holding the coin up to my face. "Heads or tails?"

I refused to answer and in protest, I turned my head. Devastatingly bad decision number three hundred. *Never flash your neck at a pissed-off vampire.*

Before the penny hit the path, Derek grabbed my hip. With his free hand, he snatched ahold of the back of my head, tangling his fingers in my hair. While he shoved his body against mine, he trapped my arms between us and lowered his mouth to my ear. "Tomorrow you will die. Whether it be by the queen. By the counsel. Or by your Change. Your death is inevitable." A flex of his wrist tilted my face to his. "I will not stand by and watch you perish at another's hands."

"You brought me here to kill me." I glared at him. "What the hell was the coin toss for?"

"I assumed it would ease your mind to let fate decide by the flip of a coin."

"Decide what? How I die?"

I slammed up my knee and freed my arms, but he blocked my attacks. Shifting his legs between mine, Derek pressed his hips tight against my lower abdomen. Wildly, I beat at his back. Pulling his hand free of my hair, he yanked my arms over my head and pinned them against the hedges. Thrashing my head, I snapped any time his face came close enough.

"Do not fight me." By my wrists, Derek jerked me to my tiptoes, forcing me to look into his black mirrored eyes. A deadly blend of compulsion and the blood-bond wrapped around my mind and body, leaving me to dangle in his hold. "I offer you a quick death, or I turn you. Choose, before I do."

"I choose to live."

He lowered his head. "That is not an option."

"Yes. It is."

His lips grazed my neck.

"You've had multiple opportunities to kill me," I whispered, flinching as each of my words bounced my jugular against his mouth, "but you didn't. You chose to save me."

"The blood-bond keeps me from killing you." His body shook against mine. "It drives me to turn you."

"You won't turn me. You hate your existence more than you hate me." I glanced at the indecisive penny wedged between two pebbles. Neither heads nor tails.

"Even the stupid coin doesn't want a part in my death. Look."

The brush of his hair against my throat signaled that he'd stolen a peek at the penny. His grip on my wrists tightened. "You should have left." He moved his lips back to my throat. "I'd rather you hate me for an eternity."

"No. You don't want to do this."

"I'll be swift," he whispered.

"Please. No. Wait." I tensed as his fangs replaced his soft lips. "Back in the room...something scared you."

"Not a *thing*." When he lifted his face to mine, the reflection of my glowing eyes filled his lifeless stare. "You."

"Why?"

"Do tell, Derek," Nathaniel said, standing behind Derek. "Please inform us what has brought the queen's hunter to quiver with fear in the presence of a dog."

Now that he'd fed, Nathaniel's third-degree burns were a distant memory. Rain fell in crimson streaks from his slicked-back hair, stained with blood. His suit, in ruins, hung off his thin frame, which was heaving with rapid breaths.

Derek dropped me to my feet, then turned to face Nathaniel. "What happened?"

Nathaniel jabbed a claw at me. "She used the link to warn the alpha. Those animals knew I was coming. However" — he flicked rain and blood from his brow — "I got one to talk before I snapped its neck."

"And?" Derek asked.

"Tell him, she-beast," Nathaniel said.

Keeping his attention on Nathaniel, Derek ordered, "Speak, Tessa."

"I—"

Nathaniel blurted, "The werewolves plan on attacking the council during the Gathering."

"How many?" Derek growled.

"Every alpha on this filthy continent, along with their packs."

With his eyes ablaze, Derek turned toward me. "Is this true?"

"Yes," I whispered.

"As I said, Derek. You have brought the final death to us all," Nathaniel growled.

Silent, unmoving, Derek stared at me.

"You are the queen's hunter. It is your responsibility and duty to protect our kind. To eliminate all threats." Nathaniel's voice shook. "Turn the Wolf Born, or I will."

"Tessa Sanders." As Derek spoke my name, power swelled around me. "You are free of my compulsion. Run."

Nathaniel charged Derek. Maneuvering around the oncoming attack, Derek countered by hurling Nathaniel down the path.

"Run," Derek screamed.

Using my monster speed, I blindly tore through the maze. The soaking coat impaired my agility, snagging on stray branches as I passed. My taking a second to tear it off gave Nathaniel the opportunity he needed.

The force of his right hook to my jaw sent me sprawling onto my back. Shoving my hands against Nathaniel's throat spared my neck from his fangs, I kneed him in the gut. Using my momentum, I spun him onto his back.

He disappeared.

A kick to my ass sent my face scraping against the path. A shoe ground between my shoulder blades, knocking the wind out of me and stopping me from rolling over. Sudden relief from the pressure came when Derek tossed Nathaniel over my head. Forcing air into my lungs, I stumbled to my feet. Pushing myself back into a run, I raced past the vampires and took a hard left.

Bright lights crippled me. Pressing my back against the hedges, I painfully waited for my eyes to adjust to the dome lights built into the path.

Nathaniel appeared.

Shoving my crossed wrists up to my throat, I blocked him. When a blow ceased to connect with my body, I lowered my arms.

Nathaniel bent at his waist, stumbled backward then took a hard seat on the circular bench that bordered the sixteen-foot-tall marble statue of a woman. What had started as a string of curses in French bubbled into wild laughter.

Derek rested his hand on my shoulder, holding me from bolting.

Nathaniel glanced at Derek. "That, my friend, is being kicked in the ass by fate." Turning his head up to the statue, his body shook again with laughter.

"Shut up," Derek huffed.

After his use of modern-day lingo, my curiosity moved from Nathaniel composing himself to Derek staring at the statue. When he caught me watching him, he motioned with his chin for me to look at the woman.

Freezing and throbbing in pain, I shuffled around to the front of the statue. The toga-clad woman rested her left hand on the head of a massive wolf seated at her side while the stump of her right arm extended to the sky. Through the thinning clouds, a soft glow from the almost full moon touched her upturned face. If her right hand were still attached, it would have appeared as if she were holding the moon. A shiver having nothing to do with frostbite ran through my veins.

"She's freezing." Fatigue layered Nathaniel's voice. "Take her back inside."

"Who..." —my teeth chattered uncontrollably—"is she?"

Nathaniel stood, pinning Derek with a do-not-go-there look.

"Fine. If you won't answer that" —I pointed at the wolf's emerald stone eyes—within the moonlight, the jewels appeared to glow—"explain to me, if vampires hate werewolves, why would they have a statue of one?"

"It amuses me," the queen said.

Chapter Twenty-Six

As the queen stepped into the center of the maze, Derek and Nathaniel lowered their heads and took to their knees. Refusing to bow, I struggled to keep my knees from knocking together while I shivered violently.

Two of the queen's tuxedo-clad vampires flanked her. One held a black umbrella over her dainty head. Unlike the other bloodsuckers, she kept up the façade that she still felt the cold. Dressed in a full-length gray fur coat, with her hair pinned back in a stylish bob, she looked the part of an Old Hollywood starlet. Thankfully, being downwind saved me from smelling her Fifi perfume.

"Why is my sheep outside?" She looked me up and down. "Ruining my blouse."

"She was close to changing," Derek answered.

The queen lifted her hand, silencing him. "So you take her outside to frolic under the near-full moon? If I doubted your loyalty, Derek, I'd think you were plotting something *very* unwise."

Refusing to take her bait, Derek stayed silent and emotionless.

She turned her attention to Nathaniel. "You stink of wet dog. Speak of your outing."

"While I patrolled the city, six wolves attacked."

"Interesting. They knew where to find you." She cast a sideways glance at me. "Why did you attack my sheep?"

Nathaniel's jaw tightened.

"I ran," I answered.

Everyone shot their glares at me while I put my focus on the queen's upturned nose.

"You ran?" She smirked. "This is how you show me gratitude?"

"You will *never* have my gratitude," I growled.

"I shelter you, give you nourishment and protection. Yet you repay me with disobedience, destroying my property, using the link to communicate with the alpha behind my back—"

She snapped at Derek, "Speak and I will take your head. I know everything, hunter." Her pointy high-heeled boots whispered against the path as she walked toward me. "You think you're so clever. I find you…simple. A letdown." She paused. "Bow."

Uncurling myself, I stood tall. "No."

Her lips trembled into a tight smile.

"Wolf Born," Nathaniel warned.

"Fear not, servant." Cold fury dripped from the queen's voice. "She will bow."

"Never," I whispered.

The queen tossed her head back. Her laughter splintered like glass shattering against concrete. Even the elements cowered from her shrill. The rain ceased and the wind changed direction to escape.

She clapped her gloved hands in front of her face. "I, myself, was on an outing tonight. First, I met with a few council members. Boring group. So stuck on their traditions." She sighed. "Being in their company left me...restless."

A gust of wind pelted my face, carrying her rancid perfume to my numb nose. Taking a sharp inhale, I caught the smell of gasoline. At a closer inspection at her gloves, specks of white shone through their blackish material. I darted my gaze to her *gold* coat, covered in a layer of ash. The queen slipped her hand into one of its deep pockets where she retrieved a white handkerchief.

"I respect humans." Blotting her ruby-red lips, she smiled. "That look in their eyes as they realize they are about to die. Such emotion. The passion they utter with their last breath. Glorious."

She ticked her index finger, and the guard holding the umbrella closed it. With a wave of her wrist, both guards fell back a couple of steps. Once again, the statue demanded my attention. A reddish-orange glow flickered along the woman's shoulders while her missing arm extended up to a sky heavy with plumes of smoke.

"What did you do?" I gasped.

The queen let the handkerchief flutter from her fingertips. As it floated down to her boots, a gust of wind rolled it across the path to my mud-covered toes. Fresh blood speckled the satin fabric. When I glanced back at her, the scent of cinnamon drifted up to my nose. "What—" My voice broke with terror. "What did you do?"

"I did what you asked of me, sheep."

I shot my attention back to the hanky entwining with my toes. Slowly, I lifted my stare to the queen's face.

"I set Andrea free." She smiled sweetly at me. "Free of her earthly body."

My knees buckled. Crashing to the ground, I buried my fingers amongst the pebbles, digging my nails into the frozen earth. My lungs burned for air, but I had forgotten how to breathe. To think. To feel.

"There," the queen said. "I told you, she would bow." She closed the distance between us and lifted my chin with her index and middle finger. "The despair in your eyes is more precious to me than eternal life. To see your tears reminds me fondly of a spring sunrise." Her cheek grazed mine as she whispered against my ear, "I accept your gratitude."

When she went to stand, a muffled gag slipped past her strained smile. My hand, clenched around her windpipe, kept her in place. Raising my stare to her bulging eyes, I smacked the back of her head against the path. She responded by stabbing her claws into my side, scraping them against my rib cage before someone yanked me off of her. Their arms slid against my slick body.

Warmth flowed from my side down to my thigh. Splotches of black tore through my vision. Still, I dove at the queen. Meeting me mid-strike with the momentum of a wrecking ball, she hurled me onto my back. Pain sliced through the back of my skull. With the overwhelming scent of Andrea on the queen straddling me, I roused myself enough to dodge her fangs.

Nathaniel pried the queen off me. Her screams morphed into a roar while he dragged her away.

Unable to move, staring upward at the statue, my vision doubled. Reality blended with nightmare. Andrea loomed over me. Blinking back tears, Derek came into focus. Another fluttering of my eyes and Andrea scowled down at me. Her mouth was moving, but Derek's voice came out. "Fight. Stay with me."

"I'm sorry…" I repeated my apology until unconsciousness seized me.

In the darkness of my mind, Andrea responded, *"No, Tess. I won't accept an apology. It's not over. Ben. Sam. Keep fighting."*

Chapter Twenty-Seven

When a finger probed my torn-up side, my eyes shot open. Tears clouded my vision, but from his scent, I knew the blob sitting in front of me was Sam.

"I'm sorry." Sam removed his finger. "But if you sleep, your wolf will try to take over…again."

Every atom in my body screamed for me to return to the comfort of darkness, yet the word *again* had me struggling to remain awake. I sat on the prison room floor with my back grinding against the pole, and my arms stretched taut over my head. Steel cuffs bound my wrists to the pole.

"Derek's gone to feed. He will use the blood-bond to heal you. Once he comes back and sees you're awake, he'll remove the chains," Sam said. "Until then, stay calm. Okay?"

When I went to answer, my throat burned from my screaming. Instead, I nodded my understanding. Rubbing my tears away on my forearm, my cheek throbbed from Nathaniel's right hook.

A few feet away, Sam sat cross-legged with his eyes puffy and red. Seeing my attention on him, he looked toward the fireplace. For the first time in a week, he was wearing clothes. Granted, it was a guard's uniform, but if Sam was at work, he'd have been dressed in an all-black attire as well. At the thought of Oblivion, tears filled my eyes.

Andrea was dead.

Shoving his fingers through his hair, Sam sighed. He glanced at me, and his jaw tightened. Grief swelled in his tense shoulders as his eyes grew slick.

"Andrea," I whimpered. "You know?"

"I heard...everything."

A tear rolled down his cheek, and my heart shattered.

"Andrea wouldn't want this," he whispered. "You and I sitting on our butts, crying." He nodded to himself. "What was that saying of hers?"

"Lifetime called...." My throat clenched.

Sam gave a sad smile while he finished Andrea's punchline. "They want their drama back."

Unable to hold my grief in check, I cried. I screamed. I laughed. Then I heaved a deep breath, sinking into blissful numbness. At some point, Sam moved over to me. Awkwardly, he folded his legs so our knees touched. Waves of his body heat flowed between us and my shivering body devoured the warmth.

"I know you think it's your fault," he said.

"Not think." I struggled against the chains at my wrists. "Know."

Pressing the heel of his hands on my thighs, Sam held me in place. No matter which way I turned my head, he mirrored me. "You risked your life to save Andrea."

"I told the queen to let her go," I snapped. "And the queen killed her. My. Fault."

"No." His eyes narrowed. "Andrea was dead the second she stepped out of Oblivion's restroom."

"What?"

"When you were being questioned by Miller, I gave her the keys to my truck. Andrea was to stay in the bathroom and wait for you. Then the two of you were to go out the window and meet up with Ben."

I slumped against the pole.

"Andrea *chose* to stay," he said, looking down at our knees. "When we were in the back of Miller's cruiser while he and James got out to check on your place, I asked her why she stayed." Sam lifted his gaze to mine. "She said, 'I don't bail. Tess needs me'."

"If she'd waited, we *might* have avoided Jason and his pack. We *might* have dodged the vampires. No guarantees."

"Still, it was her choice," Sam said.

"Like you had a *choice* to not murder someone."

Sam flinched. "If you'd let me get a word in tonight, I could have explained."

"Explained?" Unable to move away from Sam, I kicked my gaze at the ceiling. "You mean, convince me that killing someone is a good choice?"

"Not good. Right." Sam waited until I looked at him before he continued. "And I live with the consequences every second of my life. If you would just hear me out."

I tapped the cuffs against the pole. "Well, I'm not going anywhere."

After a stint of silence paired with an intense staring match, he heaved a frustrated sigh. "Jason's pack was mine."

"Why didn't you tell me?"

"I panicked." Sam's voice trailed off as he glanced away from me. "You saw what they did to that kid in the park. To you. You've seen enough monsters. I didn't want to be one of them."

Leaning forward, as far as my arms stretched, I brought my face inches from his, forcing him to look me back in the eyes. "Tell me what happened."

He shifted side to side. Rolled his neck to his shoulders. Sam drummed his index fingers on my thighs. The blatant stalling tactic drove me mad, yet I kept still and quiet. With a sharp expansion of his chest and a race of hot breath through his unclenching jaw, Sam did what I asked.

"The pack was out at some dump bar, drinking, being stupid. Reckless." His voice softened as he recounted the event. "Ethan, a new wolf, got into a brawl with a drunk human. Before we could break up the fight, Ethan smashed the man's head against the pavement, killing him. Someone had already called the cops. Sirens screamed from about a mile away. I told the pack to bounce, except for Ethan." Sam's jaw tightened. "We have to keep the race hidden. It is our duty. If Ethan was locked up in jail during the full moon..." Pausing, Sam's gaze grew distant. "I took Ethan behind the bar and into the woods. There was a ravine. I thought we were alone, but Jason stuck around." Sam's eyes re-focused on mine. "Jason watched me break Ethan's neck. He watched me toss..."

Trying to keep my expression neutral, I nodded for Sam to keep going. Still new to this monster world, some part in the depths of my subconscious knew Sam had acted out of mercy for Ethan. But the human part of me that I clung to pumped adrenaline through my veins as I watched Sam — the killer.

"So there's the answer to your question, one kill. Ethan." Sam's throat worked around a lump as he continued. "Werewolf law states, you kill a pack member, you become a lone wolf. I planned on turning over the pack to my second. That news didn't go over well with Jason. We had a ten-mile hike through the woods to meet back with the pack. About halfway, Jason took a beer bottle to the back of my head. A couple of hours later, I woke up in a ditch with my arm sliced — forearm to shoulder. The bastard left me to bleed out."

My confused look had Sam pausing to expand on Werewolf 101.

"To become an alpha, a wolf must consume the blood of his predecessor, and in doing so, the link forges with the pack." Sam rubbed the back of his neck. "After becoming a lone wolf, the first order of business is to put miles between you and the pack. Werewolf law decrees that the lone wolf receives one night to run. Then it's fair game. If the lone wolf crosses paths with the pack, they can kill him."

"You can't reason with them? Tell them what happened?"

"No. The link forces the pack to follow the alpha. They do what he says without question. 'Call the wolf,' is what we call this…"

"Control," I muttered. "How did you get away?"

"I headed east." A soft grin warmed the sadness from Sam's face. "Met a feisty brunette on the way."

"Andrea." I tilted my head. "She said she picked you up at a diner near Rochester."

"Surprised I didn't die of a heart attack. I was living off their garbage plates before she hauled me off to a tiny city to work at an eighties-themed bar with, as Andrea put it, potential."

"Oblivion," I added. My smile slipped when his eyes darkened. "Sam?"

He dropped his gaze and pushed to his knees. "You need to rest."

"Tonight, you said you heard *everything*." Reaching for him, the chains snapped my arms back against the pole. "The queen was covered in ash. She reeked of gasoline. There was a fire in the distance…smoke."

Sam's heartbeat ticked into high gear.

"Tell me what you heard!"

Sam lunged forward, pinning my shoulders against the pole. His glowing eyes locked with mine. "You have to stay calm. Your wolf is too close. You make the Change, and the queen wins."

Blood roared in my ears as an inferno consumed my body. "She won."

"Bullshit." He shoved his forehead against mine. "She massacred everyone inside Oblivion before she set it on fire. Phil. Rick…Andrea. You think she's done?"

"No," I whispered.

Sam cupped my face. "You think she'll stop after Glenwood?"

"No." I glared at him. "What do you want me to do? What can I do? I tried outsmarting her, and she killed Andrea."

"I want you to fight."

"I did. I attacked the queen, and she had her claws digging into my gut before my head hit the ground. I just lay there." Hot tears crawled down my cheeks. "I'm not a hero. I'm a coward."

"You are not a coward." Hanging his head, Sam dragged in a breath. When he lifted his head, wolf eyes peered at me from his flushed face. "You are a fighter. Fight with me. For our race. For Andrea."

Agony swept through my limbs. Clamping my eyes shut, I hissed. "I don't know how...I can't."

"Wrong and bullshit. Give up or fight on. The choice is yours, Tess."

I heard the doors open and close. Instantly, Derek's scent curled around me. However, he refused to venture away from the doors. Instead, he opened the blood-bond, and through it, he sent an endless horror show of the queen slaughtering her victims.

Each death was more gruesome as the years progressed. Although her victims were identical in one sense. The queen broke them all. After she caught the look of complete loss in their eyes, she killed them.

With her victims' screams still ringing in my ears, I opened my eyes. Moving my gaze away from Sam to the fireplace, I zoned out on the ravenous flames rolling across the logs. Images of my father's car engulfed in fire raced across my mind were then followed by one of the werewolf statues bathed in Oblivion's firelight.

Shaking my head, I sank deeper into my mind. Soon, I stood inside my trashed apartment, holding a piece of jagged porcelain. I turned it over. Ash covered its surface. I ran my thumb over to uncover the picture of the fluffy kitten. Something hot landed on my shoulder as specks of ash fell onto the piece of the coffee mug. I glanced up. Fire consumed my apartment. Flames ate holes through the curtains and melted the window frame. Outside, the city burned.

Gasping for breath, I snapped into reality. The taste of ash stuck to my tongue and the reek of smoke burned my throat, triggering adrenaline to course through my being. Every inch of skin vibrated with the raw energy demanding release.

Sam swept my drenched hair away from my eyes, giving me a clear view of Derek standing motionless by the sealed doors. His face was void of emotion as he surveyed my battered body, until his gaze connected with mine and regret shone through.

"The queen...can't...kill." I struggled against the agony flooding through my system. "Ever again. I'll —" Energy clawed at my heart and an animalistic scream exploded from my lungs.

Sam snapped over his shoulder at Derek, "Her Change is here."

Derek's gaze entrapped mine and before he could close off the blood-bond, dread prickled against me.

"Noooo." I tugged against the chains, hoping the pain would distract the monster trying to tear me apart from the inside out. The bite of metal against my fevered skin only increased the energy rolling through me.

"Control your wolf, Tessa." Derek's voice clenched. "You know how..."

Terror laced with want left me dizzy and the monster within me ticked. Claws tore through my fingertips. As I lunged forward, Sam pressed his hand against my thundering chest, bracing me against the pole to keep me from dislocating my shoulders.

"Control how?" Sam growled.

"Derek," I groaned, keeping my vision latched to the vampire stalking toward us. Anticipation buzzed through the room with each of his steps. Derek's gaze fastened to mine, burning me deep with the desire to brush my lips against his. "When he touched —"

Sam's breath pelted my cheek. "He'll never touch you again." The mixture of blood and rain coating the blouse caused his palm to slip. The new position had Sam's hand cupping my left breast. Need danced up my ribcage. "Ever. Hear me, Tess?"

I tore my focus away from Derek to lock my eyes on Sam. Sweat slid down his temples and his scent intensified around me, tightening my belly. "Help me fight this...pain."

Sam folded his bottom lip into his mouth. Lust dropped his voice into a grovel. "Do you know what you are asking?" He swallowed. "Because if I kiss and touch you again...you're mine."

My mind reeled. Looking into Sam's eyes, being in his arms, felt simultaneously right and wrong. The monster, twisting my insides, wasn't impressed with my reflections. A spasm cracked my ribs, stealing my rationality. Before I lost the only thing that was truly mine in this world, my human life, I forced my body to still long enough to speak. "Don't let me Change, Sam."

His eyes flicked to Derek. "We're not doing this in front of a vampire."

"I will kill you before you lose your shirt, Wolf," Derek warned. His attention shifted to the blood rolling down my side. "Yet I will kill her if I come closer."

"Leave," Sam ordered.

Derek's jaw tightened. He took a backstep.

"No," I whispered. That word froze both men. When a ripple of pain dug into my mind, I snapped my last thread of sanity toward Derek. "I need...you."

Sam's muscles bunched around me.

"I will kill him," Derek answered.

"No." I leveled my gaze to his. "You're not like your queen."

"I'm worse." He took a step toward us. "I will kill anyone. Anything. That—"

White-hot pain tore through my limbs. As waves of agony threatened to drag me under, Derek became my anchor to consciousness.

"We are out of time," Sam warned.

"If this doesn't work…" I gasped for breath. "Don't let me hurt…Sam."

Derek nodded and stopped in front of the fireplace. Annoyance flared through me. I wanted him touching me.

Sam was quick to flip my frustration. The press of his nose against my exposed throat sparked fevered chills to wreck my body. "I need to move you."

As Sam grabbed my hips, my eyes remained on Derek. Fury darkened his gaze, triggering my fear, which allowed the energy to swell within me. Before agony overpowered me, Derek's compulsion trailed down my throat. My eyes fluttered shut. Emotions deep and dangerous enveloped me. Derek slid open the blood-bond and the same collage of emotions crashed into me, infusing within my soul. I stiffened, and a sigh raced from my lips.

Sam dipped his lips to my ear. His hand palmed my breast, eliciting a moan from me. "Do you want me to stop?"

"No," I whispered.

Once more Derek's phantom caresses explored my flesh, running up the undersides of my taut arms. I writhed from the featherlight touches. Derek tilted his head, realization lighting in those dark eyes. He sent a heady blast of the blood-bond at me. My hips bucked and Sam was there to catch them. Suspending me in one hand, he worked at the zipper of my jeans with the other, then slowly tugged them from my body.

Derek's compulsion threaded through my fingers, distracting me and pressing my knuckles tight against the pole.

Nipping my shoulder, Sam sent want surging through me. His tongue laved over my skin, dipping into the hollow of my throat as he adjusted his position. When he sat me on his lap, his hardness ground against me through his pants. I sank my teeth into my lip, tipping back my head.

Derek's compulsion ran across my throbbing lip. His sharp intake of breath had me rolling my gaze back to him. "Now," Derek ordered.

Sam dragged his thumb down my lower belly. His mouth hot against my ear. "Are you ready?"

My gaze roamed up and down Derek. Seeing his arousal tightening his pants undid me. "Yes," I moaned.

Derek released the blood-bond, driving my lust to the heavens. Sam pressed his thumb against my core, stroking me in time with my ragged breaths. Derek's phantom caresses trailed down my arms, across my collarbones, to meet at my neck, encircling my throat, and forcing me to willingly keep my glazed eyes at the man stealing my soul.

Derek.

Pleasure built to a crescendo, drowning out the pain. Arching against Sam, I shattered with the release. Sam crashed his mouth against mine, stealing my scream, while Derek held me in his phantom embrace. The wild energy burst from my body, knocking against both men, and my orgasm soared.

As the euphoria ebbed, my mind sluggishly worked to realign with my trembling body. My vision refocused on Derek. Silent and unmoving, he stood watching me. Slowly, he withdrew his compulsion.

Sam trailed kisses along my jawline. "You okay?"

Unable to form words, I nodded. The slight movement caused the chains to clatter to the floor. Free of the restraints, I draped my arms around Sam's shoulders.

"You broke them," Sam answered my unasked question.

Nathaniel's energy prickled along my skin, announcing his presence. He stood behind me, close enough that his blood-coated breath hit the top of my head. "The queen has set her actions into motion. Tomorrow, she will attack the council. Nothing will sway her."

Refusing to take my attention away from Derek's face, I straightened my spine. "Her reign is over. Tonight, she killed for the last time." Derek's expression fell into blankness. However, trepidation screamed through the blood-bond, pleading with me to seal my lips, and for a moment I almost did. "Tomorrow, I will fight the queen."

Derek's façade cracked and anger burned in his glare. Terror flooded the blood-bond. In that moment, I realized my life meant something to Derek. Meant more to him than it did me. I tightened my fingers against Sam's shoulders, wishing I could touch Derek the same way he had touched me. But it was Sam's sigh of relief that filled the room, not Derek's. Sam's heated skin under my fingertips, not the chilled flesh of the vampire. Tears brimmed in my eyes, but I held them back by focusing on everyone in the room, on those who had suffered the queen's wrath, and all her future victims if I did not do everything in my power to stop the monster. Tomorrow night, my fight with the queen would end in death. Hers or mine. Perhaps both.

Chapter Twenty-Eight

I wished the queen's letter, which Nathaniel held, was my pardon. Sadly, it was my invitation to the Gathering, as none other than the guest of honor.

There was a glimmer of good news. Derek and Nathaniel were to be my escorts during the event. Never to leave my side, they would keep all wayward vampires from killing me. By their cussing in over a dozen dialects, they'd rather snuggle a hornet's nest.

I kept my relief hidden. They were the queen's best fighters. If they were with me, then the queen couldn't use them against me.

As for Sam...

My head hit the pillow. Panting, I rolled stiffly to my side. Sweat slid down my tailbone while my muscles screamed for a timeout.

As Sam flipped me onto my back, the stubble of his chin scraped my jaw. "Need a break?"

"Nope." His back spasmed when I jabbed my fingers into his tender side. Before he recovered, I drove my heels into his gut, kicking him clear off the bed.

Groaning, I scrambled to the edge of the mattress and dropped to the floor, where a black blur raced toward my face. The whiff of leather filling my nose registered the hostile object as the sole of Nathaniel's shoe. Dodging his kick, I grabbed his ankle and swung. Although I forgot to let go and sailed right along with him, crashing against the wall.

Chunks of ceiling plaster hit us as we struggled to untangle our limbs. Over Nathaniel's mutterings and my swearword mashup, the annoyed tapping of a shoe announced Derek had returned from his...dinner.

I would have loved to have said that in the past six hours, I'd become a vampire-killing ninja. In truth, I resembled a werewolf's squeaker toy. However, I did learn that smacking my tailbone on the floor as a werewolf hurt just as much as when I was human. Also, from my lack of clothing options, I discovered Nathaniel could pull off a woman's size four jeans.

Tugging the sweat-drenched pair of borrowed pants back into place, I glanced at the serving cart, piled high with bagels. A pulsing ache from my bruised wrists reminded me of the frequent timeouts I'd experienced chained to the pole. Although the orgasm had suppressed my Change, if the wolf attempted to hijack my body, we took precautions. Keeping the monster in check required a carb-induced coma and covering the windows to muffle the moon song, as well as a constant dose of the blood-bond supplied by Derek.

"To heal Tessa's injuries, it took the blood of nine guards." Derek looked over at Sam, who flopped down on the wingback chair next to the serving cart. "The wolf was only to teach her self-defense."

"He's too soft with her," Nathaniel answered. "Pauses before he attacks, giving her the advantage. Strikes at her limbs, instead —"

An inch from my nose, I caught Nathaniel's fist between my palms. Sweeping my foot around his ankle, I knocked him off balance.

He disappeared mid-fall. Although he was invisible, Nathaniel's earthworm scent betrayed his location. He stood in front of me.

Reappearing, he plunged his claws into the wall on each side of my face. "She's dead." Snapping his fangs at my throat, he jerked to a stop. His black-mirrored eyes glanced down to my claws poised at his heart and gut.

"Correction, Nathaniel," Derek said. "You would be dead." Over Nathaniel's shoulder, Derek grinned at me.

Sam stood rigid by his overturned chair. "Do it, Tess."

"Yes." Nathaniel glared at me. "Please. Put me out of my misery. Spare me the agony of being your escort. I can't bear the thought of pet sitting."

Derek put his hand on Nathaniel's shoulder, pulling him away from my claws. "We are finished with self-defense training."

The room erupted with protests.

"We will go into tomorrow evening assuming that the vampires will have the same mentality as Nathaniel," Derek said.

"Superiorly intelligent," Nathaniel added.

"Arrogant." Derek turned to me. "They must believe you're weak. Terrified. You cannot act or think otherwise, Tessa."

"No worries there." Retracting my claws, I limped over to the tray.

As Sam righted the chair, he spoke at me. "The wolves won't be as easily deceived."

"Jason's just as power-drunk as the queen." Biting into a bagel, I lifted a finger as I worked around a piece stuck to the roof of my mouth. "And...I pissed him off."

"Derek told us you almost killed Jason using the link." Sam held out a glass of water to me. "He'll make you pay for that."

Shrugging, I gulped down the water. "He'll need to wait his turn."

"Don't joke," Sam growled.

"I'm not." I glared at him. "I've accepted that I'm dead tomorrow. You're the one who's *joking* if you think differently."

"Tessa," Derek interrupted.

"There's been zero discussion about an escape plan." I hurled the glass into the fireplace. "Don't think I haven't noticed."

"If you let us continue with your lessons..." Making me focus on his words instead of my anger, Derek lowered his voice. "We could talk about —"

"No." I locked my glare with Derek's concern-filled eyes. "You're as delusional as Sam. Stick to the plan." If Ben were here, he would've had a master plan, a couple of backup plans and a few more just-in-case plans. Our quartet had one Hail Mary. "Get me alone with the queen before the wolves show up."

Derek's eyes drew to slits, then he turned sharply toward Nathaniel. "Go stand in front of Tessa," Derek ordered.

Huffing, Nathaniel moseyed over to me.

"When greeting a vampire." That was as far as Derek got before Sam barged in between Nathaniel and me.

"We need to plan for her escape," Sam said. "Not some bullshit lesson on bloodsucker etiquette."

"Stop," I whispered at Sam. When he made no move to back down, I touched his trembling bicep. "Please?"

Dropping his gaze to mine, he didn't hide the pain in his eyes. "You're gonna survive. After the Gathering, you'll be free. Hear me?"

"Yes." My voice sounded distant. Weak.

Gently, he cupped my face between his hands. Careful not to tug me tight to him, he tilted his lips to mine. "Say you're gonna live."

"I...I..." My throat clenched. "Can't."

As soft as his lips brushing mine, he swept away the tears sliding down my cheeks. "Say it," he whispered to my mouth. "Promise me."

Close to another meltdown, I blurted out, "I'll live."

When he pulled away, I shut my eyes. I didn't want him to see my doubt.

"Not over yet," Sam whispered.

"Not over yet." Andrea's voice echoed in my head.

Behind me, Nathaniel cleared his throat.

"Wolf, go sit on the bed," Derek ordered.

Once Sam was across the room with his arms folded over his expanded chest and butt on the mattress, Nathaniel stepped back in front of me.

Derek stood to the side with a blank expression that didn't quite reach his eyes. Before I could gauge what he was thinking, he continued, "As the honored guest, your ranking is above all humans."

My mouth fell open. "There are going to be humans at this shindig?"

"What's a party without refreshments?" Nathaniel beamed at me.

More than likely to keep from strangling the grin off Nathaniel's face, Derek grasped his hands behind his back. "There will be many in attendance. A few as guests, most as...servants."

"Refreshments. Got it." Fisting my hands at my sides, I shook my head. "Go on."

Derek nodded. "As the honored guest, you outrank all vampires, except the queen and the council members. I will inform you who is a council member."

"I can hear it now," I muttered. "This is Bob, a member of the almighty vampire council, he'll be tearing out your throat this evening."

"Very close, she-beast," Nathaniel said. "You forgot terrorize, maim—"

"Enough," Derek snapped. Turning his full attention at me, he kept the wrath in his eyes and seriousness in his voice. "When you are greeted by a low-ranking vampire, you are not to speak. Keep your head up. Focus on their chin and give them your entire attention. They will nod or bow to you. Do not return the gesture. To do so lowers your standing and is a direct insult to the queen." Derek paused. "Do not insult the queen. Understand?"

I nodded.

"If a council member wishes to greet you, keep your head up, eyes to their chin, give them your undivided attention and do not speak. If they ask a question, I will answer for you." He hesitated. "Lastly, stand still and allow their touch."

"The hell she will," Sam snarled.

I ticked my chin at him. "What he growled."

Derek sighed. "Nathaniel, greet Tessa with touch."

If looks could have killed, Derek would've been dead three times over.

Nathaniel glared at me as he bowed at the waist. In rising, he held out his hand.

"Lift your hand to him," Derek instructed.

When I raised mine, Nathaniel grabbed my wrist. Turning my hand over, he then placed his cold thumb at my pulse.

"Release," Derek said.

Nathaniel dropped my hand, then proceeded to rub his palm on his pant leg.

"I promise you, Tessa, it will be more gracefully done," Derek warned. "They may linger. Do not release yourself from their hold. Let them move away." He took a short breath. "Now, the other greeting."

Nathaniel's sapphire eyes burned with hate toward Derek. "You can describe it."

Derek angled his head down at Nathaniel. "As the queen's hunter—"

"I cannot *wait* for you to be stripped of that title." Turning his fury at me, Nathaniel bowed. Holding out his hand, he exposed the underside of his wrist to me. As Nathaniel stepped closer, he lifted his arm.

Nope. Do not like where this is going.

He slid his wrist to the side of my neck, putting our bodies a mere inch from touching. Moving his head to the other side of my throat, Nathaniel pressed his lips against my jugular. When he recoiled, I shivered. Nathaniel wanted me dead. I felt it in his kiss.

"Can I refuse?" I whispered.

"No." Derek moved between us. "To do so is a challenge to them, and an insult to the queen. Do not—"

"Insult the queen," I answered coldly.

"You're learning." Stepping out of my way, Derek motioned for Nathaniel to head back over. "Again."

* * * *

After fifteen successful vampire greetings, Nathaniel left to burn his suit and scrub himself raw. I didn't have that luxury. My constant need for the blood-bond, to keep the wolf under my skin, had drained Derek. His lingering glances at Sam's throat kept my shower cold and short. With my hair dripping wet and dressed in another pair of Nathaniel's pants and one of his ill-fitting, non-boob-friendly white dress shirts, I hustled out of the bathroom.

On the other side of the door, Sam stood guard and sidestepped to let me pass.

Derek faced the fireplace. He turned at my approaching steps. The firelight played over his gaunt face and hollowed eyes.

I froze.

"We have one more lesson before"—his gaze dropped to my neck—"sunrise."

"Keep your eyes above my throat, Derek."

"Apologies." His unfocused gaze sharpened as it connected with mine. "I'm not easily distracted."

Stopping behind me, Sam rested his hands on my shoulders. "If you were not needed to keep Tess alive, I'd have used your *distraction* to turn you into a pile of ash, bloodsucker."

"Fortunately for me, I never make the same mistake twice." The corners of Derek's eyes tightened. "Unfortunately, Tessa, you do."

Sam's fingers curled against my shoulders.

Warning sirens blared within my skull. "So, just a hunch. This lesson is about?"

"Trust," Derek answered.

I jerked my shoulders free from Sam, but he was a step ahead. Catching me in a bear hug, he pinned my arms to my sides and lifted me to my tiptoes, so I couldn't push off the floor and nail him in the shins.

"Never trust a vampire." Derek took his sweet time walking over to us. Standing just out of my foot's reach, he waited until I stopped kicking to continue, "They deceive. Manipulate. They care only for their survival. The constant craving for power drives them."

"No shit," I growled.

He ignored me. "Whereas a werewolf thinks about the survival of their pack. The greater good. Even a lone wolf is driven by this urge."

Each of my struggles knocked Sam back a foot. A few more calculated hits and we'd be at the window. I needed to keep Derek talking. Distract them both. "Explain Jason then. He cares only for power. He's leading his pack to their deaths."

"His pack is himself," Sam answered. "Jason will stop at nothing to protect his survival. You're his guarantee."

"Control me, control the race. I got that newsflash from the alphas' meeting." When I rammed my back against Sam, he stumbled another two feet, smacking against the wall. A few inches to the left, we'd have been out the window.

Nathaniel reappeared next to Derek, un-showered and still wearing his ragged suit. For days, I'd fought my Change while letting my inner idiot run wild around the monsters. It was my stupidity that had killed Andrea, not the wolf caged beneath my skin.

"Lesson learned," I said.

"Not yet," Derek said.

Feeling Sam's body vibrating against mine sparked an idea. Power swelled throughout my body, giving strength to my command. "Sam, I—"

Nathaniel surged forward, shoving his face inches from mine, trapping me with his gaze. "You will do all I *command*. Stop struggling."

Stronger than any compulsion Derek had used. Different than the queen's power. Nathaniel's compulsion destroyed my fight and free will, effortlessly.

As I went limp, Sam caught me. Adjusting his arm underneath my ribcage, he held me up while his free hand pressed against my forehead, guiding the back of my head to rest along his shoulder.

"I'm sorry," Sam whispered against my ear.

"Are not," I snapped.

Nathaniel's voice barged into my mind. *"Focus, she-beast. I'm about to make you an offer. Act as if you are listening to Derek. You can send me your thoughts. I'll hear them."*

"I need you to think like a vampire, Tessa." Derek stood behind Nathaniel. "I cannot have you worrying about the humans, the wolves…."

"While you showered, your wolf and Derek worked on your escape plan."

"And?" I sent back.

"They believe your love for the wolf will be your death tomorrow." When my eyes narrowed, Nathaniel called me out. *"Don't deny, I can smell your unfallen tears. You care for him. Look at Derek."*

I rolled my gaze up to Derek.

"During the Gathering, the queen will have you accompany her to her throne room."

"How do you know this?"

"The how is irrelevant. It's the why that matters. Shut up and listen. Once in the throne room, you will be turned over to the alpha. He will then turn over your race to the queen. While the hounds attack the council and before you make your Change, she will kill the alpha."

"With Jason dead, the link would be severed. The queen can just sit back and watch me die from my Change."

"No. Not her style. Think, she-beast. I know that it's difficult for your kind." Nathaniel lifted his gaze to Sam. *"Why was your wolf allowed to live this long? To be alone with you?"*

Nathaniel shifted his attention back to me.

"She's going to kill Sam." Memories raced across my mind, striking on each warning sign. When I mentioned us escaping, Sam steered the conversations into pep talks about how I'd survive. From the sadness he constantly tried to hide. Even in the way he touched me. Kissed me. All were distractions away from the truth now stabbing me in the heart.

Sam had known all along.

"Keep a straight face!" Nathaniel's lips flattened. *"After she disposes of the alpha, the queen will slaughter Sam in front of you. At the cusp of your sorrow — "*

"She'll kill me."

"Yes." Not a touch of remorse came with his answer. *"On to the escape plan. I am to erase all your memories of Sam. Thus saving you from becoming broken."*

"Nathaniel," Derek warned. "I gave you the order."

Nathaniel stepped closer, putting us eye-to-eye.

"The humans you see tomorrow—you will not concern yourself about their safety." As each word left Nathaniel's tongue, my eyes grew heavy. "You will have no concern for the werewolves' safety tomorrow..." He shifted back into my mind. "*I offer you a trade. I will spare your memories for a favor. No tricks. No turn of words. I give you my word.*"

"*Why?*" I asked.

"*Though I hate to admit it, we have a similarity —*"

"*Love strengthens our fight.*"

Mutual understanding and fear passed between us. Two polar opposites conspiring against those we loved.

Knowing Sam, he'd try to keep me from attacking the queen and would end up dead. We'd still be in the same predicament. "*Spare my memories and erase me from Sam's, instead.*"

"*Done. Do we have an agreement?*"

"*What's the favor?*"

"Tess." Sam's lips brushed my ear. "You promised me that you will survive."

"*Yes or no?*" Panic consumed Nathaniel's voice. "*Hurry!*"

Sam's breath shuddered against my skin. "No matter who you have to fight or kill, you will live. You will honor your promise. I trust you." He kissed my temple. "Do it, bloodsucker."

Out of time. Desperate. I made the trade. "*Yes.*"

"*Give me your word. Speak out loud the agreement.*"

"I give you, Nathaniel, my word. Sam's memories for a favor."

Power prickled along my skin.

"No," Derek screamed, but it was too late.

A blinding light exploded around Nathaniel, knocking Derek across the room.

"Samuel Lyncourt, do not move," Nathaniel commanded.

Instantly, Sam froze.

With his black-mirrored eyes still locked with my gaze, Nathaniel grabbed my wrist, then dragged a claw across the back of my hand. "Through blood, I bind Tessa Sanders to her word." Under his compulsion, I watched helplessly as Nathaniel sealed his lips to my flesh. Energy swelled around us, pulsing in time to the pulls he took of my blood. Prying his bloody mouth away from my hand, he shot his attention at Sam. The compulsion Nathaniel used squeezed the air from my lungs. "Let her go," he ordered.

Sam dropped me to the floor. Looking up, my gaze connected with the raw fear and betrayal filling Sam's eyes.

"What did you do, Tess?" he gasped.

"Samuel Lyncourt, look at me," Nathaniel commanded, and Sam obeyed. "You will forget Tessa Sanders."

Sam's eyes clouded over and his body went rigid. Then Nathaniel turned his compulsion on me. "Sleep until I wake you," he ordered.

Chapter Twenty-Nine

"Wake up, she-beast." Nathaniel's voice boomed inside my skull while the rest of my body throbbed. Both kept my eyes shut and me playing slug.

Shoving my face into a pillow, I inhaled Sam's scent. Panic crashed into me, but as fast as it hit, numbness shot itself like novocaine into my system. When I struggled against the sensation, a stabbing pain attacked my head. Tracking Nathaniel's whereabouts by his footsteps, I flung the pillow at him. The plop of it hitting the doors signaled I missed.

"Your aim is atrocious."

"Your compulsion is worse," I grumbled.

"Tonight when you are prancing around the ballroom, you'll retract that statement," Nathaniel said.

"I feel...nothing for Sam. How am I to—" I sunk deeper into my numbness, searching for a loophole to Nathaniel's compulsion.

"Really, she-beast. We don't need you exhausting your mind before sunset. If we make it to the throne room, then you can find my deliberately placed gateway within my compulsion to your feelings for your wolf."

Liquid splashed against porcelain, and the bitter aroma of espresso tickled my nose. The promise of caffeine tugged open my puffy eyes.

Avoiding the last rays of sunset with his back facing me, Nathaniel busied himself over a serving cart, loudly tapping a spoon against a mug.

Never had I seen the bloodsucker wearing anything but a three-piece suit. My stomach somersaulted. Cringing, I kept quiet as I gawked at his black tail tuxedo jacket. At the nape of his neck, a blood-red ribbon gathered his blond locks into a thick curl resting between his shoulder blades.

Nathaniel dangled the spoon from his fingertips then dropped it clattering onto the cart. When he turned to face me, I locked my gaze on the golf ball-sized pendant over his heart—a gold replica of the queen's lion necklace.

Looking away from its twinkling ruby eyes, I squinted at the glare of Nathaniel's white, skintight pants he'd tucked into a pair of black, shiny, knee-high boots.

"Here." Nathaniel shoved the mug into my hands.

"Don't want."

"Unless you want to entertain the queen on all fours with a bushy tail, drink," he warned.

Taking a swig of espresso, I propped myself against the headboard. The effort left me breathless and unable to keep the scalding beverage from sloshing onto the sheets.

Pursing his lips, Nathaniel watched me shiver and sweat. "Your Change is, at most, hours away. When

Derek wakes, the blood-bond will strengthen. He'll keep you..." — Nathaniel waved his hand at me — "in this form as long as he can. However, doing so makes Derek...parched."

Nathaniel's gaze lowered to my neck. "He craves your blood. I've caught him staring at your throat."

"Like you're doing?"

Nathaniel snapped his flinty eyes back to my face. "I would rather consume bleach than to drink your blood again."

"Good," I shot back. "The next time you try, you'll be ash."

He chuckled. "Save some of that gusto for the queen."

"What's the favor?"

His grin flattened. "You'll know soon enough."

"I'll settle for that answer, said no reporter ever."

Batting his eyelashes, Nathaniel flashed his fangs. "Precisely why they're *always* the first to die."

He had a point. Two actually. To keep pestering him about the favor I traded for Sam's memories was a waste of time and energy. Inhaling the espresso's vapors, I nailed my mission to the front of my mind — save Sam. Dust the queen. Escape.

Nathaniel snapped his fingers in front of my nose. "Is it that exhausting to think, she-beast?"

"Last night, what happened after you knocked me out?" I asked.

"Anthony took your wolf away." In the pits of Nathaniel's widening pupils, the reflection of my glowing eyes stared back at me. "No harm came to your beast," he said, lowering his gaze to my chin, Nathaniel took a step away from the bed. "He's under compulsion to sleep until he is needed." No sign of Nathaniel's tongue combusting, proving that he spoke some form of truth.

Sniffing, I caught the faint reek of Boss. Derek's scent as well. Another sniff and I pinpointed Derek's. Shoving my nose against my shoulder, his scent filled my nostrils. "Derek touched me."

"Well, you did not float onto the bed."

Pulling away, I glanced at my damp hair stuck to my shoulder. "He touched my hair."

Nathaniel's attention latched on to the mug shaking in my hands. "That I missed."

"You left me alone with Derek?" I rubbed my neck, feeling for puncture marks.

"No. I counted cracks in the windowsill paint. Eons better than watching Derek stand guard at your bedside." Bitterness tightened Nathaniel's voice. "Over three centuries, never has Derek cared for someone, animal or thing…" Raising his cold blue eyes to mine, Nathaniel whispered, "Until you. His final death."

"Derek's not going…." Unable to utter the false sense of hope, my voice trailed off.

"Hundreds of vampires. A couple hundred armed guards. A hundred or more moon-crazed wolves. A psychopathic queen bent on world domination." Looking me up and down, Nathaniel smirked. "One little self-doubting she-beast to save us all."

At his slap of reality, I shoved the mug to my mouth and chugged the espresso.

Nathaniel used my distraction for a conversational rewind. "Tonight, pay mind to the wolf below your flesh. Stay away from windows. Eat when hungry. Think pleasant thoughts when you lose your temper."

"I'll be rubbing wrists with bloodsuckers. No whimsical thoughts of pink unicorns will give me the warm-n-fuzzies. Wait." I perked up. "Adorable unicorns impaling vampires with their horns. Yes. I can work with that."

Nathaniel pinched the bridge of his nose. "May fate show mercy and see us to sunrise."

Outside, tires and footfalls crunched on the stone driveway. Between the curtain folds, the last crimson rays of dusk slipped inside the room. It was too soon for the rest of the vampire population to be out and about.

"Your *refreshments* have arrived," I muttered.

"No. These mortals have the daunting task of last-minute arrangements." Nathaniel took the mug from me, setting it on the cart. "No more delays. Get up."

"I…" My heart kicked into my throat, tightening my voice. "I need more time."

Nathaniel clicked his tongue as he cocked his head at me. "I'm going to need hours to prepare you. Thankfully, Derek takes as long as a monarch from the seventeenth century to get ready for a formal event."

Guards marching down the hallway set Nathaniel's blank face in place. He turned and crossed the room. When knuckles tapped on the doors, Nathaniel opened them enough to snatch a garment bag from a guard. After the doors closed, he spun toward me, holding the bag draped across his arms. A sliver of hunter-green satin peeked out from the bottom.

"What's that?" I asked softly.

"Your armor."

Wiping the cold sweat from my forehead, I attempted to calculate how many steps it would take for me to make it to the windows then launch myself out.

"Go bathe, she-beast." The firmness in his voice was a precursor for the compulsion to come if I didn't obey.

As I swayed to the bathroom, Nathaniel called out, "Fifteen steps."

Resting against the cold doorframe, I sighed from the relief it gave to my feverish skin. "What?"

"To the windows." Nathaniel's eyes held a weary calmness. "Five hundred to the maze. Seven hundred to the forest. Twelve thousand to the road beyond."

Without hesitating, I asked, "How many to the ballroom?"

"A perilous journey." He forced a grin. "Hurry now. Fate waits for no one."

* * * *

For two hours, Nathaniel and a small army of human attendants fussed over me, while outside, an endless caravan of vehicles dropped off guests. Floors below, an orchestra, skilled beyond measure—likely vampires—played.

The current piece dancing through my ears was Mozart's *Lacrimosa*.

Epically fitting.

After one last adjustment to my hunter-green headband, Nathaniel took a step back. Putting his hands on his hips, he nodded. "Done."

Curious to see what all Nathaniel's cursing and fidgeting had produced, I sat still as an attendant cautiously approached the backside of the vanity, tugging off the sheet draped over the mirror.

"Whoa." I didn't recognize myself. Dark-gold smokey eyeshadow brought out the gold flecks in my green eyes, while a blood-red lip gloss accentuated my ivory skin. Thankfully, Nathaniel had decided on a down hairdo of curls. The vampires would have to fight with my locks to get to my neck. The headband's inlaid pea-sized diamonds shimmered with the slightest movement.

"No touching." Nathaniel slapped my gloved hand away from a loose curl. Clapping his hands, he dismissed the humans. Eager to oblige, they hurried to gather the suitcase-sized makeup containers, then zipped out of the room.

Stealing another look at my reflection, I tugged up the strapless corset which showcased more cleavage than I was comfortable with. Once again, my hand was slapped away.

Before Nathaniel lost a finger, I took a deep breath, as much as the corset allowed, and shut my eyes, thinking back to the costume Andrea had brought for me to wear at Oblivion. I had been able to dodge the corset then. Opening my eyes, I blinked back tears as I imagined her grinning at me all dolled up.

Nathaniel draped a hanky over my shoulder. "Werewolves. One instant, rage. The next, sobbing."

Smiling, I corrected, "Nope. That's me in general."

Ignoring the hanky, I gathered the ball gown's skirt of cascading ruffles. The pull of the blood-bond signaled that Derek was nearing the room.

Nathaniel slapped his hands on my shoulders, keeping me seated. "What are you doing?"

"Derek's here. Time to go."

"No." Looking over his shoulder, he swore in French. "Stay." Spinning around, he rummaged through the piles of boxes left behind by the attendants.

Dread clung to me more tightly than the corset. I glanced down. Perspiration had already dampened the palms of my opera-length gloves. At least that was what Nathaniel had called the gloves as he tugged them on. To me, they were false artery guards. Fangs could tear through bone. During the queen's throne room demonstration, she had made sure I knew that.

"What if I fail?" I whispered.

"You won't," Derek answered.

I snapped my head up. My breath exploded from my mouth with a pop. Tall, dark and freaking handsome stood before me. With no shame, I devoured Derek with my eyes. Although Nathaniel wore an identical ensemble, Derek owned it. Except for the lion pendant. Instead of ripping the queen's emblem off his chest, I clenched a skirt ruffle resting on my thigh.

Trapping me with the intensity of his gaze, Derek knelt in front of me. "You are stunning, Tessa Sanders." His voice sent goosebumps screaming across my flesh and made my blood boil. "However, we cannot have you walking around barefoot."

As something cold touched the sole of my foot, I felt myself nod.

"The shoes!" Nathaniel tried to barge his way back in front of me. "Let me."

"I am capable." Lifting my foot, then resting it on his thigh, Derek fastened the shoe buckle around my ankle.

Unable to decipher which snapped me out of my swooning state, either the amount of my bare leg I flashed Derek or the three-inch ankle-breaker he strapped me into, I tried to tug free of his hand. "No. This is not happening."

Both vampires narrowed their eyes at me.

"You missed that opportunity hours ago, she-beast," Nathaniel muttered at me. Then he filled Derek in. "I hinted at a trip out the window."

When Derek shot a glare at him, Nathaniel shrugged his shoulders.

Once Derek locked my other foot into its shoe, I shoved my skirt into place.

"The heels," I said. "I'm a klutz."

Both bloodsuckers blinked at me.

"I'll be kissing the floor with my first step." At the confused looks cemented to their faces, I sighed. "How am I to fight the queen if I can't even walk?"

Derek extended his hand to me. "You will hold on to me."

When I slapped mine into his, he slowly lifted me to my feet. Derek pulled me against the length of his body when I wobbled. A slight tilt of his chin brought our lips dangerously close. At the caress of his chilled breath, the sweetness of blood rolled across the tip of my tongue, setting my pulse to beat wildly at my eardrums.

"War. Mutiny. Destruction. That is our agenda." Nathaniel grabbed me around the waist, jerking me free from Derek. Then Nathaniel pulled his disappearing act, which landed us in the empty hallway. "Googly eyes. No. Hell. No."

Derek emerged from the room with a red smudge on the collar of his shirt. As he made a beeline for me, his stare fastened onto my mouth.

I licked my bottom lip. Microfibers from his shirt stuck to my tongue.

Nathaniel sidestepped in front of Derek.

Overly careful not to plow into Nathaniel, Derek jarred to a stop. His attention wavered from me to Nathaniel. Hurt-anger-regret flashed across his face. Something catastrophic had gone down between the two bloodsuckers while I was unconscious.

Nathaniel fished the tube of lipstick out from his tux. Avoiding eye contact with Derek, he jabbed a finger in Derek's direction. "You, clean yourself off."

When Derek disappeared into the room, Nathaniel reapplied my lipstick. "You will have us all killed before we are even down the stairs. Derek belongs to the queen. Don't play with her toys."

Inside my head, a comeback floated somewhere behind a wicked daydream of my lips painting-by-numbers all over Derek's face. To ground myself, I took a deep breath and drew in Derek's scent. Shuddering, I grabbed onto Nathaniel's shoulders. "This is not my Change. Why am I...."

"The attraction is from the blood-bond," Derek answered. "I'll be more cautious."

Not trusting myself, I kept a death grip on Nathaniel. "It'll go away after I Change, right?"

Silence.

"Right?" I repeated.

"Correct," Derek answered as he moved to my side.

"Good." As my hormones settled down, I let go of Nathaniel. As I rolled my shoulders and readjusted my skirt, my vision tunneled onto the staircase. "Let's do this."

While Derek offered me his arm, Nathaniel moved to my back. All the Vampire 101 lessons spun through my head as we clomped down empty hallways and staircases. I knew if I bombed this monster exam, an *F* wouldn't just stand for fail. It also meant feed, as in Tessa for dinner.

A red glow from the rubies on Derek's pendant caught my attention. Taking note of what I was looking at, he brought his free hand up to the lion. "All the queen's vampires will be wearing this over their hearts.

Each council member will have their own set of vampire guards, who will wear a similar pendant over their hearts. The pendant symbolizes their tie and loyalty to their council member."

I mentally filed that tidbit next to the lesson about not moving away when a council member sniffed me.

At the top of the grand staircase, we paused. Fresh air crawled up the steps, snaking around my ankles and flooding my nose with the stench of vampire. A heady shot of terror raced through my veins and triggered the fever of my Change. Digging my fingers against Derek's arm, I shivered as sweat rolled down my neck, gathering between my breasts and turning the corset's hunter-green fabric black.

Sending me a dose of the blood-bond, Derek held tightly to my arm with his expressionless façade in place. I could've bet my diamond headband that, behind me, Nathaniel wore the same mask.

With the blood-bond's numbing effect washing through me, we descended the staircase. Overhead, the illuminated twelve-tiered chandelier spun prisms across the marble floor. My first step was more of a slide. Nathaniel grumbled while Derek righted me. With slow, precise steps, we headed away from the throne room and toward the estate's main entrance.

Derek's eyes darkened as they looked into mine. "Do not let go of me for any reason. If you do, grab onto Nathaniel. No talking."

Four of the queen's vampires stood at the entrance. Avoiding eye contact, I glanced around their tuxedo-clad bodies. Hundreds of exotic cars lined the cobblestone driveway that continued down a hill, then dipped out of sight behind a stone wall and an iron gate.

With a tug on my arm, Derek got me moving toward a set of massive wooden doors guarded by two more of the queen's bloodsuckers. Keeping my gaze at their shoulders, I froze as they reached for the bronze handles.

Chapter Thirty

Blinded by light. Choked by panic. Paralyzed by fear. Derek granted me a speck of kindness by letting me adjust to the glass-walled battlefield. From marble floor to cathedral ceiling stretched a wall of crystal-clear windows. Three enormous bronze chandeliers reflected light off the windowpanes, giving the illusion of an endless dance floor.

Though I was unable to see the moon, my skin heated with its phantom touch and its song muted the orchestra playing on a raised stage, to the left of our trio.

Nathaniel shoved a finger against my back, pushing me to the edge of the dancefloor. "Get her to the balcony."

Beyond the dancing sea of tuxes and ballgowns rose a grand staircase that led to an overlooking balcony. Derek's chilled lips brushed my ear. "That is where the queen will make her entrance. She requests you to be with her when she addresses her guests."

Behind the balcony, two of the queen's guards opened a set of doors. "Look at that huge, almost vacant entrance." I glared at Derek. "Why are you dragging me through a room stuffed with vampires?"

"What part of 'no talking' do you not understand?" Nathaniel muttered.

"It is the queen's desire for you to mingle with her guests." Derek tugged me onward. "Seal your lips. Please."

My legs refused to move me further into the bloodsucker deathtrap. Underneath exotic perfumes and colognes, their fresh-turned-earth scents filled the air. My estimated count came in at four hundred vampires.

No amount of Dolce and Gabbana could camouflage the hundred or so humans amongst the bloodsuckers. Sweat glistened on their foreheads as they danced with toddler-like grace compared to the gravity-defying vampires. None noticed the danger encroaching around them.

As my gaze lingered on the humans, hunger knotted my stomach.

"Do not fear for the humans' safety." Nathaniel's compulsion drifted into my head. Out of the corner of my eye, amusement escaped from his emotionless face. *"No eating the guests, she-beast."*

Forcing myself to see a person, not dinner, I concentrated on their faces. A plump one caught my undivided attention. Tim McKay sipped from a brandy snifter as his gaze roamed over the crowd. A group of humans with puffed-out chests vied for his attention. Some by laughing the loudest, others by standing the tallest. A woman attempted to thrust her boob job into his field of vision. Still, his beady eyes wandered past her breasts.

As Tim looked in our direction, I broke vampire etiquette and glanced at my skirt. Since he had only met me once, I was confident he'd not recognize my ducked head. Behind me, Nathaniel pressed the heel of his hand against the small of my back, shoving me forward.

When I snapped my head up, Tim was gone. In his vacant spot stood a vampire right out of the romantic era. Unsuccessfully, I struggled to tear my gaze away from the violet-eyed monster. When I zeroed in on the tuft of lace at his throat, dizziness spun through my head. A deep breath did nothing to correct my equilibrium. Instead, an intoxicating vibration ran along my spine, urging me forward.

"Tessa." Cupping my face in between his hands, Derek forced me to look into his eyes. "See only me."

The blood-bond coursed through my mind, bringing me back to the present. Halfway across the room, I spotted the doors. Within a fraction of a second, somehow, we were smack in the middle of the ballroom.

Derek answered my unasked question. "Compulsion."

Someone's skirt brushed against mine while a throaty chuckle to the left sent my heart slamming against my rib cage.

"No," I uttered. "No. No—"

"Hush." Brushing his cheek against mine, Derek whispered, "Hear only me."

Closing my eyes, I focused solely on everything Derek. From his voice to the way his scent flooded my nose. Allowing myself to be consumed with the touch of his fingers trailing down the sides of my neck, sliding across my collarbone, then tracing my silhouette to where he grasped onto the swell of my hips.

"Hold on to me." Gathering me tightly to him, Derek clasped one of my hands to his chest while working one of his legs between mine.

Memory blended with the present. Eons ago, Derek had entranced me on Oblivion's beer-slick dance floor while werewolves and vampires surrounded us. To keep from falling, I wrapped my free arm around his shoulder, curling my fingers against the back of his neck. What started as rocking morphed into a sway. Then in one graceful step, Derek led me in a waltz.

Further catching me off guard, he opened the blood-bond and a tidal wave of emotions rolled through me. Desire. Annoyance. Strongest of all…fear.

Once more, his lips brushed my ear. "Behind the staircase, there is a hallway the human servants use to enter and exit the kitchen. On the far wall, there are three freezers. The one to the left is a trapdoor. No amount of human strength can open it." Dipping his forehead to mine, Derek captured my gaze. "You could. You always could."

"Always? I—"

"Your inner strength. In the park when you bit my hand, I saw it in your eyes. I knew *then* that you were the fool that would finally challenge the queen."

"So, I'm your golden ticket to freedom." I tried to jerk away, but Derek held firm.

"That *was* all you were." He drew me closer, pressing his forehead to mine. "At the bar, when you pressed your hands against me, branding me with the challenge in your eyes…at that moment, my freedom became an afterthought."

I went to question, but his lips grazed my cheek. Arousal hummed through my body, robbing me of speech.

"I crave your challenge. Your fight," he whispered. "I desire the fear you awaken within me." At the brush of Derek's lips nearing my trembling mouth, I froze. My heartbeat hammered at my ears. My throat clenched the air between us. Struggling to focus on the words slipping from his mouth, I latched my gaze to his intense stare. "All that has been thrown upon you, yet you still stand. Your strength intensifies my fear. Last night, you asked why I fear you." Derek's eyes darkened. "You don't know what you are capable of. That is why I fear you, Tessa."

I parted my lips to protest, but he kissed me. Soft at first. Tentative. Then all-consuming. Never breaking eye contact, we challenged each other. Daring the other to sever or continue until my lungs screamed for air. When I shuddered my exhale against his mouth, he tensed.

Behind me, Nathaniel demanded, "What are you doing?"

"Let them fight. Let them die." Ignoring Nathaniel, Derek looked again into my eyes. "Let me save you."

"No." Shaking my head, I reaffirmed my decision. "I need to do this. For Andrea. Sam."

"You will die." Derek's jaw tightened. "I should have killed you in the park."

"You didn't, though." I kept right where I was, looking straight into the hate burning within his eyes. "For your sick, twisted, messed-up desire, you kept me alive." My throat tightened, forcing my voice into a clenched whisper, "Be pissed, Derek. You've had your chances to kill me. You were just too scared to take them."

Derek abruptly spun me out of his embrace and faced me toward the chest of a vampire. Over the bloodsucker's heart rested a gold pendant of two snakes entwined. "Hector." Derek kept hold of my hand while he bowed from the waist.

"Such an honor you have this evening, hunter." Lust wove harmoniously through Hector's rich European accent. "I've not been able to keep my eyes off this exquisite creature."

Keeping my vision glued to Hector's pendant, I bit my lip to remain silent.

Derek rose.

"Hector." Nathaniel moved to my side then bowed.

"Nathaniel, it is always a pleasure. I do miss our conversations."

Count Dracula likes Nathaniel. Wonderful.

"Good evening, Wolf Born."

Hector's voice courted arousal, and my mind went blank. Desperately, I scrambled to remember how I should address a council member while Derek stayed quiet and tense, giving me no lead or hints on what to do.

"You may look me in the eyes," Hector replied.

Well, that was a creepy coincidence. As soon as the thought floated from my brain, I felt the familiar sensation of a vampire inside my mind. *"Get out of my head. Please,"* I sent.

"As you wish." Seamlessly, Hector withdrew from my mind. "Now, let me see into your eyes." His tone turned to a persuasive look-at-me-or-die. "I grow impatient."

Jet-black hair framed his masculine face perfectly. Gazing into Hector's violet eyes, *anyone* would sink to the floor in a panting puddle of desire. I looked away before I became a victim.

"She is beautiful. The legend of the Wolf Born is true on that account. I await to see if all else is true." He extended his hand toward me. The ballroom fell silent.

All watched as Hector greeted me. My pulse leaped to escape from his thumb's caress. Even through my glove, his touch hummed with power.

Hundreds of bloodsuckers drew closer. Each waiting for their turn to terrorize me. Perhaps, if I was unfazed by Hector, the rest would grow bored and go back to their box stepping. When Hector's hand tightened around my wrist, I met his gaze with courage.

Wrong. Stupid. Freaking dumb.

"Your fierceness enchants me." He grinned. The tips of his pearl-white fangs gleamed at me. Drawing me closer, he spoke to Derek. "Release her."

Without letting go, Derek moved his hold to my forearm. "Queen's orders are for me to protect her guest."

"Did *your* queen ask you to kiss her guest?" Brushing my hair over my shoulder to expose my neck, Hector lowered his lips, placing a soft, lingering kiss at my jugular. "No. I think not." When he inhaled over my skin, his breath sent licks of pleasure through my blood. Fangs replaced lips, raking their way along my neck before Hector pulled away. "Keep her safe, hunter."

"As the queen demands," Derek answered.

"Save a dance for me, Wolf Born." With a devilish smile, Hector drew away, allowing the sea of waiting vampires to consume him.

Rigid next to me, Derek and Nathaniel spoke mind to mind. Focusing out toward the mob of vampires, similar energy rose over their heads. Unable to eavesdrop on any of the conversations, I relied on their subtle physical cues. Black-mirrored eyes, elongating fangs...there were a whole lot of hungry vampires glaring at me.

Trumpets blared.

Tugging me behind him, Derek made a break for the staircase, plowing through the dispersing crowd while Nathaniel circled an arm around my waist, correcting all my stumbles, practically carrying me up the steps. As we made it to the balcony, the pounding of drums rattled my chattering teeth.

Releasing me, Nathaniel narrowed his eyes at Derek, who was rubbing away the evidence of our kiss against the sleeve of his jacket.

A slight tremor came from Derek's hand clamping my forearm. Bringing up my free hand, I rested my fingertips over his knuckles. Thankfully, he loosened his hold and blood raced to my oxygen-deprived limb.

Feeling Nathaniel's glare, I raised my eyes to his. Jealousy burned through his hate. Then a temporary resolve flickered through his stare. *"When the queen enters, kneel. Do not rise until she gives permission."*

Tipping my chin, I placed my attention on the doors. *"She-beast?"*

"What?"

"After you Change, I'm going to kill you."

"What about the favor?"

"Oh. I'll collect the favor, before."

After slamming my mental door on Nathaniel, I suffered through minutes of intro music until the doors opened and the queen delivered on her grand entrance.

A gentle tug on my arm helped me, willingly, to my knees. From my vantage point, I had a clear view of the ballroom. Hundreds had taken to their knees. Only twenty-eight bloodsuckers remained standing. Among them was Hector. As I studied the council members, movement at the main entrance caught my attention. Not a vampire. No. A human stood not bowing.

Tim McKay.

As the queen made her way toward us, Tim slipped through the closing doors. I returned my attention to the balcony's marble floor. The hem of her blood-red silk gown rested on the tips of my fingers. I kept my head bowed while an eternity passed before she continued to the center of the balcony. The train of the dress slid across my fingers. In its center, golden threads wove into a lifelike portrait of the head of a roaring lion while a pair of lime-sized rubies formed the beast's eyes.

Behind the queen entered a dozen of her vampires. Since her back was to me, I stole a peek at the guards' feet as they lined up, barricading the exit. The reek of stale blood coated their shoes.

Soon, the sweet aroma of fresh blood would fill the air. How much or how little all depended on me. Bile burned the back of my throat while visions of Glenwood's charred buildings and blood-slick streets played havoc on my mind.

Carefully, Derek lifted me to my feet. Escorting me five reluctant steps, he then stopped us a foot away from the queen's left side. With one last squeeze to my arm, he released me and sank to his knees, bowing his head.

Ignoring me, the queen's attention drifted across the bowed heads below. A smile curved her crimson lips as her eyes fluttered closed.

While she relished her power-high, I collected my nerves, letting the wolf within size up our competition just as it had done with Sam in the closet. A ruby-encrusted crown of gold encircled her head. Thick braids of her ebony hair rose from the crown's center, scaling its foot-tall, golden prongs. The hairdo's faintest vibration hinted at the consistent drain on the queen's stamina for maintaining her perfect posture.

Her lion pendant sent a red hue across her alabaster flesh, catching my attention. The hideous thing's chain dug into her neck, weighing enough to press upon her full breasts. Even with her agility, the pendant would affect her balance. Speed would also be compromised. The queen's strapless gown clung to her body as if she had been dipped into a pool of blood.

When the queen lifted her hand, the music ceased. Lowering her hand, she scanned the crowd, making eye contact with each of the council members. Then, in all her vileness, she turned to face me.

My focus landed on her glossy lips. Wet lips. Blood-covered lips.

"Sheep, you look…" She moved closer, smiling. "Frightened."

Gently, she brushed my hair over my shoulder.

Hands to my sides. Back straight. Teeth biting my cheeks. I stood still.

"They taught you well." Her breath rolled across her lips, flooding my nose with the blend of cinnamon and copper. "I tire of formalities. Greet me as if we were *best of friends.*"

From its scent to her strategic selection of words, I knew Andrea's blood decorated the queen's lips. Tearing my gaze away from her mouth, I glared into the queen's eyes.

"You will" — she dropped her voice to an airy whisper, tilting her mouth to mine — "greet me."

The rustle of Derek's clothing drove me forward. I wouldn't have his blood added to Andrea's. Pressing my mouth against the queen's, I whimpered at the silken wetness of my friend's blood coating my lips.

Grasping the back of my head, the queen pulled me tight to her. Taking over, she forced my lips apart with her cold tongue. Wanting nothing more than to shove her away and dry heave, I allowed her entrance. As she glided her blood-laced tongue across mine, there was no escaping the taste of Andrea's death.

Tears stung my eyes as a sob burst from my throat.

Slowly, the queen withdrew, licking my upper lip.

"Your weeping is lovely, sheep. A worthy redemption for your pathetic kiss." Releasing me, she glared at Derek's bowed head before returning her attention to the ballroom. "Rise, my guests."

All stood.

"Enjoy yourselves. I look forward to conversations and the honor of entertaining you all." Short and to the point. When she turned away from the room, the music began again. "Come, sheep."

When she continued to the doors, the guards filtered around us in a horseshoe formation, forcing us to follow the queen.

As I went to rub Andrea's blood from my lips, Derek grabbed my wrist. "Don't."

"Please do, sheep," the queen called over her shoulder. "I have a vial filled with your dead human's blood. Nothing would please me more than to taste your sorrow again."

Once the queen slipped from the ballroom's view, she dropped her regal act. She sped down the empty hallway with purpose.

Through the hall's staggered windows, moonbeams spotlighted the narrow passageway. Each time I crossed through a patch of light, my flesh heated and my ears pulsed with the moon song. Every one of my missteps and rolled ankles sent me slamming against Derek while Nathaniel pushed me from behind.

Ahead, the hallway ended in a descending spiral staircase. Plunged into total darkness, sandwiched between vampires, my harsh exhale ricocheted off the walls.

Below, a door opened. Candlelight illuminated the stairwell. From the room beyond, a mixture of scents crawled upwards, sandalwood, pine, sweat and fear.

Holding my breath, I willed myself to strike out the scent that dominated them all. Fresh blood. Sam's blood.

Chapter Thirty-One

We entered the throne room through the side passage that the senior citizen from Hell had used the night Miller and James were murdered.

Like a metronome, the grandfather clock ticked in time to our footsteps while thousands of white candles flickered in a variety of silver candelabras fashioned in a circular pattern around the room. In the center of the halo of fire stood the throne.

Shifting to my side, Derek did his best to shield me from the candelabras. Still, my exposed skin reddened from the amount of silver inside the room. However alarming being burned alive was, the intensity of Sam's blood hanging in the air was worse.

Hunger hijacked my vision, pinpointing the source of the sweet aroma. A floor runner of Sam's blood ran the length of the room from the main sealed entrance doors and ended at the base of the throne steps, where he lay sprawled out and unconscious.

Swollen burn-blisters and a film of coagulated blood left Sam's face unrecognizable. Deep-plum bruises, in the shape and size of a fist, covered his ribs and stomach. Blood drooled from the junctures at his forearms, sliced to the bone.

Rage should've stirred within me, revving me into action to help Sam. Yet the numbness from Nathaniel's compulsion kept me at Derek's side.

"I believe she is in a state of shock." The queen waited until I gave her my full attention. "Rest your mind," she cooed. "I won't deny you from partaking in his death." Her focus moved to the guards. "Take a stance."

Obediently, they formed a vampire corral the length of the throne room. Hands fisted at their sides, jaws tight and bodies humming with hunger, the guards kept a forced watch at the main entrance doors.

A brisk whisper from the queen to her nearest guard, and he bowed. Then he moved to the serving cart positioned against the wall across from our group.

"Food, drink, dress and jewels." Lowering herself onto her throne, she spoke to me while her gaze fell to the cart the guard rolled past. "Tell me how unpleasant my hospitality is compared to what awaits you."

Once the guard stepped away and retreated to his prior position, Nathaniel and Derek ushered me to the cart. A syringe filled with an amber-colored liquid sat next to a coil of chains thick enough to restrain an elephant.

Dragging my gaze away from the cart to her lips coated with Andrea's blood, I answered, "Anything is better than kissing you."

The corner of her mouth twitched. "Nathaniel."

In a fluid motion, he grabbed the syringe and plunged it into my jugular. A pinch, then liquid fire tore through my body. Numbness wove through my limbs while simultaneously Nathaniel yanked free the needle, and Derek caught me.

"Continue with the preparations." The queen's voice cut through the drugs. "Undress her, hunter."

"Is this necessary?" Derek asked.

"You *dare* question me?" she snapped. "Nathaniel."

"No." Stopping Nathaniel mid-reach for me, Derek growled, "I'll do it." Guiding my face to rest against his chest, Derek's stiff fingers fumbled with the lacing at the back of my corset.

Allowing the drugs to further enable his progress, I collapsed to my knees. Unable to crawl with my noodle arms, dropping to my belly, I wiggled away from Derek.

Behind us, metal clicked against the floor.

"No need for the chains, Nathaniel. You practiced too much caution with the tranquilizer. Look at the pathetic creature." The queen chuckled. "Like a worm writhing beneath a sparrow." Cutting her laughter, her voice hardened. "I'll not tell you again."

Grabbing ahold of the corset, Derek jerked me to my hands and knees. Then he leaned over me. "I'm sorry."

"Liar. Liar," I stated, bitterly adding, "tongue on fire."

"For not killing you," he whispered.

When I cranked my head over my shoulder, through the combination of drugs and tears blurring my vision, by the scent of his fear, from the stillness of his hands to the rush of his breath, Derek showed me the truth of his apology.

"Send in the alpha," the queen ordered.

At the click of the door locks, Derek's grip lessened.

My impaired vision buffered the finer details of Jason barging through the doors. Still, his wild blond hair and the disheveled, blood-drenched tux covering his heaving bulk tipped off his agitated state.

"Alpha." The queen's use of his prized title lurched Jason to a stop. "Naked, chained and drugged is how your kind keeps the Wolf Born. Correct?"

Ignoring the queen, he spoke at me. "On your hands and knees. Crying before your enemies. You will pay for your disgrace." Jason jabbed his finger at the floor in front of him. "Come."

"Nathaniel and hunter, guard my sheep," the queen ordered.

With their claws drawn, Derek and Nathaniel stood at my sides.

Stretching out his arms, Jason bared his broad chest toward the queen. "Afraid of me, vampire?"

The queen's glare smoldered. "Guards, leave us."

With their exit, Jason stood unfazed as the fang-baring guards passed inches from his outstretched fingertips. When the doors closed, Jason lowered his arms. "Those two sticking around to powder your ass?"

Ignoring Jason, the queen ticked her chin at Sam. "The animal barely lives."

"Bastard got soft." Jason obnoxiously pulled air through his nostrils. "Smells good. Doesn't it, Red?"

"No," I snapped at his blurry mug.

"Tranquilizer won't last long," Jason said. "A couple of minutes." The link stirred between us, clearing my vision, and a knowing grin pulled his split lip back from his bloodstained teeth. "Then…" Pointing in the direction of Sam, Jason paused. When I refused to drop eye contact, Jason's stare intensified. "Liver is the tastiest part. On the right side of his belly."

"Not until the blood oath is sated," the queen interrupted. "Swear the wolves to me, Alpha."

Tipping his chin, lowering his eyes, Jason muttered, "I swear —"

"No." She cut him off. "Kneel."

"I bow to no one," Jason snarled. "I am alpha."

"Indeed." She leaned forward. "Leader of the fools. Commander to the weak. Ruler amongst the enslaved."

"Get your head out of your bony ass." His eyes flashed. "Listen."

I narrowed my hearing past the ticking clock. Outside, hundreds of feet hammered the earth, nearing the estate.

"We surround you." When he stepped right to the barrier of the candelabras, Jason's face reddened and blistered. Not one flinch or hitch of breath wavered his voice. "Your spies following my pack these past weeks. Exterminated."

"You gave blood oath," the queen said over Jason. "Without my protection, your race will die tonight."

"Your vampires bordering the forest," Jason drawled. "Exterminated."

"Guards," she hissed. "Guards!"

Jason waited until the echo of her shout dissipated before he whispered, "Exterminated."

A solid knock at the doors ceased their verbal battle.

Seconds passed before the queen pulled her focus away from Jason to the doors. With her face expressionless, she sat pin straight. "Enter."

Shadows masked the identity of the short sword-bearing man as he slipped inside the throne room. Not bothering to turn and see who entered, Jason took a few steps backward. Away from the silver, his burns faded. Derek and Nathaniel ceased breathing, focusing all their attention on the approaching stranger, whose stagnant water scent engulfed the room.

Candlelight illuminated Tim McKay's flushed face when he stopped beside Jason. A coating of vampire ash clung to the contours of his tux while blood dripped from the sword he held at his side. Although Jason physically dwarfed Tim, the authority Tim possessed knocked Jason down a few pegs on the bad guy ledger.

Lifting her dainty nose, the queen drew in Tim's marsh scent. "State your purpose, troll."

"Korrigan," Tim corrected. Grinding the tip of the sword against the carpet, Tim leveled his stare at me. "I offer a trade."

"You have *nothing* I desire. My sheep informed me of your meddling with the city's water, Mr. McKay." She relaxed against her throne. "Your stench confirms your part."

"Surprising," he mumbled. "Honestly, Ms. Sanders. You are the *worst* reporter. I left you alone in my office with my desktop calendar. Made sure that you had a front seat to my soirée at the park. You had one job, Ms. Sanders." Tim's face soured. "One."

Masking my growing strength, I faked a tremble through my voice. "You *wanted* me to expose you?"

"Wrong," Tim said. "I wanted you to die."

"Why?" Derek asked.

"Speak without my permission, and I will silence you permanently, hunter." The queen's power snapped against my flesh with her threat. "What do you gain by her death?" she asked Tim.

"Currently..." Pausing, he looked at the ceiling, muttering a two-sided conversation to himself. "Yes?

No. Maybe? Agreed. For now, Ms. Sanders lives."

The queen tapped her fingernail against the armrest of her throne. "Her death at the park served you how, troll?"

"Korrigan." Returning his attention to the queen, Tim's grip tightened around the hilt of his sword. "Before I knew Ms. Sanders was the Wolf Born, she was a prop. A pretty reporter, torn apart by werewolves, grasping a phone with a couple of my pictures, makes one hell of a calling card for a vampire queen." He raised his voice at Jason. "But werewolves think with their stomachs, attacking the first human they see. Seems your hunter does, too," Tim mused. "Blood was pouring from Ms. Sanders's neck when she emerged from that tunnel."

"Humans bleed easy," the queen said.

"Two puncture marks in a throat does tend to spill blood." Tim nodded. "I've been pondering over that evening. The deliberate avoidance of serious irony on your hunter's part by saving the Wolf Born from being eaten by the werewolves." Shifting his attention to Derek, Tim asked, "Why did you offer her, your sworn enemy, protection?"

"Do not address my servant." The tremor in the queen's voice triggered a grin from Tim.

"Oh. You did not know, your highness?" He smirked. "I'll wait while you ask him."

A slow exhale passed her lips. "The trade?"

"Getting down to business. I respect that." Using his free hand, Tim unfastened the button of his tux jacket. Below, his dress shirt stretched taut over his gut. Stuffing his index finger into his breast pocket, he retrieved a rectangular plastic object. "Wolf Born, pretend you're still a reporter. Inform the queen what this is."

"A zip drive." Her blank stare prompted me to continue. "It stores information. No—"

Raising his eyebrow, Tim twirled the zip drive between his thumb and index finger. "Keep going."

"It stores files…." Stalling out loud, I sent Nathaniel, *"The list of Glenwood's half-bloods is on that zip drive."*

"Are you certain?" Nathaniel asked.

"Tsk-tsk," Tim interrupted. "Share with the room, Ms. Sanders." Tapping the zip drive against his temple, he ratted us out to the queen. "Telepathy between her and the half-blood vampire."

The queen's eyes drew to slits. "I don't recall a troll's ability to use mind speech."

"Korrigan." Air whistled through his flared nostrils while Tim molded himself into his good-ole-boy persona. "It's my pleasure to educate you."

The sick power the queen had used to strangle James rolled from her body, snaking itself around my skull and constricting. Gripping my head, I squinted at her.

"I will kill you," she warned. "What is in that *thing* he holds?"

"A list." Blood trickled from my nose to my lips. Hunger joined the queen's mental assault, stabbing me in the gut. "Half-bloods."

"Give that girl the Pulitzer Prize." Tim tossed the zip drive onto the queen's lap.

With everyone's attention on the zip drive, Tim charged Derek faster than a vampire, hurling him at Jason.

Driving his claws into Derek's throat, Jason pinned Derek to the floor. The slightest of struggles and Derek would decapitate himself.

Cold metal pressed against the back of my neck, forcing me flat on the floor.

"Don't move," Tim said under his breath.

My position gave me an unobstructed view of Sam. Sweat beaded across his furrowed brow while shallow, yet controlled breaths passed between his elongating fangs.

"Well." Tapping the blade against where Nathaniel had injected me, Tim smirked. "Someone got needle happy."

Silence.

"Come on, Queen. Does Ms. Sanders appear the type who needs subduing?" Sliding the sword to rest against the base of my neck, Tim sighed. "Then again, I overestimated you."

"You mock me?" the queen asked.

"No," Tim answered. "You're doing an impeccable job yourself." Simultaneously, he kept the pressure on his sword while shifting his weight.

Thump.

The queen gasped.

I strained my peripheral vision to the base of the throne. A rivulet of black blood rolled down the steps.

"Half-blood, chain your queen. Careful around that dagger sticking out of her chest," Tim warned. "You dust your queen, the hunter follows."

"You think chains can bind me?" Her voice shook. "I will destroy you."

Instantly, her power retracted from around my head.

"Queen, keep your vampire voodoo to yourself. Let me remind you, there are twenty-nine council members," Tim stated. "I only need one. Do you want that crown to rest upon a pile of your ashes?"

Tick. Tick. Tick. The clock counted the tense-filled seconds.

"No," the queen answered.

"Smart," Tim chirped. "Nice and tight."

Chains clattered against the throne as Nathaniel worked in silence.

"If you could see the looks on their faces," Tim spoke to me. "I'll summarize. Queen is stone-faced. Yet I see defeat burning in her red eyes. Alpha wants a piece of you. The hunter wants a piece of me. Half-blood wants the whole bloody alpha. Interesting."

"My packs grow restless," Jason growled.

"My packs," Tim corrected. "You needed refuge from the vampires. I provided. You asked for my aid to take out the queen. Done. I have a sword at your race's throat." Blood trickled down the side of my neck from the added pressure Tim inflicted. "I own you, Alpha. I own you all."

"The trade?" the queen asked.

Tick. Tick. Tick…

"The trade." Collecting himself, Tim exhaled. "Do my bidding or die."

"That's an ultimatum," I said.

Stepping on my hand, Tim ground his shoe against my knuckles. An abrupt twist from his ankle sent his full weight crushing my fingers. Pain fired through my hand as my pinky snapped under his heel. With the sword against my neck, reflexes snapped my head forward, smacking my nose against the floor.

"Lips pressed to the marble, Wolf Born, or I break another." Keeping his foot in place, Tim continued to fill the queen in. "The werewolves will cripple the vampire council. One by one, the members will be dragged to your throne. You will drain them. After you acquire their power —"

"Not even a thousand wolves could catch them all," the queen said.

"Enslave the werewolves. Destroy the council. This was your plan," Tim argued.

"Plans are frail concepts. Whimsical pathways easy enough to stray or abandon." Her voice darkened. "Endings. They are inevitable. Powerful. Success is found in endings."

"Do you envision your *ending* tonight?" Tim asked.

"The council will feed off the wolves." I could hear the smile in her voice. "Gorged on their blood, the vampires will turn to the city. After every human is slaughtered, Glenwood will burn. Ashes and blood will taint your lake. Then you shall wither away and die, *Korrigan*." The chains groaned with her movement. "I'll enjoy your death."

"Or," Tim interjected, "I behead your two vampire puppets. Leave with my werewolf packs, while you're still impaled to your throne. Perhaps a council member will stumble upon you." He grunted. "If you somehow manage to avoid being dined on, in a few hours, you'll have a marvelous view of the sunrise through those windows. Meanwhile, I'll rendezvous with an intelligent council member. Hector seems like he has a sound mind." Tim spoke at me. "Bet he'd turn a couple of half-bloods for a playdate with you."

"She's mine," Jason snapped.

"Another word, Alpha, and I'll give her to you, piece by piece." Then Tim gave me a warning. "Scream, and I'll sever your spine." He rolled his heel back and forth over my pinky. I bit my lip. "Understand, Alpha?" Tim asked.

Silence.

"Good." Tim's foot stilled. "Now, see? Here we all are being respectable. Nice, isn't it? I'm gonna keep it that way." He paused. "Tonight, the war between werewolf and vampire ends. Done. Finished. Tonight, a new era begins. A reckoning."

Silence.

"For too long, the humans have been allowed their false sense of entitlement while the other races have sunk into submission or death. Time for us to put the humans back where they belong on the food chain." The sword ticked against my neck from Tim's erratic heart pumping blood through his hand. "Let me make myself clear. I'll be directing your races while you tear this internet-gluten-free-reality-show-loving world asunder." He paused. "Because I know you two won't play nice together, you'll need...babysitters. Powerful ones. And look what's sitting on the queen's lap. A list of thirty-eight half-bloods. Well...twenty-three that'll be able to keep your races in line. The youngsters and grannies, you can eat them. That'll save me the expenses of braces and dentures."

"Vampire half-bloods are too powerful." The queen spoke with caution. "Uncontrollable. Compulsion is useless against them. Human or turned, half-bloods are destroyed. It is our law."

"Yet there one stands." Tim shot his voice in Nathaniel's direction.

That's why Nathaniel is special. I craned my neck to stare at him. *He's a freaking half-blood vampire.*

"Nathaniel remains because he serves me." She hesitated. "Except all present, no one knows he is half-blood."

"About that…" Tim paused. "A few days ago, in front of the alpha and his pack, half-blood disappeared your hunter and the Wolf Born right out of her apartment. Now, I know vampires. Being able to disappear not one but three bodies aren't part of an average vampire's repertoire. Not even a council member could muster that escape."

"She had a list of the half-bloods," Nathaniel whispered to the queen. "I — "

"I did not ask for an explanation," she replied. "You will be killed."

"I'll guard your secret, Nathaniel," Tim offered. "What do you say? I'll free you from your queen. If you serve me."

"No," I blurted.

"Really, Ms. Sanders?" Tim's foot smashed my ring finger.

Through the surge of pain, clarity hit. "Council members get their abilities from their victims. Even with the entire council's blood, the queen will never be as powerful as you. Tim will have her feast on the council members, and then he'll have you drain her." Lifting my head toward Nathaniel, I rushed to finish. "You're who he wants to turn the half-bloods."

"There're smarts in your brain, Ms. Sanders. Too much. Such a pity. I was gonna keep you." Instead of breaking my middle finger, Tim removed his foot from my hand. "You're a risk," Tim said, zig-zagging the sword across the back of my neck. "I can't have you make the Change. You'll end up getting yourself killed, and there goes half of my army."

While Tim's foot landed between my shoulder blades, he lifted the sword. At the same instant, Jason unleashed the link. A current of energy tore through me, driving the drugs completely from my system.

"Let her hunter serve you as well," Nathaniel said.

When the tip of the sword kissed the floor next to my neck, my gasp elicited a chuckle from Tim. "If the hunter consents."

"He will." Panic strangled Nathaniel's voice into a whisper. "You have my word."

"All must come willingly to me. Yes. Sometimes, persuasion is involved. The choice is there all the same. Life or death. Eternal servitude or the nothingness that awaits you when you turn to ash." Tim paused. "Alpha, let the hunter answer."

At the wet sucking of Jason's claws extracting from Derek's throat, I closed my eyes and kissed my human life goodbye. Rolling to my side dislodged Tim's foot from my back.

Tick.

As the sword struck the floor, sparks flew at my face. When I rolled the other way, the blade nicked my earlobe. Another dodge spared my heart.

Tick.

Jumping to my feet rewarded me with a slice to my collarbone. Dropping back to my knees, the sword sent diamonds from my headband skating across the floor.

Tick.

Tim grabbed me by my hair. Twisting his wrist, he spun me to face him and jerked me to my feet. Steel pressed underneath my ribcage.

Tick.

Our eyes met.

"Do your job," he said, thrusting the sword through me. "Good girl—"

Tim's eyes widened. Then his attention slid to my claws buried in his chest cavity.

"Success in endings," he whispered, returning his glossy eyes to mine. "Chaos in beginnings." Shoving himself deeper onto my claws, impaling his own heart, Tim dissolved into an explosion of swamp water.

Drenched in the remains of Tim McKay, I sank to my knees, clenching the sword buried in my side. Behind me, several fights erupted while the tipped-over candelabras set the curtains and walls on fire.

"Use the alpha's link to heal." Nathaniel, blood-covered, loomed over me. Dropping to his knees, he tore off his jacket. "Hurry."

"Can't," I groaned.

"We need to move." Without warning, he pulled the sword from my side then wrapped his jacket around me. Knotting the sleeves and giving the makeshift tourniquet a final tug, Nathaniel nodded to himself. As he stood, a drop of blood fell off his nose and splattered onto my cheek, carrying the scent of sandalwood.

"Jason?" I asked.

Nathaniel looked away.

Tilting my head to the side, a few feet away, was my answer. Blood bubbled from the gaping hole in his throat. Still, Jason fought to take a breath.

"Stupid she-beast. You left me with no choice. He was going to kill Derek." Folding his arms around me, Nathaniel struggled to get ahold of me, but the blood-saturated dress resisted any efforts to get me to my feet. "I had it under control. You had to interfere. Had to be the hero."

"Kept you from becoming a troll's bitch-boy." I winced. "Sam?"

"She knows my name?" Sam growled.

"Stay back," warned Derek.

Off to my right, Derek blocked Sam. Locking my stare with Nathaniel, I tuned them out. "Before Jason dies—" Agony ripped through my spine. "Sam needs to drink Jason's blood. Then Sam will become the pack's alpha...Sam can call off the packs."

"Too late." Embers floated around the queen, still chained and impaled, to her throne. "He draws his last breath."

Jason seized.

Terror flashed through Nathaniel's eyes.

Closing mine, I concentrated on the last thread of energy I had left. "Sam, I command you to drink the alpha's blood." As my command left my lips, the link forged between Sam and me.

"Derek, we leave now." Nathaniel propped me against his chest as he stood.

"No." Clenching my side, I pushed away. "We have to stop the wolves attacking."

"Let Sam." Nathaniel's gaze slid from my side to the growing pool of blood at my feet. "You have minutes at most."

"What you've wanted all along," I whispered.

"There is still time..." Nathaniel's voice trembled. "Derek will turn you."

Shaking my head, I turned to Sam. "Call off—"

Jason's lifeless eyes stared at me, while at his splayed throat, Sam feasted. Behind them, Derek gave me a nod to keep speaking.

Swallowing hard, I continued, "Call off the packs. I command you."

Sam went rigid over his prey. The power of Sam's link, sent outward, tossed me against Nathaniel.

While howls bellowed outside, glass shattered. Screams from the hallway followed.

"Why isn't it working?" I asked.

"Their beasts are in control. Your alpha is too weak." The queen chuckled. "Your race will die. Your city will burn. Your humans and half-bloods will perish. The council shall crumble." She smiled. "Success."

I shoved Nathaniel off balance. The glint of steel propelled my charge. Leaning down, I plucked McKay's sword from the carpet and staggered up the throne steps.

The queen's smile grew. "Yes, give me my ending, sheep."

As she bared her neck to me, I froze. My hesitance sent fury blazing through her eyes. "Give me my end," she roared.

"No." I let the sword clatter against the floor. Dizziness attacked me while I leveled my stare at hers. "I'm not like you."

"You're weak." A tremor consumed her voice. "You're a coward—"

"No, I'm a fighter." Pain cut through my broken fingers as my claws lengthened once more. Andrea's blood covering the queen's lips gave me the strength to rush forward, and score my claws across the queen's face. "Not a spineless killer. Like you."

Terror flooded her eyes. "You can't leave me here."

I let silence be my answer.

As she struggled against the chains, blood seeped from the five slash marks across her ruined face. "I will destroy you."

"No. You *never* will," I whispered. Snatching the zip drive off her lap, I crushed it under the sole of my ankle-breaker.

When I staggered around, I met Nathaniel standing with his mouth hanging open.

"You bested her." His face went slack.

Over the wave of fatigue strangling my heart, I asked, "How does one free a vampire from a queen?"

"You drew her blood. You outrank the queen." He raised his eyes to mine. "By your orders, you may grant freedom."

"Derek." Standing at the throne steps, I turned to face him. "You're free."

Relief and admiration entwined through the blood-bond, but it was the clarity within his eyes that stole my breath. "I knew it would be you," he whispered.

Before I became lost in the depths of Derek's emotions, I glanced at Nathaniel. "You're free too."

Nathaniel shot his attention at his ex-queen, hitting her with his compulsion. "You will stay seated on the throne until you are ash."

Holding out my bloody hand, I motioned to the sword grasped between his shaking palms. "Give it to me. I've got some vampire ass to kick."

Too fast for me to follow, Nathaniel lifted the sword into an attack position. Then he tipped his head toward the doors. "Lead on, she-beast."

Nodding, I wobbled down the steps.

"No." Derek grabbed me by the arm. "You'll —"

Using the blood-bond, I pulled Derek's energy from him until his hand slipped. Turning away, I finished his sentence to my liking. "Save the wolves."

A warm, familiar hand rested on my shoulder. *Sam.* When I turned, his eyes met mine. Within their depths, Nathaniel's compulsion shattered.

I found my loophole.

My heart throttled into gear, pumping adrenaline through my dying body while Andrea's voice thundered a battle cry through my mind. *"Not over yet. Fight."*

Nathaniel was right—love strengthened our fight.

"She must make the Change," Sam said.

Shaking my head, I hissed as every muscle along my back tore.

"She needs the moon." Sam's gaze went to my side. "She will die if she Changes here."

Derek picked up a candelabra, launching it through the glass wall.

Sam's eyes narrowed to mine. He hissed in pain. "Compulsion," he gritted. "I know—"

"Don't let him break the compulsion," Nathaniel warned.

I grabbed Sam by the back of his head. Closing my eyes against the gore covering Sam's mouth. Summoning the link, I pressed my lips to his. Before he could react, I drove the link into my kiss. As the blast of light from Sam's Change engulfed the room, I used its cover to crash through the doors.

Chapter Thirty-Two

Smoke engulfed the hallway littered with blood and vampire dust. Death assaulted my nose...and my lips. Rubbing Jason's postmortem from my mouth, I gave a pep talk to my esophagus to hold the bile down a bit longer.

Out of the smog, a wolf charged.

Nathaniel moved to my side. "Know how to call a wolf?"

Before I could answer, Sam bounded forward, blocking us. My skin prickled from the link he used. Lowering his head, Sam faced off against the other wolf.

Flattening its ears, the wolf lowered its head to Sam. Sam growled.

The wolf responded by turning away, then charged toward the ballroom.

"I do now," I said to Nathaniel.

Sam looked over his shoulder at me.

"Stay alive," I commanded. "Go."

Lowering his head, Sam chased after the other wolf.

"You can't command someone to live," Nathaniel muttered. "Call the wolves, she-beast. I'll—"

"We will take care of the vampires." Derek moved to my side. "None will make it to the city."

"Thank—"

Derek pressed me between the wall and his body.

"Let me turn you." His eyes searched mine. "Do not choose death."

"I need to save as many lives as I can, and there is only one way." In the reflection of his eyes, mine set aglow. "I choose the Change."

With his stare intensifying, Derek tilted his head, bringing his lips close to mine. "Our paths *will* cross again, Tessa Sanders. Not a thousand werewolves will keep you from me."

"When that night comes, are we...enemies?" I whispered against his lips.

"If—"

"I hate ifs." Closing the distance, I slanted my mouth to his. Derek took over the kiss. Careful not to brush against my side, he arched his chest away from me. Needing Derek's touch, strength...him, I grabbed his shirt, pulling him tight to me. He groaned, releasing the blood-bond, easing the pain seizing us both. Passion ignited through my being, racing through the bond, searing my soul to his.

Derek tensed. His lips trembled against mine as he whispered, "Stay safe, my wolf."

As suddenly as the embrace started, it ended with me, in the empty hallway, gasping for breath. Leaning over, I tore off the ankle-breakers. Groaning through the pain consuming me, I pushed away from the wall.

The grit of vampire ash clung to my feet as I staggered around the fallen chandelier. Ahead, screams poured out from the smoke-filled ballroom. Shoving my self-doubt down to my pinky toe, I stepped through the entrance. With my eyes forward, I kept a slow pace so as not to attract attention. I needed to get to the center of the room. That way I'd be surrounded when I called the wolves. Out of the corner of my eye, I caught a glimpse of Nathaniel wielding the sword.

Metal pressed against the back of my head. When the trigger clicked, I dodged to the side as a bullet tore past my ear. I spun to face Boss loading another round. Too close to escape another shot, I kicked his kneecap, which sent the bullet grazing my shoulder.

A blur of brown fur rocketed against Boss. Mid-fall, Boss unsheathed a knife at his shin.

"Sam!" I screamed.

Driving the blade into Sam's gut, Boss then yanked the blade upward.

Sam went lax, spurting blood.

Boss's gaze rose to mine. Sam had taught me well. My attention locked onto Boss's trigger finger concealed underneath Sam's body. I dodged and the bullet missed me. Before he fired again, I grabbed his wrist. Bone snapped under my fist, and shock replaced the smug grin on his face. Making sure he'd never again shoot at anyone, I tore his hand from his body.

Boss looked at his detached appendage, and his gaze blurred before he passed out.

"Call the wolves," Nathaniel screamed across the room.

As I sank to my knees, time slowed. Shaking, I put my palms flat against the floor. Energy swelled throughout me.

Sam groaned.

Relief surged through me, driving my adrenaline to pulse through my being, giving me the courage I needed. Lifting my head, I stared into his eyes as I released the link.

Intense heat rolled into agonizing pain while a blinding light filled the ballroom. When the light dimmed, a stillness consumed the room. Then, the presence of every werewolf flowed through my mind. With command, I willed them through my thoughts. "*Leave.*"

Under the spotlight of the full moon, I rose to all fours. With the Change humming through my new form, I raced across the ballroom. Wolves surrounded me, breaking off only to attack oncoming threats. The group in front bounded ahead, shattering through the wall of glass.

Out on the grounds, bullets whizzed overhead. As important as it was for me to put distance between the vampires, their guns and myself, I needed to escape the wolves as well. Using my speed, I pulled away. Then I closed off the link to the packs. Dropping my head, I raced toward the woods. Nathaniel said that the forest led to a road. Roads led to new beginnings.

Freedom.

After endless miles of frozen terrain, I slowed my pace. The smell of exhaust filled my nose. Tilting my ears, I strained to hear over the wind. Static from a radio buzzed through my ears. The clattering of a muffler hinted a car sat idling yards away. To gauge how many people, I sniffed the air.

Two scents. Earthworm and lavender.

Nathaniel's tired voice traveled to my mind. *"Best Change, she-beast. You don't want to kill Benjamin."*

I closed my eyes. No one had told me how to reverse the Change. Using the link to turn wolf came to me naturally, so I prayed going human would too. When I willed the Change, heat flooded my body while energy swirled through my blood.

Light flashed against my eyelids, leaving me gasping for breath while on my hands and knees. I lifted my trembling hand. Shoving my face into my palms, I giggled. I cried, then laughed some more, until a gust of wind sucked the sweat from my naked flesh. Wrapping my arms around my shivering body, I cursed.

A werewolf would've been less scary to Ben than seeing me naked.

"Benjamin has not stopped searching for you. I read his memories. He is loyal. Brave. And knows far too much about science-fiction weaponry. Best you care for him, fiercely." Ash-covered, knee-high boots appeared next to me as Nathaniel switched to talking out loud. "He followed McKay. Tonight, Benjamin was almost eaten twice by wolves and once by a vampire. He's been briefed on the current events. He took it well for a human. Only used a touch of compulsion to keep him from fainting." Nathaniel dropped a coarse blanket over my shoulders. "The wolves are still tracking you. Hustle, she-beast. Unlike the hounds, Derek is impeccable at tracking down...the enemy."

When I rose to my feet, Nathaniel was gone. Sinking into my thoughts, I closed my eyes and whispered, "If." Holding out that maybe, just maybe, *if* we met again, Derek wouldn't kill me. As a mournful country song drifted through the pre-dawn air, once more I whispered, "If."

Epilogue

Three months later

Rubbing my eyes from the hours in front of the laptop, I blinked at the snow falling outside the window. Beyond the curtain of flurries, the Adirondack Mountains rose to the twilight sky.

"You know all the squinting will land you with another migraine." Ben dropped a log inside the woodstove.

"Yep." As I stretched, my gaze roamed across the desk to the photo of my family before drifting to a photo of Andrea.

Ben came up behind me. "Anything new?"

"No attacks. No wolf sightings. No more illnesses." I turned the screen so he could glance at the Glenwood Press webpage. Then I clicked on the local hotspot for paranormal news — MostyGhosty — our website.

Run by our alter egos, the website fueled my reporting obsession while letting Ben's inner comedian run wild. Bonus points for the website keeping food in our guts and a roof overhead. People freaking loved monsters. Well, the made-up ones.

Rolling my shoulders, I offered my latest findings. "No bloodsuckers. No trolls. Looks like Bigfoot was spotted by the skating rink." Nodding, I sighed. "The only real monster around here is me."

Ben's heartbeat ramped up. For the most part, he handled his best friend being a werewolf pretty well. As for being my roommate in an eight-hundred-square-foot log cabin with the world's smallest water heater, not so much.

Falling into my thoughts, my mind took up its hourly battle of tug-o-war with its desire to open the link to Sam. Which I always resolved with a hell no, fearing I'd be answered by an alpha who would drag me off to some vault, or just as awful, his silence.

"Sam made it, Tess. That Nathaniel said so." Ben patted my shoulder, knowing, as usual, what I was thinking about in my sulk mode.

Well, half of the time.

I never talked about Derek, who resided in my dreams. Where he'd chase me, catch me, then all the kissing… Swallowing, I let my thoughts drift outside to chill with the blizzard.

A knock at the door had Ben unholstering his pistol.

I grabbed his free arm, and Ben groaned. Mouthing, "*Sorry,*" I let go and held my hand out to keep Ben where he stood. After seconds passed with no foreign scents or heartbeats, I nodded to him.

Ben crept to the cabin door. Gun ready, he twisted the handle then peeked outside. He paused. Then he bent down. As he stood, tension vibrated from his shoulders to his earlobes. After closing the door, he turned to face me.

With his eyebrows hugging his hairline, Ben handed over a box of dog treats. Scrawled in permanent marker across the front of the Labrador retriever's head was a message.

You owe me a favor.

Want to see more like this?
Here's a taster for you to enjoy!

Sin City Wolf: Howl
January Bain

Excerpt

Cristaldo

I stared out at the night, the pull of the waxing moon yanking hard. Taking a gulp of my Dalmore 62, the finest single malt whisky ever produced, I raked a hand through my hair. The need to run free was building, growing stronger by the hour. I ached to let the clean, dry desert wind blow everything else away.

Blame it on the blood moon, an ominous portent to all my wild forbearers, scheduled to rise over Las Vegas's towering skyline in a matter of days. All my billions couldn't stop that trickster from wreaking havoc on my kind. Not that I would trade places with any otherworldly creature. *Nothing beats being a werewolf. Nothing.* Especially being a billionaire werewolf, with more money and possessions than any other wolf — and most humans — on the planet.

I savored the final gulp of the fragrant whisky with its drumroll and smooth finish. It would prove amusing to see what my rivals at the House of Ribelle had planned during the event, necessitating me showing those mongrels their low rank in the pecking order. My wolf bristled at the very idea, prepared to strike.

I dropped my glass onto the proofs of the recent interview I'd done for *Business Leader Quarterly*. The founding of the Royal Bank of Luceres and the recent expansion of our casino enterprises into several new countries was the stuff of legend and warranted a huge center spread in the magazine. Amusing really, humans being unable to see even that which what was right in front of their noses. My photo stared from the piece, all *GQ* to the public, but the slick surface hid a beast, one ready to burst forth at a moment's notice.

And that beast, bored and weary at the sameness of the days, needed a change. Where was the excitement? The new challenge? Having gathered all the riches the world had to offer didn't fill the deep void of longing, growing stronger by the day, of wanting something more. Only to myself would I admit that my life was lacking, that surrounded by so many, I was lonely.

Maybe it was time to choose a mate? Even if she wasn't the famed Forever Mate so valued by the pack, at least I would have company at night. Someone to share my victories with. *No.* I wanted the real thing. A true mate at my side, anointed as being the chosen one of destiny. I raised my head and closed my eyes, catching a sense of change on the wind. Something was coming...

Thud.

My office door slammed wide open, causing a low growl of warning to escape my throat before I caught sight of the intruder who'd broken my concentration. *Ah, Lucius. My identical twin.* He'd come bearing dubious gifts, by the look of it.

Two frightened young women preceded my brother inside the penthouse offices of the Glitter Palace casino.

They should be scared. Lucius might have been named for the light, but his heart was filled with darkness.

"I caught this pair skulking about, asking the dealers questions about our operation and generally making a nuisance of themselves. I intervened when they bribed one of our staff into letting them into the restricted area...bribed with the promise of a free blow job."

"That's not fair," the taller of the pair objected. They were beautiful women, tall and blonde and done up in the stock-in-trade of those looking for a good time. *Or to provide one.* I raised a sardonic eyebrow at her as she continued her protest.

"I'm just a student of hotel management, trying to get some pointers from those working in the real world. My friend Brandi only came along for company. I'm Jill, by the way."

Even from twenty feet away I could smell the smoking lie that scented her skin. Normally I would tell them both to strip, to prove themselves innocent. Today, I found the idea abhorrent. Lucius gave me a strange look, waiting for my reaction. I nodded at him. *You want this, go ahead.*

"Strip."

They both stared at Lucius with huge doe-like eyes.

"What?" Jill asked, her gaze flitting back and forth between me and Lucius.

"You heard me. If you're innocent, strip," Lucius said.

"I'm not wearing a wire."

"Prove it. I'll let you leave if you're clean."

The one called Brandi shook her head. "I'm not doing this. You can't make me." She hugged both arms around her upper body.

"I can and I will. We're the only authority here at the Glit." Lucius used the shortened version of the Glitter

Palace, our casino's name. His demands had aroused the taller one — her scent saturated the air with a sweet musk. My nose twitched, ambivalent about the odor.

"What's it to be, Jill? Strip or banishment?"

"So ban me. I don't care," Brandi said.

Jill looked my twin straight in the eyes, challenging him. She raised her arms in a graceful arc and undid the strings tied at the back of her neck, letting her short blue chiffon gown fall in a shimmer of fabric the length of her body to puddle on the floor. Underneath, she was naked except for a tiny pair of white lace panties. Her luscious double Ds were firm and upraised, the nipples tight and protruding out a good half inch, begging to be pinched and sucked. Apparently, Jill liked to be told what to do, like a long string of Jills before her. Bored now, my mind drifted. Even my wolf seemed to find the display less interesting than usual, just sitting back observing instead of wanting to play.

"See, no wire," she said. She twirled in a full circle, her long blonde hair cascading around her, her breasts swaying with the graceful ballet-like movements of her body.

"How about under those panties?" Lucius asked, the challenge clear. One thing we did agree on — there was nothing on earth more beautiful than the female body. But today, I sat and contemplated having another strong drink, drumming my fingers on my desktop.

She hooked her fingers into the elastic waistband and eased the panties down her long tan legs, exposing her complete Brazilian wax job. Then, slipping the lace over her four-inch platform heels, she threw them at Lucius. He caught them and took a deep whiff of their fragrant dampness. "Nice. Now you." He pointed at the other girl.

She shook her head. "No way."

I suddenly realized I'd prefer to go for a run than be here. The pent-up lust from the pull of the coming wolf moon made my skin ripple with the urge. If this female was reluctant, then banning her from the premises would suffice. Neither I nor Lucius would force a woman. Why should we, when they all came of their own accord? Not that I wouldn't mind a good chase for a change — as long as I won. *And I always win.*

"Fine. But be advised, a photo will be taken and shared with the staff," Lucius said. He was dragging this out and I wanted it over and done with. I tried to catch his eye to let him know.

The female hesitated, biting her bottom lip. I could see through the sham. I had to give it to them — the Ribelle dogs were attracting better-looking spies. Not brighter, perhaps, unless they were looking to be caught? They'd have to be checked over thoroughly before they could leave the premises. I'd leave those honors to my twin.

Lucius glanced my way, lust darkening his complexion. He, perhaps more than I, enjoyed our couplings with willing women in the immediate vicinity of the other. Our more studious younger twin brothers, currently in Rome, enjoyed having the *same* woman, but I did not imagine that ever being the case for me and Lucius, with me being alpha.

Spy number two shimmied out of her tight minidress, exposing another spectacular set of large breasts and a lack of underwear, her reluctance an obvious game. *And a lure.*

"I'll need to check you for bugs," Lucius said.

Jill, spy number one, offered herself to my brother, raising her hands high above her head in the surrender position. He caged her wrists between one of his hands, then ran his other hand through her hair, then down her supple flesh, tweaking her nipples before slipping his fingers down to her pussy. She arched her back.

From the corner of my eye, I caught the slight shimmer of the cosmic disturbance in the air around Lucius, his eyes flashing blue before returning to brown. He wanted the change. I got it. Business had been all-consuming of late, especially concluding the arrangements on the acquisition of the new bank.

A loud knock sounded at the door. "Come in," I called.

"Sorry to bother you, sire," Serge said with all due respect.

My right-hand man, second in line after Lucius and similar to a mafia don's *consigliere*, looked unusually agitated, though he was doing an admirable job of attempting to hide it. But *my* job was to miss nothing that might affect those I was in charge of. Every little nuance meant something.

"Yes?"

"Just advising you that the all-girl band, The Sirens, has arrived and is set up in Nero's." Serge was fully aware of my standing order to make sure I knew *everything* going on in my casino. The online contest we'd run for the chance to win three nights' playing at Nero's had drawn a lot of media attention — good for business, and good for the group that would benefit from the exposure.

I nodded. The sense of change in the wind tonight grew stronger. *Time to pay close attention*, it seemed to say.

The lights in the room dimmed. My twin was making preparations to fuck the women.

"Check their jewelry, Lucius. Remember the last time." Hiding a bug in an earring had worked until I'd had the penthouse swept for electronic devices.

I made a quick decision in the moment, born of my urge to get out of the office and check on the band that had drawn so much attention.

"Let's go," I said to Serge.

I led the way to my private elevator across the hall and punched the lobby number. We rode in silence, my wolf somewhat annoyed about losing out on the easy tail waiting upstairs in my office, now that I had chosen to move on. But my mind went back to thoughts of my own Forever Mate and what that would mean in my life.

I shook my head with finality, pushing the idea away. The chances of that happening after all this time were slim to none. But that didn't mean I couldn't enjoy the company of a female, under the right circumstances, to keep the urges at bay.

Moon madness is a bitch.

About the Author

When not writing stories, where the villain and heroine fall madly in love, I can be found daydreaming, singing all the 80's songs, drinking copious amounts of coffee, reading books in headstand, protecting wildlife, and advocating for students with disabilities.

M.J. Klipfel loves to hear from readers. You can find her contact information, website details and author profile page at https://www.totallybound.com

Home of Erotic Romance

Sign up for our newsletter and find out about all our
romance book releases, eBook sales and promotions,
sneak peeks and FREE romance books!

www.ingramcontent.com/pod-product-compliance
Lightning Source LLC
Chambersburg PA
CBHW030809260626
47169CB00001B/255